The Robe of Sincerity

The Robe of Sincerity
and Other Stories

by
Marie-Jeanne
L'Héritier de Villandon

Translated, annotated and introduced by
Brian Stableford

A Black Coat Press Book

Visit our website at www.blackcoatpress.com

ISBN 978-1-61227-732-5. First Printing. April 2018. Published by Black Coat Press, an imprint of Hollywood Comics.com, LLC, P.O. Box 17270, Encino, CA 91416.

TABLE OF CONTENTS

Introduction

The first four stories in this collection are translated from *Oeuvres meslées* [Miscellaneous Works], which was published with the by-line Mad^{elle} de L'H*** by Jean Guignard in 1696. The appendix comes from the same volume. The remaining stories are taken from the version of *La Tour ténébreuse et les jours lumineux, Contes Anglois* [The Dark Tower and the Luminous Days: English Tales] reprinted in volume 12 of Charles-Joseph Meyer's 41-volume collection *Le Cabinet des fées* (1786), credited there to "Mademoiselle Lheritier." The original volume bearing that title had been published in 1705.

No copy of the 1705 version of *La Tour ténébreuse et les jours lumineux* is available for consultation in any location accessible to me, nor can I find any secondary account of its exact contents, so I cannot be certain whether or not it contains more material than the version reproduced in the *Cabinet des fées*, but whether or not the latter is complete in the sense that it reproduces the entire text of the original volume, it is certainly not complete in the sense that its framed narrative is concluded and contains all the inserted stories that were originally intended to be inserted into that frame. I suspect, however, that the work was never completed in the second sense, and that a projected second volume, or perhaps more than one, never appeared. One other collection of stories by the author, *Les Caprices du destin* [The Caprices of Destiny] (1718), is reproduced on the Bibliothèque Nationale's *gallica* website, as is her translation of *Les Épitres héroïques d'Ovide* [The Heroic Epistles of Ovid] (1732), but it is difficult to estimate the extent of the author's other publications, let alone her writings; at least some of the former, and perhaps many of the latter, appear to have been lost. That is not surprising, given the context in which they were produced.

7

Marie-Jeanne L'Héritier de Villandon (1664-1734) is nowadays best known as the "niece" of Charles Perrault (1628-1703)—she was actually a more distant relative—and one of the members of a group based in the salon culture of the reign of Louis XIV who initiated the development and popularization of what came to be known as *contes de fées* [tales of enchantment, but usually mistranslated as "fairy tales"].[1] Because Perrault reaped the lion's share of the celebrity subsequently associated with that popularization—only shared to any considerable extent with Madame d'Aulnoy—some subsequent historians suggested that his cousin got the idea of writing such tales from him, but it was almost certainly the other way around. In all probability, Perrault did not merely take some inspiration from L'Héritier's propagandizing, but also appropriated some of her tentative pioneering materials, along with materials from other female writers involved in the initiation of the practice.

Because of the manner of the second-stage popularization of *contes de fées*, which shaped and marketed the material specifically as tales to be read to children, the actual origins of the vogue in the salons of Versailles and Paris have not only been obfuscated but somewhat misrepresented. The whole picture is now impossible to reconstitute, but certain aspects of it can still be discerned, albeit vaguely, and L'Héritier's published writings provide some of the most significant evidence of the process by which the salon tales came to be written and the various things that their producers were attempting to achieve. The tales themselves tell a story of sorts, but after the

---

[1] The French *féerie* means "enchantment," so a *fée* is, literally, an agent of enchantment. Because the noun has the feminine gender, however, it is frequently assumed that the agents in question are female, and the word has a masculine equivalent in *enchanteur*. It is perfectly clear in Mademoiselle L'Héritier's stories that her *fées* are human enchantresses, not supernatural beings, as implied by the English word "fairies." It is for that reason that I invariably translate *fée* as "fay."

first four "*nouvelles*" reproduced in *Oeuvres meslées*, and before the collection of her poetry that fills most of the remainder of the volume, the author took the trouble to reproduce a brief explanatory essay in the form of a letter, a translation of which I have appended to the present volume, which casts a little more light on the detail of her thinking. If her work is to be fully appreciated and understood, however—or, at least, appreciated and understood to the extent that it can be—it is first necessary to have a better appreciation of the historical and social context in which it were produced, and the enormous influence on that context, and on L'Héritier herself, of Madeleine de Scudéry.

Madeleine de Scudéry (1607-1701) was orphaned at the age of six and was raised, along with her brother Georges, by her uncle, a clergyman. She and her brother settled permanently in Paris in 1640, having already become members of the salon that was hosted at the Hôtel de Rambouillet by Catherine de Vivonne, Marquise de Rambouillet (1588-1665) from 1608 until her death. The Hôtel de Rambouillet was a place of rendezvous for the high society of the era, and hosted all kinds of social events, but it was the literary salon guided by Catherine—anagrammatically nicknamed "the incomparable Arthénice"—and dominated by its female members that made it notorious even in its own day. It was the cradle of a primitive feminism that was transferred to Scudéry's own salon, launched in 1652, which became the heart of the movement in question for more than half a century, formally inherited after her death, by L'Héritier. The literary and feminist aspects of the movement were parodied by Molière, initially in the brief farce "Les Précieuses ridicules" [The Ridiculous Precious Women] (1659)—as a result of which the key salon members became known as the *précieuses*—and more elaborately in the five-act comedy, "Les Femmes savantes" [The Savant Women] (1672).

The subject-matter of the 1659 farce is the supposed effect on its young female protagonists of reading the works of Mademoiselle de Scudéry, who was then by far and away the

9

most popular writer in France, although her works were published under her brother's name. The books that obtained the unprecedented popularity in question are no longer read, partly because of their enormous length. Begun with the relatively modest four-volume *Ibrahim, ou l'illustre Bassa* (1642), they reached their peak of achievement and celebrity in the prodigious ten-volume *Artamène, ou le Grand Cyrus* (1649-1653)—if it is reckoned a single work of fiction, the longest ever published—and the ten-volume *Clélie, histoire romaine* (1654-1660). The latter endeavors were, in effect, potentially-interminable serials, and are ancestral in their narrative technique and concerns to modern TV soap operas, as well as having given birth, more directly, to the modern novel. Another reason why they are no longer read, however, is that they also pioneered the strategy of the *roman à clef*, in which contemporary individuals are satirically disguised as fictional characters, in these cases in the context of a Classical pseudohistory.

The primary—in fact, the only—subject matter of Scudéry's proto-novels is an idealized version of amour, and although she did not invent that idealized image, which had long had prolific literary representation in lyric poetry, she certainly provided it with a new narrative context, a new rhetorical strategy and a new analytical depth, in what was promptly labeled the *roman*. The word *roman* eventually became the standard French term for what are known in English as novels, causing problems for English commentators who wanted to distinguish "novels" from "romances." There is, however, a direct line of descent from Scudéry's works to what are now known in English as "genre romances": formularized love stories that still feature the same mythology of idealized amour that she favored, albeit somewhat diluted.

The success of Scudéry's works was extremely important in terms of the literary marketplace of her era; indeed, it can be said without exaggeration to have been the crucial factor in the subsequent reorientation of that marketplace toward prose fiction, and the consequent changes in its financial reorganization that occurred over the next three centuries. Although seventeenth-century printers did occasionally pay authors for the privilege of printing and selling their works, it was still far more common for authors to have to pay printers, or to persuade patrons to pay on their behalf, for the distinction of publication. Whether Madeleine or Georges de Scudéry made any money out of the spectacular sales of her works it is difficult to tell, but the printers certainly made lots of it, and probably more than they had ever made out of printing poetry, plays or works of philosophy, in spite of the prestige attached to the latter genres. In a just world, that success might have raised the prestige of prose fiction to equal that of poetry, but no one can be in the least surprised by the fact that did not happen in the 1650s, because we are still living amid the residue of the backlash of contempt that not only inspired Molière but thousands of other hostile assaults.

That hostility is unsurprising, but is worth noting one other particular circumstance that has some relevance to the contemporary attitude to Mademoiselle de Scudéry and perhaps also to the precise nature of the ideology promoted by her works. In the same way that she used dozens of other contemporary individuals as the bases for characters in her works, she also inserted herself into them. The final volume of *Clélie* is a fictional biography of the poet Sappho, which is also a kind of autobiographical allegory, and Scudéry consistently referred to herself as "Sapho" (the French spelling of Sappho). Exactly what she meant to imply by that appellation is not entirely clear, because she only wrote about herself in carefully masked terms, nor can we be sure what exactly what inference her contemporaries took from it, although many of them presumably supposed, rightly or wrongly, that it referred to her sexuality as well as her poetic talents.

The vast majority of those who took that inference, however, certainly had no idea whether, or how, that sexuality might have been translated in terms of practice, and the person who was presumably in the best position to know, her principal protégée—Marie-Jeanne L'Héritier, who similarly never married—never gave any explicit indication. To complicate the matter further, Scudéry had a notoriously close relationship for much of her life with the historian Paul Pellisson (1624-1693), although whether it was sexual is open to doubt. What is certain, however, is that the particular idealization of amour developed by Scudéry and embraced wholeheartedly by L'Héritier put an immense emphasis on the cult of virginity, which might seem extraordinary if it were not still clinging stubbornly to a residual role in the mythology of contemporary romance, in both literature and in life.

Even though she is no longer read, and few people now alive have even heard of her, it is arguable that Mademoiselle de Scudéry was the single most influential figure in the entire history of European literature, partly because of the crucial influences her works had on the subsequent development of prose fiction, its obsessions and its marketing, but also because of her furtherance and perfection of the salon tradition that she inherited from the Marquise de Rambouillet. In addition to her fiction and her poetry, Scudéry was a prolific writer of non-fiction, a great deal of which was devoted to the art of conversation, and the application of classical analyses of rhetoric and eloquence to contemporary oral and written discourse. She not only inherited from her predecessor the idea that the principal focal point of salon conversation should be literature, but she attempted to dictate how that conversation should be organized and conducted; she made her salon into a literary workshop, in which she sought to define what the works produced by its members ought to be attempting to contrive, and she strove to establish rules for their discussion and evaluation. As with the modern literary mythology of "romance," a direct line of descent connects Scudéry's endeavors with modern writing workshops; she was the ancestress not only of the subsequent evolution of French literary salons and Romantic cenacles, but of their English and American spinoff, and thus played a crucial role in the development of countless cauldrons of subsequent literary inspiration.

The importance of the latter point, in respect of L'Héritier's work and, more specifically, the emergence from

Scudéry's salon of modern *contes de fées*, is that the process of that emergence was entirely conscious, strategically contrived in the context of a particular literary theory. It is perfectly obvious that L'Héritier's "Les Enchantemens de l'éloquence" (tr. herein as "The Enchantments of Eloquence"), which gives every appearance of being the immediate source text of two of Charles Perrault's most famous stories, "Cendrillon" ("Cinderella") and "Les Fées" (tr. as "Diamonds and Toads"), is not an adaptation of folklore, but an attempt to recycle motifs that the author attributes to the literary inventions of troubadours, in order to illustrate and develop an argument about the essential purpose of fiction and the rhetorical role that ought to be played in fulfilling that purpose by "eloquence."

There are no dates in *Oeuvres meslées* to indicate when the works it contains were originally composed, but they probably antedate its publication considerably, perhaps by more than a decade in some instances. The collection looks like a sample chosen from what was already a substantial body of work, which had had some difficulty reaching print, partly because of the problems inherent in obtaining the royal "privilege" that was necessary for publication at the time. Although L'Héritier, like everyone else at court, flattered the King and his family outrageously in the numerous works she dedicated to them, the very fact that everyone did it made that a necessary but far from sufficient condition of obtaining such a warrant, in the face of all kinds of prejudices.

Although *Oeuvres meslées* was published a year before Perrault's *Contes de ma mere l'Oye* (1697; tr. as "Tales of Mother Goose"), and its privilege is dated 1695, the prefatory note attached to the first "nouvelle," addressed to Charles Perrault's daughter, makes it clear that L'Héritier already knew that the latter collection had been compiled, ostensibly by his young son. The note is somewhat tongue-in-cheek, as there is no way that a historical *nouvelle* of transvestism could have been added to such an assembly of *contes*, and it is probably best interpreted as a wry response to the fact that Perrault had borrowed from her work. Perrault had previously published a "*nouvelle en vers*," "La Marquise de Salusses, ou la Patience de Griselidis" (1691) and a "*conte en vers*," "Les souhaits ridicules" [The Ridiculous Wishes] (1693), so he had already done adaptations of fanciful material, but he had done so very much in the vein of the fables in verse—with some later ventures into prose—penned by his fellow Academician Jean de La Fontaine (1621-1695), issued in several volumes between 1668-1694, which were mostly adapted from Classical fabulists, including Aesop and "Pilpay" (Bidpai).

That work obviously influenced L'Héritier, who similarly wrote a "*nouvelle en vers*," and she often used the term "*fable*" to describe her stories as well as "*conte*," "*nouvelle*" and "*historiette*"; what distinguished her work was not so much is the desire to adapt previous fantastic materials as her determination to fit such materials into the context of Scudéry's literary theory. In that context, her choice of terminology is not insignificant; although she used all the available terms for short prose works more-or-less interchangeably, as many others did and still do, her distinct preference for "*nouvelle*," which I have elected to render as "novelette" emphasized the fact that her stories were considerably longer than Perrault's *contes*—much longer, in the cases of "Ricdin-Ricdon" and "La Robe de sincérité"—and not adapted to be read aloud in a single session.

Although La Fontaine was a cardinal influence of both her uncle and herself in terms of published work, L'Héritier presumably took a more immediate influence from her collaborators in Scudéry's salon, on the basis of oral representations. As to what she heard and when we can only speculate, but in the early 1690s she must have been exposed to the work of Baronne d'Aulnoy (1650-1705), who followed up the success of Perrault's initial collection with the almost immediate release of the four-volume *Contes de fées* (1697), rapidly supplemented by *Contes nouveaux ou Les Fées à la mode* (1698). D'Aulnoy had been exiled from France for many years, after allegedly conspiring to frame her husband for a capital crime, but she was allowed to return to Paris in 1690 and readmitted to court because of "services rendered to the crown," where she threw herself back into salon culture with enthusiasm. Her life continued to be a popular topic of scandal, but she was the most successful member of the Scudéry-L'Héritier coterie following her return, publishing three volumes of slightly salacious fake memoirs in 1691-96.[2] Her scandalous reputation—supported by such evidence as the fact that two of her six children were born some time after her separation from her husband—does not seem to have deterred Scudéry and L'Héritier from maintaining her in amity; it was presumably with the latter's permission, as well as her knowledge, that d'Aulnoy incorporated elements from two of L'Héritier's tales in "Finette Cendron" (1698), admittedly with far greater variation and elaboration than Perrault had.

How much Madame d'Aulnoy owed to L'Héritier and *vice versa* it is impossible to determine, but d'Aulnoy was certainly the more inventive as well as the more prolific writer, and the fact that she was largely unhampered by the moralistic restrictions that L'Héritier trumpeted so loudly undoubtedly assisted the appeal of her work. D'Aulnoy always seemed perfectly comfortable working with and devising the fantastic and extravagant elements of her plots, whereas L'Héritier, no matter how much she propagandized the virtue and utility of the *merveilleux*, always seemed more comfortable doing without; none of the stories in *Les Caprices du destin* have any fantastic content, and it is significant that "La Robe de

---

[2] The fake memoir was a significant step in the evolution of prose fiction within salon culture, which saw the light almost simultaneously with the development of *contes* and *nouvelles*. Another of the most significant pioneers of *contes de fées*, Charlotte-Rose de Caumont de La Force (1650-1724), who published her collection of such tales in 1698, had built her reputation with a series of "*histoires secrètes*," mostly featuring notorious women. Like Scudéry and L'Héritier, she never married.

sincérité" only admits apparent magic, insisting quite forcefully that any magic that is not a mere confidence trick must be the production of science, and invoking anachronistic and improbable mechanical devices to supply the seemingly supernatural events introduced into the complicated plot in a miserly fashion.

If L'Héritier's influences are a trifle difficult to calculate, her influence on other writers is even harder to estimate with certainly. There is no way to prove decisively that the exceedingly close resemblance between the opening of "Cendrillon" and the whole of "Les Fées" to sections of "Les Enchantemens de l'éloquence" results from Perrault borrowing from her rather than *vice versa*, and we can probably be sure that the similarities between the central motif of "La Robe de sincérité" and Hans Christian Anderson's story known in English as "The Emperor's New Clothes" (1837) are coincidental, but the case of "Ricdin-Ricdon" and its resemblance to the Brothers Grimm's "Rumpelstiltskin" is much more intriguing.

"Rumpelstiltskin" was first published in 1812, and was allegedly based on an old German folktale, but the Brothers Grimm's claim to be recording authentic folktales is largely a pretence. There is, in any case, no such thing as a "written folktale" because the process of writing obliges various modifications of oral discourse, but so far as can be judged from their notebooks, the Grimms did a great deal of rewriting in "adapting" the tales they collected (mostly from middle-class neighbors, not from peasants) and they certainly published straightforward adaptations of several tales originated by the French salon writers, including a recycling of "Cendrillon" as "Aschenputtel" and a recycling of Mademoiselle de La Force's "Persinelle" as "Rapunzel."

Even if "Rumpelstiltskin" did incorporate some material collected locally, however, there was plenty of time during the previous century for oral recyclings of "Ricdin-Ricdon" to have traveled quite extensively, and the Grimms were almost certainly familiar with the written version.

Whatever the exact reasons are for the resemblances between "Ricdin-Ricdon" and "Rumpelstiltskin," however, the two stories certainly make an interesting comparison, in terms of the contrasted reasons for the heroine's involvement in what is represented by L'Héritier as a straightforward diabolical bargain, and the role played by the lovestruck Prince in getting her out of it. The main reason why "Ricdin-Ricdon" is much longer that "Rumpelstiltskin" is its intense and complex analysis of the psychology of amour, in the manner of Mademoiselle de Scudéry's novels, from which it also borrows the device of the heroine's abduction by what would nowadays be described as a stalker—always Scudéry's favorite plot lever.

The same fascination with the psychology of amour is responsible for the elaboration of the even longer "La Robe de sincérité," where the blatant obsession with the significance of virginity provides the symbolism of the eponymous artifact. The scrupulous narrative detailing of the obsession in that story makes an interesting contrast with "L'Adroite princesse, ou les Aventures de Finette" ("The Clever Princess") where a cruder symbolic motif is displayed in an abbreviated and graphic fashion, culminating in the bizarre blood-letting of the story's climax, which would have delighted Sigmund Freud. It is interesting to note that in her letter to Madame de G***, L'Héritier claims to have toned down the original version of the story[3] considerably in regard to the immorality of Finette's sisters, given the garish quality of its other imagery.

In general, however, L'Héritier does seem to have been ever ready to tone down the fantastic elements of her work in the interests of what she called *bienséance*, which I have normally translated as "decorum," although "propriety" or "decency" would have done as well. It is not without reason that

---

[3] Although L'Héritier does not specify that original, she undoubtedly borrowed the template of her story from the French translation of Giambattista Basile's *Il Pentamerone* (1634-36; Fr. tr. 1762), also a source of prolific borrowing by the brothers Grimm.

her study of "Les Enchantmens de l'éloquence" is alternatively titled "Les Effets de la douceur," which I have translated as "The Effects of Mildness" in preference to "Sweetness" or "Kindness," although *douceur* and *douceureuse* crop up so often in her work that I felt obliged to employ variants on occasion.

By way of further contrast, however, I have included a translation of another work of fantastic fiction contained in *Oeuvres meslées*, which is not categorized as a *"nouvelle"* and shows the author in a mood that is anything but mild: "Le Parnasse reconnoissant, ou the Triomphe de Madame des Houlières" ("Grateful Parnassus"), a flamboyant celebration of another author now forgotten, although she was regarded in her heyday as the leading lyric poet of her era. The story is interesting not only for its fervent feminism, but for its graphic imagery and the sly wit of some of the comments made in passing on the personnel of the Underworld and Parnassus.

It is perhaps the case that L'Héritier's insistence on maintaining a scrupulous *douceur* in so much of her work did not work to her advantage in obtaining publication, or in recommending her work for enthusiastic preservation by posterity. If, as seems likely, the publication of *La Tour ténébreuse et les jours lumineux* was interrupted and the latter half aborted, that might have had something to do with its relatively slow pace and lack of melodrama, particularly conspicuous in the frame narrative, which represents the tales that it contains as the work of Richard the Lionheart, whiling away the time with Blondel while imprisoned. It is perhaps ironic that the version reproduced in the *Cabinet des fées* ends abruptly at the moment when something actually happens potentially capable of disrupting their quietude, although the fact that the ending in question is reported to be the *Fin de La Tour ténébreuse* suggests that the luminous days were yet to come, and one cannot help suspecting that they too might have been a trifle mild.

In spite of their frequent mildness and occasional preachiness, however, L'Héritier's stories are certainly not tedious, and their interest is by no means merely historical.

They remain very readable, aided by their inventiveness and also by their idiosyncratic wit, whose deft irony is not always obvious at first glance but is nicely pointed when its thorns penetrate their polite disguise. Her feminism is bound to seem primitive by the standards of that movement's subsequent heroism, but it is not craven, and her other varied literary accomplishments serve, alongside those of several of her associates, demonstrate that the intended sarcasm of Molière's description of "femmes savantes" should not be allowed to obscure the fact that the leading members of Mademoiselle de Scudéry's salon really were savant, as well as eloquent.

The translation of the stories from *Oeuvres meslées* were was made from the copy of the 1696 edition reproduced on *gallica*, and the translation of *La Tour ténébreuse et les jours lumineux* from the copy of the 1786 edition of volume 12 of the *Cabinet des fées* reproduced on the same website, with the assistance of the London Library's copy of the same text.

Brian Stableford

MARMOISAN;

or, Innocent Deceit
A Heroic and Satiric Novelette

To Mademoiselle Perrault

A few days ago, Mademoiselle, I found myself in a company of persons of distinguished merit, in which the conversation fell upon poems, tales and novelettes. It paused for a long
time on the last-named sort of work; various examples of it, in
verse and prose, were examined, and infinite praise was given
to the charming novelette of Griselidis,[4] in which the advice of
a sage fay gives rise to a thousand incidents in which there is
the marvelous. Someone said thereafter that however beautiful
those works might be in their genre, they are the slightest productions that could emerge from the hand of their illustrious
author, who had given marks of his great talents for poetry and
eloquence and whose vivid enlightenment in the sciences and
all the fine arts were known to everyone.

A few reflections were then made in which people hastened to render justice to the merit of the savant man of whom
you are so fortunate to be the daughter. Mention was made of
the fine education he gives his children; it as said that they all
show much intelligence, and finally, of the naïve tales that one
of his young pupils put on paper not long ago with so much
charm.[5] A few were recounted, and that led insensibly to the
recounting of others.

---

[4] By Charles Perrault, as noted in the introduction.
[5] This reference to Charles Perrault's son as the ostensible
author of the as-yet-unpublished collection is reflected in the
warrant that the King issued for its publication, which is made
out not to Perrault but to his son Pierre Darmancour, then sixteen years old; it was not until sometime after its publication

It was necessary to tell one in my turn. I told that of Marmoisan, with some embroidery that came to mind at the time. It was new for the company, which found it very much to its taste, and judged it so little known that I was told that it was necessary to communicate it to the young storyteller who occupies the amusements of his childhood so intelligently. I am making it a pleasure to follow that advice and as I know, Mademoiselle, the liking and attention you have for all things in which there is some moral, I am going to tell you that tale very nearly as I recounted it. I hope that you will impart it to your amiable brother, and that you will judge together whether the fable is worthy of being placed in his agreeable collection of tales.

In the time when France was divided between several kings—I have not been told under which reign or in which century, but it does not matter—there was a Seigneur named the Comte de Solac, who was very brave, very rich and full of intelligence. He had married at a very advanced age and his wife died young, leaving him six children, including a son and a daughter who were twins. That son was unique; there were three older daughters of the two twins and one three years younger.

The Seigneur did not want to marry again, and devoted all his care to bringing up his children well. He only succeeded with the smaller number, however.

A few years after he became a widower, his eldest daughter was of an age to be married, but, in spite of the desire that her father had for her to do so, she did not want to enter into that engagement, and she did well. Her character was composed of a hypocritical devoutness and an excessive prudishness. She was very ugly, and weak enough to have a great

---

that Charles Perrault was "exposed" as the true author, although L'Héritier must have known full well when she wrote this paragraph that her "uncle," and not his son, was its originator.

deal of chagrin in consequence, which rendered her so ill-humored that she held the scant liberality of nature in her regard against everyone. She expressed an aversion so affected for the sex different from her own that when hazard had brought some man into her room she opened the windows in order to expel the bad air, and then burned pastilles. She did not want to give herself the slightest trouble or undertake any domestic chores, and never came back from the church, where she went in order to criticize everyone, without scolding someone on returning home, not even sparing her father.

The Comte de Solac, abandoning that excessive prude to her eccentric character, thought that he could console himself with the merit of the two daughters who followed that eldest one. The next one had beauty, but that beauty was not supported by intelligence or joviality. An insipid indolence reigned in all her actions, and as she did not know, or do, or think anything, for want to finding funds at home to amuse herself, gambling became her dominant passion. She devoted herself to it to such an extent that it became a fury, and, abusing her father's good will, at least four card-tables were always seen in her room, surrounded by people whose minds were as disorderly as their morals, who, at the slightest dispute, continually voiced the most frightful verities. Those kinds of people won immense sums from her, and, in addition to all the money that her father's complaisance furnished her, she carried out a thousand rapines on everything submitted to her direction, and showed a sordid avarice for everything that was not gambling, in which she spent the greater number of her nights.

The Comte's third daughter was not beautiful; however, she had a lively and frivolous air about her that was nevertheless pleasing. Joviality and fire were evident in her spirit, but she had neither judgment nor good conduct, and was recklessly fond of all pleasures. She would have been in despair if a day had gone by without a ball, a spectacle or a fête. Her magnificence in matters of furniture and clothes was boundless. Not only did she gave herself blindly to all sorts of fashions, however bizarre they might be, but she gave birth to some herself, and my chronicle relates that she was the sensate young woman who had the solid glory of inventing all the steenkerques, firmamens and furbelows of her century.[6] The most fragile ornament and the most infantile trinket excited her envy, and in order to furnish those futile expenses she would even have pawned her father's dressing-gown. And in addition to all those faults, she also had the one of being unable to live if she did not have a dozen insipid Blondins running after her, who paid her vapid compliments that they knew by heart, by virtue of having repeated them to a hundred beauties.

The gambler and the coquette chagrined their father scarcely any less than the excessive prude, especially when he saw that a more mature age did not correct their dangerous penchants.

He had reason to be content with his fourth daughter, however. She was a charming brunette, all of whose features, as regular as they were piquant, were further embellished by an admirable complexion. A tall and shapely figure, sustained by an air as noble as it was relaxed completed rendering her entirely likeable, and the charms of her wit and her humor even surpassed those of her body. She had a lively, solid and well-regulated mind, was both generous and thrifty, and undertook all the little domestic chores to which her sex engaged her with a good grace, making it a pleasure and a study to fulfill all her duties well.

Her brother, who was her twin, resembled her entirely in his face and stature, and as he had dark hair, like hers, if the difference in their sex had not been evident in their clothing it would not have been possible to tell them apart.

If the young Seigneur, whose name was the Comte de Marmoisan, resembled the amiable Leonore, his sister, in terms of personal charms, however, he scarcely resembled her intellectually. He had assembled within him the diversity of

---

[6] A steenkerque [Frenchified as stinquerque in the original] is a kind of cravat, a firmamen a kind of jacket.

the tedious faults of all his other sisters, except for the hypocrisy of false devoutness and bizarre prudishness. On those two articles one would have been wrong to accuse him, for he gave himself to entirely opposite excesses. And to all the bad character of his sisters he had also added certain foolish and irresponsible manias to which the liberty of his sex permitted him to devote himself.

However, in spite of his vanity, his love of gambling and his foolish expenditure, he loved Leonore, who was modesty and common sense personified, in preference to all his other sisters, whose inclinations resembled his own, so lovable is virtue even to those who have no desire to follow it. It is true, however, that his twin sister and he found themselves in accord in being very fond of the pleasures of hunting.

Leonore was naturally lively and indefatigably active. She found time to fulfill all her duties, to read and work on tapestry while still finding moments to mount a horse, fire weapons and hunt. Those occupations were a very touching diversion for her and reflected her courage, which was of a rare firmness for persons of her sex. When the Comte de Solac knew all her merit, he combined the tenderness of a father with a great esteem, which caused him to develop an attachment for her that it would be difficult to express.

He would have liked to see the same qualities in his son, but even though his son was far from possessing them, because he was unique, and likeable in spite of his faults, the good father loved him passionately even so. He had put his youngest daughter into a convent at the age of three, and, as he was unaware of her humor, he did not have any design of taking her out of it until she was of an age to marry, for fear that she might follow the bad example of her other sisters rather than that of Leonore.

Meanwhile, the good Seigneur de Solac, who was overwhelmed in old age by inconveniences that he had contracted in bearing arms gloriously for a long time, saw with chagrin war reborn in the realm. He was no longer in any condition to serve and he was reluctant to expose his only son to it so soon.

As for Marmoisan, he was eager to be on campaign; he had a desire to distinguish himself and to be the master of his action. In addition to that, his father enjoyed several good governments and a quantity of other royal benefits, which the young Seigneur wanted to render himself worthy of inheriting; and to animate him further, he knew that the name of his family was greatly revered in the army.

Solac saw all that, and would have been very sorry if his son had not inherited all those royal benefits, especially the governments, in which he had always made his residence and where he had lived as a petty sovereign. To complete that good fortune, all his lands in the Languedoc were placed around cities where he commanded. In addition, he was very zealous for the service of the King. In spite of all those considerations, however, he was hesitating between glory and tenderness when he received a positive order from the King to augment his regiment, which had been mobilized again, and to send his son to head it, because the name of that son was known and loved.

It was already some years since the Comte de Solac had taken Marmoisan to the court; he had been thought very handsome there, and had showed signs of spirit and courage above his age on several occasions. In any case, it did not matter if he had bad qualities; it was only a question of going to shine in the army, and he had what was required for that. The need of the State was pressing and all the considerable nobility was required to serve it well.

In order to animate the young seigneur, and to bring his father to see him depart with joy, they were promised the conclusion to their advantage, as soon as the first campaign, of a just lawsuit that Solac had against an ancient enemy of his family, which the credit of a minister had prevented from finishing for a long time. The Comte de Solac, who was one of those worthies of antiquity sensible to excess regarding points of honor and vengeance, flattered by triumphing over an enemy he hated, having the positive word of the King, which he knew to be inviolable, hesitated no longer to consent to his son's departure and thought about equipping him magnificent-ly.

Marmoisan was radiant with joy. However, he was not so strongly occupied with it that he did not have anything else in his mind. For some time he had been in love with a pretty woman, the wife of a rather considerable gentleman. That woman was virtuous and loved her husband. She had told the young Comte several times, in very vigorous terms, that he would give her great pleasure by not importuning her any longer with his foolish pretentions, of which she advised him to rid himself; but, far from profiting from her advice, he got it into his head to complete his designs before his departure.

To that effect, he employed various schemes that were futile, and, finally, having learned that it was believed that the beauty's husband was to be absent for a few days, he resolved to introduce himself by night into the young lady's bedroom by means of a rope-ladder, hoping to succeed in rendering himself fortunate by means of that unworthy artifice. Full of that pernicious project, he paid no heed to certain reflections that strove to horrify him, and, his natural imprudence always accompanying him, he got ready to climb up to the bedroom of the object of his desire went it was not yet ten o'clock in the evening.

The gentleman had concluded his business sooner than he had expected, and by a strange freak of chance, he was about to go back into his dwelling at the moment when the extravagant Marmoisan was climbing the rope-ladder. The night was too dark to discern faces, so the husband, seeing a man in that occupation, did not know whether he ought to take him for a thief or suspect his wife's virtue. As he thought about what he should do to punish him immediately without making a noise, the unfortunate Marmoisan, whom that unexpected arrival had troubled so much that he no longer knew what he was doing, lost his footing and fell to the bottom of the ladder. The jealous husband ran him through with his sword, and the thrust was so fatal that he lost his life an instant later.

27

All of that happened in a manor house near that of the Comte de Solac. The noise of the gentleman's action caused everyone to emerge from the manor with lights, including the wife, who had thought that she had heard her husband's voice and was astonished to see the spectacle. She found incontestable means to prove her innocence in the affair, but when she and her husband were in accord, they were very embarrassed as to how they were going to exculpate themselves with the Comte de Solac, whom they esteemed, and of whose credit they were apprehensive.

They could think of no better way than to ask the Comte to come to their house in order to tell him what had happened and to prove it to him by means of the rope-ladder, which was still in place, and various other items of evidence. All that was done, and in spite of the mortal dolor that the loss of his son caused the Comte, his equity made him see that he ought not to hold anyone responsible for the fate of the young fool except evil destiny. What caused him even more despair were the shameful circumstances under which he had died. Thus, by virtue of I know not what impulse, he begged the two spouses to hide that catastrophic adventure completely, and had the body carried away secretly. Then he went to discharge his dolor in the heart of his daughters, who were scarcely less afflicted than him, particularly Leonore.

The worthy old man exaggerated the cruel circumstances that accompanied the undignified death of his son, and was utterly in despair at seeing the loss of the advantageous decision in the great lawsuit, which was to have been the fruit of Marmoisan's first campaign. His daughters consoled him as best they could, but as their dominant passions occupied each of the others too much for them to be as sensible as Leonore to the tenderness of blood, they did not acquit that task as well as she did. Furthermore, her tenderness and her courage inspired a very generous design in her. As she resembled Marmoisan completely, she proposed to her father, if he would consent to it, that she would quit the costume of her own sex and go to play the role of her brother at court and in the army.

The good Seigneur, charmed by her resolution, applauded it immediately, and there was no longer any question but that of making precise arrangements in order to carry out the project cleverly.

They put about the rumor that Marmoisan was absent, and at the same time they published the news that Leonore was going to spend some time in a distant convent, and that her little sister Ioland would accompany her there. A masked young woman was made to depart, who was said to be Leonore, and Leonore put on Marmoisan's clothes.

Young Ioland was, indeed taken out of her convent, but it was in order to disguise her as a page, with the design of sending her with Leonore, because it was necessary that she had someone in her retinue who knew the secret of her sex, and they could not do better than to confide in that young sister, who was not known to anyone in society, where she had never appeared. She was not yet fifteen years old, and her sisters thought that the costume of a page suited her admirably. Although she was not as beautiful as Marmoisan, her manner was very lively and very piquant; she had intelligence, and was very jovial, but nevertheless had prudence. She was beginning to get bored in the convent and was delighted with the scene that she was to play with Leonore, whom we shall call Marmoisan henceforth, and who departed for the court as soon as her carriage was ready.

He[7] was very well received by the King, who was a wise prince full of good will, and attracted the particular good will of the monarch's only son, a very brave and very lively young prince, but not amorous, to the great astonishment of the entire court and the great regret of all the coquettes there who thought themselves beautiful.

The Prince, however, was so devoted to the love of war and violent pleasures that he seemed to have no time to think

[7] From this point on, the original text sometimes refers to the protagonist as "il" [he] and sometimes as "elle" [she], depending on the circumstances of the plot.

of tenderness. Balls, spectacles, hunting parties, masquerades, equestrian events and fêtes occupied him entirely while awaiting the opportunity to distinguish himself by means of arms. He attached himself with such good faith to the young Seigneurs who approached him in whom he found merit that he treated them more as friends than subjects, and his father the King feared that he might acquire the habit of becoming too obsessed with his favorites. He involved Marmoisan in all his pleasures, and that agreeable Comte attracted the approval of everyone by his good grace and skill.

The young Prince was often surrounded by a troop of hare-brained, coarse and brutal young men full of a ridiculous vanity, ever ready to draw their swords inappropriately, ever ready to speak ill of the human race and all women. In sum, those people only lacked the name of "fop"; as for their manners, they were similar; for society has always been similar, and in those days, as they are now, courts were full of men of that sort.

Marmoisan had a great deal to suffer in their conversation. He had taken on their cavalier air marvelously, but not their extravagances. Thus, sometimes fatigued by the impertinent tales they told of their bravery and their good fortune with beauties, he was able to tease them in a delicate and piquant manner. He soon succeeded in making himself hated, and as they had noticed that coarse remarks of a certain character made him blush and disconcerted him, they took pleasure in making them before him and making mock of his restraint at every opportunity.

They did not fail to tell stories to the Prince, and the Comte de Genac, one of his more meritorious favorites said that he was, in fact, surprised to see Marmoisan so well-behaved and modest at court, because, having seen him some time before in the province, he had not seemed so reserved. As the Prince was very reasonable, the tales he was told about Marmoisan in that regard only augmented the favor he showed him.

The Comte de Genac contributed something to that. He had an extreme esteem and amity for Marmoisan. He praised the young knight's good qualities incessantly to his young master, and gave him pleasure, for he felt his penchant drawing him to like Marmoisan a great deal. The Prince was not alone in the court in having that penchant; many of the ladies resembled him. I shall not amuse myself by recounting all the affectations and falsities that one of them adopted to please our pretended cavalier, nor all the page's tricks that Ioland played on them.

Ioland was delighted to exercise her enjoyment in a thousand petty acts of mischief, which suited the costume she was wearing admirably. She played even more on the fops than the coquettes, and acquired the reputation in a very short time of being the boldest page in the kingdom, but in that character was full of wit and charm, and had a marvelous talent for imitating all those she thought ridiculous. The Marquis de Brivas, a young friend of Marmoisan's, found so much charm in the lively manner of the page that he often said to his master: "My poor Comte, I would gladly give my most beautiful piece of land to have such a witty and amusing gentleman with me as your page."

Eventually, the season of war succeeded that of pleasures. The Prince left for the army and all the young nobility with him. As the dangerous mind of the Queen, the Kings second wife, had formed more than one turbulent cabal in the State, which were always seeking a quarrel, the monarch remained in the heart of his kingdom in order to thwart those factions by means of his presence.

Meanwhile, the campaign was murderous. There were three great battles, in which Marmoisan distinguished himself in an entirely heroic manner, and in one of which he was fortunate enough to save the life of the Prince. He also had the good fortune of discovering by means of his prudence a terrible treason that would have delivered half the army to the enemy. Those splendid actions acquired him such a great reputation and completed bringing him into the greatest favor with the Prince, such that he gave rise to a great deal of jealousy, among those who only sought to harm him.

The Comte de Richevol was one of those who resented him with the most malignity. That Seigneur had valor, but it was the only good quality he had; he was also eccentric, as imprudent as he was prodigal, and although he had married one of the great heiresses of the real and had an immense income from royal benefits, there never was a man who had so many creditors, such huge debts and the intrepidity of not paying a single penny of the millions he owed. However, the spirit of expense, which drew him to poorly calculated magnificence, and the gifts full of profusion that he made to his mistresses, put him perpetually in such shortage that he fatigued the King incessantly with his requests.

There were no charges, privileges and confiscations for which he did not hasten to ask; anything seemed proper to him, and the King, who esteemed his bravery and liked his character by virtue of a natural penchant, always had the generosity to grant him what he requested. The rumor of that had spread through society. Thus, when Marmoisan appeared at the court, having remarked that the irresponsible Richevol was wounded by the approval that we given to him, and had tried to thwart his nascent favor, he did not have much regard for him.

One day, when had learned that Richevol had made a few bad jokes, the immediately paid his back with a good one. They were both in the King's apartment, where there were a great many people, and Richevol, contrary to his habit, remained pensive, not saying anything. When, in that lethargic state, he opened his mouth to yawn, Marmoisan said in a loud voice: "The King grants it to you."

"What do you mean by that?" said Richevol.

"That you've never opened your mouth here," Marmoisan retorted, "except to request something of the King, who has the goodness never to refuse you. So I said that the King grants it to you in order to spare you a longer speech."

That quip amused the whole court greatly, and Richevol, cut to the quick by it, caused his resentment to burst forth on an occasion of which I shall speak.

A town had been attacked, and the soldiers, irritated by too much resistance on the part of the inhabitant, wanted to abandon themselves to all the furies of war against them. The Prince gave orders to retain them, but they would have been very poorly executed if Marmoisan's generous compassion had not employed a thousand stratagems to guarantee the life and honor of the large number of people. He even strove, as far as was possible, to prevent pillage; and that was a further offence for Richevol, for, although he was a great lord, he loved pillage more than the least soldier in the army.

He made terrible complaints to the Prince against Marmoisan and said that the soldiers were murmuring aloud, with reason, since it was just that those unfortunates should be compensated by pillage for all that they suffered during a campaign. He claimed that Marmoisan had over-extended the Prince's orders regarding the brake that he wanted to put on them. Then he added: "Personally, I believe that the handsome Comte is a woman in disguise, so tender and pitying is he. We have already remarked enough manners to give rise to that suspicion." Richevol had a strong desire to add that Marmoisan was not brave, but no occasion could be presented when he had not given proof of valor, so he dared not tell such a gross lie against him.

The Prince stopped all those differences by his authority, but what Richevol had said came back to him mind more than once. "Have you noticed," he said to the Comte de Genac, "what has been said to us about Marmoisan's manners, and have you not reflected on what we have seen a hundred times ourselves? I do not know whether Richevol has not stumbled on the truth, and that Marmoisan might, in fact, be a woman in disguise."

Genac, who had known the true Marmoisan in Langue-doc and could have furnished a long list of his amorous flings, assured the Prince positively that he was a was a man, and had even been very flighty when he had emerged from child-hood, but that he must no longer be thinking about that, since he had corrected himself so well that he could pass for the sagest young man in the army.

The prince was in despair at those assurances, for he would have liked, by virtue of some unknown impulse, Marmoisan to be a different sex than his own.

However, Richevol, still animated by hatred, took pleasure making that rumor run through the army in order to cause chagrin to Marmoisan, whom he believed in the depths of his soul to be veritable a cavalier. The rumor spread far and wide among the soldiers, and Marmoisan saw incessantly that people were looking at him, following him and observing him; and the more one is observed, the more one is disconcerted. They said a hundred times over to his servants that their master was a girl; Ioland informed him of it, but told him that his mildness, his modesty and his compassion for the wretched were the only subjects that gave rise to those rumors.

Marmoisan was penetrated by chagrin to see that those malicious rumors were apparently about to defeat all the measures that he had taken so cleverly. He decided to return to his father's house as soon as the campaign was over, there to feign an illness, and then declare publicly that Marmoisan was dead and reassume the costume of the other sex. The King had already granted his father the favor that he had promised him, but our heroine had too much courage to disappear before the campaign was over, and furthermore, her departure, in the state that things were in, would not have failed to disclose the secret she wanted to keep.

Full of those various anxieties, she left the camp on her own, in order at least to have the relief of being able to think freely, for her intrepidity made her scornful of the perils that might ensue from separating herself thus.

How great the ferocity of men is! she thought. *And how convinced they are of it themselves, since a little mildness and restraint is capable of making them glimpse that I am not of their sex! If they had seen me swear, strike my servants, never*

mention the divinity except to blaspheme, and drink with
shameful excess, no one would have doubted that I was a man,
and I would not find myself in the cruel chagrin that I am in,
merely for having lived with too much regulation. But even if I
have to suffer more, I cannot resolve to live in an extravagant
manner, whatever costume I wear; for, except for wild and
libertine appearances, have I not acted as men do? Have I not
risked my life? Have I not....

Marmoisan, in that ill humor, was about to make many
other bitter moral judgments against the male sex when confused voices and cries interrupted her in the middle of her argument. Scarcely had she emerged from her reverie than she
saw a young woman whom two soldiers were tugging back
and forth violently, each from one side.

He ran to them and commanded them to let the unfortunate woman go, but the brutes, excited by wine, seeing that he
was alone, replied insolently that since she was their prisoner,
only the two of them ought to dispute her. At the same time,
one of them began to drag her toward a nearby wood.

Marmoisan, only consulting his courage, drew his sword,
and the brutes did the same. By means of a valor accompanied
by good fortune, he slew the first and laid the other out, dangerously wounded, and then took the young woman, who appeared to him to be very beautiful, to his tent, wanting to protect her against the danger she might have run elsewhere.

In spite of the strange fear that the young beauty was in,
she testified her gratitude to her liberator with all the sentiments of a well-placed heart, and those thanks were made in
terms that showed that she was a person of quality.

The soldier who had been wounded was the first to pub-
lish the extreme valor of Marmoisan, and the rumor of that
adventure, quickly spread, destroyed entirely the one that
Richevol had put around, for, by the care that Marmoisan
showed for the health and honor of the beautiful prisoner, no
one doubted that he wanted to make her his mistress, so he
was thought to be very cavalier.

The Prince was in despair, and the fops, who thought that Marmoisan was finally in the process of resembling them, esteemed him more. Personally, he was very afflicted by the wrong that those foolish beliefs were doing to the reputation of the young woman, although he flattered himself that he would find means to prove her innocence without committing himself, and in the meantime he had the joy of seeing that he was no longer suspected of not belonging to the sex of which he wore the costume.

The Prince alone could not resolve to believe that, and planned more than ever to take measures to clarify the matter. He made Marmoisan a thousand presents of magnificent trinkets and rare flowers, bagatelles that ordinarily charm women, but the person to whom he addressed them, penetrating the design that he had in giving him presents of that sort, showed the greatest possible indifference for them. She let it be glimpsed that she was only accepting them because of the hand from which they came, and even sometimes let it slip that a fine horse or a good sword would have given her greater pleasure than all those vain trivia.

The desire for clarification that the Prince had put her to a further proof. He gave her several large repasts all composed of compotes and jams, solid and liquid, frangipane tarts, buttered cakes, biscuits, almond cakes and sweet liqueurs; for although that century resembled ours in a thousand ways, it differed in some, and there was no lady who was accustomed to perfumed tongues, Boulogne sausages and ratafia, as some are nowadays. Still playing her character well, although the feasts the King gave her were veritably to her taste, she pretended as much as decorum permitted to find all those things very insipid, and took the liberty of asking the Prince, in jest, whether he took them for beauties to regale them thus.

The Prince no longer knew where he was. All Marmoisan's words and actions charmed him; he could not live without him, and he sensed clearly that if all the merit he saw in him were found in a young woman, she would become the subject of a violent amour for him. However, he could no longer imagine that Marmoisan was one; everything assured him to the contrary.

How unfortunate I am! he exclaimed. *My heart has always been inaccessible to tenderness, and I get it into my head to find it for an idea. I say to myself over and over: If only Marmoisan were a young woman, how pleasant it would be to love her!' Oh, I am ashamed of these chimeras.*

The Comte de Genac was no less occupied by them than him, since a certain day when he had engaged Marmoisan to sing, who had not dared to refuse for fear of suspicions. The voice was so beautiful, and so soft, that the enchanted Genac could not believe that such a charming high register was the voice of a man. All the proofs that he had advanced to everyone of Marmoisan's sex vanished from his mind, and he became as charmed as the Prince. His passion opened his eyes, but he understood that if Marmoisan really was a heroine, he would not fail to have a rival in his master, so he was careful not to let his sentiments appear.

Meanwhile, Marmoisan, delighted to see his cavalier reputation well established, perhaps observed himself less than usual, and had the imprudence to express much chagrin in the presence of the Marquis de Brivas regarding poorly bleached linen and poorly folded clothing. In spite of his natural mildness, he criticized his servants forcefully on that subject, and his ill humor was further augmented when he saw that his tent was untidy.

He paid such great attention to those things, and entered into details of neatness so full of bagatelles, that he showed perfectly well on that occasion the ordinary character of women, the majority of whom affect in their clothing and furniture a propriety that they sometimes take as far the most ridiculous eccentricity, and of which they make a merit as an extended delicacy. Those who have a firm mind are ordinarily exempt from those faults, but Marmoisan, with all his greatness of soul, had not had the strength to rise above them, so deeply is the penchant rooted in certain individuals of the sex.

Brivas, who counted among Marmoisan's particular friends, could not prevent himself criticizing him. "Is it possible," he said to him, "that, having such great intelligence and heart, you can enter into such pettiness? It's assuredly to punish you for it that Heaven determined that you had the reputation of a woman for a few days; for I do not know if it reached as far as you, but that rumor ran around the army at one time, and to be honest, you merit it, for it is not usually a fault of men to be so small-minded."

Marmoisan blushed cruelly, and tried to prove that extreme neatness ought to be to the taste of both sexes, but Brivas still sustained, by strong arguments, that only the median was praiseworthy on that chapter, and regarded that stubbornness in Marmoisan as a weakness mingled with his great qualities.

A few days later, as people were talking in the Prince's tent about the rumor that had run through the army regarding Marmoisan's sex. Brivas stated naively what he thought had given rise to that rumor: he believed that others had remarked Marmoisan's feminine neatness, and drew attention to it while excusing it; for those times also differed from the present in another respect than the one I have already mentioned. Ladies it is true, did not drink champagne or ratafia then, but men did not take three hours dressing, put on essences and pomades, or compete with one another for celebrated coquettes by means of the quantity and extravagance of their fashion. Far from it: they were scorned as soon as they were seen to have manners that smacked slightly of triviality.

Thus, Brivas employed all his all his eloquence to disculpate Marmoisan, and as he was liked by the Prince and all the considerable persons who were there were his friends, those faults were passed over in favor of his merits. The Prince and Genac, however, were delighted by what they had just heard.

The Prince was no sooner alone with that favorite than he exclaimed: "Genac, there is no more doubt about it; Marmoisan is a young woman, and if he is one, I sense that I shall love her as long as I live. What beauty! What virtue! Mildness and courage combined!" Then he projected seeking means to convince himself of Marmoisan's sex not matter what the cost, and shortly thereafter, he thought he had found a favorable opportunity.

The commencement of autumn in that year was excessively warm, and much more so than the middle of summer had been. The Prince, being in the company of Genac, Marmoisan and several other seigneurs one day, proposed that they all go to bathe in a beautiful nearby river. He was convinced that Marmoisan was a young woman, and a modest young woman, who would not fail to be alarmed by such a proposal and would excuse herself, but he intended to press her so forcefully that she would be constrained to admit her sex.

However, he was mistaken; Marmoisan agreed, like the others, to what he proposed, although penetrated by dolor. He saw clearly that if he refused to take part, he would be discovered, and his modesty made him shiver with horror in thinking about the consequences of being exposed. He therefore followed the cheerful troop sadly, resolved to feign a violent illness when they reached the river bank, if some fortunate accident did not deliver from the danger on the way.

They arrived and wanted Marmoisan to be the first in the water; he joked for some time about that preference, and then slowly began to remove his scarf, his cravat and the most superficial parts of his attire. Then he tied a ribbon in a thousand knots while pretending to try to untie it. As he was attentive to undoing the knot once more, he and the entire company heard a loud voice that seemed to be coming from mid-air, and which shouted three times in a lugubrious and emotional tone: "Marmoisan! You are bathing, and your father is dying!"

The entire troop was extremely surprised. No one could be seen in the entire plain, and no one doubted that the voice was supernatural. Marmoisan repaired his attire with precipitation, and ran to his tent in order to find out whether a courier had arrived. He was told that no one had come. However, the bathing party had broken up; everyone, including the Prince, had accompanied Marmoisan, and, the emotion he had had having given him a slight indisposition, he feigned a considerable one, in order to get rid of all those importunate individuals.

He was no sooner alone than Ioland told him that, having heard the proposal that had been made to go and bathe, without being perceived, she had racked her brains for some means of getting him out of the dangerous situation, and, having furnished herself with a bronze cornet,[8] had followed him at a distance, and then had climbed to the top of the highest tree, from where she had cried into the cornet in a lamentable voice the words that he had heard.

Marmoisan, charmed by his amiable sister's presence of mind, embraced her a thousand times, and both were greatly amused by that stratagem; but the reflection that Marmoisan would soon be tormented by some other proof arrested their joy, with the result that, in order to put his mind at rest, as he had performed enough deeds of valor for his courage no longer to be doubted, he resolved to feign illness for the rest of the campaign, in order not to be exposed again to bathing or other disgraces.

Having kept the beautiful prisoner for some time with all the decorum that can be observed in a camp, he had eventually taken her to a celebrated abbey in a nearby town, where he often went to see her. The young woman, who was an heiress of great quality, had lost her father in the war, and her relatives, who would have liked to see her dead or a nun, were in no hurry to come to take her out.

---

[8] I have transposed the word *cornet* directly, although it cannot refer to the modern musical instrument known by that name, and probably refers to a simple funnel, here used as a loudhailer. L'Héritier seems to have had an exaggerated idea of the utility of such artifices, as the reader will observe later in the present volume

While Marmoisan was feigning illness, he asked Genac, of whose sagacity he was aware, to visit the beautiful individual occasionally in his stead, in order to console her for her misfortunes. Genac acquitted that commission like a gallant man, and, as he wanted to rid himself of the penchant he had for Marmoisan, whom he no longer doubted to be a young woman, he attempted to acquire one for the lovely foreigner.

Finally, the campaign ended and Marmoisan asked the Prince for leave to go and see his father, who was not dead, in spite of what the lugubrious voice had said. The Prince, however, did not want to give him that permission, and told him that the King, charmed by his valor and all the great services that he had rendered him, wanted to show his gratitude in the court and heap him with benefits.

Solac, meanwhile, really had need of Marmoisan's presence, in order to be consoled for the terrible chagrins that two of his daughters had caused him.

Scarcely had Marmoisan departed than the gambler had recommenced tormenting her father more than ever to extract immense sums from him, and the worthy Seigneur, who liked peace, had given her all the property that she could claim from her mother's estate for her to dispose of as she wished, in order no longer to be fatigued by her eternal demands. When she was mistress of it, she gambled with so much fury and ill luck that she lost all her capital in a matter of months. She perceived her folly when there was no longer time to repair it, and she felt so much shame and dolor that she went to throw herself into a convent, where she took the habit of a nun.

The coquette soon followed her. Her ridiculous penchant for flirtation always drawing her into some intrigue, she had a liaison that caused a scandal and made her the subject of all gossip. Perhaps she was innocent, but in sum, her reputation was ruined, and, although she was fundamentally well-behaved, her imprudence and the lack of concern for her glory merited that punishment. Seeing that the scandal had tarnished her forever, overwhelmed by despair, she did as the gambler had done and went to take the veil in the same place, to her great regret.

No one any longer remained to the Comte de Solac but the ridiculous prude, savage and eccentric, with whom no one could live and who was only good for causing her father chagrin at all hours of the day. The virtues and heroic actions of Marmoisan, however, consoled his father for all the defects of his other children. He was also very content with Ioland, and only hoped to see both of them return.

They had no less desire to do so. However, it was necessary to go to the court, where everyone regarded Marmoisan as a prodigy of valor and conduct. The King heaped him with caresses, honors and benefits. The Queen, who had not lost the desire to form parties against the State, was annoyed to see a young man of that merit so attached to her handsome son, the Prince, and resolved to take measures to detach him and to recruit him to her own interests. Thus, for different reasons, Marmoisan was caressed on all sides.

Although all those honors flattered him agreeably, he was no less eager to quit the court, where he still trembled that he might be recognized. He thought he had deduced what the sentiments of the Prince would be if he admitted that he was a young woman, and the good looks, the agreeable intelligence and the other qualities of the young Prince rendered him sufficiently likeable to be appropriate to inspire similar ones. Our heroine was not insensible, but she was able to reign over her passions, and when she reflected on the inequality of their conditions, she told herself that the Prince would only think of her to provide him with an amusement.

The mere idea of that put her pride to the torture, so she fought more than ever the secret penchant that she had always had for him, and only thought of forgetting him in her province. She was therefore waiting impatiently for time to furnish her with an opportunity to quit the court decorously, when the Prince hosted an equestrian event attended by everyone of importance in the court.

Everyone made full use of their magnificence and gallantry in order to succeed in giving themselves an agreeable adornment. Finally, the day of the display arrived, and there was a question of breaking lances against one another, in accordance with the fashion of the century. Marmoisan caused his skill to appear several times, but after having carried off the honors so many times in combats with lances, the least adroit man in the court broke one against him that shattered into several pieces, one of which wounded him so unfortunately that he fell unconscious from his horse.

That accident troubled the entire fête; Marmoisan was carried into the palace at which the games were being held. The Prince quit them and ran to the bed in which he found Marmoisan unconscious. As attempts were made to bring him round, blood was perceived that revealed that he was wounded in the stomach. The wanted to see of what the injury consisted, but how astonished those present were when they saw a cleavage charming in its beauty.

The Prince, simultaneously seized by joy and dolor, uttered a cry, which he was unable to suppress, as Ioland came into the room. She had not witnessed her sister's accident, for she was occupied at that moment in preparing a ballet that was to be put on in the evening. When she saw her sister unconscious, covered in blood, and her sex discovered, the spectacle threw her into such despair that she could no longer control herself.

"Oh, my dear sister," she cried, "is it necessary for you to lose your secret and your life in a vain amusement, after you have been able to conserve both in the midst of the most frightful perils?"

Those words gave a further enlightenment to the Prince.

The rumor of the adventure having spread instantly through the Palace, the court rendered in a crowd to Marmoisan's room. She had not emerged from her unconsciousness in spite of all the efforts that had been made to bring her round.

The King, who expressed an infinite consideration for the charming heroine, instructed his wife, the Queen, forcefully to get rid of the crowd, and withdrew. The Queen, who saw that it would take her a long time to come round, left her in the hands of her women, and also withdrew. In spite of his anxiety, the Prince was obliged by decorum to leave, and to escort the Queen to her apartment. It did not take him long, however, to return in order to seek information about the health of a person so dear to him.

He found Ioland with his sister, still inconsolable for the condition in which she found her. She believed that it was no longer a time to hide anything from the Prince, and, in spite of her dolor, she told him, with a great deal of intelligence, about the measures her sister had taken in order to maintain her disguise and thus ensure that her secret would be buried eternally, in order to give her brother the glory of all the courageous actions she had carried out. Then the young woman added that the hereditary zeal in the family for the King had, more than any other reason, engaged Leonore to take that course of action.

Finally, sentiment returned to her, and the confusion that she felt on seeing the Prince beside her is indescribable.

"How much alarm you have given us, Madame," he said to her. "It is only the joy that we shall have in seeing you recover that can equal it."

She replied to him in a fashion that was as witty as it was modest, but it was easy to discern that she was deeply troubled. Then the Prince left her in order to leave her at liberty.

Meanwhile, the entire escort was resounding with the merit of Marmoisan, who had become Leonore; people were praising to the skies her valor, her virtue, the solidity of her mind, the charm of her wit, and could not be sufficiently astonished in seeing the qualities of the two sexes so well united in the same subject. The rumor of the praise that was being lavished on the heroine delighted the Prince, secretly, and caused him to applaud his choice again; but he was strangely anxious to know how he figured in Leonore's mind.

44

He went to seek clarification on hat matter the next day, as soon as possible, and found Ioland in the costume of her own sex.

Leonore was in bed, in the negligence of an invalid inattentive to her adornment, but in spite of her negligence and dejection she appeared admirable beautiful. The Prince learned that the wound the lance had inflicted was not dangerous, and would not take long to heal.

As everyone had gone away out of respect, he approached her and said to her tenderly: "How happy everyone will be, Madame, if all wounds were as easy to cure as the one that has caused me to shed tears for you! But there are some that are more dangerous, about which I can speak from experience, and, generous as you are, I fear that you might not have the sensibility for me that I have had for you, and that you might only see that they are making me suffer without being touched by them."

Leonore, very disconcerted by that speech, replied in an embarrassed fashion: "Sire, the zeal and respect that I have for you will always make me take a keen interest in everything that concerns you, but there are certain wounds that consist more of imagination than they are real, and of which, in fact, I confess that that I do not have to complain."

The Prince only wanting to explain himself partially, told her in terms as passionate as they were gallant about the presentiments that he had had regarding her sex, exaggerating the impressions that they had made in his soul, and ended up by saying that he would be the unhappiest of all men if she were insensible to a tenderness that would last as long as he lived.

Leonore replied to him that she dared to remind him of the marks of firmness she had often given in order to make him reflect that she was not subject to many weaknesses of which other women were capable, and that, in order to avoid the greatest of all those weaknesses, she would never share the sentiments that he had just expressed to her, since the interval between their conditions prevented her from ever being able to respond without injuring her glory.

"Your merit alone, Madame," replied the Prince, impatiently, "renders you worthy of filling the throne of the foremost sovereigns in the world, but in addition to that merit, I am in your debt for a thousand reasons: the striking services that you have rendered to the State, the life that I owe you...."

"You exaggerate those feeble services too much," said Leonore, interrupting him, "but even if they were as great as you deign to say, your father the King would not...."

"Reply to me with your heart," the Prince said, interrupting, "and I will answer for the King's consent. I know what his esteem for you is, and his good will toward me."

The arrival of the two princesses put an end to that conversation. Meanwhile, the Prince ran to report to the King on Leonore's health. He gave an advantageous account of the manner in which she sustained the character of her own sex, and the King praised her unreservedly. Noticing the excess of joy that the praise in question cause to appear in the eyes of the Prince, he said, smiling, that Leonore had disarmed many of his enemies costumed as a man, but that she had disarmed his son in the costume of a woman.

The young Prince blushed and remained nonplused, but he soon pulled himself together and told the King that it was true that he had not been able to refuse his esteem to so many virtues. He added that if he deigned to approve his penchant, he would find himself the most fortunate of princes, in seeing him united with a heroine so accomplished. The King told him with kindness that he had no opposition to that inclination, and that he would consent to him marrying her as soon as she had recovered. The Prince, transported by joy, threw himself at his feet to thank him, and ran to take that news to Leonore.

As soon as her sex had been recognized, the whole court was full of the rumor that the Prince was charmed by her. The King had been immediately alerted to that, and had made the decision at the same time to allow his son's choice to act. The late Queen, the mother of the young Prince, was a foreign Princess who had always conserved such an eccentric inclination for her homeland and the princes of her house that she had never acquired a sincere attachment for her husband the King, or even for her son, and had taken that strange caprice so far as to betray the State. The King's second wife was a Princess with an unquiet and turbulent mind, who wanted absolutely to have a part in its affairs, although the pettiness of her mind rendered her incapable of conducting any. She formed cabals incessantly, which divided the court, and allowed herself to be governed by women of low intelligence and obscure condition, all of whose impulses she followed.[9]

The King, fatigued by the mental annoyances of those two Princesses, convinced of the uselessness of foreign alliances and convinced of Leonore's elevated, tranquil and reasonable character, had no difficulty in resolving himself to seeing her become his son's wife, all the more so in thinking that the young Prince so easily took impressions from those he considered. The King preferred that he abandoned himself to the advice of a cherished wife whose sentiments only seemed to aspire to virtue than to that of some ambitious favorite.

The people, who had been charmed by Marmoisan's fine deeds and transported with joy when they learned that they were those of a young woman, heaped the King with blessings for the consent that he gave to the marriage. The court seemed delighted by it, and the Marquis de Brivas, one of the greatest Seigneurs in the realm, was doubly so, obtaining for a wife the lovely Ioland, whose joviality had charmed him so much in the days when she wore the costume of a page. The Comte de Genac married the beautiful prisoner, whose merit and wealth rendered her a very fine match.

Leonore and the Prince savored together for many years all the pleasures of good fortune accompanied by virtue, and that heroine was the glory and consolation of her father, with

---

[9] Any perceived resemblance between these fictitious wives of a fictitious King and Maria Theresa of Spain and Madame de Montespan (whose "secret" marriage to Louis XIV was known to the entire court) is, the author would doubtless have declared, purely coincidental.

47

whom the false prude had finally quarreled publicly, thus rendering herself a topic of gossip in her turn by allowing her bizarre caprices to be discovered.

But in telling you, Mademoiselle, the memorable story of Marmoisan, I believe, on extending my reflections further, that I was not thinking. It seems to me that my narration did not last as long when I made it to the company that I mentioned to you. But in sum, no matter; what I have just told you is fundamentally and naively the tale of Marmoisan, such s it was told to me when I was a child.

Moral

A hundred times my nurse or my darling
Told me that fine tale by the fire
I only have added a little embroidery
One sees clearly by such accounts
That the wisdom of our fathers
Without embarrassing us with severe maxims
Teaches us fine lessons.
That those who blur the mind
With fire of criminal ardor
Always perish shamefully
And those who follow blindly
Gambling, false prudery
And eccentric coquetry
Always and infallibly
Pay for their foolish mania;
But those who do all in their power
To follow reason, glory and duty
Can finally vanquish destiny
And see their virtue crowned. [10]

---

[10] L'Héritier's snatches of poetry, whether attached to her stories as "morals" or inserted within them as "songs," always rhyme, but are erratic in their scansion. I have translated most

THE ENCHANTMENTS OF ELOQUENCE

or, The Effects of Mildness
A Novelette

To Madame la Duchesse d'Épernon[11]

Beautiful Duchesse, please interrupt your serious and savant occupations for a few moments in order to listen to one of those Gallic fables that apparently come in a direct line from the storytellers or troubadours of Provence, once so celebrated. I know that minds as great and as well made as yours do not neglect anything, that they find in the slightest bagatelles subject for important reflections, which not everyone is capable of discovering; and I cannot help thinking that you will be able to do so right away. You, whose profound science is never astonished, will doubtless be astonished that these tales, incredible as they are, have come to us from age to age without anyone taking the trouble to write them down.

> *They are not easy to believe,*
> *But as long as there are children*
> *Of mothers and grandmothers,*
> *The memory of them will remain.*

---

of them literally, except in one brief instance where the rhyme seemed more necessary than the exact conservation of the meaning.

[11] Louise-Anne-Christine de Foix de La Valette d'Épernon (1624-1701) spent a riotous few years at court before entering a Carmelite convent, from which she maintained a prolific correspondence with various notable individuals; she might have become a saint but for vague and unspecific rumors concerning the authenticity of her vocation.

A lady, very learned in Greek and Roman antiquities, and even more knowledgeable about Gallic antiquities, told me this tale when I was a child, in order to imprint it in my mind that honesty has never done any harm to anyone, or, as the old proverb says, "a fine talker does not skin his tongue," and that often

Mild and courteous language
Is worth more than a rich heritage.

She strove to prove the truth of that maxim, very sensate, although Gothic, by means of the marvelous story that I am going to tell you.

In the time when there were fays, ogres, follet spirits and other phantoms of the same kind in France—it is difficult to specify that time, but it does not matter—there was a gentleman of great consideration who loved his wife passionately, and that is another reason why I cannot divine what time it was. His wife loved him no less; he was a good man and he merited it. They lived together quite happily for fifteen or sixteen years, but death separated them. The lady died, and only left a unique daughter.

She had been very beautiful, and her daughter was no less so; and, with a thousand charms that appeared in her infancy, she had a complexion so dazzlingly white that it inspired her name, which was Blanche.[12]

Her mother had not had any wealth, but her father had had a good deal. However, he no longer had it when his wife died, because his affairs had turned bad during his marriage, and his daughter found herself reduced to having nothing for

---

[12] "Blanche-Neige" [Snow White] is the French title of "Schneewittchen," a story by the Brothers Grimm published in the same collection as "Rumpelstiltskin," which similarly seems to have no substantial basis in Germanic folklore.

her dowry but her white skin and her beauty, which are not usually a great help in finding a considerable match.

Blanche's father, being greatly afflicted by his wife's death, thought that he would not be consoled until he found another, and as his daughter still seemed young enough to have time to find an establishment at her leisure, he concluded that it was necessary to think of himself first, and he thought seriously about making his choice. The poor state of his affairs made him lean in the direction of wealth, so he attached himself to a widow who was neither beautiful nor young, but very opulent.

Like him, that woman had only one daughter, and she was the widow of a financier, who had not neglected any of the tricks of his métier in order to maximize wealth, and had succeeded in doing so. They had nothing for which to reproach one another with regard to birth, so the point of honor never caused any division between them, but as she had carefully conserved the sentiments and the manner of the family to which she belonged, she had given her daughter an education similar to the one that she had had. Her daughter having a rude character very apt to receive vulgar impressions, it was almost impossible to find two persons more vulgar and more rustic than them. In that character they did not fail to include an excessive but ill-extended ambition; they had ideas so ridiculous that they committed a hundred extravagances, in which one saw and discovered the aberrations that their ostentations and vanity inspired in them.

With those dispositions, it is easy to judge that Blanche's father, who bore the title of Marquis, was welcomed with joy by the widow, whose desire to have a great name caused her to make the marriage in a matter of days. Her new husband, who had only envisaged her wealth in marrying her, saw with a great deal of chagrin, as soon as they were married, how numerous and fatiguing the Marquise's faults were, but as he was naturally inclined to be at peace with everyone, and he also had a character of allowing himself to be governed by his wife, such as she was, they lived together quite happily, on condition that he made it a principle never to contradict her and to leave her the absolute mistress in all things. He consoled himself for her inconvenient humor by means of the comforts that the great wealth she had brought him procured. He supported her fits of temper philosophically, and when he saw her begin to scream, as he liked reading, he went to read in his study.

It was only the lovely Blanche who had every reason to complain. Her stepmother had an inconceivable aversion for her; she was in despair in seeing that her beauty caused all her daughter's deformity to appear and rendered her the scorn of society; for Alix—that was the name of the financier's daughter—was a monster of ugliness as well as vulgarity. Such as she was, however, her mother nevertheless loved her to the point of idolatry; she would have sacrificed anything for her satisfaction; and to complete Blanche's misfortune, Alix hated her a hundred times more than her mother. In consequence, she employed all imaginable means to cause her chagrin.[13]

The mother wanted Blanche to be put in a convent, but Alix, who was determined always to see her the victim of her caprices, deflected her mother from that design, fearing that Blanche would then no longer be under their eyes, that some obliging friend might bring all her merit to light and procure her some splendid establishment—which Alix feared more than death.

It was therefore resolved that Blanche would stay in the house and not make or receive any visits. They took measures to hide her carefully from all honest people, and in order to tarnish her beauty they obliged her to occupy herself with the employments of a chambermaid, housekeeper, and even cook.

---

[13] As well as being reproduced in Perrault's "Cendrillon" (with the addition of an extra ugly sister) this situation is also very obviously reflected in Madame de Villeneuve's 90,000-word "*conte*" "Les Nayades" (1765; tr. as *The Naiads*), Black Coat Press, ISBN 978-1-61227-626-7), which seems to have taken considerable inspiration from L'Héritier's story.

If I wanted, Madame, to tell you this story entirely in the terms that the storytellers of Provence taught it to our grand-mothers, I would tell you a thousand astonishing details about Blanche's cleverness, but there is no need; I shall only tell you that, by virtue of an admirable docility very rare in such a beautiful person, she had the complaisance to employ herself in all the disagreeable tasks that her stepmother prescribe for her; that Blanche added luster to everything she touched; and that no one had ever seen ruffs so well starched and high collars so well-dressed. She acquitted all those things so skillfully that I am sure that if she had lived nowadays she would have been perfectly able to straighten hats, and would have attract-ed a large court of women who are always in mortal chagrin because their hats go stubbornly askew no matter how much care that they take in giving proof of straightness in their at-tire. Blanche would have given to that ornament, so useful to women in the land of pygmies, all its symmetry, and she would have outdone Monsieur D***, with whom no coquette dares to quarrel, because she had the fortunate talent of arrang-ing headwear and showing off cornettes better than the finest hairdresser in the world.[14]

That fine prerogative attracted the admiration and com-plaisance of a large number of women because she did their hair and enabled them to turn heads as she turned them; but let us leave those remarks in order to continue our story.

Not only was Blanche given a thousand fatigues, but she was left in a negligence that would have gone as far as the most disgusting dirtiness but for the natural disposition that she had to be neat in no matter what way she was clad. So, in

---

[14] The wordplay in this paragraph does not translate, but the references to clothing that I have translated literally could all be construed metaphorically at the time of writing to refer to a woman's character in derogatory terms, in much the same way that many similar terms still can. The term *cornetet* refers here to a kind of head-dress, typically but not exclusively worn by nuns.

spite of the care that was taken to give her clothes capable of deforming her, whatever they did, her flat hair and her garments coarse cloth did not prevent her from appearing as beautiful as Amour, while Alix, covered in gold and precious stones and with her hair carefully made up, frightened everyone who looked at her, for the excess of her adornment only rendered her uglier and surlier.

However, Alix could not stay at home; she was seen incessantly on the promenades and at balls; she never wearied of displaying her pomp everywhere; but if she found pleasure in attracting the gaze of a few bourgeois women, she was also very mortified to hear the pages and musketeers of that era incessantly voicing the most piquant verities behind her. For even in those days, many musketeers, students, young officers and other harebrained individuals had the ridiculous habit of coming to look all the women they thought poorly adorned in the face, and saying a thousand impertinent things loudly when they did not find them sufficiently beautiful for their liking. Thus, one can imagine how many of those young fools exercised the fine talent they had for cold mockery when they saw Alix's repulsive face. But what one cannot easily imagine is how she avenged herself on Blanche for all the insults she had received; calculating that if there were no beauties in the world, ugliness would not be exposed to such scorn, she redoubled her aversion for that lovely individual and engaged her mother to cause her further chagrins.

In spite of Blanche's natural mildness, so much illtreatment sometimes embittered her so much that she made plans to get out of the house no matter what the cost, but the hatred she had for outbursts, the love she had for her father and the hope of finding an opportunity to escape from of her slavery with decorum took away the resolution to leave noisily. She therefore prepared once again to be patient, and her father, who loved her dearly but did not have the firmness to oppose the barbaric manner in which she was treated, softened her chagrins by sharing them, praised her virtue, and consoled

her by promising her on behalf of Heaven that she would find
herself in a happier state one day.

Those consolations sustained Blanche's constancy in her
misfortunes, but as society and all sorts of diversion were forbidden to her, she found the means to obtain it in her room by
reading. She amassed a large number of novels,[15] I do not
know how; but she did not get as much satisfaction from them
as one might think, because she could only read by night, her
stepmother occupying her relentlessly while the daylight lasted. Although it required her to cut down on her sleep in order
to read, however, that did not stop her; she believed that she
was reposing in reading, and when she could slip away for a
few moments by day, she returned to her books with haste.

Her stepmother, who kept watch on her incessantly, took
umbrage at the ardor that she had to be alone in her room, and,
seeking clarification of what it was that attracted her there so
powerfully, she surprised her one day as she reached one of
the most beautiful passages of a novel as well-written as it was
pleasantly invented. The Marquise ought to have been touched
to see the innocent amusement to which Blanche was reduced,
but although she could scarcely read, she threw herself upon
the book and snatched it from her hands, and after having read
the title, with a great deal of difficulty, because it was a forbidding Greek name that she pronounced very poorly, she
finally understood that the book was a novel, and commenced

---

[15] Translating *romans* as "novels" is in this context is undoubtedly anachronistic, but the anachronism is clearly delib-
erate on the author's part, as subtly signaled by a little inter-
jection on the subject of another anachronism that she with-
draws ostentatiously. It is certain that the works the author has
in mind are those of Madeleine de Scudéry, and the following
passage is a spirited defense of them against contemporary
prejudice. The reference to a Greek title offers the specific
suggestion that the book in question might by *Artamène, ou le
Grand Cyrus*, whose protagonist is borrowed from Xenophon.

to scream strangely at Blanche, when, fortunately for the poor girl, her father came into the room.

Without giving him time to speak, his wife shouted at him with all her might: "Well, Monsieur Ruinous, with all your chic and sugared arguments. Look how well you have brought up your slut of a daughter. I have just caught her reading an amorous book on the sly."

The Marquis found a little more courage than normal that day, responded to his wife after looking at the book: "Blanche does very well to amuse herself with this reading. You have taken all pleasures away from her; she cannot do better than to take one that will open her mind to politeness. I am delighted when I see young women of quality occupying themselves in reading; if they all applied themselves to it, one would not see them so embarrassed in their pleasure, they would not be running so much from one spectacle to another and one card game to another."

The Marquise, who knew full well how avid her daughter was for gambling, as well as all other pleasures, thought that her husband had the intention of attacking Alix in what he had just said, so she resumed in an even louder tone: "Truly, I am of the opinion that women of quality, who have wealth in thousands, ought not to be prevented from diverting themselves at their whim; it is as well for paupers,[16] who are of ruined nobility, to entrench themselves in such pleasures, but it is permissible for ladies who have more pistoles than those sluts have pennies to do whatever seems good to them. As for demoiselles who do not have a sou, they only ought to know how to do housework and to be always occupied with it; at least, if they want to be readers, it is necessary that it is in good books, not those in which one learns mischief."

"One does not learn mischief," retorted Blanche's father, brutally, "in these beautiful novels that I see my daughter

---

[16] The literal translation of *gueuses* [female paupers] diminishes the insult, the term also being frequently used as a description of common prostitutes.

reading"—for he had loved them even more than her, and he still loved them. "On the contrary," he said, "one only finds great sentiments in them and fine examples; one always sees vice punished therein, and virtue always recompensed. One can even say that for young persons, the reading of novels is in some ways better than reading history itself, because history, being entirely subject to the truth, sometimes presents images very shocking for mores. History paints men as they are, and novels represent them as they ought to be, and seem by virtue of that to be aspiring to perfection. At least one cannot deny that well-made novels teach social graces and politeness of language. Blanche already had a disposition to speak properly, and I hope that the reading of these agreeable works will finish giving her the habit of it."

The stepmother, who did not understand anything of that philosophy, and who was a surly creature who had no intention of relaxing her severity to Blanche in the slightest, could not allow the apology for novels that the Marquis was about to continue to reach completion, because it was all Greek to her.

"What a seeker of midday at four o'clock!" she replied. "Mercy of my life! Let your daughter read as much as she likes, since that game pleases her, and you too, but if the affairs of my house are not done as punctiliously as usual, I shall be able to turn her to that end." She quit them, and the angry conversation finished in that manner.

You, Madame, who only occupy yourself with sublime reading, might perhaps find that Blanche's father was a little too prejudiced in favor of novels. I do not know what you think about it, but I will not tell you what I think either; I will only report what my chronicle contains; I am a historian, and a historian, male or female, ought not to take sides. Do not make fun of these reflections, I beg you, for if you are going to lose your seriousness you will also make me lose mine. I need it, however, in order to have the strength to recount to you tranquilly the rest of this surprising history.

Blanche's father was not mistaken. In very little time, that beautiful girl combined an achieved politeness with her natural mildness; no one can express themselves with greater charm and precision that she did, either by virtue of the commerce that she had with the productions of the intellect or for some other reason. Neither Alix or her mother envied those new advantages; they were too vulgar to sense the delicacy of what they heard her say, so they only continued to be wounded by her personal charms and no longer thought about anything but causing her to lose them forever.

At the height of the summer the Marquis and his family went to the country. It was there that Blanche's stepmother exercised all the talents she had in order to torment her. She employed her in all the most rustic labors, but in spite of the care she took to expose her at every moment to the sun, her complexion, which was naturally incapable of sunburn, still conserved its whiteness.

Her stepmother was dying of chagrin in seeing that nothing was capable of rendering her ugly and could not give up that deign. Finally, after all the means she had attempted, which had not succeeded, she took it into her head also to charge her with going to fetch water for the usage of the entire household from a rather distant spring.

Blanche, who had devoted herself to patience, did not receive that commission with any more repugnance than those that were ordinarily given to her; to go in quest of water was not for her an employment more humiliating than a hundred others to which she had been subjected. In addition, she saw demoiselles who also went there, for the customs of that time were in some ways quite different from the manners of the present time, and the example might have been able to console her if she had been going there of her own free will, like the country demoiselles, or because of the indigence of her father's household.

Although she was well armed with patience, however, she had difficulty holding back her tears when she considered that the crushing toil that was imposed on her was only intended to drive her to despair and destroy her. That was her chagrin. However, not only did she have the example of her neighbors but she had read somewhere that he daughters of kings did the laundry in the times of Homer, and that Achilles did the cooking quite happily; Blanche therefore went, without saying anything about it, to fetch water whenever it was needed.

The spring to which she went to fetch it was surrounded by the most beautiful landscape in the world, but the place was dangerous because it was close to a forest from which wolves often emerged to make brief excursions as far as the water. Muffled rumor published that it was for that reason that Blanche's mother liked sending her there so much. The likeable young woman had been warned several times about the danger to which she was exposing herself, but, although the wolves were not what she feared the most, the warnings were quite useless to her, because she could not make her stepmother hear reason.

After having been there several times without finding either beasts or men—to speak like my author—one day, after having drawn the water, she saw a furious wild boar coming toward her, although it was not being pursued by anyone. She was seized by fear, as one inevitably would be, Madame. She was not so frightened, however, that she did not think of self-preservation; she took flight, and had already reached the brushwood when she was struck in the shoulder by a blow that knocked her to the ground. At the same moment, the boar passed by without doing her any harm and hid in the wood.

As she made efforts to get up, in spite of the pain that she felt, she heard someone cry: "What! Beautiful child, it's you that I've wounded instead of the boar! How unfortunate I am!"

At the same time, Blanche saw a richly clad young man, who approached her in order to help her up. Although the blood she had lost rendered her very pale, the hunter had no sooner looked at her than he saw that she was extraordinarily beautiful and felt touched by the gentle and engaging appearance that he found in the young woman, in spite of the rusticity of her clothing.

He did not amuse himself paying her compliments; he was more judicious; he thought about helping her promptly. He tore up his handkerchief and his cravat—or his ruff, if you prefer—in order to try to staunch the blood from the wound. The history says that Blanche's eyes also inflicted a wound on the hunter, but I have difficulty believing that it happened at the first moment, or, if the chronicle is telling the truth, it is necessary that the hunter caught fire as easily as his rifle.

Some critic might say that the hunter could not have had a rifle because, in the days of fays, people did not yet have the use of artillery. I know scrupulous savants who would never let a tale finish without protesting against that anachronism, but if I wanted to get into an argument with such an insensate storyteller, could I not say that Mesdames the fays had performed one of their tricks? One sees many other marvels, so they could well have contrived that one, especially in favor of the hunter in question, who was the godson of Melusine, Logistille and I don't know how many others among the most celebrated of those obliging ladies.[17]

However, it is true that the weapon that had wounded Blanche was not a firearm, for a historian must always tell the truth, although I am rather sorry that one is lacking here; it was a dart, or a javelin, that the prince had tried to throw at the boar…but I think that I have not yet told you that the hunter was a prince? Well, no matter; I will tell you soon what his genealogy was, for at present it is necessary to return to poor Blanche, whom we have left too long semi-conscious on the grass.

As she found herself in the hands of such a surgeon, she was not afraid, and in a confusion that gave her as much pain

---

[17] Logistillle is a fay who protects the knight Roland in some of the romances detailing his adventures. She appears as a character in the lyric tragedy *Roland* (1685), whose libretto was by Philippe Quinault and music by Raymond Lully, both close associates of Mademoiselle de Scudéry's salon. Quinault is cited by the author a few paragraphs hence.

as the harm she was suffering. The obliging hunter gave her all the help that he could, and was so penetrated by admiration and dolor that he did not have the strength to say a word.

Finally after having put the best dressing on the beauty's wound that he could contrive and had thrown water in her face ten or twelve times, in such a manner that she no longer appeared to be in danger of fainting, the young stranger said to her: "How extreme my good and ill fortune are today! What good luck to have seen a person as charming as you! What bad luck to have been the case of the woes she is experiencing!"

"You are an innocent cause of those woes," replied Blanche. "So, Seigneur, such a misfortune does not merit troubling your tranquility."

"Even if you were only an ordinary young woman," replied the stranger, "I would be very sorry to have wounded you; imagine my despair regarding the accident, then, on seeing you as lovely as you are."

"Without responding to your honeyed words," Blanche retorted, "I will tell you, Seigneur, that you are pushing generosity too far. If you had killed me, it would only have been necessary to blame destiny and not yourself. And even then, the loss of the life of a girl like me would not have been anything to merit agitating yours, which appears to me to be one of those fine lives that are ordinarily so useful to the State. I can answer for the fact that people of my character would sacrifice their useless lives with pleasure for gentlemen as necessary to the public as you appear to be. Grant me then, Seigneur, the favor of asking you not to be afflicted by my adventure, for in my turn, I would reproach myself for the chagrin that it would be causing you."

The stranger, who had initially judged Blanche, on the basis of her clothing, to be a peasant, or at most a demoiselle from the village, was extremely surprised by the manner in which she spoke, but he was even more touched by her mildness than her politeness. The young prince was naturally very violent, and he felt strongly that if anyone, even innocently, had done him as much harm as he had just done to that beauty, nothing that could have stopped him becoming terribly angry against the author of that harm. The less he was capable of such moderation, the more he admired it; by virtue of that, Blanche rendered herself the absolute mistress of his soul, and that example proved admirably in advance the truth of one of the maxims of Quinault, who said with so much justice:

> It is beauty which commences to please,
> But tenderness that completes the charm.

The Prince was enchanted to such a point that the host of thoughts that presented themselves to his imagination made him remain silent for a few moments, and he only broke the silence in order to say a hundred more gallant things to Blanche. Nevertheless, he did not testify to her any of the impressions that she had made on his heart, because he feared alarming a beautiful person who put as much modesty into her responses as mildness and politeness.

However, the prince was very anxious in seeing that his followers were not catching up with him. He had been separated from them during the hunt, and he was very impatient for someone to find him because he wanted to send immediately for a carriage, to take Blanche wherever she wanted to go.

The beauty, however, to whom he expressed his anxiety and his design, said to him: "Seigneur, I beg you with the utmost urgency not to give orders for that, and if you have as much consideration for me as you have made me see, I assure you that you could not give me a more sensible pleasure than by quitting me without giving me any further thought, and without talking to anyone about encountering me or my wound. I have the strongest reasons in the world for making you those pleas, and I hope that I can return very quietly to my father's dwelling when I have rested here for a little longer."

After a few very obliging protestations on the part of the prince, he said to her: "Well, if that is what you want; I am submissive to your orders; but as for not thinking about you, do not believe, charming person, that one can obey you in that regard."

With those words, the prince quit her, remounted his horse and left Blanche astonished, weak and very anxious about what people might be thinking at home, from which she had been absent for such a long time.

Finally, she set forth, and after much difficulty she arrived at her father's dwelling just as someone was being sent to see what was retaining her at the spring. The stepmother commenced by making a great deal of noise, but when Blanche had said that she had had an accident, that she had been wounded by a wild boar, and that, but for a passer-by who had helped her, she might have died on the spot, the stepmother was constrained to shut up. The Marquis, greatly troubled by that news, ran to his daughter, had her put to bed and resolved not to rely on his wife with regard to the care that Blanche would need.

Since the beautiful young woman is in good hands, let us return to the Prince and his genealogy.

He was related to Urgande, the cousin of Maugis, the great-nephew of Merlin, and also the godson of the wise Lirgandée and the most savant fays, as I have already said.[18] In any case, it is not known exactly of what land he was the future sovereign, for certain narratives say that he was the son of the Duc de Normandie, others affirm that it was the Duc de Bretagne and other memoirs that it as the Comte de Poitiers that had given him birth. That lack of clarity comes from that no one knows where the spring was to which Blanche went in quest of water. In the final analysis, it does not matter much; it is sufficient that all the narratives agree that the hunter who

---

[18] A tragedy entitled *Urgande*, probably by Quinault, was performed in front of Louis XIV's court in January 1679. She also features prominently in his lyric tragedy *Amadis de Gaule* (1684), again with music by Lully, based on the Spanish romance of that title. Lirgandée is featured in French translations of *Don Quixote* as a relative of Urgande.

wounded the beauty was the son and heir of the sovereign of the land.

As the young prince was very occupied by the adventure he had had, as soon as he had rejoined his companions he charged one of his squires, who was very clever, to go and make inquiries in the village regarding Blanche's destiny. The squire acquitted his commission skillfully and came to render an exact account to his master of the birth, the inclinations and the misfortunes of the young beauty. The prince was delighted to learn that she was of illustrious nobility, and thought about taking measures to render fortunate a person who seemed to him to be so worthy of being so.

Blanche was loved in the village of which her father was the Seigneur, as much as Alix was hated, so the peasants had told the squire a hundred amusing tales regarding the fine qualities of the one and the shocking faults of the other. The gentleman, who was quick-witted and jovial, had not forgotten a single word of all the things that had been said to him, and he recounted them to the Prince in the same terms, with a naivety that had the ability to divert a lover who was as occupied with tenderness as the heroes of novels usually are.

The first concern of the Prince was to seek to cure Blanche of the wound he had inflicted, but even though he belonged to a family very knowledgeable in the art of enchantment, he was no more skillful for that in that art, so he had recourse to one of his godmothers, to whom he recounted his adventure. He did not confide to her the amour he had for Blanche; he only requested that the beautiful young woman be cured, but did so with so much ardor, and spoke about her merit with so much exaggeration that any woman with some knowledge of the world, without being a fay and knowing necromancy, would easily have divined that he was in love. It was therefore not difficult for the good fay to make that discovery, and as she loved her godson veritably she was very glad that he had put the affair in her hands, making it a pleasure to see Blanche, and to examine whether she was worthy of the sentiments that she had inspired in a heart insensible until then to tenderness.

Dulcicula,[19] as the fay was named, therefore went to prepare a marvelous balm that cured the most mortal wounds in less than twenty-four hours. Then she adopted the guise of an old peasant woman, and in that apparel she went to present herself at the door of Blanche's father.

The first person she encountered was Alix, to whom she said very civilly in a village style that, having an admirable secret, she had come to offer her services to the Marquis for his daughter.

"What has this old madwoman come to tell me?" replied Alix, brutally. "I believe that all the village vermin are frantic to intervene on behalf of that she-ape Blanche. I don't know who they think they all are, to get demented like idiots; this old beast would do better to go make her a box for the cemetery; if it were some good sheepdog, its death would be a greater loss than hers."

Dulcicula was extremely surprised to see a demoiselle covered in gold and gemstones speaking such a strange jargon, but the fay, who was mildness personified, was even more indignant at her evil nature than her vulgarity. She did not make any reply to that brutality, and, having learned that the Marquis was not at home, she addressed herself to the woman whom he had charged with looking after Blanche.

The woman took the fay to the invalid's bedside. Dulcicula said to her, still in terms that were in conformity with her attire, that, her accident having touched her, she had come expressly from her village to offer her a balm that she had, which cured all sorts of injuries very promptly.

Blanche, who had a great deal of intelligence and who was not preoccupied with popular errors, thought that the balm that was being mentioned to her was one of those remedies of which the people are fond, which are known as "innocent little

---

[19] Dulcicula is the Latin word from which the French *douceureuse* [sweetness, or mildness] is derived.

remedies" because they are, in fact, very innocent in their usage. The amiable young woman, however, still retaining her character, replied to the fay: "You're very kind, my good mother, to quit your affairs like this to come and give me pleasure; I don't know how I can recognize what I owe to your zeal, being so far from the state that I would like to be in, but I will mention you to my father, and I hope that he will reward you for your good will. As for the balm, I thank you for it, but I am in the hands of surgeons, and it is necessary not to change remedies every day."

Dulcicula, charmed by Blanche's mildness and honest manners, nevertheless penetrated the poor opinion she had of her balm, but she pressed her to make use of it with so much ardor and confidence that the beautiful young woman consented to do so, purely out of complaisance for the peasant woman whom she saw so affectionate for her. The fay therefore put her enchanted balm on Blanche's wound, and, by a marvelous effect, it was not long before the beauty began to feel greatly soothed.

They entered into conversation then. Dulcicula could not cease admiring privately the mildness and other good qualities that she saw combined with so much beauty, and that admiration produced a good effect. The fay was holding a stick on which she seemed to be supporting herself, but it was the enchanted wand of which she made use to accomplish all the prodigies of her art. She touched Blanche with that wand, as if by chance, and gave her a gift of always being more gentle, amiable and decorous than ever, and having the most beautiful voice in the world.

As soon as she left the beautiful invalid's room, accompanied by the woman who was caring for her, she made inquiries regarding Alix. She learned that the scold in question was as coquettish as she was ugly and malevolent, and that because she was always in splendid attire and made a hundred grimaces and contortions in order to make herself seem charming, she was known everywhere, by virtue of irony, as "the beautiful Alix." The woman added that in a thousand places, when a young woman was seen putting on impertinent and affected airs, people said that she was "behaving like the beautiful Alix."

Thus informed, the fay once again encountered the person they had just been discussing in such fine terms in the courtyard, on her own. She approached Alix and said to her, civilly: "Mademoiselle, I beg you to tell me where I can find the back door of this dwelling."

Alix responded angrily: "Can one see anything more ill-informed than this old hag, who comes to ask me such a stupid question?"

Without making any response, the fay began walking behind Alix, and, letting her wand fall on her, as if unintentionally, she made her the gift of always being ill-tempered, disagreeable and ill-behaved. That was only to assure her of qualities that she already had. So, she entered into such a fury at the fall of the wand that she thought about beating the good peasant woman; at least, she vomited against her a torrent of insults. The fay, who had done what she had come to do, withdrew.

Meanwhile, Blanche, who no longer felt such intense pain since the application of the enchanted balm, recalled the adventure in the wood to her memory. The agreeable manners and handsome face of the hunter presented themselves vividly to her idea, and it seemed to her that in all the novels she had read she had never seen anything more marvelous than that incident. She would very much have liked to know who the hunter was, but all her impulses were born of simple benevolence and curiosity. Do not believe, I beg you, that other sentiments played any part in it; you would be doing Blanche wrong.

As for the Prince, he was entirely delivered to amour. What Dulcicula had told him about Blanche's merit further stimulated his fire, and he was so transported that, without the apprehension of his father the Duc, he would have gone in quest of the unfortunate beauty immediately, in order to bring her triumphantly to his palace; but he was able to moderate his transports, not without searching his mind a hundred times for means to content them.

At the end of twenty hours, Blanche found herself completely healed, and a few days there after her pitiless stepmother casually sent her back to the spring. As he was about to draw the water she saw a lady coming toward her who was even more brilliant in her noble attitude and her good grace than in her adornment, although she was dressed in a manner as magnificent as it was gallant. The lady approached Blanche and said to her: "My beautiful child, I beg you to give me something to drink."

"I am in great confusion, Madame," replied Blanche, agreeably, "not to be able to present you with anything but this pitcher, which is scarcely convenient for that." At the same time, the beautiful young woman leaned over the edge of the spring, rinsed out the pitcher carefully, and then presented it, with good grace, to the lady, in order that she might drink.

After drinking, she thanked Blanche very civilly. She found her so amiable in her manners that from thanks she progressed to conversation with her, throwing into it a thousand agreeable and delicate subjects, by which Blanche was not at all embarrassed; she responded to them with so much intelligence, mildness and politeness that she completed charming the person to whom she was talking.

The lady, as I believe that you have already suspected, was also a fay, but you will not have suspected that the fay was named Eloquentia Nativa. That name might appear to some people to be as strange as a Greek name, but, charming Duchesse, you will see clearly that it is very Latin; but, Latin or Greek, it makes no difference, it was by that forbidding name that the fay in question was known, and it is necessary not to be astonished by that; all fays have always had unusual names. Eloquentia Nativa therefore, penetrated by Blanche's eloquence and obliging manners, resolved to recompense her magnificently for the small pleasure that the beauty had given her with such good heart and such good grace.

The savant fay put her hand on Blanche's head and gave her for a gift that pearls, diamonds, rubies and emerald would emerge from her mouth every time she made a finished sentence in her speech. Then the fay bid adieu to the amiable young woman, who returned home carrying her pitcher full of water.

Blanche was no sooner in her stepmother's presence than the woman asked her in a shrill tone what had kept her so long as the spring again. Blanche replied that it was the arrival of the most amiable lady she had ever seen. With those words, a dazzling mass of pearls and precious stones emerged from her mouth.

"What's this!" cried the Marquise.

Blanche recounted to her, eloquently and ingenuously, he encounter she had had with the lady and the conversation that she had had with the admirable stranger, but that story was not told without, at the end of every sentence, no matter how short it was, a rain even more precious than the one that vanquished Danaë falling on to the floor.

Everyone hastened to pick up what Blanche distributed from her mouth; no one was frightened of the pills that she spilled. She started collecting them herself in her turn, and although she was not mercenary she gradually acquired the habit of speaking in a curt style. The joy of the Marquis was indescribable, which is why I shall say nothing about it.

The Marquise, however, as surprised as she was consternated, resolved to send her daughter to the fountain the next day, flattering herself that she too would find the unknown lady there and that she would do her the same favor as Blanche. People in those days were as they still are today: they did not do themselves justice, and wanted favors without taking the trouble to merit them.

The mother informed Alix of her design, who, being more brutal than ever, replied to her in impertinent terms that she had to be joking in wanting to give her that fine employment, and that she would not do it. The mother told her that she wanted absolutely that it be done and that it was for her own good that she was sending her for water. Finally, Alix, after saying a thousand stupid things, got ready to go.

She adorned herself with as much care as she would have done in order to go to a ball, picked up the most beautiful golden vase there was in the house, and in that pompous display she arrived at the spring. Eloquentia Nativa was, in fact, in the vicinity of the stream; the savant fay had discovered that beautiful solitude a little while before and took great pleasure in it. That day, however, she was strolling in the guise of an agreeable peasant woman, whose naïve attitude and rural costume she had adopted, for Eloquentia was no less beautiful in simple garments than beneath the most brilliant ornaments. On the contrary; when she put on affected attire, it obfuscated her beauty.

Alix sat down on the edge of the spring, and the pretty peasant woman, who was thirsty, because she had been walking for a long time, immediately approached the bank. Alix, whose vulgar mind was only impressed by the glamour of magnificent clothes, to which she rendered the only honor that she was capable of rendering, looked at the pretended peasant with scorn, and did not deign to honor her with a nod of the head, even though Eloquentia rendered her a profound reverence.

The fay was not put off by that; making another curtsey, she said to Alix: "Mademoiselle, I beg you to have the goodness to suffer that I make use of your vase in order to draw water, for I have a violent thirst."

"Look at this small fry," replied Alix, furiously. "One comes here expressly to drink; truly, they need golden vases in order to put their dog's muzzle in. Go away, stupid scrap, show me your back, and if you're thirsty, go drink from your cattle's trough. "

"You're very brusque, Mademoiselle," replied the fay. "Have I offended you, for you to treat me thus?"

Alix stood up then, and, putting her hands on her hips, shouted with all her might: "I believe that you want to argue, pestiferous slattern, but I advise you not to warm my ears, for I'll have you beaten whenever you go past our door."

The sage fay, full of indignation at the creature's brutalities, wanted to punish her in a manner that conserved a memory full of horror at the insulting torrent of her venomous tongue. She threw Alix to the ground by touching her with the tip of her wand, and in that state she gave her the gift, or rather the punishment, that every time she spoke, toads, snakes, spiders and other vile animals, whose venom would cause everyone to shudder, would emerge from her mouth.

Eloquentia went away immediately, and left Alix full of rage against her.

That malevolent individual waited a long time for the brilliant lady for whose favors she hoped, but, seeing that she was waiting in vain she finally wearied of it and returned home. Her mother was burning with impatience to see her again, and the moment she perceived her from the doorway the Marquise ran toward her.

"Well," she said, "have you had a fortunate encounter?"

"Yes," said Alix. "It was very necessary send me there to run into a whore."

At these words, a host of snakes, toads and mice emerged in a flood from Alix's mouth.

"Where did you get that, wretch?" cried her mother.

Alix tried to respond, and produced another deluge of vile creatures.

The mother and daughter went back into the house, where it was seen that the fine gift that Alix had was an evil without remedy, and everyone ended up taking that unworthy individual in the utmost aversion. Even her mother could not help doing so.

Meanwhile, the Prince, who was very attentive to everything regarding Blanche, was soon informed of the fortunate gift that she had received from a fay, and as he was aware of the power and generosity of Eloquentia Nativa, who was another one of his godmothers, he had no doubt that the prodigy was due to her. Taking the pretext of wanting to witness it, he manifested a strong desire to have Blanche come to the court and went to ask Eloquentia to go in quest of the beautiful young woman about whom so many marvelous things were said.

"Did you know," the fay said to him, smiling "that it was me who was responsible for it?"

"No," the Prince replied, "but I render you a thousand thanks, for I have an ardent passion for that young beauty."

"You know the zeal I have to oblige you," said the fay, "but you need not thank me on this occasion; I was unaware of the interest you had in Blanche; you had no part in what I have done for her; the mildness and politeness of that amiable young woman charmed me. Her conversation is entirely admirable; nothing equals the fortunate turn of her expressions, and I wanted pearls and gems to emerge from her mouth in order to mark the sweetness and brilliance that one finds in her speech."

The prince was delighted to hear Blanche's eloquence praised by a fay whose good taste and talents he esteemed a thousand times more than those of rhetoric.

In the end, Eloquentia Nativa quit her godson and went to the house of Blanche's father. It was besieged by an incredible crowd of people. The brilliant things that emerged from her mouth attracted even more people than those which emerged from the mouth of Monsieur de ****, beautiful as they were.

Those people were right; was it not more agreeable to see precious stones emerging from a beautiful small mouth like Blanche's than it was to see flashes of lightning emerging from the wide mouth of that thunderous orator, who was nevertheless so sought-after by the Athenians?[20]

To the great regret of the crowd surrounding Blanche, Eloquentia had her climb into a carriage and took her to the

---

[20] The reference is presumably to Jacques-Bénigne Bossuet, Louis XIV's court preacher, reputed to be the greatest orator of his era, and an habitué of the Hôtel de Rambouillet.

court. There the prince expressed the transports of is tenderness to her. Blanche was not insensible to that, and as the fortunate gift that the beauty had received rendered her richer than the foremost princesses in the world, the Prince married her with the applause of the Duc his father and all the people of his estates.

Blanche's father, who was at the peak of his joy, had great credit in the court, and no longer had to suffer the caprices of his wife; she no longer dared cause him chagrin since the elevation of his daughter.

The envious Alix, whom Blanche's good fortune would have been sufficient on its own to drive her to despair, also had that of seeing that neither her mother nor anyone else could tolerate her presence any longer. She quit her mother's house in a rage and went to wander from one province to another, where she was an object of aversion to everyone and where she experienced all the rigors of necessity. Finally, after having suffered a great deal she died of poverty "under a bush," while Blanche was triumphant.

The happiness of that beautiful person lasted as long as her life, which was long, and her destiny and that of Alix prove what I said to begin with, that often,

Mild and courteous language
Is worth more than a rich heritage.

I do not know, Madame, what you think of this tale, but it does not appear to me to be more incredible than many of the histories that ancient Greece has left us, and I would rather say that pearls and rubies emerged from Blanche's mouth to signify the effects of Eloquence than to say that lighting flashes emerged from that of Pericles. Tale for tale, it appears to me that those of ancient Gaul are worth very nearly as much as those of ancient Greece, and fays have no less right to work prodigies than the gods of fable.

I leave you to make that dissertation, about which I am quite tranquil. What I fear is that those who hear these tales of fays, and who know your fine talents, will only imagine that it is by the art of enchantment that you speak with so much charm and justice; yes, for in seeing so much knowledge and eloquence in you, one can scarcely believe that there is not a little enchantment therein. However, it is necessary for me, who knows of what your charms consist, to render justice, and I assert here in good faith that it is not by virtue of the gifts of the fays, but only the gifts of Heaven, that you personify Eloquentia Nativa.

THE CLEVER PRINCESS

Or, The Adventures of Finette
A Novelette

To Madame la Comtesse de Murat[21]

It is to you, who make the prettiest novelettes in the world in verse, but in verse as sweet as it is natural, that I would like, charming Comtesse, to tell one in my turn; however, I do not know whether it can amuse you; today I am of the humor of the Bourgeois-Gentilhomme;[22] I would not like to employ either verse or prose in order to relate to you: no fine words, no brilliance, no rhymes; a naïve tone suits me better: in brief, an unpretentious narrative, as people speak; I only seek some morality.

---

[21] Henriette-Julie de Castelnau, Comtesse de Murat (1668-1716) was a close friend of Baronne d'Aulnoy and another important contributor to the vogue for *contes de fées*, and it is said to be at L'Héritier's urging that she published three volumes of them in 1697-99. In 1699 she was accused in a report by the King's Lieutenant of Police of "scandalous practices"—lesbianism was specifically cited—estranged from her husband, to whom she had been married by arrangement when she was allegedly about to take the veil, and imprisoned.

[22] The reference is to Molière's comedy *Le Bourgeois gentilhomme* (1670), which had musical interludes supplied by Lully. The protagonist, Monsieur Jourdain, remained notorious for his declaration that he had been surprised to learn, at the age of forty, that he had been speaking prose all his life without being aware of it.

75

My short story furnishes enough of that, and might be agreeable to you in consequence. It rotates around two proverbs instead of one; that is the fashion, and you like it; I accommodate myself to the usage with pleasure. You will see how our ancestors were infinitely well aware that one falls into a thousand disorders when one pleases oneself doing nothing; or, as they put it: "Idleness is the mother of all vices," and you will doubtless like their manner of persuading that it is necessary always to be wary; you will understand that I mean that: "Suspicion is the mother of security."

No, Amour hardly ever triumphs
Except over hearts that have no occupation.
You, who fear that your heart might become
The dupe of some adroit conqueror,
Beauty, if you want to conserve your heart,
It is necessary that your mind be occupied.
But if, in spite of your care, your fate is to love,
At least do not let yourself be charmed
Without knowing the person that your heart
Wants to give itself for a master.
Beware of the sweet-talking Blondins
Who fatigue the alcoves of beds
Only knowing what to say to beauties
And how to sigh without being in love.
Mistrust the flirtatious storytellers,
Know the depths of their minds well;
To all Irises, they say a thousand things.
Finally, mistrust the abrupt lovers
Who say they catch fire at first sight,
And swear a vivid flame;
Make mock of those vain oaths;
To fully subjugate a soul
Necessarily costs time.
Be sparing with complaisance,
Do not disarm your austere pride too soon;
On your just suspicion

Your repose and your security depend.

But I am not thinking, Madame! I have made verses! Instead of holding to the faith of Monsieur Jourdain, I have rhymed in the manner of Quinault! I shall resume the simple tone as quickly as possible, for fear of having a part of the old hatred people have of that agreeable moralizer, and for fear that I might be accused of pillaging him and tearing him to pieces, as so many pitiless authors do nowadays.

In the time of the first crusades, the King of I know not what kingdom in Europe, resolved to go and make war against the infidels in Palestine. Before undertaking such a long voyage, he put the affairs of his kingdom in good order, and confided the regency to a minister so skillful that he was tranquil on that matter. What caused the prince the most anxiety was the care of his family. He had lost the Queen his wife a short while ago; she had not left him any sons, but he found himself the father of three princesses to marry. My chronicle has not told me their veritable name; I only know that, as in these fortunate times, the simplicity of the people casually gave nicknames to eminent individuals, in accordance with their good qualities or their faults. The eldest of the princesses had been nicknamed Nonchalante, which signified Indolent in modern parlance, the second Babillarde, and the third Finette: names that had an accurate rapport with the characters of the three sisters.

Never had anyone been as indolent as Nonchalante was. Every day, she did not get up until one o'clock in the afternoon; she had to be dragged to church, as she emerged from her bed, her hair in disorder, her dress crumpled, with no belt, and often with her slippers on the wrong feet. That difference was corrected during the day, but the princess could never be persuaded to go out in anything but slippers; she found it an insupportable fatigue to put on shoes.

When Nonchalante had dined, she attended to her toilette, which lasted until evening; she employed the rest of her time, until midnight, playing cards and having supper; then it took almost as long to undress her as it had taken to dress her; she could never succeed in going to bed before dawn.

Babillarde led another sort of life. That princess was very lively, and only devoted little time to her person, but she had a desire to talk so strange that, from the moment she awoke until she went to sleep, her mouth was never shut. She knew the stories of the troubled households, tender liaisons and gallantries not only of the entire court but the pettiest bourgeoisie. She kept a register of all the women who exercised certain rapines in their domestic budget in order to gave themselves a more splendid adornment, and was precisely informed as to the exact pay of the maidservant of such and such a Comtesse or the butler of some Marquis or other. In order to be informed of all those trivia she listened to her nurse and dressmaker with more leisure than she would have done to an ambassador, and then she bored everyone with those stories, from her father the King to the lowliest footman. For, provided that she was talking, she did not care to whom.

The itch to talk produced another bad effect in that princess. In spite of her high rank, her overfamiliarity encouraged the boldness of the Blondins of the court in flirting with her. She listened to their sweet talk casually, in order to have the pleasure of replying to them, for at whatever price, it was necessary for her to be listening or cackling from morning till evening. Babillarde never occupied herself with thinking, or any other reflection, any more than Nonchalante did; she did not embarrass herself with any domestic concerns, nor with the amusements provided by the needle and the spindle. In sum, the two sisters were in an eternal idleness that never caused their mind or their hands to be active.

The younger sister of those two princesses had a very different character. Her mind and her person were incessantly active; she had a surprising vivacity and she applied herself to making good usage of it. She knew perfectly how to dance, sing and play musical instruments; succeeded with admirable skill in all the kinds of petty handiwork that normally amuse individuals of her sex; put order and regulation into the King's household, and prevented by her cares the pilfering of petty officers, for even in those times they were involved in stealing from princes.

Her talents did not stop there; she had a great deal of judgment and such marvelous presence of mind that she immediately found means of getting out of all kinds of trouble. The young princess had discovered, by means of her penetration, a dangerous trap that an ambassador of an evil king had set for her father the King in a treaty that the prince in question was ready to sign. In order to punish the perfidy of that ambassador and his master, the King changed the article in the treaty by putting it in the terms that his daughter had inspired, and tricked the trickster in his turn.

The young princess also discovered a knavish trick that a minister wanted to play on the King, and by the advice that she gave her father he was able to make the infidelity of the minister rebound on him. On several other occasions, the princess gave evidence of her penetration and mental finesse, to such an extent that the people gave her the nickname of Finette.

The King loved Finette much more than his other daughters, and had such great trust in her good sense that if he had not had any other child than her he would have departed without anxiety, but he distrusted the conduct of his other daughters as much as he trusted Finette. Thus, in order to be sure of his family, as he thought he was sure of his subjects, he took the measures I shall detail.

I have no doubt that you, charming Comtesse, who are so knowledgeable about all sorts of antiquities, have heard mention a hundred times over of the marvelous power of fays. The King about whom I am talking, being an intimate friend of one of those clever women, went to find that friend. He told her about the anxiety he had regarding his daughters.

"It is not, the prince said to her, "that the elder two about whom I am anxious have ever done the slightest thing contrary to their duty, but they have such scant intelligence, they are so imprudent and they live in such great unoccupation that I fear that, during my absence, they might entangle themselves in some foolish intrigue in order to find amusement. As for Finette, I'm certain of her virtue, and yet I shall treat her like the others, in order to make everything equal. That is why, sage fay, I beg you to make me three glass distaffs for my daughters, made with such art that each distaff cannot fail to break as soon as the person to whom it belongs does anything contrary to her glory."[23]

As that fay was one of the most skillful, she gave the prince three enchanted distaffs, worked with the necessary care for the design that he had; but he was not content with that precaution. He took the princesses to a very high tower, which was built in a deserted place. The King told his daughters that he ordered them to make their residence in that tower throughout the time of his absence, and forbade them to receive any other person there whatsoever. He took away all their servants of both sexes, and, after having made them a present of the enchanted distaffs, whose qualities he explained to them, he embraced the princesses and closed the doors of the tower, taking the keys away with him. Then he departed.

Perhaps you will think, Madame, that the princesses were in danger of dying of hunger there. Not at all. Care had been taken to attach a pulley to one of the windows of the tower; a rope had been fitted to it, to which the princesses attached a basket, which they lowered every day. Their provi-

---

[23] The glass distaffs are an innovation of L'Héritier's; in Basile's version of the story the three princesses are given rings that will tarnish if they do anything to tarnish their reputation. The symbolism of the distaff is echoed in "Ricdin-Ricdon," and constituent material in the famous slipper in Perrault's version of "Cendrillon." Before the advent of the spinning-wheel, the distaff, which held the unspun fibers while the spindle accumulated the wound thread, was usually held in the spinner's left hand.

sions for the day were put into the basket, and when they had pulled it up again, they drew the rope carefully into the room.

Nonchalance and Babillarde led a life in that solitude that drove them to despair; they were bored to a point that it is difficult to express; but it was necessary to be patient, for the distaff had been made so terrible to them that they feared that the slightest slightly equivocal step might break it.

As for Finette, she was not bored at all in the tower. Her spindle, her needle and her musical instruments furnished her with amusements, and in addition to that, by order of the minister who was governing the State, letters were put into the princesses' basket that informed them of everything that was happening within and outside the kingdom. The King had permitted that, and the minister, in order to pay court to the princesses, did not fail to be exact in that matter.

Finette read all that news eagerly and was diverted by it. As for her two sisters, they did not deign to take the least interest in it; they said that they had too much chagrin to have the strength to amuse themselves with something so trivial; at the very least they needed playing cards to distract themselves during their father's absence. They spent their time, therefore, murmuring against their destiny, and I think they did not even neglect to say that, in order to be happy, it would be better not to have been the born the daughters of a King. They were often at the windows of the tower, in order at least to see what was happening in the surrounding country.

One day, when Finette was very busy in her room with some pretty needlework, his sisters, who were at the window, saw a poor woman dressed in tattered rags at the foot of the tower, who cried out to them in the most pathetic manner. She begged them with joined hands to let her into their tower, telling them that she was an unfortunate foreigner who knew all sorts of things and could render them service with the most exact fidelity.

At first, the princesses remembered the order their father the King had given not to let anyone enter the tower, but Nonchalante was so weary of serving herself, and Babillarde

81

was so bored with only having her sisters to talk to, that the desire of one of them to have someone to have her hair properly arranged and the other to have another person with whom to chatter engaged them to let the poor foreigner in.

"Do you think," said Babillarde, "that the King's prohibition extends to people like that poor woman? I think that we can receive her without any consequence."

"Do as you please, my sister," Nonchalante replied.

Babillarde, who was only waiting for that consent, immediately sent down the basket. The poor woman got into it, and the princesses pulled it up with the aid of the pulley.

When the woman was in front of them, the horrible dirtiness of her clothes disgusted them. They wanted to give her others, but she said that she would change the next day, and that for the moment, she would think about serving them.

As she finished speaking, Finette came into the room. That princess was strangely surprised to see the unknown woman with her sisters. They told her the reasons why they had brought her up, and Finette, who could see that the thing was done, dissimulated the chagrin that the imprudence caused her.

Meanwhile, the princesses' new servant made a hundred tours of the tower under the pretext of their service, but in fact to observe the disposition of the interior. For, Madame, I don't know whether you suspect it already, but that pretended pauperess was as dangerous in that swelling as the Comte Ory was in the convent into which he entered disguised as a fugitive abbess.[24]

---

[24] The reference is to a legendary tale of which numerous versions exist, in which a nobleman, or the Devil, disguises himself in order to infiltrate a nunnery and wreak havoc there, but the specific reference to "*le Comte Ory*"—subsequently featured in the title of an opera by Rossini—is enigmatic. It might be an abbreviation of "le Comte d'Ossory," meaning "the Irish Earl." It is unlikely to refer to the Inquisitor Matthieu Ory (c.1492-1557) r the economist Jean Orry (1652-1719).

In order not to keep you in suspense any longer, I will tell you that that creature covered in rags was the eldest son of a powerful King, a neighbor of the princesses' father. That young prince, who had one of the most cunning minds of his time, governed the King his father entirely, and he did not need much finesse for that. For the King had a character so mild and facile that he had been given the nickname Very Benign. As for the young prince, as he only acted by cunning, and deviously, the people had nicknamed him Rich-in-Guile, abbreviated to Richguile.

He had a younger brother, who was as full of good qualities as his elder was of faults; in spite of the difference in their temperaments, however, such a perfect union was seen in those two brothers that everyone was surprised by it. In addition to the good qualities of the soul that the younger prince had, the beauty of his face and the grace of his person were so remarkable that he had been nicknamed Handsome.

It was Prince Richguile who had inspired in his father's ambassador the trick of bad faith that Finette's cleverness had turned back on them. Richguile, who had not liked the princes' father before that, had completed his aversion in consequence, so when he heard about the precautions that the prince in question had taken with regard to his daughters he took a pernicious pleasure in deceiving the prudence of such a suspicious father. Richguile obtained permission from his father to make a voyage, under a pretext that he had invented, and took the measures that enabled him to enter the princesses' tower as you have seen.

On examining the edifice, the prince remarked that it was easy for the princesses to make themselves heard by passers-by, and he conclude that he ought to remain in his disguise all day, because they might well, if they took it into the heads, summon people and have him punished for his reckless enterprise. He therefore kept the costume and character of a vagabond woman by day, and in the evening, when the three princesses had had supper, Richguile cast off the rags that covered him and revealed the costume of a cavalier, covered with gold and gems.

The poor princesses were so frightened by that sight that they all hastened to flee. Finesse and Babillarde, who were agile, had soon reached their bedrooms, but Nonchalante, who was scarcely habituated to walking, was immediately overtaken by the prince

Immediately, he threw himself at her feet, told her who he was, and declared that the reputation of her beauty and her portraits had engaged him to quit a delightful court in order to come and offer her his prayers and his faith.

At first, Nonchalante was so bewildered that she could make no reply to the prince, who was still on his knees, but as he paid her a thousand compliments and made her a thousand promises, he implored with ardor to receive her as a husband from that moment on, her natural laxity did not leave her the strength to argue. She told Richguile that she believed that he was sincere, and that she accepted his faith. She did not observe any greater formalities than that in the conclusion of the marriage, but she also lost her distaff in consequence; it shattered into a thousand pieces.

Meanwhile, Babillarde and Finette were in strange anxieties. They had gone to their rooms separately and locked themselves in. Those rooms were some distance from one another, and as each of the sisters was entirely ignorant of the designs of her sisters, they spent the night without closing an eye.

The next day the pernicious prince took Nonchalante to an apartment that was at the end of the garden, and there that princess expressed the Richguile how anxious she was about her sisters, although she dared not present herself before them for fear that they would criticize her marriage. The prince told her that he would take charge of making them approve of it, and, after various speeches, he went out, and locked Nonchalante in without her perceiving it. Then he went to search carefully for the princesses.

It took him some time to discover the rooms in which they were locked. Finally, the desire that Babillarde always had to talk, having caused that princess to talk to herself while lamenting, the prince approached the door of her bedroom and looked through the keyhole.

Richguile talked to her through the door and told her, as he had told her sister, that it was to offer his heart and faith to her that he had undertaken the enterprise of introducing himself into the tower. He praised her beauty and her intelligence with exaggeration, and Babillarde, who was quite convinced that she possessed an extreme merit, was foolish enough to believe what the prince said to her. She replied to him, uttering a flood of words that were not overly disobliging.

It was necessary that that princess had a strange fury to talk in order to behave as she did at that moment, for she was in a terrible dejection, apart from the fact that she had not eaten all day, for the reason that there was nothing edible in the room. As she was extremely idle and never thought about anything but talking perpetually, he did not have the slightest foresight; when she needed something she had recourse to Finette, and that amiable princess, who was as laborious and prescient as her sisters were not, always had an infinity loaves of bread, pâtés, and solid and liquid preserves in her room, which she had made herself. Babillarde, therefore, who had no such advantage, feeling herself pressed by hunger and by the tender protestations of the prince through the door, finally opened it to her seducer. When she had opened it, he played the actor perfectly again with her; he had studied his role well.

Then they both emerged from the room and went to the tower's larder, where they fund all sorts of refreshments, for the basket always furnished the princesses in advance. At first Babillarde continued to worry about what had become of her sisters. But she got it into her head, on I know not what basis, that they were doubtless both locked in Finette's room, where they would not lack anything. Richguile made every effort to confirm her in that thought, and told her that they would go to find the princesses in the evening. She was not of that opinion;

she replied that it was necessary to go and look for them when they had eaten.

In sum, the prince and the princess ate together in very good accord, and after they had finished, Richguile asked to go and see the most beautiful apartment in the tower. He gave his hand to the princess, who took him there. When they were there, he recommenced exaggerating the tenderness that he had for her and the advantages that she would find in marrying him. He said to her, as he had said to Nonchalante, that she ought to accept his faith at that very moment, because if she went to find her sisters before having accepted him as a husband, they would not fail to oppose it. Since he was incontrovertibly the most powerful neighboring prince, he appeared to be a more plausible match for her elder sister than her. Because of that, the princess in question would never consent to a union that he desired with all imaginable ardor.

After many discourses of no significance, Babillarde was as extravagant as her sister had been; she accepted the prince for a husband, and only remembered the effect on her glass distaff after that distaff had shattered into a hundred pieces.

In the evening, Babillarde returned to her room with the prince, and the first thing the princess saw was the glass distaff in pieces. She was troubled by that spectacle; the prince asked her the cause of her disturbance. As the rage to talk rendered her incapable of saying nothing, she stupidly told Richguile the mystery of the distaffs, and the prince had a rascally joy in knowing that the father of the princesses would be entirely convinced of the bad conduct of his daughters.

Meanwhile, Babillarde was no longer in a humor to go in search of her sisters; she feared, with good reason, that they would not approve or her conduct; but the prince offered to go in search of them and said that he would not lack means of persuading them to approve it.

After that affirmation, the princess, who had not slept during the night, became drowsy, and while she was asleep, Richguile locked her in, as he had done with Nonchalante.

Is it not true, Comtesse, that Richguile was a great scoundrel and those two princesses loose and imprudent individuals? I am very angry against all those people, and I have no doubt that you will be too; but don't worry; they will soon be treated as they deserve. It will only be the sage and courageous Finette who will triumph.

When the perfidious prince had locked Babillarde in, he went to all the rooms in the tower, one after another, and as he found them all open, he concluded that the only one that he found locked from the inside was surely the one in which Finette remained. As he had composed a circular speech, he went to recite at Finette's door the same things that he had said to her sisters. But that princess, who was not a dupe, like her elders, listened for quite a long time without making any reply. Finally, seeing that he was enlightened as to who was in the room, she told him that if it were true that he had a tenderness as strong and as sincere as he wanted her to be persuaded, she asked him to go down into the garden and to close the door behind him, and after that she would talk to him as much as he wished through the widow of her room, which overlooked the garden.

Richguile did not want to agree to that, and as the princess was still obstinate in not wanting to open the door, the wicked prince, out of patience, went to look for a log and broke down the door. He found Finette armed with a large hammer that had been left by chance in a wardrobe that was in her room. Emotion animated the complexion of the princess, and although her eyes were full of wrath she appeared to Richguile to have an enchanting beauty.

He wanted to throw himself at her feet, but she said proudly as she recoiled: "Prince, if you come near me, I shall split your head with this hammer."

"What, beautiful Princess!" cried Richguile, in his hypocritical tone, "the amour that one has for you attracts such a cruel hatred?" He started to tell her again, but from one end of the room to the other, about the violent ardor that her reputation for beauty and her marvelous intelligence had inspired in him. He added that he had only disguised himself in order to come and offer her his heart and his hand, and begged her pardon for the violence of his passion and the boldness that had led him to break down the door. He finished by trying to persuade her, as he had her sisters, that it was in her interest to receive him as a husband as soon as possible. He also told Finette that he did not know where her sisters had retired, because he had not taken the trouble to search for them, having only thought of her.

The clever princess, pretending to soften, told him that it was necessary for him to search for her sisters, and that they would make arrangements together afterwards, but Richguile replied that he could not resolve to go and look for the princesses while she had not consented to marry him, because her sisters would not fail to oppose it on the grounds of their right as her elders.

Finette, who was rightly suspicious of the perfidious prince, sensed her suspicion redoubled by that response. She trembled at what might have happened to her sisters and resolved to avenge them with the same coup that would enable her to avoid a fate similar to the one that she judged that they had had. The young princess therefore said to Richguile that she consented without difficulty to marrying him, but that she was convinced that marriages made in the evening were always unhappy, and that she begged him to postpone the ceremony of giving one another a reciprocal pledge of faith until the next morning. She added that she assured him that she would not tell the princesses anything, and that she begged him to leave her alone for a little while in order to think about Heaven, and that afterwards she would take him to a room where there was a very good bed, after which she would return to lock herself in until the next day.

Richguile, who was not a very courageous person, and saw Finette still armed with the large hammer, which she was wielding as one does a fan, consented to what the princess wished, and withdrew in order to give her some time to meditate.

He had no sooner gone than Finette ran to make a bed over the hole of a drain that was in a room in the tower. The room was as clean as any other, but into the opening of that drain, which as spacious, all the rubbish in the tower was thrown. Finette crossed two weak sticks over the hole and then made up a bed very neatly on top of them, and immediately returned to her bedroom.

A moment later, Richguile came back, and the princess conducted him to the room where she had made the bed, and withdrew.

Without undressing, the prince threw himself down on the bed precipitately, and, his weight having caused the sticks to break suddenly, he fell to the bottom of the drain, without being able to retain himself, and sustaining twenty bumps on the head and breaking his ribs.

The Prince's fall made a loud noise in the shaft; in any case, it was not far distant from Finette's bedroom. She knew immediately that her artifice had had all the success that she had promised herself, and she felt a secret joy that was extremely agreeable to her. The pleasure she had in hearing him splashing about in the drain is indescribable. He merited that punishment fully, and the princess was right to be satisfied.

Hr joy did not occupy her so much, however, that she no longer thought about her sisters. Her first concern was to search for them. It was easy to find Babillarde. Richguile, after having locked her in her bedroom, had left the key in the lock. Finesse went into the room in haste, and the noise she made woke her sister up with a start. Babillarde was very confused on seeing her; Finette told her the fashion in which she had defeated the villainous prince who had come to outrage them.

Babillarde was struck by that news as if by a thunderbolt, for, in spite of her loquacity, she was so scantly enlightened that she had believed everything that Richguile had said to her. There are still dupes like her in the world.

Dissimulating the excess of her dolor, Babillarde emerged from her room in order to go with Finette to look for Nonchalante. They went to all the rooms in the tower without finding their sister; finally, Finette thought that she might be in the apartment in the garden. They did, indeed, find her there, half-dead from despair and weakness, for she had not had any nourishment during the day. The princesses gave her all the necessary help; then they made mutual clarifications that put Nonchalante and Babillarde into a mortal dolor. Then all three of them went to bed.

Meanwhile, Richguile spent the night very ill at ease, and when day came he was scarcely better off. The prince found himself in caverns of which he could not see all the horror because daylight never reached them. Nevertheless by dint of tormenting himself, he found the outlet of the drain, which emptied into a river some distance from the tower. He found a means of making himself heard by people who were fishing in the river, and was taken out in a state that excited the compassion of those worthy folk.

He was transported to the court of his father the King, in order to heal at his leisure, and the disgrace that he suffered caused him to acquire such a strong hatred for Finette that he thought less about recovering than avenging himself on her.

That princess spent very sad moments; glory was a thousand times dearer to her than life, and the shameful weakness of her sisters put her in a despair of which she had difficulty rendering herself the mistress. Meanwhile, the poor health of the two princesses, which was caused by the consequences of their unworthy marriages, put Finette's constancy to a further proof.

Richguile, who was already a skilful rogue, gathered all his intelligence after his adventure in order to become a supreme rogue. Neither the drain nor his contusions gave him as much chagrin as having found someone cleverer than him. He suspected the consequences of his two marriages, and in order to tempt the ailing princesses he had large crates filled with beautiful fruits transported to beneath the windows of their tower.

Nonchalante and Babillarde, who were often at the windows, did not fail to see the fruits; they were immediately gripped by a violent desire to eat them and they persecuted Finette to go down in the basket in order to go and collect them. That complaisance of that princess was great enough to want to content her sisters. She went down and brought back the beautiful fruits, which they ate with the utmost avidity.

The next day, fruits of another species appeared, giving rise to a further desire on the part of the princesses and a further complaisance on the part of Finette. But Richguile's servants were hiding, and, having missed their coup the first time, did not miss it this time. They seized Finette and took her away out of sight of her sisters, who tore their hair in despair.

Richguile's satellites took Finette to a country house to which the prince had gone in order to complete his recovery. As he was transported with fury against the princess he said a hundred brutal things to her, to which she always replied with a firmness and a grandeur worthy of a heroine like her.

Finally, after having kept her prisoner for a few days, he had her conducted to the summit of an extremely high mountain, and he arrived there himself shortly after her. There, he announced to her that she was going to be killed in a manner that would avenge him for the tricks she had played on him.

Then the perfidious Prince showed Finette a barrel bristling within with knives, razors and barbed nails, and told her that in order to punish her as she merited she was going to be thrown into that barrel and rolled from the top of the mountain to the bottom. Although Finette was not a Roman, she was no more frightened of the torture that had been prepared for her than Regulus had once been at the sight of a similar destiny.[25] The young princess conserved all her firmness, and all her presence of mind.

Instead of admiring her heroic character, Richguile became further enraged against her, and thought of hastening her

---

[25] The Roman consul Marcus Atilius Regulus was said to have been atrociously tortured by the Carthaginians in 250 B.C. or thereabouts, who completed the process by rolling him down a hill in a spiked barrel.

death. With that end in view he bent down over the opening of the barrel that was to be the instrument of his vengeance in order to check that it was furnished with all the murderous weapons.

Finette, who saw her persecutor looking attentively, did not lose any time; she tipped him cleverly into the barrel and sent it rolling down to the bottom of the mountain, without giving the Prince time to collect himself.

After that coup she ran away, and the Prince's servants, who had seen with an extreme dolor the cruel manner in which their master wanted to treat the lovely princess, refrained from running after her in order to stop her. In any case, they were so frightened by what had just happened to Richguile that they could not think of anything else but trying to stop the barrel, which was rolling violently. Their efforts were futile; it rolled all the way to the bottom of the mountain, and they took their Prince out of it covered in a thousand wounds.

Richguile's accident put King Very Benign and Prince Handsome in despair. As for the people of their estates, they were untouched by it; Richguile was hated by them, and everyone was astonished that the younger prince, who had such noble and generous sentiments, could love his unworthy elder brother so much. But such was Handsome's natural goodness that he was strongly attached to his blood kin, and Richguile had always expressed so much amity to him that the generous prince would never have been able to forgive himself for not responding with vivacity. Handsome, therefore, experienced a violent dolor because of his brother's wounds, and put everything to work to try to cure him promptly.

In spite of the urgent care that everyone gave him, however, nothing soothed Richguile; on the contrary, his wounds seemed to become increasingly envenomed, and to make him suffer for a long time.

After having escaped the frightful danger she had run, Finette had been able, fortunately, to return to the tower where she had left her sisters. It was not long before she was delivered to new chagrins. The two princesses each brought into the world a son, by which Finette found herself very embarrassed. The courage of the young princess was not diminished, however. The desire that she had to conceal her sisters' shame caused her to risk herself once again, even though she could clearly see the peril.

In order to ensure the success of her plan she took all the measures the prudence could inspire. She disguised herself as a man, and put her sisters' children in boxes, and made little holes opposite the infants' mouths in order to allow them to breathe. She acquired a horse, took those boxes and several others, and with that equipment she went to Very Benign's capital city, where Richguile was.

When Finette was in the city she learned that the magnificent manner in which Prince Handsome recompensed remedies that were given to his brother had attracted all the charlatans in Europe to the court; for in those days there was a quantity of adventurers without employment and without talent, who passed themselves off as admirable men who had received the gifts of Heaven for curing all sorts of ills. Those men, whose only science was bold knavery, always found a great deal of belief among peoples. They were able to impose upon them by their extraordinary external appearance and the bizarre names they adopted. Those sorts of physicians never remained in their birthplace, and the prerogative of having come from far away, often took the place of merit in the minds of the vulgar.

The ingenious princess, informed of all that, gave herself a name perfectly strange for that kingdom: the name of Sanario. Then she had it announced everywhere that the Chevalier Sanario had arrived with marvelous secret for curing the most dangerous and the most envenomed wounds. Immediately, Handsome sent people in quest of the pretended Sanario.

Finette arrived, and played the part of the empiricist physician perfectly, making five or six speeches about the art in a cavalier manner; nothing was lacking. The princess was surprised by the fine appearance and agreeable manners of Handsome, and after having talked to the prince for some time on the subject of Richguile's wounds she said that she would go in search a bottle of an incomparable liquid, and that in the meantime she would leave two boxes that she had brought, which contained excellent unguents appropriate for the wounded prince.

With that, the pretended physician left, and did not return. People became very impatient in seeing him so long delayed. Finally, as they were about to send someone to press him to return, the cries of small infants were heard in Richguile's room. They listened, and discovered that the cries were coming from the empiricist's boxes.

They were, in fact, Finette's nephews. The princess had given them a good deal of nourishment before coming to the palace, but as they had been there a long time they wanted more, and were explaining their needs by whining in a plaintive tone. The boxes were opened, and everyone was very surprise to see two babies therein, who were thought to be very pretty. Richguile immediately suspected that it was a new trick on the part of Finette, and he conceived a fury in consequence that is indescribable. His injuries were augmented by that to such a degree that it was evident that he was going to die of them.

Handsome was very afflicted by that, and Richguile, perfidious to the end, thought of abusing his brother's tenderness. "You have always loved me, Prince," he said to him, "and you are mourning my loss. I have no more need of proofs of your amity in relation to life. I am dying; but if I have been veritably dear to you, promise to grant me the prayer that I am about to make to you."

Handsome, who was in a state in which his brother could see that he could not refuse him anything, promised him with the most terrible oaths to grant him anything he asked of him. As soon as Richguile had heard those oaths he embraced his brother and said to him: "I am dying consoled, Prince, since I shall be avenged. For the prayer that I have to make to you is to ask for Finette in marriage as soon as I am dead. You will doubtless obtain that malign princess, and, as soon as she is in your power, you will plunge a dagger into her breast."

Handsome shivered with horror at those words; he repented the imprudence of his oaths, but he no longer had time to take them back, and he did not want to testify his repentance to his brother, who expired a short time thereafter. King Very Benign was deeply afflicted by that. As for his people, far from regretting Richguile, they were delighted that his death would ensure the succession of the kingdom to Handsome, whose merit was universally cherished.

Finette, who had once again returned fortunately to her sisters, soon learned of Richguile's death, and a short time later the return of the King their father was announced to the three princesses. That prince hastened to come to their tower, and his first concern was to ask to see the glass distaffs. Nonchalante went in quest for Finette's distaff, showed it to the King, and then, having made a profound curtsey she returned the distaff whence she had taken it. Babillarde did the same, and Finette brought the distaff in her turn; but the King, who was suspicious, wanted to see the three distaffs at the same time. Only Finette could show hers, and the King entered into such a fury against his two elder daughters that he sent them immediately to the fay who had given him the distaffs, asking her to keep them with her for as long as they lived, and to punish them as they deserved.

In order to commence the punishment of the princesses, the fay took them into a gallery of her enchanted castle, where there were paintings of the histories of an infinite number of illustrious women who had rendered themselves celebrated by their virtues and their laborious lives. By a marvelous effect of the art of enchantment, all those figures were capable of movement, and were in action from morning until evening. Visible on all sides were trophies and mottoes to the glory of those virtuous women, and it was not a slight mortification for the two sisters to compare the triumph of those heroines with the deplorable situation to which their imprudence had reduced them.

95

To complete their chagrin, the fay said to them gravely that if they had occupied themselves as well as the women they saw in the pictures, they would not have fallen into the unworthy errors that had doomed them, and that idleness was the mother of all vices and the source of all their misfortunes. The fay added that, in order to prevent them from ever falling into such misfortunes again, and to enable them to make up the time they had lost, she would occupy them in a useful fashion. In fact, she obliged the princesses to employ themselves in the most vulgar and degrading tasks, and, without regard for their complexion, set them to pick peas and tear up weeds in the garden.

Nonchalante could not resist the despair she had in leading a life so little in conformity with her inclinations; she died of chagrin and fatigue. Babillarde, who found a means shortly thereafter of escaping by night from the fay's castle, broke her head on a tree branch, and died of that wound in the hands of peasants.

Finette's good nature caused her to feel a very sharp grief at the destiny of her sisters. In the midst of her chagrins she learned that Prince Handsome had asked the King her father for her hand in marriage, which he had granted without consulting her, for in those times the inclination of the parties was the least consideration in the arrangement of marriages.

Finette trembled at that news; she feared, with reason, that the hatred that Richguile had for her might have passed into the heart of a brother by whom he was so cherished, and she was apprehensive that the young prince only wanted to marry her in order to sacrifice her to his brother. Full of that anxiety, the princess went to consult the sage fay, who esteemed her as much as she had despised Nonchalante and Babillarde.

The fay did not want to reveal anything to Finette; she only said to her: "Princess, you are sage and prudent; thus far, you have taken just measures for your conduct by always keeping in mind that suspicion is the mother of security. Continue to remember actively the importance of that maxim, and you will succeed in being fortunate without the aid of my art."

Unable to extract any further clarification from the fay, Finette returned to the palace in a state of extreme agitation.

A few days later, the princess was married by means of an ambassador in the name of Prince Handsome, and she was taken to her spouse in a magnificent carriage. She made her entry in the same way into the first two frontier towns of Very Benign's realm, and in the third she found Handsome, who had come to meet her on his father's orders. Everyone was surprised to see the sadness of the young prince at the approach of a marriage for which he had expressed the desire. The King had even criticized him for it and had sent him to meet the princess in spite of his reluctance.

When Handsome saw her he was struck by her charms. He paid her compliments, but in a manner so confused that the two courts, who knew how intelligent and gallant the prince was, thought that he was so deeply affected by the force of being in love that he had lost his presence of mind. The entire town resounded with cries of joy, and nothing was heard from all directions but concerts and fireworks.

Finally, after a magnificent supper, it was time for the two spouses to be taken to their apartment.

Finette, who still remembered the maxim that the fay had renewed in her thoughts, had a plan in mind. The princess had bribed one of the maidservants who had a key to the cabinet of the apartment destined for her, and had given that woman instructions to take into the cabinet, straw, a bladder, some sheep's blood and the entrails of the animals they had eaten at supper.

The princess went into that cabinet on some pretext and composed a figure of straw into which she put the entrails and the bladder full of sheep's blood. Then she dressed that figure in female night attire and a bight bonnet. When she had finished the marionette in question she went to rejoin the company, and a short time later the princess and her husband were taken to their apartment. When the necessary time had been devoted to the toilette, the maid of honor brought candles and withdrew. Immediately, Finette put the straw woman into the bed and hid in a corner of the room.

After having sighed loudly two or three times, the prince drew his sword and passed it through the body of the pretended Finette. At the same moment, he felt the blood flowing in all directions, and found the woman of straw motionless.

"What have I done?" cried Handsome. "What! After so much cruel agitation! What! After having hesitated so long as to whether I should keep my sworn oaths at the expense of a crime, I have taken the life of a charming princess whom I was born to love! Her charms delighted me the moment I saw her, but I did not have the strength to liberate myself from an oath that a brother possessed by fury had demanded of me by means of an unworthy surprise! Oh, Heaven, can one think of punishing a woman or having had too much virtue? Well, Richguile, I have satisfied your unjust vengeance, but I shall avenge Finette in her turn by my own death. Yes, beautiful princess, it is necessary that the same sword...."

By those words, the Princess understood that the prince, who had dropped his sword in his transport, was searching for it in order to pass it through his own body. She did not want him to do something so stupid, so she shouted: "Prince, I am not dead. Your good heart has enabled me to divine your repentance, and by an innocent deceit, I have spared you from a crime."

With that, Finette told Handsome about the foresight she had had regarding the woman of straw. The Prince, transported with joy in learning that the princess was alive, admired the prudence she had had on all sorts of occasions, and had an infinite obligation to her for having spared him from a crime about which he could not think without horror. He could not understand how he had had the weakness not to see the nullity of the evil oaths that had been demanded of him by artifice.

However, if Finette had not always been persuaded that suspicion is the mother of security, she would have been killed, and her death would have been the cause of Handsome's, in consequence of which people would have discussed at their leisure the eccentricity of that prince's sentiments. Hurrah for prudence and presence of mind! They preserved those two spouses from disastrous misfortunes, in order to reserve for them the sweetest destiny in the world. They always had an extreme tenderness for one another, and spent a long sequence of fine days in a glory and a felicity that would be difficult to describe.

That, Madame, is the marvelous story of Finette. I confess that I have embroidered it, and that what I have told you is a little long, but when one tells tales, it is a sign that one has not much else to do; one seeks to amuse oneself, and it appears to me that it costs nothing to extend them, in order to make the conversation last longer. In any case, it seems to me that circumstances are more often than not the charm of these playful stories. You can believe, charming Comtesse, that it is easy to shorten them by abridging them; I assure you that if you wanted, I could tell you the story of Finette in very few words. However, it was not thus that it was told to me when I was a child; the narration lasted at least a full hour.

I have no doubt that you know that this tale is very famous, but I do not know whether you are informed of what tradition tells us about its antiquity. It assures us that the troubadours, or storytellers, of Provence invented Finette a long time before Abelard or the celebrated Thibaut de Champagne had produced ballads.[26]

---

[26] Thibaut, Comte de Champagne (1201-1253), and later King of Navarre, was also known as Thibaut the Troubadour; a volume of songs attributed to him was published some time after the present story, but L'Héritier could only have know of them by reputation; The attribution of ballads to the philosopher Peter Abelard is probably apocryphal, although he certainly figured as a subject in many because of his ill-fated infatuation with Héloïse.

These sorts of fables enclose a good moral. You have noticed, with a great deal of justice, that one can perfectly well tell them to children in order to inspire them with a love of virtue. I do not know whether anyone has talked to you about Finette nowadays, but for me:

> *Hundreds of times my governess,*
> *Instead of animal fables*
> *Told me the moral features*
> *Of this surprising story.*
> *One sees the evils defeated there,*
> *Of a dangerous prince whom black malice*
> *Drew into the horror of vice.*
> *One sees there naturally*
> *That two impetuous princesses*
> *Who spent every day in vain idleness*
> *And fell unworthily*
> *Into a frightful aberration*
> *Received for the price of their loose weakness*
> *A prompt and just chastisement.*
> *But as much as one sees in that story,*
> *Unfortunate vice punished,*
> *One also sees virtues*
> *Triumphant and covered in glory.*
> *After a thousand unforeseen incidents,*
> *The age and prudent Finette*
> *And the generous Handsome*
> *Savor a perfect glory.*
> *Yes, these tales are often more striking*
> *Than the deeds of the monkey and the wolf;*
> *I took an extreme pleasure therein,*
> *All children can do the same;*
> *But these fables also please great minds,*
> *If you wish, beautiful Comtesse*
> *To ornament such tales with your talents*
> *Ancient Gaul presses you to do so.*
> *Deign therefore to bring to light*

The ingenuous tales, but filled with art
That the troubadours invented.
The mysterious meanings that envelop them,
Certainly equal that of Aesop.

GRATEFUL PARNASSUS

Or, The Triumph of Madame des Houlières

To Mademoiselle de Scudéry

Illustrious Sappho, whose airs
With so much sweetness enchant the universe,
Famous Scudéry, who knows Parnassus
And the highways and byways,
Keen intelligence that nothing embarrasses,
Garden where so many flowers are reborn every day,
Although in the vast adornments of the Temple of Memory,
In beautiful gilded characters,
An immortal sculptor has engraved our memory
And your revered talents
In all times are honored.
By the frequent commerce of the Immortal Troop
I will go to the Sacred Mountain to bring you news
Of which you might be unaware.
But will my voice be strong enough and fine enough
To sing it to you as is necessary?
No; let us fear the reefs of that reckless project;
To speak like the gods is no small affair;
Let us not take a tone so high
And follow the ordinary language of mortals.

Yes, savant favorite of the gods, admirable Scudéry, I am going to tell you the story that I promised you and tell you about the honors with which Apollo wanted to render the illustrious Madame des Houlières after passing from this life to immortality; but I will tell you the story in vulgar language, so

102

do not expect anything from me in this little discourse but a naïve simplicity.[27]

Know, then, immortal Sappho that as I reviewed this morning the loss that the Empire has suffered of the intelligent and knowledgeable Madame des Houlières and I was thinking that all those who love beautiful productions of the mind ought to render funeral honors that illustrious shade, I saw the Muse Urania, who was shining with a splendor that dazzled my eyes, and in the adornment that all her sisters wear when they attend some extraordinary ceremony, advance toward me, and I was about to ask her the reason for that attire when she anticipated me by saying this:

"I am too attached to the party of women, and I take too much account of the interest you take in those who have merit, not to some to inform you of the destiny of Des Houlières. I will make you party to what has happened in her favor on Parnassus, of what we have seen ourselves and what Mercury has told us.

"As soon as Des Houlières, that delicate and profound genius, had seen her immortal soul separated from the fragile shell that coved it, Pluto had no application stronger than thinking of placing it in the part of the Elysian Fields that he thought most appropriate to her, and in order to receive it with more honor he took Proserpine, with her chariot harnessed to her black horses, and they went together to meet that great shade just beyond the frontier of their realm.

---

[27] Antoinette des Houlières died on 17 February 1694. This item is the last included in *Oeuvres meslées*, in a slightly different typeface, and must have been a belated addition while the volume was already in press. A prominent figure at court, famed for her beauty, Madame de Houlières had numerous flatterers there, but Voltaire subsequently proclaimed her the best of female poets. A volume of her poetry published in 1688 included her most famous poem, "Les Moutons," to which reference is made in the story.

"A large number of the population of that fatal darkness from which one never returns accompanied them, and the illustrious shade was received by that host of the dead with a thousand marks of admiration, especially the poets, whose strove mightily to sing her praises, some with an impromptu epigram, others with a sonnet and others with a rhyming couplet.

"Proserpine, Queen of the Underworld as she is, did not think that she was lowering herself by descending from her chariot, and Pluto, who has done the same thing, offered her his hand with the intention of taking her into it and placing her between the two of them, in order that she could enter in triumph into the Elysian Fields.

"Before she could climb up, however, the god thought it necessary to decide in which part of the blessed Fields he should place her. He consulted Proserpine, and they both found themselves greatly embarrassed.

"The established order in that Empire is to sort out all the shades in an exact manner and Des Houlières had shone in the world in so many different ways that it was difficult to determine how she ought to be classified.

"He thought he would be doing an injustice to the beauties not to place with them a woman whose beauty had acquired so much reputation.

"Those whose lively, touching and joyful airs had acquired a quantity of lovers even without beauty could claim that Des Houlières, by her vivacity, tenderness and joviality, ought to be placed in their category.

"He presumed that it would not even be to the gamblers that it would be difficult not to cede her, since, in order to relax from more serious occupations, gaming had been one of the amusements of her life.

"But with the most just entitlement, the pleasant satirists protested that she belonged to their troop, being able to put into a lively satire, without wounding anyone, with so much delicacy and wit, the faults of men and the foibles of the century.

"He felt keenly that the savants would say that her writings, full of science and good taste, showed clearly enough that it would be an injustice to remove her from their company.

"And finally, the witty would show that she had shone so brightly and that she owed to the extent of her wit so much acuity and so many various talents that she had employed so well.

"Pluto explained to Proserpine the embarrassment into which these reflections put him, which impeded his decision, and his irresolution was beginning to make Mercury impatient—who, as you know, is charged with placing the shades in the abode destined for them.

"You know that he is a god who, like the metal over which he presides, is in a continual state of agitation, and does not settle easily. The confidence of Jupiter and the negotiation of humans gave him so many affairs in Heaven and on Earth that one cannot see without surprise that he had so much time to spend in the Underworld and that he had agreed to accept that charge of Grandmaster of Ceremonies.

"However, the particular consideration that he had for the shade of a woman whom he had regarded as being born under a very favorable aspect blunted his impatience, and he resolved not to leave until Pluto had made up his mind. That god perceived, nevertheless, that he had some anxiety, and in order not to prolong it, he ordered that Minos be summoned promptly in order to obtain his advice and settle his irresolution thereby.

"Minos made them wait longer than the respect he owed to Pluto seemed to permit him. The judge of the subterranean regions, although very prompt to do justice to those of the earth, was tied up by the examination of a strange case, which was that of a misanthrope of a new species, who had been the irreconcilable enemy of women throughout his life, and who had only hated them because he could not suffer their joviality and their natural mildness.[28]

"The novelty of that crime chagrined Minos all the more in that he had wasted considerable time on it, because, instead of the established custom of the Underworld of assembling all those guilty of the same crime in order to pass one sentence on all of them, he was obliged to judge him in isolation, not finding any similar individuals in Pluto's empire. It is true that he would have liked to wait, having bent told that many men still remained in the world possessed by the same misanthropy and who would soon arrive.

"Finally, Minos judged him and condemned him to receive from Cerberus as many bites as the insulting darts his malevolent tongue had launched against women and then to take on the livery of the Furies in order to be their lackey in perpetuity; a torture too light for a crime of that class, although he would have a great deal to suffer in the service of the terrible sisters, and the aspect of their serpentine tresses was capable on its own of causing shivers to the man who carried the tatters of their lacerated train.

"As soon as Minos had expedited the cynic, he left and went to find Pluto, but he had no sooner arrived, and excused himself for the delay by the difficulty he had had in relation to the trial before Aeacus and Rhadamanthus, than Ovid appeared.

"Ovid, as you know, was not put in the Underworld like other humans; he was too favored by Apollo during his life to be separated from him after his death, and that god had always

---

[28] The important one-time courtiers who died in the year preceding Madame des Houlières' death included Roger de Rabutin, Comte de Bussy (1618-1693), who had been sent to the Bastille in 1665 for writing *Histoire amoureuse des Gaules* [Amorous History of the Women of France] (1660), which satirized the ladies of the court, unwisely including members of the royal family; he had been exiled to his estates after his release.

kept him with him in order to be the secretary of his commandments of Parnassus and perform for him the functions that Mercury performs for Jupiter.

"That famous Roman, who was still an adorer of the fair sex, told Pluto that he had come on behalf of the King of Parnassus in order to ask for the illustrious Madame des Houlières, for whom he destined a place in the company of the nine Muses more agreeable than any that could be prepared for her in the Elysian Fields.

"At the first glance she had cast upon that illustrious shade, Proserpine had felt one of the prompt effects that extraordinary merit produces on a good heart, and she was very chagrined by that compliment, but the daughter of Ceres was careful not to quarrel with the gods, otherwise the earth would not have any wheat. In consequence, after having kissed her tenderly and made her promise not to forget her, she could not avoid handing over to Ovid a shade whom, having not yet crossed the fatal river, was not yet within Pluto's power.

"Ovid had no sooner received the precious deposit of that shade from Proserpine's hands than he perceived Minerva on the bank of the infernal river, who had brought her chariot at Apollo's request in order to take that friend of the Muses to Parnassus. She had her take her place beside her; as the goddess of wisdom and science had been the guide of all her actions during her life, she wanted to serve as her guide after death, in order to put her in the hands of the god who had always cherished her tenderly.

"She therefore took her to the summit of Parnassus and descended to the peak of the rock, from which the celebrated spring flows from which the poet take such various intoxications. Nothing there seemed new to Madame des Houlières; she had made so many excursions in that beautiful abode and slept so many times in the shade of the laurels, which conserve an eternal verdure there, that nothing was unfamiliar to her.

"Never had the air one breathes there seemed so sweet to her, however, and one can believe that the comparison she made with the sulfurous air of the bank of the Cocytus, which she had just quit, contributed a great deal to increasing the pleasure that she found on Parnassus. The welcome that she received there and the eagerness that was shown to give her glorious signs of a veritable joy touched her even more, but she reached the peak of her own joy when, presented by Ovid at the foot of Apollo's throne, she heard the god speak to her in these terms:

"'A long time ago my nine sisters have explained, as well as me, the confusion we feel in not being sufficient to sing the glory of the hero who governs the foremost monarchy in the world, and the most beloved by the gods. The number of his exploits is so great that it is impossible for us, in spite of all our talents, to celebrate half of them, and my penetration into the future has allowed me to discover that, far from letting us respire, that monarch will overwhelm us even more with the host of his great deeds. His august son will continue to combine his own with them.[29] What will happen, then, when the three young heroes formed of the blood of that son will march in the great tracks of their grandfather? Their exploits will provide enough subjects to keep our lyres forever taut, and our voices will scarcely be able to follow them?

"'I see the first of those amiable princes whom all the auspices of the monarch his grandfather will take his victorious arms as far as Africa and Asia, and, in the footsteps of Alexander will extend his conquests as far as India. To the valor of a conqueror he will be able to join a sublime knowledge, of which he will show a hundred splendid signs, and the future is preparing no fewer triumphs for his brothers. How, then, shall we able to avoid succumbing under the weight of so much illustrious material if we do not seek help?

---

[29] L'Héritier could not know that Louis, the "Great Dauphin" (1661-1711) would not live long enough to succeed his father, nor that his own eldest son, the "Petit Dauphin," would die a year later, similarly unable to fulfill Apollo's optimistic hopes.

"'I declare, then, that with the applause of Minerva and the unanimous suffrage of the nine sisters, we are appointing Des Houlières the tenth Muse.

"'The various talents that have shone in that illustrious woman have done us much honor among mortals, but since it is the verdict of destiny that she has not remained there any longer, we want to make it seen with ostentation how grateful Parnassus is, in assuring her, with that title, which she has acquired by her merit, the eternal honor that we want to do her.

"'We hope that, disengaged from the cares of the body, clad in the immortality that is her due, and further enlightened by the continual conversation of the nine sisters, who will take a particular pleasure in confiding to her all the secrets unknown to mortals, she will give us considerable relief in our labors.'

"The god of eloquence said a hundred other obliging things in favor of the savant woman, and then ordered a fête to celebrate the reception of Des Houlières in the ranks of the Muses.

"All the Arts hastened to employ their most ingenious talents to contribute everything that depended in them to the celebrity of the fête, and there was not one that did not show a glorious competition to please the god of verse in honoring the heroine who had just been adopted.

"Poetry, which had always been a delight of that amiable woman, was charged by Apollo with doing the honors of the fête, and appeared there in her most magnificent attire. She was followed by all her nymphs and various genii, each of whom had charming beauties of her character. They were wearing their most beautiful ornaments, and nothing more gallant or magnificent had ever appeared on Parnassus.

"The Epic, which had only rarely found the means, as yet, to dress in the French style, appeared with her long Grecian robe; she walked supported at her right hand by Homer and at the left by Virgil, and had her train supported by Tasso.

"Tragedy, shod in her cothurnes and wearing her royal mantle, came next, preceded by Sophocles and Euripides, like a rector and his mace-bearers; but Corneille, as her dearest friend, served as her squire, dressed as a Roman Emperor and sustaining in all his grandeur the character of those masters of the world.

"Comedy appeared by her side in a bourgeois costume, mocking and censuring human ridicule. Aristophanes, Menander, Terence and Plautus formed her cortege, but Molière, who had preceded them, laughed like Scaramouche while unmasking a Tartuffe, and had dressed as a Mamamouchi in order to render himself worthy of giving his hand to a goddess.[30]

"Satire, clad in the skin of a porcupine and throwing handfuls of salt in all directions, drew after her Juvenal, Persus and Martial. Horace would have been at their head had he not taken his place among the lyric poets, but the nymph was seen to refuse her hand to Régnier and D***, the former because he had made descriptions to full of coarse and shocking images and he latter because, not moderating his overly caustic salt, he had reduced the number of women of honor to three, to the great scandal of the fair sex.[31]

"The nymph Lyric, who mingled gods, heroes, amours and wine, appeared next in a pompous and gallant costume, holding her lute in her hand, whose chords she accompanied with her voice. Anacreon followed her; Pindar was at the right hand of the goddess, followed by Horace; and finally, after those illustrious ancients, Quinault was seen walking—who, after being an excellent operator of ordinary tragedy, had

---

[30] The protagonist of *Le Bourgeois gentilhomme* is persuaded that the Grand Seigneur has appointed him a Mamamouchi, a knight of an imaginary order.

[31] Mathurin Régnier (1573-1613) is the first of the two rejects; the other is "Despréaux," a variant of the name of Nicolas Boileau-Despréaux (1636-1711), singled out for specific criticism later in the story, still unnamed but there unmistakable.

pushed French lyric poetry as far as it could go—humming an air by Lully, which had served as a canvas for very pretty words that he had just written.

"In sum, in order not to bore you, all the different genii of Poetry were there to render homage to the savant Des Houlières and honor her apotheosis, and, just as paintings of subjugated places, rivers and mountains were carried in the triumphs of the Romans, all those genii carried in different tableaux the names of the various works of the tenth Muse

"The Heroic genius carried on a blue satin gonfalon, heightened with excellent gold embroidery, the title of the sublime ode in which she celebrated the homage that the sovereign of a superb republic came to render the greatest of kings, and those of the admirable epistles which sang so nobly the glorious conquests of Mons and Namur.

"The serious genius put in view the savant ode made to console La Rochefoucauld for a rigorous woe, the idyll that regretted the death of the generous Montausier and the elegy to Lycidas.

"The moral genius displayed a host of idylls, the force of which equaled their beauty, and put in the balance whether she ought to have given the first rank to *Les Moutons*.

"The gallant genius caused to appear on a standard woven from linden-bark harvested from the banks of the Charente the charming eclogues in which Celimène laments so tenderly the absence of her shepherd and Iris the ingratitude of hers, and an infinite number of fine, delicate and touching songs all full of new thoughts.

The jovial genius carried in triumph those agreeable epistles written on the banks of the Lignon, others full of fine pleasantries on the aberrations of harebrained youths of all times, and a hundred other brilliant pieces of a joviality as it as it is gallant.

"The genius that frolics lightly and to whom La Fontaine has lent the naïve turn of admirable fables and Marot his clownish simplicities, bore the titles of her ballads full of

111

agreeable naivety, and the amusing rondeaux whose salt is never out of place.

"I shall leave," Urania continued, "the detail of many of the extraordinary pomps that were put on to honor that fête. I will only describe a few of the triumphal arches that were erected over the passage of the new muse. Seen on the first were excellent figures of the most celebrated savant women of antiquity, and the actions that had brought glory to those illustrious women were represented in bas-reliefs carved with all the cares of sculpture.

"The figure of the ancient Sappho was remarked immediately. That learned individual has conserved an immortal memory, although she has been as far surpassed by a new Sappho as she herself surpassed the most famous poets of antiquity. One saw beneath her a bas-relief representing the honors that the Lesbians rendered in a public fête to that admirable citizen. Troops of young women were seen throwing flowers over her route, while young men dressed as Apollo put laurel crowns on her head and others in similar costumes followed her, playing various instruments.

"On another side one saw the Mytilenes and the people of Smyrna, who had put the face of the heroine on their money. And on the border of the bas-relief, the busts had been added of the great men who had striven to render justice to the merit of Sappho in their savant writings; one recognized Socrates, Aristotle, Strabo, Dionysius of Halicarnassus, Plutarch, Longinus and the Emperor Julian.

"Erinna, to whom Lesbos has given birth as well as Sappho, was beside her. And in the bas-relief that was at her feet, one saw the Graces in miniature, enchained in a narrow circle, to signify that they were able to put all the graces into the small space of a madrigal.

"Then one saw Corinna holding a medallion in her hand, which represented Myrtis, from whom she had learned the precepts of the poetic art, but as the pupil had had surpassed the mistress, one saw in the bas-relief a troop of judges who appearance was as intelligent as it was sage, who were ward-ing Corinna the prize that she had won over a hundred learned rivals, including Pindar, and far from any chagrin marring the physiognomy of the great poet, an expression of agreeable surprise and satisfaction was visible in his features.

"After Corinna, Aspasia appeared, who was holding a lyre. But as Poetry had not been the only one of her talents, a large number of the most illustrious Athenians were represented beneath her, who had come to obtain from that clever woman the rules of eloquence and lessons in politics. The famous Pericles was the most eager among that number.

"One remarked with pleasure the figure of Praxilla; her lively and childlike expression rendered her very gracious; a group of Games and Amours were at her feet, in order to depict the playfulness and tenderness of her writings.

"The last statue on that triumphal arch was the figure of Telesilla. She had an expression full of wisdom and majesty, was holding a helmet in her right hand and had a large quantity of books at her feet. It was thus that the people of Argos once represented her when they erected a statue to her in the most beautiful of their public squares

"In the background of the bas-relief beneath her, Telesilla could be seen touching a lyre in a gallery surrounded by books, to mark her talents as a poet. Then, in the foreground of the bas-relief, one saw the illustrious savant woman on horseback, and, having animated all the women of Argos with her songs, defending her city against the Spartans who hoped to take it by surprise while the men of the city were on campaign. On another side the flight of all the Spartans was seen, and finally the triumph of Telesilla, as illustrious for her courage as her science.

"To complete the ornaments of that triumphal arch, the medallions had been placed of the mother of Gracchus and Zenobia, as famous for her eloquence and her love of science as for a quantity of other fine qualities.[32]

---

[32] The motherhood in question is metaphorical, the reference being to Scudéry.

"Ovid would have liked there also to be a place there for his Roman Corinna, but, in spite of the credit he had with Apollo, he had not been able to obtain hat favor, for there is not on Parnassus the unjust complaisance that certain fine minds have had on earth, and as it is well known in our court that the Roman Corinna only owes her reputation for knowledge to the writings that Ovid and a few other adorers have composed under her name, it is not tolerated that such a usurpatrix of glory should be placed with the illustrious women who were true savants.

"After that triumphal arch in which the merit of all the savant women of antiquity was displayed came another on which modern savant women were represented. One saw there, firstly the judicious Christine de Pizan, then Catherine Desroches and her mother, the learned Schurman, Elisabeth, Princess Palatine, Madame de Malnoue, Princess de Rohan, Arthénice, Julie, la Suze, Ville-Dieu, Cornaro and many others.

"As with the ancient savant women, the illustrious moderns had bas-reliefs at their feet in which their principal deeds were represented; there was none that did not show clearly enough that those heroines had given striking proofs that their sex is capable of the highest sciences and the most excellent productions of intelligence.

"On the pedestals of all those figures of illustrious women ancient and modern, inscriptions had been put that made agreeable allusions to their various talents and those of Madame des Houlières, and if I wanted to enter into a description of all the other triumphal arches that were erected in her passage I could fill a volume of the most illustrious symbols and mottoes in the world, which were taken from the streams, flowers, birds and sheep that the rural muse of the heroine had rendered so celebrated.

"That pomp made in honor of our sex filed all Parnassus with joy, and my sisters and I, interested in the honor of that sex, took the first opportunity to animate the bilious against the bilious individual who has had the temerity to spread with too much bitterness the fateful bile of his peevish rhyme against women.[33]

"'Hey, goddesses,' Apollo said to us, 'What's the matter with you? Don't worry about the excessive insults with which that new Juvenal is heaping you. Your admirable sex, whose interests I always take, is already avenged. Have you not seen me indignant at the ill-use he has made of the talents of which I gave him a share? What I had given him I have taken back, with no hope of a return, and as a jut punishment I have determined that he, that grandmaster of the art, who has given such fine lessons to others, has followed them so poorly. Yes, I have taken pleasure in letting him fall into embarrassing obscurities, and insupportable repetitions, and finally running into the reefs that so many others have avoided by virtue of appropriate instruction.

"'When the Latin satirist published the licentious satire that lacerated women from the Empress to the humblest citizen's wife, ladies were no less honored and the names of virtuous Roman women have nevertheless passed to posterity. But if in the century of the first Emperors so many women were rendered celebrated by her science and the strength of their genius, the modern century furnishes so many sublime examples of virtue that the fair sex has no reason to regret or envy the past, and the heroine who is coming to take her place among the muses is not the only one who places her sex at least in equality with that of men.

"'Very far, then, are the portraits of women from the portraits of the likes of Laïs that the satire has made for us; they are, on the contrary, only full of false traits that render them unrecognizable. How many heroines one finds who have virtues so pure that their imagination cannot conceive anything beyond it? And the illustrious and virtuous Scudéry will permit me to tell you without wounding her modesty that I know

---

[33] The reference is to the satire "Sur les femmes" included in *Les Satires* (1694) by the aforementioned Nicolas Boileau-Despréaux.

one of them who possesses more merit on her own than is required to render ten women very illustrious, since one sees shining within her simultaneously wisdom, grandeur of soul, generosity, rectitude, intelligence and knowledge—in sum, all the great qualities that have been so variously divided between all the individuals of her sex. But it would be of little account if those advantages were not sustained and embellished by an admirable modesty that is wounded when one renders them justice ostentatiously.

"'So many others rendered themselves famous by a solid piety, by an inviolable modesty, by a sage economy, by a well regulated science and by an infinity of other advantages that it is astonishing that someone has wished by frightful libel to scandalize them in such a cruel manner, and to assassinate all of them for the weaknesses of a few; it is to avenge that sex in some manner that I want today to render it a singular honor in the person of this new Muse that I am adopting, and ladies have already avenged themselves in their toilette for the insult of that libel by tearing it up in order to make curlers.'

"Thus it was," Urania continued, "that Apollo spoke, and we all applauded it. Then he made Madame des Houlières mount a magnificent chariot of extraordinary form, and in that machine, pulled by Pegasus, she was carried over the foothills of Parnassus in the midst of the cries of joy of an innumerable crowd of Amours, Games and Genii, which accompanied her in order to honor her triumph, which would not have had its perfection if Apollo had not commanded Music to assemble under the conduct of Lully a magnificent choir of the most beautiful voices in the world to sing around her chariot the voices that I shall recite for you.

> *May beauty, wit and science forever*
> *Desire to reign over ladies,*
> *May we always see their souls*
> *Submissive to the laws of duty.*

> *You who possess a hundred lustrous talents*

That will outshine in all their light,
The poisonous darts of crude satire,
Triumph, illustrious heroine,
Triumph is this beautiful abode,
To the glory of your sex mortal women will be
Ever amiable, ever beautiful,
Always worthy of a pure amour,
And in spite of D***, always intelligent.

In vain his harsh, satiric, malign spirit
Pours over the cherished sex a frightful venom.
In vain with a bloody verse he shocks and wounds,
If the hero, and if the savant
Has good taste and politeness,
He will owe it to the delicacy
Of that charming sex.
To the commerce of Des Houlières,
Full of joviality,
Full of sagacity and charm,
How many minds have received their brightest light!

You whose desolate, defeated hearts are seen,
Tender objects that weep for the fatal loss
Of the one who rendered your enemy confused;
Console yourselves, those still remain
Who will be able to defend your virtue.

It is in vain that he rants and rails against you,
Sex that is the better half of the human race.
His piece, which everyone attacks
Engenders less harm than pity,
And in spite of his intimations
Your attractions will last as long as the world.

"Those songs complete the glory of a sex that can only be hated by pedants; Parnassus as a whole put Des Houlières in possession of immortality.

117

"You see me still," said the Muse, "in my ceremonial garb, and I have come to tell you the story, which I believe will not have displeased you."

Urania ceased speaking at that point and disappeared. And I thought, illustrious Scudéry, that I ought to make you party to this news immediately, which will doubtless give you some pleasure.

If I have not made that narration in the terms the Muse employed, it is because the divinities speak with so much rapidity that it is impossible for mortals to retain their discourses word for word; all that they can do is retain the meaning, and I assure you that in that regard my memory is very faithful.

THE DARK TOWER AND THE LUMINOUS DAYS

The intrepid Richard, King of England had signaled his courage a hundred times over in Palestine with the valiant Philippe Auguste, King of France. After being covered with further glory since the departure of that monarch, he was obliged to return to his estates, of which the spirit of faction and revolt had taken possession almost entirely. But as that prince, who had powerful reasons for not making himself known in Germany, was traversing that vast country in disguise, he had suddenly disappeared, without anyone being able to discover what had become of him.

In vain the leaders who had remained his faithful subjects had made scrupulous searches to discover the place where he might be hidden; they had not learned anything new. After sixteen months of futile effort they had almost lost hope of recovering that generous king, and had enounced the design of searching. That had given a not inconsiderable joy to the Prince, his brother, the Earl of Mortagne and Lancaster, who was secretly stirring up the rebel faction, and had inspired by underhand means the resolution that no further searches for Richard would be undertaken.

The savant Blondel de Nesle was the only one who could not resolve himself to abandon that quest.[34] That French gen-

---

[34] This "Blondel de Nesle" can only be identified with Jean I de Nesle (c.1155-1202), who fought in the crusades, although some historians suggest that the author of the songs credited to that name were the work of his son, Jean II. Only the former could have been associated with Richard I of England, as in the legend in which he helped to free him from imprisonment in 1192—a fiction invented some seventy years later. In fact,

tleman owed his fortune to King Richard, to whom he had devoted himself several years before, with the permission of King Philippe Auguste. Animated by zeal and gratitude toward an illustrious master to whom he owed all the good fortune of his fate, he had resolved to search the world incessantly until he had discovered the destiny of that Prince. Blondel had already made an entire tour of Europe without having collected the slightest fruit of his labor. He had begun his travels in Germany, had then traversed Italy, France and various other countries, and had then returned to Germany again.

After having visited all the provinces, during a rather considerable time, one day when he found himself in the town of Linz in Austria, while he was conversing with his host, as was his custom, he learned that near the town, at the entrance to a wood, there was an extremely strong ancient tower, in which they was a prisoner who was being guarded with the utmost care. Blondel shivered at that news; a secret presentiment seemed to him to announce that the prisoner in question was the King of England, and he no longer thought about anything else other than determining whether his presentiment was accurate.

Immediately, he directed his steps toward the tower, the mere sight of which made him shudder. He made the acquaintance of a peasant who was going to take food supplies there and questioned him ardently. Although he gave many liberalities to the peasant to engage him not to keep quiet, however, and although the good man did, indeed, tell him all that he knew, he could not tell him the name or the quality of the prisoner. He only knew that he was guarded with great exactitude, and he had no communication with him at all, only with his keeper and servants. He also told Blondel that the prisoner had no other distraction than often looking out at the countryside through a tiny barred window, which was the only one that illuminated his apartment. Then the peasant gave him,

---

Richard's place of imprisonment was never secret, and he was released on payment of a ransom

as best he could, a description of the entire tower, which he declared to be a frightful abode, in which all the apartments and staircases were so dark that one needed torches to guide oneself even in broad daylight.

Blondel listened with an extreme attention to everything that the peasant said, and tried to take advantage of it. Although he adopted various disguises, however, and racked his brains, he got no further forward in making the discovery that he desired.

Finally, one day when he was walking at the entrance to the wood near the tower, he heard someone coughing at the little window that the peasant had mentioned. Full of hope that it might be his dear master, he was burning with the desire to see the prisoner's face, but the smallness and the height of the barred window did not permit him to flatter himself that he might have that pleasure. He could see clearly that it was no longer possible to seek to obtain any enlightenment regarding the prisoner by speech; he could only have made himself heard by shouting very loudly, which could not fail to attract the attention of the guards and the tower's keeper and make them suspicious. In order for him to be useful to the prisoner, it was necessary that no one perceive that he had the intention of entering into communication with him.

In the agitation that all these thoughts gave him, his presence of mind did not abandon him. He remembered that he had once composed the beginning of a song, of which the King of England had finished the last five lines. He knew that the King had been greatly diverted by that amusement, so he had no doubt that, wherever he was, he would have conserved the memory of it. In that persuasion, he believed that it was a sure means of discovering whether the prisoner was King Richard. Full of that idea, in spite of his anxiety, he nevertheless found his voice, and sang loudly and very pleasantly the four lines:

Corise has been very severe with me,
I shall always remain in her charming thrall.

She is proud and indifferent to my love,
But at least she loves nothing at all.

After having sung those four lines, Blondel stopped short and listened, delightedly, to a voice that came from the little window, taking up the song where he had left it and continuing it.

Since she flees conversation with rivals.
Rather would I suffer her eternal rigor
Than sigh for one of those beauties
Who flatter with their tender choice,
Five or six lovers at a time.

Blondel was transported by joy, being convinced by those lines and the sound of the voice he had just heard that it was his master the King who was enclosed in the tower. He no longer thought about anything else but introducing himself into it.

In order to succeed in that he disguised himself better than ever and learned various things regarding the keeper and his family. He knew that the man had a daughter whom he loved very much, and that he desired greatly that she be taught to sing. He also knew that the keeper had a servant who was dangerously ill and was looking for someone to take his place.

Dressed in a manner appropriate to the estate that he claimed, Blondel went to offer himself to the keeper as a servant, not forgetting to announce that he knew music. His physiognomy pleased the whole family so much that he was immediately accepted, and on the very day that he was received in the place as a servant his new master took him with him to take food to the prisoner he desired to see so passionately.

What a delight it was for the faithful Blondel when he recognized the august features of the great King for whom he felt such an ardent attachment and such a keen gratitude! The King, whose ideas regarding his subject had been forcefully awakened by Blondel's song, recognized him as soon as he appeared, and was scarcely less joyful than the zealous favorite, but both of them hid the movements of their soul perfectly from the keeper.

The keeper, who was very idle by nature, soon handed over to Blondel completely the care of going to the prisoner's room to attend to his needs. He acquired an extreme confidence in the new servant, who seemed to him to be full of intelligence and prudence. In any case, he was so convinced of the excellence of the tower's locks and the fidelity of the guards that he believed that if anyone ever tried to free the prisoner their efforts would always be futile. He contented himself with telling Blondel that the prisoner was a criminal who had been recommended to his care, but that he was very polite and civil, and that he took pleasure in seeing that he did not lack anything.

Blondel thus had the touching satisfaction of speaking to the king alone. He thought he would expire of joy at his master's feet. The Prince lifted him up benevolently, embraced him tenderly and said a hundred obliging things to him. Richard was burning to know the means by which Blondel had discovered his prison and how he had introduced himself into it. Blondel told him briefly, and then assured him that he still had many faithful subjects in England. He added that he had no doubt that, as soon as there was certain news of him, his brother's party would dissipate.

He asked the King what misadventure had led him to lose his liberty.

"It was by an act of strange perfidy," the Prince replied. "But, my dear Blondel, it is necessary that you do not stay with me too long, for fear that they will suspect our understanding, and I will tell you the story you desire another time."

Blondel agreed with the King and withdrew, but as the talents he had for singing and playing instruments—for he played the lute and the spinet as agreeably as he sang—gave him a great luster among all those inhabiting the tower, the King pretended to be equally struck by it, and asked the keeper to permit him to come to him often in order to play and sing, in order, he said, to relieve the tedium of his imprisonment slightly.

The keeper consented to that gladly, so no one was surprised any longer to see Blondel remaining with the prisoner for a long time. He did not just amuse himself there with musical exercises; he listened with avid attention to what his illustrious master had to say, and responded to the questions that he was asked.

In order to satisfy the strong desire he had to learn the manner in which the King had become a captive, the Prince told him this one day:

"A short time after the departure of the King of France I had a great quarrel with Leopold, Duke of Austria.[35] The good fortune I had had in conquering the Kingdom of Cyprus in such a short time, and the glory I had acquired in sharing with the King of France the success of Christian arms in Syria, had given birth in Leopold's heart to a secret envy, which often gave rise to impulses that he sought to cover with other pretexts.. Thus, during the quarrel that we had, in which that prince was completely in the wrong, he acted with such a strange impetuosity that he seemed frantic. As I had justice on my side, all the crusader princes and lords in Palestine took my side, and the angry Leopold, without informing anyone, abruptly returned to Austria.

"The Emperor, as you know, has been my implacable enemy for a long time. The Duke of Austria, who was only seeking to do me harm, reawakened his hatred by telling him that when the crusader princes had rendered themselves masters of the city of Acre, my troops had erased the imperial arms in several places in order to replace them with mine. The

---

[35] Leopold V (1157-1194), nicknamed the Virtuous, quarreled with the Kings of England and France during the Third Crusade, and complained bitterly about Richard to the Holy Roman Emperor Henry VI (1165-1197), who collected the enormous ransom for the English King after Leopold had captured him, and released him in 1194.

Emperor and the Duke formed a thousand projects of vengeance against me, and resolved to use any means to execute them. To that effect, they sent their emissaries to Palestine and gained one of my servants, Varnery, by means of large bribes. I learned all these details in a way that I shall tell you son.

"Meanwhile, all the crusader princes still showed an esteem and deference toward me that heaped me with glory, and they had a confidence in my conduct that contributed more than a little to enable everything we attempted to succeed. The taking of Gaza, that of Jaffa, and the great victory that we won over Saladin made a noise in Asia and Europe very favorable to us, and I was preparing to lay siege to Jerusalem when I received news of England's troubles.

"The fatality of those seditious troubles gave me chagrin, as you can imagine, seeing that the necessity of my presence in my kingdom was about to oblige me to abandon the continuation of my conquests in Palestine; for you know that the most zealous subjects I had in England had written asking me to hasten my return as soon as possible. You doubtless remember that you were not the least ardent in telling me that it appeared to you to be absolutely necessary.

"I therefore resolved to depart, and, after having negotiated a truce with Saladin and handed over the care of all affairs in Asia to the Comte de Champagne, I embarked; but a violent tempest drove me toward Dalmatia and to run aground on that coast. The misfortune of my shipwreck obliged me to continue my route via Germany, and I disguised myself in order to traverse it.

"As my retinue was reduced to a very small number of persons, and I was not unaware of the hostile sentiments that the Emperor and the Duke of Austria had in my regard, I thought that prudence dictated that I take that precaution. It was, however, futile; the traitor Varnery gave information of all my steps to the Duke of Austria, and, in spite of being costumed as a merchant, I was arrested near Vienna as I was in a wood some distance from the village to which Varnery had sent all my men under pretexts regarding my service, thus remaining alone with me.

"It was in vain that I tried to defend myself against Leopold's men; they overwhelmed me in spite of my resistance. As soon as the perfidious Duke had me in is power, he handed me over to that of the Emperor, with whom I requested a conference in vain; he never wanted to grant it to me. I forgot to tell you that during the time when I was being transferred from Leopold's hands to the Emperor's, I chanced to overhear a conversation between the Duke and Varney, from which I learned all about the treason of that perfidious servant, who was preparing to give new information on my subject to the Emperor.

"I wrote to that prince regardless that, although it was true that having no war with him or the Duke of Austria, my detention was absolutely contrary to good faith and the rights of people, I would nevertheless submit with good grace to my destiny and that I would pay scrupulously the ransom that he put on me. I asked him to fix it promptly, however, because I had urgent affairs recalling me to my estates.

"The Emperor did not deign to respond to my letter, and had me informed insolently that he would not limit the vengeance he wanted to extract from me to the light penalty of paying a ransom, but that, since he was the absolute master of my fate, no one in the world knowing what had become of me, he would make me spend my entire life in prison without my friends or my subjects being able to obtain any news of me.

"That cruel response afflicted me greatly at first, but after putting my confidence in the protection of Heaven, I convinced myself that justice would not allow me to spend my days in an obscure prison, since I had never committed any action that ought to attract such an unfortunate fate to me. I therefore hoped that some stroke of Providence would exact me from my captivity; and as you know that, by virtue of my temperament, I only abandon myself with difficulty to a violent chagrin, I have supported by destiny with constancy for a long time, and even sought to charm the tedium of my imprisonment by amusing myself in composing various tales and various gallant stories in the same taste that I had in composing them in my early youth.

"In spite of the disposition I had in hoping for all sorts of events, however, and in spite of my natural firmness, the length of my imprisonment, always in the impossibility of informing my friends about it, finally exhausted my constancy; I saw the months going by without any change occurring in my sorry fate. At the end of a year I was still in the same situation, and several months ago I had the dolor of seeing myself ready to attain another. Such a long duration of misfortune had finally triumphed over the strength of my soul and I would have entered into the ultimate despair without your arrival here; but since Heaven has deigned to bring to my proximity a generous heart as devoted to me as yours, I want to give myself entirely once again to the natural penchant I have for joy. I feel that all my hope is reborn; I am convinced that by your efforts, I shall not take long to recover liberty."

Blondel responded with as much intelligence as zeal to all the obliging things that the King had said to him. Then he rendered an exact account to the prince of the situation in his kingdom, and informed him in detail of the actions of all the English lords who had remained faithful to him. He was no less instructive in detailing the hidden intrigues and overt conspiracies of those animated by a spirit of rebellion.

Then, seeking out of generosity to justify the Earl of Mortagne, he continued: "I assure you, Sire, that the prince your brother has not deliberately formed parties against your authority; the insolence of the Chancellor, whose audacity has already been punished by the equity of your orders and the zeal of your barons, initially engage the Earl of Mortagne in the movements, almost involuntarily; afterwards, the secret solicitations of the King of France and that monarch's brilliant promises ended up drawing the Earl into a few actions contrary to the obedience he owes you, but it is evident that he is ashamed of going astray, since he only enters those factious intrigues covertly, and his reason disavows publicly the unjust steps that a blind ambition has caused him to take in secret."

"You have no need," Richard replied, "to seek to excuse the ambitious vagaries of the Earl of Mortagne to me; as soon as I am free and I have recovered all my authority, I shall only listen to the sentiments of nature, which will speak to me in favor of a brother, and will be very forgiving when he is no longer in a position to harm me. But as long as I am a captive and I see a seditious party in England I want all faithful subjects to regard the Earth of Mortagne as an ingrate to his brother and a rebel against his King."

"It is true, Sire," Blondel continued, "that your good will and your generosity redouble the crime of which the Earl de Mortagne is guilty toward you, for no King has ever heaped his brother with as many marks of amity and as many magnificent benefits as you have lavished in that prince. Everyone remembers that a few imprudent steps that an excessively frivolous youth led him to take in the time of the late King, your father, had lost him the good graces of that monarch, who, having wanted to punish him by not giving him any prerogatives, had caused him to acquire throughout Europe the disagreeable nickname of John Lackland.

"They also remember, Sire, that when you succeeded to the throne, not only did you heap that prince with riches and titles, but overwhelmed him with them. They have not forgotten that, in addition to the county of Mortagne and the conquests that our father had made in Ireland, you gave him the counties of Cornwall, Devon, Somerset, Dorset, Nottingham and Lancaster, with the result that it would not have taken much for the grandeur if his property to equal the power and glory of the crown.

"But Sire, it is the same generosity that you had toward the Earl of Mortagne that engages you to have indulgence for him; that prince owes you all the happiness of his life, you will be delighted to conserve your work; the splendor of his fate in the effect of your liberality, the repose of his days will be the effect of your clemency."

"Let us think," the King said, "about putting me in a position to exercise that clemency. But tell me, what is my mother the Queen doing in all these troubles?[36] Is she not very afflicted by their excess, and is my sister not very afflicted also?"

"The Queen Mother," Blondel replied, "is still very full of zeal and tenderness for you, it is would be desirable, for the good of our affairs, that she had over the minds of the factious all the credit and authority that she ought to have. As for the Queen of Sicily, although greatly chagrined by the audacity of the rebels, she is even more afflicted by not knowing the destiny of a brother like you, to whom she has such great obligations.[37] But Sire," he added, "you are not asking me for news of Queen Alys."[38]

"Do not give the title of Queen to Princess Alys," said the King. "You know that she would be irritated to bear it is it were necessary to have, along with the title, the name of being veritably my wife."

"However, Sire," Blondel went on, "Princess Alys has always appeared to take a great interest in the success of your arms. Smiling, he continued: "But if you have not hastened to ask me for news of the Princess of France, at least ask me for that of Navarre, for I cannot believe that all your victories in

---

[36] Richard's mother was Eleanor of Aquitaine (1122-1204), the richest woman in Europe.

[37] The Queen of Sicily was Joan, the youngest of Richard's three sisters.

[38] Richard was contracted to marry Alys of France (1160-1220), the daughter of Louis VII (Eleanor of Aquitaine's former husband) and Constance of Castile, when they were both children, but the marriage never took place, amid rumors that Alys had become the mistress of Richard's father, Henry II. Richard had actually married—although some historians have taken leave to doubt that the marriage was ever consummated—Berengaria of Navarre (c.1170-1230) in 1191, before the present story is notionally set.

Syria, nor the loss of your liberty, have made you forget the charms of the amiable Berengeria."

"I confess," the King replied, "that I still render to the attractions of the Princess of Navarre the same justice that I have rendered to them all my life; but you are much mistaken, my dear Blondel, if you imagine that her attractions, brilliant as they are, have ever made any impression on my heart."

"What, Sire!" said Blondel. "It is not the Princess of Navarre that is the cause of the reluctance you have had in uniting yourself in an eternal bond with the Princess of France!"

"No," retorted the King, "Princess Berengaria has never had the slightest empire over my heart, in spite of the desire that my mother has always had to make her reign there; but in order to extract myself entirely from the prejudice you have in that regard, I shall confide a secret to you today; know that the charming Princess of Flanders, the wife of the fortunate Comte de Hainaut, is the only person that has ever inspired amour in me, and the only one with whom the bonds of a sacred union would have made the happiness of my life.[39] Now that you know my secret," Richard added, "it is up to you to inform me of everything you know about the situation of that adorable Comtesse."

"On learning that it is the Comtesse de Hainaut that is the object of your tenderness," said Blondel, "I feel very sorry for you, Sire, for that Comtesse appears to be very attached to her husband the Comte and lives with him in perfect union. It is true, however, that although that princess is beautiful, one sees in her face and in her manner a certain languor, which might well be the effect of a certain unfortunate passion. Thus, Sire, I have a great inclination to believe that you are loved tenderly by the beautiful Comtesse de Hainaut, and that while you have all her inclination, she is only attached to her husband by the sentiments that virtue inspires in her."

---

[39] The reference is presumably to Marguerite d'Alsace (1145-1194), wife of Baudouin V, Comte de Hainaut (1150-1195), but the allegation seems highly unlikely.

"Alas," exclaimed the King, "You have divined correctly. And that is what makes my dolor and my joy in such a tender passion; I know that the princess I adore shares my woes; I know that she sighs in secret over the fatal knot that attaches her to someone other than me; but if I feel a thousandfold tenderness in having the prayers of that admirable person, I also suffer a mortal dolor in the chagrins to which she delivers herself, for I know that by her delicate virtue she reproaches herself incessantly for not being able to bring her heart and her faith into accord."

"I have, in fact, remarked," said Blondel, "that she is very melancholy; I passed through her court not long ago, and the confidence with which you have just honored me, Sire, is presently causing me reflections that I did not make in that court. The Comtesse asked me for news of your fate with a particular urgency, and when I had replied to you that everyone was still in a sad uncertainty as to what had become of you, she maintained silence and seemed extremely dejected. At the time I did not pay those things the attention they merited, but now I am convinced that you are cherished more than ever by the charming Comtesse de Flandres.

"I believe, Sire," Blondel continued, "that you suspect that that name is given now to the princess that you love. As soon it was known for certain in Europe that Philippe, Comte de Flandres, had died in Asia, Baudouin, Comte de Hainaut, seeing his wife the heiress of that beautiful sovereignty, quit the title of Comte de Hainaut in order to take that of Comte de Flandres, and everyone admires the fate of Comte Baudouin, who, thanks to his lucky star, finds himself the wife of such a beautiful princess and such a rich heiress; but when the good fortune of that Comte is proclaimed, no one knows that he does not possess the heart of his lovely wife, which is uniquely filled with the image of the great King Richard."

"What use to me is the tenderness of her sentiments," Richard exclaimed, "since, in the interest of her glory, which, because of the purity of my ardor, is dearer to me than my own, I cannot even aspire to be happy?"

"It is necessary to hope," said Blondel, "that fortune will engender a few events that will be favorable to you. You and the Comtesse de Flandres have too many virtues and too many likeable qualities to lead a life traversed by misfortunes forever, and it is certain that Heaven will give its protection to a tenderness as noble and innocent as yours."

"May just Heaven decide that your prediction is accurate!" exclaimed the King again. "I would like to think so; you know the facility with which I abandon myself to hope; I would dearly like to deliver myself today to its most agreeable ideas. My mind and my heart, mortally fatigued by what despair has made them suffer, avidly grasp that which imagination can show them of a happy future. I shall even seek to divert myself with the past; I shall recall the memory of all the sweet moments that you and I spent talking about history and poetry, and I want to pass through my memory again the gallant and tender verses you came to show me when you had composed them for young Berthelide. But give me news of that charming person," Richard added, "and tell me whether you have finally vanquished her indifference."

"Sire," Blondel replied, slightly disconcerted, "I have to render you an account of so many important things regarding your service, that you will permit me not to employ the precious moments that I am permitted to spend with you with bagatelles that concern me. I am beginning to perceive that perhaps I have stayed too long today, and it is therefore necessary that I tear myself away from that please, in order to be in a position to conserve it."

"I consent to your quitting me," said Richard, "when you have told me whether you know what has become of the Comte d'Estanfort, from whom Varnery separated me when I was captured."

"No, Sire," said Blondel, "no one has had any news of that Comte, for which I am very sorry."

After those words, Blondel quit the King and went to fulfill the employments to which the position he occupied in the keeper's household obliged him. He continued to obtain the increasing consideration of that man and his entire family, and in very little time he acquired such a perfect confidence in their regard that he was able to spend full half a day with the prisoner without provoking the slightest anxiety. He took advantage of that favorable disposition like the clever man he was, but whatever care he devoted to it, and whatever secret attempts he made to discover a means of saving Richard, he still could not glimpse any appearance. His happiness was still limited to sensing the pleasure of consoling the prince and of sometimes making him forget, in their conversations, the chagrins and inconveniences that his frightful imprisonment caused him.

One day, when he was able to remain for a long time with that heroic master, he said to him: "I have not forgotten, Master, that you have done me the favor of telling me that in this dark tower you have composed various tales and petty stories. I hope that the same generosity that once engaged you to make me party to the excellent productions of your intelligence, might lead you once again to honor me with that mark of your benevolence."

"I confess," the King replied, that it would give me pleasure to read or recount to you all the fables of various species that I have composed here; I have never been left lacking the things necessary for writing; that amusement has been a great help to me. I assure you that if the diversion that it has given me had not been sustained, there were certain moments when I would have expired of tedium. I will, therefore, make you party to the only pleasures that my forced leisure has been able to permit me."

After saying that, the King recited to Blondel a tale that I shall report in all its depth and substance, but I shall not conserve overly extensive terms or narrations. I believe, however, that it will be permissible for me to add a few small reflections; at the same time, I shall suppress various circumstances that are not to the taste of our century; it is, therefore, not King Richard that is speaking, but me.

RICDIN-RICDON

In one of the most beautiful realms of Europe, of which historians have nevertheless not recorded the name, a prince reigned who, by virtue of his equity, the rectitude of his soul and his paternal love for his subjects, had acquired the glorious nickname of the King Prudent—which, in those days signified perfectly a king full of probity and honor.[40]

That King was united with a spouse who also had a great deal of virtue, and as that princess, who as naturally lively and active, was incessantly occupied in some amusing endeavor, the people had nicknamed her Queen Laborious.

The King and the Queen in question only had one son, whose inclinations bore him no less toward the virtue of those from whom he had received birth, but as the young Prince, who had the vivacity of his mother the Queen, did not yet have any occupation, he sought one in pleasures, and he showed so much liking for balls, spectacles, carousels and magnificent hunting-parties, and, in brief, was so enthusiastic about everything that could contribute to furnishing him with agreeable diversions, that he had been nicknamed Prince Lovejoy.

The King and Queen, who saw that the pleasure that amused him were innocent, did not oppose the penchant he had for them, and assumed that the perhaps excessively ardent enthusiasm he had conceived for them would pass with his first youth. In any case, the prince had a very agreeable face,

---

[40] The literal reference of the King's nickname, *Prud'homme*, which I have rendered as "Prudent," is to a careful and honest man, but it is very often used sarcastically to refer to an individual characterized by an unwarranted self-satisfaction and pomposity. In the same way, *Laborieuse* [Laborious] has a double meaning that the transcribed word retains in English, able to signify not merely hard-working but tedious.

and made it visible by all is actions that his spirit was no less penetrating than it was ardent.

What surprised everyone was that such a vivacious prince was not yet amorous and did not include the amusement of the heart among the number of those which he was so sensible. But festivities and hunting were the only objects of his desire, and they alone furnished him with certain pleasures that seemed to him very piquant by virtue of their singular novelties and their variety.

Sometimes, while chasing a deer, he went astray from his retinue, and sometimes, before any of his companions could find him, he was so forcefully gripped by hunger pangs that he went into the home of the first country gentleman or peasant that he encountered. As he did not usually make himself known, he sometimes had bizarre adventures that amused him greatly, and which he recounted to his father and the court with an extreme pleasure.

One day, when he had been separated from his companions in that fashion, as he was traversing a hamlet that appeared to be deserted, he saw a young woman of dazzling beauty emerging from a garden, whom an old woman with a very ugly face was dragging violently toward a rustic house that was opposite the garden on the other side of the public highway.

The young woman had a distaff charged with flax at her side, and was holding a bunch of flowers in one of the folds of her dress, which she had just picked in the garden. The old woman snatched them away, threw them into the middle of the road, gave the beauty a few rather hard slaps, and then, seizing her by the arm again, said: "Come on, you little wretch, let's get back to the house quickly; it's there that I'll make you feel what you deserve for having the insolence to disobey me."

The Prince, who had stopped short in order to consider that spectacle, approached the old woman as she was about to go back into her dwelling and said to her mildly: "How is it, my good woman, that you are treating that young woman so badly? What has she done, to attract your anger thus?"

The peasant woman, who, naturally, was very excited, and did not like people interfering in her affairs, was about to reply insolently to the prince, but, having cast a glance over his garments and judging by their extreme richness that the person wearing them must be of great importance, she retained her temper and contented herself with replying, in a bitter tone: "Sire, I am angry with my daughter because she always does he opposite of what I tell her to do. If I do not want her to spin, she spins from morn to night, and does it with a diligence that has no equal, and I am only making her the remonstrations that you see because she spins too much."

"How is that a reason for scolding the poor child like that?" said the Prince. Truly, my good woman, if you hate daughters who like to spin, you have only to give yours to my mother, the Queen, who diverts herself so much with that amusement and likes spinners a great deal; the Queen will make your daughter's fortune."

"Alas, Sire," replied the old woman, "if that pretentious chit, with her fine skill, appears to you to be so appropriate for our good Queen, you have only to take her away with you right away, if that seems good to you, for she has weighed upon my shoulders for a long time, and I desire to be rid of her."

As she finished speaking, a part of the Prince's retinue came to join him. He told one of his valets to lift the beauty on the rump of his horse.

The young woman still had a face covered with the tears that the old woman's threats had caused her to shed, but her tears did not hide her charms. The Prince tried to console her, assuring her that with the skill that she had she could not fail to attract the Queen's benefits abundantly. The poor girl, however, was so bewildered to find herself surrounded by so many men that she did not hear half of what he said to her.

Her mother watched her leave without showing the slightest concern for her fate, but the inhabitants of the hamlet found that they did not have eyes wide enough to consider her in the midst of all those lords covered with gold. They were petty officers of the Prince, who were taking her to the Queen, which made all the young peasant women in the vicinity envy her fate.

On the way the Prince learned that the beauty's name was Rosanie; as soon as he had arrived at the palace he introduced her to his mother as the most skillful and diligent spinner in all her estates. The Queen welcomed her generously, considered her attentively, and praised her modest and touching charms highly, which was not a slight mortification for certain women of the court who were envious of her perfect beauty.

The Queen had Rosanie lodged in an apartment where there was a sequence of rooms filled with an accumulation of the most celebrated textile fibers in the world. There was hemp from Syria, flax from the isle of Ithaca, hemp from Brittany and flax from Picardy and Flanders, and even the famous incombustible flax, from which a marvelous cloth could be made that the most ardent fire could not damage. Rosanie was told, as good news, that she had only to choose between all those fibers the one with which she wanted to commence; it was added that it ought to be indifferent to her because, as she was very young and more adroit than anyone else, the Queen, who wanted to keep her for a long time and treat her very well, had destined them all for her.

When the poor girl was alone, she abandoned herself to the most violent despair; she had an insurmountable aversion to spinning, which caused her to regard as a frightful torture the obligation to devote a few hours to that work. It is true that when she had the courage to make a sufficiently great effort for her to occupy herself with it for some time, she performed the task with an infinite skill. The thread was perfect in its slenderness and evenness, but she spun with such an excessive slowness that even if she had been able to force herself to devote herself to it assiduously, she would scarcely be able to spin enough in a day to half-fill a spindle.

Given those dispositions, it is easy to judge the dolor caused to her by the sentiments that the Queen had in her regard. She could not see how she could get out of the embarrassment into which her mother's malice had thrown her. She was, however, delighted to be out of the hands of that mother, who treated her with barbaric harshness. The gracious kindness with which the Queen had treated her delighted her imagination. The court in which she had just arrived, and of which she had only caught a rapid glimpse, already appeared to her to be a very pleasant abode; all the objects presented to her eyes had charmed her, but she understood well enough that she would only be able to sustain herself in that court on the basis of being a skillful spinner, and she sensed all too clearly that she would never have the talent for it.

Occupied with those cruel anxieties, she did not have a moment's sleep all night.

The Prince did not sleep either; the touching attractions and the naïve grace of Rosanie had struck his eyes so forcefully and made such a deep impression on his heart that, full of the idea of that charming young woman, he spent the entire night thinking about her.

As soon as it was daylight, however, the Queen sent word to Rosanie that she wanted to talk to her. There was a formal reception in the apartments of the princess, so when Rosanie arrived, a host of ladies avidly attached their gazes to her face. The King, who had not yet seen her, and who was in the Queen's apartment at that moment, looked hard at the young beauty and lavished various praises on her. The Prince, who was also there, and who thought even more highly of her than his father, nevertheless did not say as much.

It is true that Rosanie, in spite of the simplicity of her violet corset and the rustic arrangement of her hair, enchanted the eyes of everyone who looked at her. They saw that she had a slim and shapely figure, accompanied by such an easy manner that, in spite of the education she had had, there was no village awkwardness about her. Her hair, which was the most beautiful ash-blonde, ornamented an alabaster forehead, beneath which large blue eyes shone, as full of tenderness as they were of vivacity; she had a nose in the most exact proportion, a small, agreeable fashioned mouth and, as was fitting to complete her perfect beauty, admirable teeth. Her complexion was dazzlingly white, heightened by a light incarnadine, which gave her every possible splendor. Along with all the regularity of her features and the lively color of her complexion, the unspecifiable piquant charms were also visible in her face and throughout her person that are the very soul of beauty.

Although she had not slept all night she did not appear the worse for wear. The confusion that she felt in being thus exposed to the gaze of a numerous court gave her a blush that only served to cause her attractions to shine forth with all their gleam, and it was obvious that her métier as a spinner, which had obliged her to remain indoors, had preserved her complexion from the ravages of sunburn. All the ladies who had pretentions to beauty were animated by an extreme chagrin, and tried to find fault with her face or her figure. Young fools formed a thousand ridiculous designs in her subject. All in all, in various ways, she attracted the attention of the entire court.

As he went away, the King was moved to tell the Queen that he advised her to give the beautiful spinner different clothes, because her own were too bizarre and too different from those of all the other young women of his household. The Queen replied that she had already thought of that; and, in fact, a few hours later, Rosanie was brought a very proper costume and coiffure, perfectly in keeping with the fashion then reigning in King Prudent's court. The Queen's maidservants dressed her and arranged her hair with a great deal of care, and showed her in detail what she ought to do henceforth in order to adorn herself in a similar fashion.

They did it admirably well, and she appeared in that condition in the temple, where the Prince saw her. He thought her even more beautiful than he had thought her before, and gave her limitless praise behind her back. All the courtiers who had not seen her in the Queen's apartment looked at her with an urgent curiosity, and, as a thousand people had not remembered her name, and the King had called her the Beautiful

139

Spinner, that flattering nickname stuck. She became so fashionable that in less than twenty-four hours, there was not a single conversation in the court or the city in which the Beautiful Spinner did not feature.

While a hundred young beauties, fatigued by hearing incessant mention of her, envied her good fortune and her glory, however, the young woman who had given birth to so much jealousy sometimes had sad moments. In the course of the first day that she spent in the palace, in order to exempt herself from the occupation of spinning that as so insupportable to her, she said that she had cramp in her fingers, and during that day, the pleasure of being richly adorned and that of having a thousand praises addressed to her beauty suspended the anxiety that the inconvenient toil for which she was destined gave her.

The Queen's ladies-in-waiting, the majority of whom were no longer young and not gifted with beauty, had initially conceived a good deal of affection for Rosanie, to which the young woman responded with an extreme docility and complaisance; they showed her over the entire palace and even part of the city, which greatly diverted the new inhabitant of the court, whose eyes were not accustomed to objects so magnificent.

Once she had returned to the fatal apartment so full of fibers, however, that odious sight plunged her back into all her despair. Nevertheless, she recovered some tranquility and slept much better than she had the previous night.

The following day, as soon as she got up, she thought about ornamenting herself with all the beautiful accoutrements that the Queen had given her. Far from having retained the lessons that the maidservants of the princess had given her, however, she could never get to the end of placing them in tolerable manner, even though she undressed and undid her hair twenty times over in the attempt.

Finally, after much wasted effort, she remained coiffed and dressed awkwardly, and with very ill grace. Chagrined by the lack of success that her cares had had in that direction, she sought to compensate for it another. She loaded her distaff and began to spin, but her hand was still as slow as usual, in spite of all the efforts she made, and she did not succeed in spinning a quarter of a spindle of thread between ten o'clock, when she had finished her adornment, and half past twelve, when someone came to tell her that the Queen would like to see her work.

As soon as Rosanie had heard that order, she dissolved in tears; then, eventually, she tried to find in her mind some apparent excuse that might still get her out of trouble. She presented herself before the Queen with a dejected expression and told her that she was in despair because a violent rheumatism, which had put her arm out of action had prevented her from showing her zeal by her work. She added that she had made every effort to vanquish her illness, but having taken up the distaff and the spindle twenty times in vain, in spite of all her perseverance, she had only been able to spin the small amount of thread that she showed the Queen.

Queen Laborious found it admirably fine, which confirmed the idea she had of Rosanie's skill, and as the princess was good, she sympathized with her, told her that she did not want to force her arm, and added that she would send her foremost physician to see her. Rosanie, who was afraid that it might be discovered that there was nothing wrong with her, told the Queen that she had no need of any remedy, and would surely be better before long, since every time the trouble afflicted her, it only required rest to make it pass.

The Queen was content with those reasons, but as soon as Rosanie was no longer before her eyes, her seamstresses, who were very envious of the great distinctions that had suddenly been given to the newcomer, opined loudly that the cramps and rheumatism were only maladies of convenience, and that there was every appearance that the beauty who was said to be so skillful and so diligent was simply a maladroit idler.

Poor Rosanie, who heard those speeches, was extremely afflicted by them, and on the other hand, the Queen's maidservants and the ladies of the court, who saw the excessively poor appearance that her clothes and hair presented, burst out laughing and made a thousand jokes about her violet corset and her skirt, claiming that it had been a great mistake to take them away from her, since they suited her far better than the attire of a demoiselle.

Rosanie could not hold firm against such upsetting things; she left the palace and went into the gardens, and was still walking there when she found herself in a dense wood was at the end of the park. When she was in that place she felt so weary that she sat down promptly on the edge of a rapid stream that snaked through the wood. There she started thinking sadly about her unfortunate destiny and the decision she had to take regarding the position she was in.

Sometimes, she resolved to return to her mother, harsh and barbaric as she was, but when she came to think of the ill-treatment that she had always received since she had lost her father, she criticized herself for having the slightest idea of returning. Furthermore, young and devoid of experience of the world as she was, she felt for that abode and the manner of village life an aversion that the atmosphere of the court had not diminished, even though she had been breathing it for such a short time.

On the other hand, she saw very clearly that she was going to attract the indignation of the Queen, to be expelled from the palace shamefully, and perhaps punished, when the princess realized that she had misrepresented her talents as a spinner. She also saw, however, that the truth was about to become obvious; she had reached the end of her resources and there was no longer time to feign cramps and rheumatisms successfully. She had only to wait for the moment when she would be the butt of the jokes of all the young women by whom she had been so envied

In those cruel reflections, utterly abandoned to her despair, she told herself that there was no other course of action for her to take but that of killing herself. Full of that thought, forgetting her lassitude, she got up in order to go to a high pavilion that was at the other extremity of the wood, which the Queen's ladies-in-waiting had pointed out to her the day before while showing her around. She intended to go up to the top of the building, which was open, and then throw herself out of a window.

Nevertheless, the natural love one has for life, memories of her tender youth, and, most of all, the secret pleasure she felt in her beauty, caused her to shed tears at the thought of her death, and to go toward the fatal place where she was condemned to perish at a very slow pace.

As she was going along a path that led to the pavilion she suddenly saw a tall brown-haired man appear in front of her, very well dressed, with a rather somber physiognomy, but who adopted a cheerful and gracious expression when he spoke to her.

"Where are you going, my beautiful child?" he said. "It seems to me that I can see tears trickling down your cheeks. Tell me what your affliction is; it would need to be very strange for me not to be able to give you assistance."

"Alas," Rosanie replied, "there is no remedy against the chagrin that is overwhelming me, so it is quite pointless for me to tell you the cause."

"Perhaps," said the stranger, "the difficulty is not as desperate as you think, but at least troubles can be relieved by recounting them, so tell me yours. You could not tell them to anyone who would be more interested in them than me."

"Since you press me so insistently," said Rosanie, "I will inform you of all my destiny. I have the misfortune of being born in a very obscure condition. My father was a worthy peasant, full of probity and common sense, who had acquired such great trust among the inhabitants of his hamlet and all the surrounding villages that he was taken as an arbiter in all disputes; and as he was very secretive and never in a hurry to speak he was nicknamed Taciturn. That father, who loved me with an extreme tenderness, had once borne arms, and had even had the full confidence of his captain. That was because there was nothing in his speech or manner of the tedious rusticity of those who have never left the village.

"From early childhood he took a thousand cares to give me all the education of which I was capable, and if I have a great love of virtue and am not completely stupid, it is to him alone that I have the obligation; as for my mother, she is frightfully vulgar, and furthermore, she never took the trouble to give me the slightest instruction about anything whatsoever; she never had anything for me but harshness and aversion; all her tenderness was for my brother.

"In spite of residence in the village and the feeble enlightenment of my education, I found that I had sentiments and inclinations far above my birth, the baseness of which drove me to despair. Only the features of my face were capable of consoling me; fortunately, they gave me flattering hopes for my fortune, and I was not yet twelve when I did not find any pool or spring by means of which I could not tell myself that I would surely not remain under thatch.

"With such ideas, I was very scornful of the complaisance of boys of my condition. I was scarcely past my fourteenth year than several better parties than a person of my estate could aspire to asked my father for me in marriage, but I shed so many tears when he proposed them to me, and said so forcefully that I would rather have death than such marriages, that his amity for me bore him not to constrain me to accept them.

"My mother scolded him a great deal for that, and said that he had spoiled me by his blind indulgence to my will. In spite of all she said, though, he did not become any more terrible toward me; on the contrary, he often reproached her for not loving me, and because it was only her son who was dear to her. Alas, it was not long before I was to see how truly he spoke. He undertook a journey, the reason for which he did not tell us, assuring us, however, that he would soon return, but he must have perished in that unfortunate voyage, for a long time passed beyond that which he had indicated to us for his return.

"Since my mother has found herself the absolute mistress of my fate, there is no sort of ill-treatment that I have not received from her. Finally, two days ago, after having quarreled with me cruelly because I had not spun sufficiently, as she was dragging me back to our house, threatening me with a great deal of anger, the son of the King of this country was passing our door, and he asked her why she was maltreating me so badly. She replied, making mock of me, that it was because I spun too much. The Prince thought she was speaking seriously, and as our Queen takes pleasure in all sorts of workmanship, and diverts herself with spinning more than anything else, the Prince immediately asked my mother for me, for his own mother, the Queen. Mine, delighted to be rid of me, immediately handed me over to his servants.

"I was introduced to the Queen as the best and most diligent spinner in her entire kingdom, and never was anyone more distant than me from having those qualities. However, the Queen, informed that I possessed them, destined for me such a horrible quantity of work that the mere sight of it made me tremble. I believe that she assembled all the fiber there ever was in the world in order to overwhelm me with it. With the terrible hatred that I feel for spinning, and the slowness I have in that métier, I do not know where to start or finish such annoying and tedious work; however, I have no other means of remaining in the court, which pleases me so much, but being a seamstress for the queen.

"Alas, when I was first seen in the palace, and I had heard my beauty given so much praise, I recalled the idea that my vanity had given me in my childhood; I flattered myself that some lord of the court, or at least some officer of the King, would have sufficient inclination for me to want to share his fortune with me by marrying me. I even thought, for a few moments—oh, what a proud thought!—that the Prince was looking at me with eyes animated by passion.

"Well, of all that, what remains to me, except the despair of sensing that by virtue of my lack of skill in adorning myself I am disfiguring the gifts that nature has given me, and that, by virtue of the same lack of skill, for want of spinning quickly enough, I am going to be thrown out shamefully by the Queen, and to serve as the victim of the envious companions, whom my beauty and my nascent favor caused to tremble?

"You see, kind stranger," Rosanie concluded, "that there is no remedy for my woes. However," she added, with a sigh, "I hope to spare myself that torture by a fatal means that I shall not specify."

"But instead of a fatal means," said the stranger, "if someone were to give you a comfortable and agreeable means to avoid those woes, would you not be very obliged to them, and would you not do something in their favor?"

"Everything that I could do reasonably," replied Rosanie, precipitately. "Except for honor and duty, there is nothing I that I would not sacrifice to gratitude."

"Since you have that sentiment," said the stranger, "I will engage myself with pleasure to serve you, but first let us settle the terms of our agreement precisely. Look at this wand I am holding in my hand, and take it in yours."

Rosanie took the wand and studied it. It was very small, made of an exceedingly shiny gray-brown wood, the name of which was unspecifiable. It was garnished with a changing stone, which was neither an agate nor a cornelian, nor any other familiar stone. In sum, it was no easier to specify the name of the stone than that of the wood.

When Rosanie had considered the wand for some time, she handed it back o the stranger, who said to her: "You see, this little wand has admirable qualities. As soon as you touch any sort of hemp or flax with it, it will spin by day as much as you like, as fine as you could wish. It also has the gift that as soon as one touches wool, silk or cloth with it, one can make the most beautiful tapestry in the world, and works of petit point that can compete with the most excellent miniatures."

He continued: "I will lend you this marvelous wand for three months, provided that you remain in accord with what I say to you. If, three months from today, when I come back in quest of my wand, you say: 'Well, Ricdin-Ricdon, here is your wand,' I will take back my wand without you being engaged to any obligation toward me; but if, on the appointed day, you cannot remember my name, and you simply say to me: 'Well, here is your wand,' I shall be the master of your destiny; I shall take you anywhere it pleases me, and you will be obliged to follow me."

Rosanie thought for some time about what she ought to reply; but it appeared to her that the name Ricdin-Ricdon was so easy to remember that it did not seem that she was running any risk in accepting the favorable help of the wand. She was already taking a secret pleasure in being able to confound the pride of her competitors by means of the beautiful thread that the wand was going to spin. However, there was another chagrin that made her anxious. She had savored too well the advantages that her beauty gave her to lose any of them, and she imagined that the poor manner in which she adjusted her hair and her garments took away a great deal. She therefore envisaged with extreme dolor the displeasure of remaining permanently in the palace coiffed and clad so gracelessly.

The host of those thoughts suspended for some time the response that she wanted to make to the man who had spoken to her. Finally, she said: "Lord Ricdin-Ricdon, I will accept the agreement that you want to make with me, if you can add one more condition to it, which is that in addition to the gift of making fine thread and fine tapestry, I would like your wand to have that of putting into coiffure and attire all the good appearance and good grace that is necessary for them to please. If you can enrich that wand, already so useful, with a gift as necessary to beauties as nourishment, our treaty is made."

"Oh," exclaimed Ricdin-Ricdon, "nothing is easier than to grant you what you ask; my comrades and I never refuse persons of your sex the talent of making the best of themselves, as soon as they want to reach any sort of understanding with us. That is why one often sees little girls of twelve, who cannot be taught anything, coiffing themselves with such admirable artistry, and already placing a beauty-spot as judiciously as women of fifty. I announce to you that as soon as my wand touches your coiffure and your clothing, all the charms and the fashionable appearances in the world will shine there, as well as all the fluttering graces that are able to enchant handsome men."

"I accept your treaty, then," said Rosanie.

"But it's necessary to swear it," said the negotiator.

"Well, I swear it," she said, "And by the most inviolable oaths."

"That being so," said Ricdin-Ricdon, "since I have your promise in such good form, I am your servant, my beauty, until I see you again."

As he spoke, he placed the wand in her hand again, and then he went away.

As soon as Rosanie had the mysterious wand at her disposal, the first thing she did was to touch her hair and clothing; then she looked at herself in the nearby stream, where she found herself so beautiful, and dressed so well, that she was very pleased with the bargain she had just made—for she remembered very clearly the individual with whom she had concluded it, and, in gazing lovingly at the officious wand, she told herself with an extreme pleasure that she had just acquired an extremely useful implement at very little expense.

While she was occupied in these various thoughts she was still walking, returning to the palace. She had not yet arrived in the flower garden, however, when she met the Prince. He had not seen her all day, but certain malevolent jokers, with whom the court as always inundated, had not failed to tell him tales of the gauche manner in which the Beautiful Spinner put on the costumes of a demoiselle. The Prince had listened without smiling to everything that was said to him on that subject, but he had not dared to tell them how convinced he was that Rosanie was still charming, no matter how she was dressed, for he was too fearful that the sentiments he had for the beautiful girl would be revealed.

As soon as he perceived her he was, as usual, enchanted by her attractions; then, examining her attire and seeing that it was perfectly adjusted, he turned to one of the tedious jokers who had fatigued him some time before with a tiresome story that he had thought very comical. The Prince made a hundred fine and pointed remarks about the calumny and tastelessness of his story. Then he saluted Rosanie with as much politeness as if she had been one of the most qualified persons in the court, and asked her obligingly, as he passed close to her, whether she had seen the fountains playing. When she replied that she had not he told her that he would have them activated for her the following day.

After having made a profound curtsey, she withdrew to her apartment, so transported by joy at the possession of the marvelous wand that, in her transports, she lost the memory of the name of the individual who had given it to her.

Joy prevented her from sleeping, as chagrin had on the first night that she spent on the palace, and during all the hours she ought to have given to sleep she only occupied herself with agreeable ideas, which gave her much more pleasure than the most flattering dreams could have done.

When it was broad daylight, she got up, and her wand, in an instant, served her as the favorite chambermaid of the most skillful coquette would have done. Then she hastened to test the gift of the same wand on a small parcel of the Queen's flax; which, by virtue of the power of the enchanted wood, immediately became a pile of thread as fine as the most beautiful Flanders thread.

Charmed by the fortunate success of the wand, Rosanie put away a part of the thread that she had spun and only retained, to show it to the Queen in the evening, a little more than the most assiduous and diligent seamstress in the world could have spun in one day.

After having gone to see the fountains playing—which, in accordance with the orders that the Prince had given, did so better than they had for a long time—when the day was over, she waited for the Queen to pass, who ought to be going for a walk. When the princess appeared, she told her that, her cramps and rheumatisms having quit her, she had employed her day, and had taken the liberty of coming to present her work to her.

The Queen took it eagerly and looked at it, but as the daylight was fading and the apartments were not yet illuminated by candles, the Queen had them lit immediately. She was enchanted by the beauty of the thread in question, and amused herself for so long considering it and talking about fabric that she let the hour of her walk pass and said that she no longer wanted to go—which caused some of the ladies of the court to murmur against the Beautiful Spinner, to whom the Queen, in the meantime, said a thousand gracious things, and ordered her to come to see her when she got up in the morning.

Rosanie, having slept very well all night, did not fail to do that punctually, and took with her the other part of the cotton thread that she had spun.

"Madame," she said, in presenting it to her, "as I saw that my petty work had the god fortune to please you, and that it might perhaps contribute sometimes to your amusement, I spent the night making more in order to demonstrate my zeal."

"Oh, the poor child!" cried the Queen, turning to her maid of honor. "She is as affectionate as she is skilful and diligent. But," she added, addressing Rosanie, "I don't want you to make a custom of staying up late, my girl; it would damage your health, which seems so firm and so brilliant."

"No, Madame," replied Rosanie, "I shall have the honor of working hard for you without it doing me any harm; I have the health and strength of my seventeen years; at that age, nothing is inconvenient. I only beg you to have the kindness to permit me to divert myself for a few hours every day; if I have that permission, it will cost me nothing to pass the nights."

The Queen assured Rosanie that even if she did not spend a single moment working late, she would be given time to amuse herself every day.

After such an assurance, the beautiful girl went on: "Before having enabled you to see, Madame, what I can do with the distaff and the spindle, I had not dared to inform you that I have no less talent for tapestry than I have for spinning, but now that you have seen my work in spinning, I shall take the liberty of telling you that if it pleases you to have me given wool, silk and canvas, I will make you all kinds of works of tapestry and petit point, as you wish."

"Truly," said the Queen, exclaiming again, "this little girl is a prodigy of skill! Go, my child," she went on, "Go and pick strawberries in the fruit garden with my women. Soon I will have you given everything you need for making tapestry, and you can work on that tomorrow."

"I still have one more favor to ask you, Madame," said Rosanie, "which is that you have the kindness to order that, when I am shut in my apartment, I will be left tranquil and solitary there, without anyone coming to trouble me or watch me work. Company is uncomfortable when one works with as much application as I do."

"I approve of your request," the Queen replied, "and I will give orders that you be left in complete liberty and full repose."

After that speech, Rosanie withdrew, and spent the day amusing herself and the night sleeping.

Although she had forgotten the name of the individual of the wand, she did not give much thought to that forgetfulness, and when she did think about it, it was with scant anxiety, for she had no doubt that the name would return to her memory when she took the trouble to remember it; and in any case, the three months that she saw before her in order to profit tranquilly from all the wand's gifts appeared to her as long a time as half a century might have seemed to someone else.

Meanwhile, the Prince was no longer occupied with anything but his amour; the amusements that had once seem to him to be the most enjoyable no longer gave him any pleasure. Hunting and spectacles appeared to him to be insipid amusements, and he was bored everywhere that he did not see Rosanie. Seeing her, speaking to her about his tenderness, proving it to her by some great service, and touching her heart, were now the object of all the young Prince's desires. Nevertheless, he dared not attach himself to her footsteps as much as his penchant impelled him to do, for fear that the court might notice his enthusiasm.

In spite of the precautions he took, however, the majority of the old courtiers had already divined his veritable sentiments, which contributed more than a little to attract to Rosanie, on their part, a great deal of complaisance and regard. As for the young men, they did not imagine in the slightest that the Prince was sensible to the young beauty and only thought about her as an agreeable conquest for themselves.

In the meantime, the Queen instructed one of her maid-servants, named Vigilentine, to take Rosanie everywhere she might want to go and to serve her as a mother. Vigilentine was delighted by that commission; she found Rosanie utterly charming and it was a great pleasure for her to put her care into teaching her everything she knew about politeness, and inspiring her to conduct herself well in everything she did. As the woman had a great deal of intelligence and knew the usages of society, she formed Rosalie's manners agreeably in a very short time.

In King Prudent's capital there was a public garden to which the beauties of the court and the city came in order to make a pompous display of their attractions. Gallantry had great days there; coquetry held various tribunals. One breathed an inflamed air in that garden, which the breath of zephyrs barely refreshed, and one ran the risk there of being more intoxicated by flirtations than flowers. Vigilentine only took Rosanie there after having instructed her in the manner in which was necessary to conduct oneself in order to avoid reefs.

Thus, in spite of the good taste and the gallant air that the assistance of the wand extended over Rosanie's accoutrements, Vigilentine's lessons enabled her to present a modest exterior, which, combined with her charms and her brilliance, made her appear an entirely admirable person, as appropriate to inspire respect as amour.

She was regarded with exceedingly jealous eyes by four or five young fashionable beauties who had come to the capital from all the provinces of the realm with the design of attaching fortune to their chariots with fine knots. Having faith in their attractions, they had imagined that as soon as they appeared in the big city, all the men there most elevated by their wealth and rank would come in haste to offer them their heart and their hand. They had been convinced by sad experience however, that in that kingdom, as in so many others, people were far more touched by the gleam of gold than that of two beautiful eyes.

In vain they had made a thousand movements to announce their charms loudly in all directions, hardly anyone had thought about them for a solid bond, and in spite of all their cares, all that remained to them was the frivolous glory of being run after by foreigners, pestered by young fops and secretly evaluated in monetary terms by financiers. The only advantage that they had was that the public rendered justice to their virtue and because it was true, they were able to avoid many dangerous traps.

Those competitive beauties, who were ordinarily at odds, were all united against Rosanie. The incense lavished on her from all sides, the acclamations that she provoked as soon as she appeared in public, embittered them strangely; they could not suffer without getting angry that a rustic shepherdess could come to steal the empire of their beauty, which each of the claimed to merit alone but wanted at the very least to divide between themselves.

As each of them had a party, those various parties took great care to decry Rosanie's charms in all their speeches. One elongated her nose, another magnified her mouth, a third shrank her eyes and burnished her complexion, and they spread those rumors in all directions with so much artistry that all those who had not seen Rosanie or had only seen her imperfectly were duped by their false depiction and said to one another that the Queen's Beautiful Spinner, of whom there was so much talk, was not such a marvelous beauty—that, on the contrary, her face had many faults, and that a great deal of prejudice entered into the admiration that people had for her.

However, no matter how much trouble was taken to establish those ideas, as soon as Rosanie appeared, they all disappeared. Those who had seen her before, looking at her more attentively, found her more beautiful than the first time they had envisaged her, and those who had only heard mention of her protested on seeing her that there had been a great deal of malice or bad taste in the descriptions that had been given to them.

Vigilentine took her to spectacles, and the crowd that filled the vast edifice in which they were put on heaped her noisily with so much applause that she was embarrassed by it, and even chagrined. Not that she was sorry that people were admiring her; she had the same humor as most beauties, ever avid for incense, but Vigilentine had told her there is nothing so fatal for a young woman as to attract too much attention, and because people looked at her so much, she only took her occasionally to public promenades and spectacles. Such a resolution irritated Rosanie intensely, for she enjoyed herself greatly in places where a great many objects struck her sight.

She was soon able to console herself for that petty annoyance by virtue of the great success of her wand. Although she employed almost all her time going out and amusing herself, she always found enough to make use of the officious wand on a daily basis, to do all the work of the most skillful seamstress. Thus she continued to show the Queen the most beautiful thread in the world, and when eight or ten days had gone by since she had been given wool, silk and canvas, she also showed the princess tapestries more beautiful and more expertly woven than those of Arachne.

The Queen, who had a passion for all those kinds of work that sometimes went as far as excess, was transported at the sight of them; she lavished Rosanie with her praises and caresses, and from that day on she heaped the beauty incessantly with benefits and marks of her favor. It even seemed that the extreme baseness of her birth was forgotten, for in all the fêtes held in the court, she was placed with the Queen's maids of honor, and in that company she was not one of those who received the smallest marks of distinction.

All those young women were very irritated by that, except for one, who was nicknamed Siren. The Siren in question had a very pretty face and a very generous soul; she rendered justice to Rosanie's beauty and skill, and, far from being scornful of her for the baseness of her birth, she said that she ought to be given more credit for her virtue and her mildness than ought to be given to someone born of illustrious blood, who is bound to have nothing but nobility in her sentiments and behavior. The equitable young woman had such a beautiful and touching voice, and sang so pleasantly, that the precious advantage had earned her the name of Siren, but what acquired her so much suffrage at court was that she had a humor as sweet as her voice.

Rosanie, who sensed very clearly that favorable dispositions she had in her regard, conceived a veritable amity for her. Siren always responded to in a very gracious and obliging manner, and did by virtue of inclination and with joy what her companions only did for political reasons and with chagrin. Not only did the politeness that they were obliged to show Rosanie cost them a great deal, but, as I have said, they were in despair at the distinguished honors that they saw rendered to her and the flattering eulogies that she was given.

The Prince was delighted by the regard that everyone had for the object of his amour, but the satisfaction that he felt was troubled by the difficulty he found in talking to her about his tenderness. He had succeeded in the good fortune of seeing her often without anyone finding anything to criticize in that, but he could not converse with her for a single minute in private. No one was permitted to enter her apartment, and as soon as she was no longer shut up therein, Vigilentine never quite her for a moment.

It was in vain that balls were held, where one ordinarily finds the means of talking to the person one loves, as poor Rosanie did not know how to dance—for, although she had been given a master as soon as she was in the palace, she had scarcely had enough lessons to have learned to make a curtsey properly. As she did not know how to dance, she was obliged to be nothing but a spectator and to remain in the middle of a crowd, where it was impossible to find a few moments appropriate to tell her how he felt.

It was not that the Prince, by means of a thousand gallant actions and various veiled remarks, had not sought to make her understand the passion that he had for her, and had not remarked by virtue of a hundred small things that she had said and an even greater number that she had not, that he had been understood—but it was not enough for an amour as intense as his to be known to the person who had given birth to it; he wanted to know whether it had made favorable impressions on her heart.

He saw, with extreme chagrin, that even under Vigilentine's eyes, many men of the court and the city had already dared to hazard formal declarations in Rosanie's regard; he even knew that an ambassador, forgetting the dignity of his position, had been bold enough to tempt her virtue by the offer of a considerable sum of money—which had irritated the young woman extremely, in whom one never saw, with regard to all essential things, anything but noble and elevated sentiments.

In any case, she was quite childlike in her inclinations and her amusements. She liked ribbons, dogs and birds with an unmitigated passion. The conversation of serious women did not take long to make her impatient, and she only found the company of young women of her own age amusing. If she liked spectacles, it was not because of the spectacles themselves; she was only touched by the pleasure of seeing such a large number of people assembled and in movement. The poor girl understood very little of the satirical wit of a comedy, and even less of the political metaphors and poetic tenderness of a tragedy; and if it were not for the pleasure of seeing and being seen, far from being enthusiastic to go to theatrical performances, she would have preferred to all the *Cinnas,*

Iphgenias and *Misanthropes* of her era the piquant diversion of a game of Tag or Blind Man's Bluff.

Nevertheless, although she still had such infantile inclinations in some regards, as she was naturally affectionate, she was very sensible to the ardent enthusiasm of the Prince. The penchant she had for virtue, however, was opposed to what she might have felt for such a likeable Prince. She told herself incessantly that the elevation of his rank ought to close her eyes to his amour and his merit, since the elevation question was an invincible obstacle that would prevent them from ever being united by a sacred bond.

In the midst of all those reflections, the beauty still continued to have her wand spin and make tapestry with a marvelous success, and was no less admired at all times for the good grace of her adornment. She also succeeded in learning to dance, although no enchantment entered into the lessons she was given in that art; she had no other advantage than that of being guided by a good master. Although she was shown with a similar care how to read and write, however, she only succeeded in making feeble progress therein. Assembling letters and tracing characters appeared to her to be very tedious things and she did not have the strength to put much application into something that did not amuse her.

Meanwhile, the Prince was still burning with impatience to talk to Rosanie about his ardor without constraint, at least for a few moments. The restriction in which he found himself obliged to live gave him a chagrin that changed his humor. Among his most assiduous courtiers there as a very witty young knight nicknamed Good Advice, who had a large part of his favor; he made him the confidence of his desires, and Good Advice, who was ingenious, quickly found a means to be of use to him.

As he followed his master everywhere, when the Prince found himself in the places where Rosanie was, Good Advice occupied Vigilentine so cleverly by talking to her about matters that seemed to her to be consequential that the Prince had the leisure to speak to Rosanie for some time about his amour.

He did so in depictions so vivid and so tender that she was touched, but, however sensible the beauty was, she did not neglect to tell him that he would do better to stifle that ardor, since, in spite of all the merit of which he partook, she did not have a soul sufficiently base ever to resolve to become his mistress, and that she was not enabled by birth ever to become his wife.

The Prince replied that there was nothing new in seeing kings marrying shepherdesses, and that no one would see anything strange in a bond of which amour and merit tied the knots. Rosanie, who did not understand figurative ways of speaking in the theater, understood them perfectly when they came from the mouth of a lover who as dear to her. The Prince assured her very frequently that his love as more ardent than that of all those who had ever loved before; he protested so loudly that he would a thousand times rather renounce the throne than her; and he swore so many oaths that, whatever might happen, he would never have any other wife than her, and that in the meantime, he would only offer her his prayers with the same respect as he would have offered them to the foremost princess on earth. In sum, he spoke in a manner so passionate and so natural, that the beauty allowed herself to be persuaded that his love was sincere and pure, and permitted him to talk to her about it sometimes, provided that he did so with the respect that he promised and that he was firmly resolved to maintain the fidelity to her that he had sworn.

The amorous Prince swore once again that he would never think pleasing anyone but her, and that he would never have any sensibility for anyone but her—and he swore it with the most terrible oaths.

From the day when the hearts of the two lovers had a perfect intelligence, so did their eyes, and often gave one another tender explanations of their secret sentiment. Good Advice contrived various conversations for them, but he could not always succeed in that with so much skill that the Prince's attachment was not divined. The King and Queen were alerted to it at the same time. The King was not overly anxious about his son's inclination, which he regarded as a temporary amusement, and as for the Queen, she had so much confidence in Rosanie's virtue that she did not fear anything fatal in such an attachment.

The Prince made every effort to hide it from the eyes of the court, but he did not succeed very well; amour is one of those turbulent passions that one can only rarely hide beneath the veil of discretion.

As soon as Rosanie's competitors were informed of the illustrious conquest she had made, their jealousy and hatred in her regard were increased by more than half. But among those who delivered themselves to such unjust sentiments there was none more tyrannized by them than one of the Queen's maids of honor, who had been secretly in love with the Prince for a long time.

That young woman, who was nicknamed Bleakthought, had some beauty, a great deal of ambition, a violent amorous inclination and a black soul, as vindictive as it was cunning. So long as she had seen the Prince indifferent to all beauties, she had consoled herself for not being able to touch a heart that no one had the gift of rendering sensible, and had flattered herself that if ever he turned toward amour he would not fail to be softened in her favor; she counted extremely on the strength of her charms, and she had made so many advances to the Prince that she could not resolve herself to believing them wasted, for she was not unaware that they had been noticed by the person to whom they had been addressed.

When, therefore, she was convinced that the Prince whom she had made the object of all her prayers was only repaying her tender steps with ingratitude, and had given himself to an odious rival that she already hated more than death, all her amour turned to fury, and she no longer occupied herself with anything but forming projects of a barbaric vengeance.

In order to succeeded in that, she went to find a pernicious witch, who was active in her interests but who had not been able to succeed, by means of the secrets of her art, in making the man she wanted to please love her.

"In spite of your good intentions," she said, on approaching her, "you have not been able to serve my amour, but I know that you will be the mistress of serving my vengeance; so, cause the ingrate who has scorned my fires perish, and cause to perish at the same time, in a terrible manner, the unworthy rival whom he has preferred to me."

The witch assured her that she would enter with her into the sentiments of her vengeance, and promised to do her best to serve them.

In the meantime, the Prince, whose tenderness was more content than it had ever been, resumed his ordinary amusements. He went hunting in the depths of a forest, in which, as often happened, he was separated from his followers while pursuing a beast with too much ardor.

After having wounded it mortally he found himself unexpectedly before the door of a palace of an admirable structure and magnificence. He was very surprised to see an edifice so pompous in that deserted place, but his astonishment was much further augmented when he saw a lady of great beauty, magnificently dressed, emerge from the palace, followed by several other ladies who appeared to hold her in great respect.

The beautiful lady approached him in a gracious manner and said: "Prince, if you love glory and if you are sensible to the woes of the unfortunate, for your interest and theirs, come into this palace with me and do not refuse to listen to me."

Only responding with a profound bow, the Prince gave hr his hand and they both went into an apartment where gold and precious stones were seen glittering in abundance. The Prince expressed to the lady the impatience that he had to learn whether he might be fortunate enough to have the opportunity to render her some service, in the misfortune of which she complained. After she had begged him to sit down, she spoke to him thus:

"You see before you, Sire, an unfortunate princess, the nearest relative and heiress of a king, the master during his life of a fertile neighboring realm, of which a cruel tyrant has taken possession for more than fifteen years. By that description you will doubtless recognize the realm of Fiction, of which the barbaric Hollowdream has taken possession after having defeated and killed King Finedesign in the last battle he fought against that amiable prince. Finedesign's wife, Queen Smilingimage, was taken prisoner; she was pregnant, and the tyrant had the child to whom she gave birth killed, and has held the poor Queen captive for many years.

"I was almost in the cradle when King Finedesign was dethroned, and by the death of that prince and his child, I found myself the heir to the realm of Fiction. My mother, who was the foremost princess of the blood, was fortunate enough to be able to protect me from the power of the tyrant, and a sage magician, the master of this palace, gave us a refuge in a solitary manor, which often serves as the shelter for illustrious unfortunates. My mother raised me in that place with all possible care, but since I had the misfortune to lose that princess a year ago the magician has been my sole support.

"He brought me to this superb palace, where I am served with a splendor appropriate to my rank; but he discovered a short time ago, by means of the secrets of his art, that the time has come when I shall be able to enter into possession of my realm and punish the usurper, provided that I can find a protector born of royal blood who will employ for me the value of his arm, and who will adopt my interests on certain conditions, which the savant magician will propose to him.

"I have seen your portrait, Sire," the unknown princess added, lowering her eyes, "and on the strength of the greatness that it offers to our eyes, I begged my sage guardian to make you the proposals in question. I shall withdraw for a few moments and he will come to talk to you. I shall be fortunate if, without the eloquent discourse of that generous old man, the sight of me disposes you somewhat to take an interest in my party."

After saying that, the princess retired, and immediately, an old man of benevolent appearance, but dry and fleshless, seemingly weighed down by the burden of the years, appeared before the prince.

"Prince," he said to him, bowing to him in a respectful manner, "the great qualities of which you partake have given me such a strong inclination for you that I will consider myself fortunate if I can employ the power of my art for your happiness and your glory. Deign, then, to allow yourself to be guided by me. The beautiful princess that you have just seen has the most tender penchant for you; she is the heir of a great kingdom, and it only depends on you to unite her crown with the one that Heaven has destined for you, if you want to receive the advice and the gifts of Cutlamboy—that is my name.[41]

"Here," he continued, taking a ring from his finger, "is a ring that has the power of rendering its wearer incessantly victorious; even if you have a host of enemies, they will all succumb under the force of your arms, as long as you have this ring; there is no valor that can hold firm against it. If you want to love our princess and swear an eternal love to her, I will make you a present of this rare ring; as soon as you put yourself at the head of a powerful party that has been formed in the realm of Fiction against the tyrant Hollowdream, you will triumph, and then, adding to his defeat a hundred further triumphs, you will render yourself master of the estates of a host of kings, and become one of the greatest conquerors there has ever been on earth."

The Prince had listened to that speech with an extreme astonishment, but as soon as the magician had stopped speak-

---

[41] Given that the other names in the story translate with relative ease, this one—*Labouréelamboy* in the original—seems odd. *Labourée* [labored] usually refers to a plowed field, although it can mean cut or dug by extension. It is conceivable that "lamboy" is a disguised derivative of the verb *flamboyer* [to blaze], given the character's infernal nature.

ing and was awaiting his response, without hesitating for a single moment he said to him: "I cannot offer amour to any lady; my heart and my faith are engaged to a charming person, whom I shall love until my last sigh; but even if I were in a position to offer by tenderness to the beautiful princess that I have just seen, I would present my vows to her and would fly against her enemies without waning to accept your ring; I like glory, and that given by the triumph of arms appears to me the most touching of all. I will seek it ardently as soon as it is possible for me to do so, but I only ever want to owe victory to my courage and the strength of my arm, and I would refrain from accepting the help of a supernatural power."

"You are very delicate, Sire," said Cutlamboy. "I know many princes and generals who have sought very ardently for what you are refusing; but if you disdain the aid of my art, and least do not scorn the advice of my experience; I have lived for such a long time that I seem to have acquired some right to give it to persons of your age. Suffer then that I tell you that the vain scruple of the oath you have made to another beauty ought not to prevent you from offering your heart to the heiress of the realm of Fiction; that princess has a powerful party in her estates; you have only to put yourself at its head and it is certain that, without the help of the ring that you are refusing, you will nevertheless triumph over the tyrant. After his fall, you will marry the princess and by that marriage you will acquire a crown that you will one day combine with the one that is your due; in addition, you will perform a generous action toward an amiable princess who has the most vivid and tender ardor for you. "

The Prince still replied that his heart and his faith were no longer his and he could no longer dispose of them; but he was very surprised when he saw the princess come in, covered with tears, who came precipitately to throw herself at his knees, saying to him: "Oh, Sire, if my feeble attractions cannot touch you, be sensible to my woes and my tenderness; I shall die if you continue to scorn the ardent testimonies that I am giving you."

The Prince was in an extreme confusion and embarrassment. He had been on his knees as soon as the princess, but when he had lifted her up and he had raised himself up too, he maintained an anxious silence in looking at her. He saw a face brilliant with attractions, on which dolor was nevertheless painted. He accused himself secretly of barbarity, in only responding with coldness to the prayers of such a charming person. On the other hand, the tender amour and the sacred oaths that engaged him to Rosanie were vividly present in his imagination, and could not permit him the slightest spark of ardor for any other object. He therefore made the decision that his inclination and good faith inspired; and the thought that he could satisfy generosity and at the same time.

"A beauty such as yours, Madame," he said, "merits an undivided amour and an entire heat; mine is no longer in my power; the most powerful bonds and the faith of my oaths have attached it forever to an object worthy of all my tenderness. But Madame, although I cannot give you my heart, I can dedicate the most profound respect to you, and I can destine all the effort of my arm to you. Let us depart, then, Madame; I shall be delighted to support the zeal of your faithful subjects and I shall shed my blood with joy in order to bring down the usurper of your crown."

"I acquit you of that, ingrate!" cried the princess, angrily. "I do not want your services if you refuse me your heart; it is your heart alone to which I aspire, alas! My amour, my wrath...."

As she pronounced those words, a young child of radiant beauty suddenly appeared in the room; in his hand he was carrying a kind of golden scepter, with which he struck the princess and the magician, who immediately fled with terrible howls. He also struck the walls of the room, and at the same moment the entire palace disappeared.

The Prince found himself in the forest, surrounded by trees, having no one with him but the charming child.

"Prince," said the latter, "I have just dissipated the fatal illusion that was obfuscating your senses, in order to reward you for the faithful generosity you have just shown in keeping your oaths. If Heaven punishes perjurers severely, it is no less exact in recompensing good faith. That you have just shown toward Rosanie has merited celestial grace. Know that the object that just appeared to your eyes as a beautiful princess was a demon clad in a fantastic body by the conjurations of a perfidious witch who wants to doom you.

"That spirit of darkness, disguised as a princess, took her measures poorly in saying that she was the heir to the realm of Fiction. King Finedesign had no relative who was not presently in old age when he died, but he has left a child who will be made known to you one day. As for the figure that appeared to you here as an old man, it was a demon, like the pretended princess. If your heart, seduced by the beauty of the one and the flattering promises of the other had violated the oaths you have made to the object of your tenderness, those cruel demons would immediately have taken possession of you and you would have remained subject to their power until the end of days. But since you have triumphed generously over all their attacks, as the prize of your victory and to crown your good faith, Heaven wants to free you forever from their traps.

"Here, sincere lover," the amiable child continued, presenting a ring to the Prince, "this is a ring that is in absolute contrast to the one that the seductive spirit offered you just now. That one was the ring of deceit and this one is the ring of truth. Always wear it; it will prevent the dangerous illusions of Hell from having any power over you, and you will see magicians and demons performing their black operations without them being aware that you can see them."

After those words, with an entirely gracious action, the charming child put the ring on the Prince's finger, and then disappeared.

The Prince had still been in a state of such great surprise that he had not been able to find the use of his voice, and he had only testified his sentiments to the child, who had seemed to him to be divine, by a few signs of respect and gratitude. Finally, his departure leaving him a little more to himself, he rendered thanks to Heaven, with a great deal of ardor, for having avoided the frightful perils that had menaced him that day.

After that he started walking, and sounded his horn in order to find his companions, whom he did indeed find.

When he had returned to the palace, the charms of the presence of Rosanie and the innocent tenderness that he detected in her beautiful eyes made him forget all the anxious emotions that had agitated him during the hunt.

Meanwhile, Bleakthought and the witch were in despair at having failed in their vengeance. They had expected a great deal on the place in the solitary forest, for it was indeed a production of their malice; having counted so much on the enchanted palace it was with a mortal dolor that they saw the Prince escape their net. Bleakthought, irritated by the feeble power of the magic art, resolved to avenge herself by human means, the most pernicious that artifice and perfidy could inspire. As she had spies watching Rosanie and all those who took an interest in the beautiful girl, she knew that the ambassador who had made her offers that had so offended her was more infatuated with her than ever; she even knew that he did not retain any control over his passion and that he was capable of sacrificing the greatest interests of his fortune to it.

In fact, that minister, being convinced that it was impossible to succeed in the possession of Rosanie except by marriage, had resolved to marry her. After having begged her pardon for the offensive views that he had initially had for her, he offered her his hand, assuring her that the slight chagrin she might have in going to spend her life in a foreign country would be entirely soothed by the splendor of rank and the limitless complaisance that her husband would have for her eternally.

Rosanie told the ambassador that she was much obliged to him for the honor that he wanted to do her by marrying her, but that she declined with thanks, not being able to resolve to leave the Queen, her mistress, to whom she was attached by such an ardent zeal, and who had treated her with so much kindness.

The ambassador, who was violent, was extremely angered by that response, and contented himself with the resolution to satisfy his amour no matter what the cost might be.

*

As King Richard was at that point in his story, someone came to tell Blondel that the keeper was asking for him. It was necessary for that generous favorite to quite he conversation with the vanquisher of Syria in order to go and receive his orders from a vile jailer.

The latter told him, in an urgent fashion, that the Emperor was in Linz, and that Princess Sophie, his sister,[42] having come to walk in the woods nearby, had heard mention of his voice from inhabitants of the village who had been to take her fruits, and that she wanted to hear him sing.

Blondel went to find the Princess, and presented himself before her with a attitude both respectful and assured. Her surprise was great at seeing a man of the sort she believed him to be so well made, and hearing him express himself with much intelligence and politeness—for he spoke the Teutonic language as well as he spoke the Romance language, which was the French language at that time.

He sang for Princess Sophie a song for which he had written the words himself. Those words, in the Romance language—which the Princess understood well—had the following meaning:

> *If amour did not deliver the same adventures*
> *To sincere lovers and perjured lovers;*
>> *If that redoubtable vanquisher*
> *Were able to recompense the confidence of a heart*
> *I would spend my life in a thousand sweet pleasures;*
> *But pity therein being forever asleep*
>> *It cannot cure me,*
>>> *Nor let me die.*

---

[42] No such individual is recorded in history.

Princess Sophie was extremely content with Blondel's voice and manner of singing. She gave him a great deal of praise, but she would doubtless have given him even more if she had known that the lines he had sung and the tune were his own compositions. She sought to engage him to come to the imperial count, by means of engaging promises, but although he found the Princess very beautiful and very gracious, he refused with thanks the protection that she offered him at court, and appeared to Sophie so heedless of fortune that as she had been told that the keeper has a rather pretty daughter, she thought that Blondel must be in love with her, and imagined that the infatuation of which he was full was making him neglect an opportunity that others would have sought eagerly.

The Princess resumed the road to Linz without making any longer reflections, and Blondel returned to the tower, where he was not long delayed in informing the King of his conversation with Princess Sophie. Then, as soon as it was convenient, he begged the prince to be kind enough to satisfy the strong curiosity he had to learn the remainder of Rosanie's adventures.

Smiling, the King said that the occupation of making stories and listening to them was very pardonable in people whose life was as sterile in pleasures as theirs. After those words, the prince, whose politeness equaled his valor, resumed his tale.

When Bleakthought heard about the refusal that Rosanie had made to a marriage that seemed so advantageous to a person of her condition, she entered into a rage that it would be difficult to describe.

"How," she cried, "can that audacious peasant girl find that a young and well made lord as considerable as the ambassador is not good enough for her? From what I can see, it is the throne that she wants, and nothing less than lovers who are to wear crowns. Truly, I shall be able to lower the sights of her insolent pride."

Full of that idea, she prompted the ambassador's confidant, who was entirely hers, to act. The confidant inspired his master with the design of abducting Rosanie, and the master, frantic with amour and chagrin, approved entirely of that reckless project. His embassy was concluded, in quitting the estates of King Prudent, he sensed that he would be delighted to carry away that beautiful prey. He no longer thought about anything but taking all the measures necessary to succeed in it.

He picked a time when the King and the Prince were making a journey to a house of pleasure, to which the Queen had not gone because of some indisposition. The palace was therefore less crowded than usual.

One evening, when Rosanie was returning after taking a stroll with Vigilentine in the public garden that we have mentioned, as she was coming back into the palace through the kitchens, four masked men seized Rosanie abruptly and dragged her away through a hidden door. She suddenly found herself in a deserted street in which, in spite of her cries and her resistance, she was put into a carriage, which immediately drew away with as much speed as if it were flying.

After it had been traveling for some time, escorted by several horsemen, it stopped and the horses were changed. Then the sad Rosanie, who was in despair, saw the audacious ambassador, the author of her abduction, climb into the carriage. At that sight she redoubled her cries and her tears.

"Don't be afflicted, Madame," he said to her. "I am very far from any design to submit you to any outrage; I only want to take you to my country in order to make you a very agreeable fate and give you a rank worthy of you by marrying you."

"Oh, Sire," cried Rosanie, in a voice punctuated by sobs, "whatever your intentions might be, they cease to be legitimate as soon as you employ violence to accomplish them. In the name of all that you hold most dear in the world, deign to take me back to the Queen, my mistress; the obligation that you will have given me will doubtless make me more sensible to your desires than I have been until now, and might determine me to quit my Queen in order to go spend my days with you, but if I do not go back, what will that great princess think of me? Alas, she will believe that I have consented, without her consent, to dispose of my destiny. In the name of God, Sire, permit me to destroy that suspicion in her mind."

"No, no, ingrate," replied the ambassador, "I shall not let you out of my hands; I see your artifice; once you were out of them you would mock my amour again. After having taken so much trouble to render myself the master of my happiness, I shall be careful not to let it escape."

"Perfidious individual," replied Rosanie, "since you have so little regard for my prayers, I shall not lower myself any longer to addressing them to you; but I hope that Heaven will take my defense; I flatter myself that it will extract me from your unworthy hands and that it will not leave your treason unpunished."

While they were making these speeches, the carriage was still traveling with an inconceivable speed, but the coachman was so occupied in guiding it rapidly that he strayed from the route that his master had ordered him to take. He perceived that, and tried to get back on track, but when he attempted to do that with application, the carriage broke and threw Rosanie into the middle of the road near a dense wood. As she did not feel any injury, far from being frightened by the accident, she took it as a favorable augury.

Meanwhile, the ambassador was swearing with a terrible fury at his squire and his coachman, and all the rest of his men got down from their horses in order to try to lift the carriage up. Rosanie, her courage redoubled by that embarrassment, started shouting with all her might in order to attract a few peasants to her rescue.

She would have like to flee, but it was impossible, the ambassador having ordered one of his servants to hold her by the arm. She trembled, therefore, that her cries might be uttered in vain, and, suspended between hope and dread, she looked incessantly by means of the moonlight, which was very bright that night, to see whether anyone might appear.

She did not have long to wait before three men emerged from the wood.

"Sires," she shouted, in a loud voice, as soon as she saw them, "deign to lend assistance to an unfortunate girl who is being abducted against her will."

Immediately, the three unknown men drew their swords and came to fall upon the ambassador and his men, who did not have time to mount their horses again. All the thrusts that the three strangers delivered were mortal; one of them, in particular, called attention to himself by an unparalleled valor and skill; he killed the confidant and two more of the ambassador's men.

The latter, transported by rage, came in his turn to fall upon him like a furious lion; the brave stranger received him with the same vigor as he had commenced the combat, and although he was wounded in the left shoulder, he delivered a thrust so terrible to the ambassador that he laid him dead at his feet.

As soon as the minister's men saw their master dead, they all took flight. Then the valiant unknown approached Rosanie, who was chilled by fear, and was shivering in horror at seeing so much blood shed on her account.

"You are free, beautiful girl," he cried. "Your kidnappers have scattered."

At the sound of that voice, Rosanie was suddenly seized by the most vivid transport of joy that one can feel, for she recognized her dear Prince in the person of her liberator.

One can imagine all the tender things the two lovers said to one another; the Prince was enchanted to have rescued the object of his amour so fortunately, and Rosanie could not cease to give thanks to her illustrious defender. Of the two men who were with him, one was his faithful Good Advice and the other a gentleman of his household who also had a considerable part of his confidence. Thus, neither he nor Rosanie constrained themselves before them.

The Prince's wound, which proved, fortunately, to be only a slight contusion, was bandaged. When that lover, as brave as he was tender, recognized the ambassador, he was initially afflicted to have killed a man whose person ought to have sacred rights because of the title that characterized him, but when he reflected that the unworthy minister had derogated all the privileges of his position by an odious abduction, he applauded himself instead, for the fact that Heaven had chosen him to punish the other for having so audaciously violated human rights in his estates, and even in the palace of a King who had treated him with so much generosity and consideration.

Meanwhile, the Prince, although inconvenienced by his wound, assisted the amiable Rosanie to walk, in order to take her to the King's pleasure palace, which was on the far side of the wood from which he had emerged. While walking she gave him a detailed account of her abduction, and in his turn, he told the beautiful girl that, downcast by the chagrin that her absence caused him, and judging that he would not be able to sleep, he had decided to spend the greater part of the night taking the fresh air in the wood while chatting to the two men that she saw.

The Prince had scarcely put Rosanie into the hands of two ladies at the manor when someone came to tell him that one of the Queen's gentlemen, who had been sent as a messenger, was asking to speak to him.

The gentleman announced that Rosanie had been abducted from the palace, almost under the eyes of the Queen, and that the princess in question, irritated and chagrined to the highest degree by the insolence of the kidnapping was sending the information to the King and him, in order that they could take the measures necessary to arrest the kidnapper and punish him, although she had already given the sternest orders that had been possible for her.

The Prince charged the gentleman with returning immediately to inform the Queen of the fortunate hazard by which he had saved Rosanie and punished her abductor.

The next day, the King decided that they would return to the capital and take the Beautiful Spinner back to the Queen. The amiable girl was received with so much kindness and so many marks of benevolence that the envious Bleakthought was ready to expire of rage; but what completed her despair was seeing that her rival only owed the good fortune of having avoided the abduction to the valiant assistance of the Prince. Although she saw clearly by various glaring signs that Heaven was opposed to hr vengeance, she persevered nevertheless in the design of satisfying it, and took new measures in order to succeed.

Meanwhile, in spite of the joy that Rosanie had in being saved from her abductor by a cherished lover, who had covered himself in glory, she was agitated by a secret anxiety that he had difficulty hiding. Siren, who still testified an increasingly tender amity to her, perceived her agitation and asked her the cause of it, but she did not want to confide in her.

She was not wrong to maintain reserve in that matter; her chagrin was caused by the infidelity of her memory; she sensed that the term that the man with the wand had prescribed for coming to fetch his precious piece of wood was getting nearer by the day, and the bizarre name of the man did not return to her mind. For some time, in vain, she had been making a thousand efforts to discover it, but they were always futile. However, she understood that if she could not rediscover that fatal name, an inviolable promise would oblige her to follow the donor of the wand wherever he wanted to take her; and her abduction by the ambassador had made her sense more than ever the mortal dolor that she would have in being separated from the Prince forever.

However poorly she formed the characters of writing, she wanted to see whether they might aid her to rediscover he name so ardently desired. She therefore tormented herself greatly, with all the application of which she was capable, and wrote *Racdon*, then *Ricordon*, and finally *Ringaudon*. But if, at certain moments, she had the joy of believing that she was about to find the name that she needed, at other times, she was

173

in despair, convinced that it was in vain that the ones that presented themselves to her memory seemed to approach it, since they contributed nothing, in the end, to recalling a sure idea of the veritable one. Weary of racking her memory with such scant success, she abandoned the assistance of writing and plunged back into her sad reflections.

Bleakthought intended to give her a subject for even more dolorous ones soon. That cruel person, beside herself because, not only had the Prince avoided her vengeance, but had also enabled Rosanie to avoid it, wanted to slake her fury by means of the death of the young hero. As the perfidious young woman had beauty, birth and fairly considerable wealth, she had a great many lovers, but the majority were men devoid of title, devoid of wealth and devoid of decency, whose character was even worse than their fortune.

Among those ruined and knavish lovers, Bleakthought chose three, to each of whom she said individually: "I will render you master of my person and my wealth by marrying you as soon as you have rendered me a service that I want of you. The Prince has offended me and I can only appease my anger by his death; it is therefore necessary that you observe his steps and that you take his life during one of those moments when he goes astray while hunting. Two of my friends are ready to accompany you in order to assist you; I will give all three of you enchanted swords, of which a savant witch, one of my friends, made me a gift. By the power of her art she has ensured that you will always wound and never be wounded; and by means of the same power, she will prevent it from ever being discovered that it was you who have killed the Prince."

Bleakthought having made that speech separately to each of the three said lovers, none of the scoundrels refused her horrible proposal. She did indeed give them swords, over which the witch had mumbled a few words from a grimoire, and all three of them prepared to execute the detestable assassination that she requested of them.

Since the Prince had escaped the traps that had been set for him in the enchanted palace, Bleakthought no longer dared count reliably on the power of the magical art, so, in the perfidious project that she had planned, she only had a mediocre confidence in the assistance of that art, but she was convinced that, without any supernatural power, it would be easy for three well-armed men to take the life of a single one that they attacked advantageously. Consequently, she had only had recourse to the witch as an additional precaution, not doubting that it would be easy for her three lovers to make the Prince perish under their thrusts without enchanted weapons.

Meanwhile, for particular reasons, the King made a journey to his country house without the Queen or the Prince, and the young lover, entirely recovered from his wound greatly troubled by the anxiety that he remarked in Rosanie, went hunting in order to dissipate the chagrin that the beauty's caused him.

More occupied with his reveries than the concern of pursuing the beast, he was separated from his companions and went so far astray from them, while still dreaming, that nightfall surprised him before he could rejoin them.

Passing through an utterly deserted area near an old ruined palace that seemed uninhabitable, he noticed that there were a great many lights in the palace in question. He approached the windows of the halls, which were all open and all broken, and looked through the trees that surrounded them. By the glimmer of violet light he saw several individuals with frightful faces and bizarre costumes. In their midst there was a desiccated and bronzed man of sorts, who had a wild gaze and a frightful physiognomy, but who appeared to be exceedingly cheerful and was making leaps and bounds with an inconceivable agility.

The Prince sensed a secret shiver at the sight of those frightful objects, and did not doubt that they were denizens of Hell. Remembering that he was wearing the ring of truth, however, he did not fear their odious power. There was a woman in the troop who was making great supplications to the frightful human figure, who was in the middle.

"No," he said, "my power does not extend over him; a celestial spirit, my sworn enemy, defends him against me and made me experience it not long ago when, in my enterprises, I was unfortunate under the name of Cutlamboy. My other name is much more favorable to me; I've already acquired a great many young beauties under that name, and I hope that tomorrow, I'll acquire another, worth more than many others.

After those words, the frightful man recommenced his capers, singing this song in a terrible voice:

If a young and tender female
Only liking childish frolics,
Had kept it in her head,
That Ricdin-Ricdon is my name,
None would come into my lakes;
But the beauty will be mine
For such a name is unknown.

After the demon, for he was indeed one, had sung that fine song, he addressed the woman who had spoken to him, saying: "As men have an education more cultivated than women, we ordinarily have more difficulty in seducing them than we have in duping the credulous sex, unless we make use of persons of that sex to make men fall into our traps, just as, on the other hand, it is often men who are the cause of women giving themselves to our nets. I alone have acquired more young women by the desire that they have to appear more beautiful, and to be able to adorn themselves well, than twenty of my comrades have acquired by a hundred different means, and the violent passion that makes them seek so ardently to acquire beauty and good grace is only born of the enormous desire that they have to charm men. That is why I said that it is often men who are the cause of women becoming our spoils.

"For example," the hideous orator continued, still addressing the same woman, "it's certain that your good friend will not escape us. Well, is it not the inordinate fury she had in wanting to please a man that will render her our prey? But who would have believed that the young Prince who had charmed her would render devoid of effect all the batteries that we have set up against him? Nothing, however, has been able to engage him to beak the oaths of fidelity that he had sworn to his mistress, and it has never been possible to tempt him by a wealth or a glory due to magic art. Those two efforts of virtue have acquired him a defender who presently renders all the power of Hell futile against him. Thus, it is vain for you to implore my help today to make him perish; neither you nor I can harm him any longer; everything in his regard will proceed naturally."

By this speech, the Prince understood clearly that this was the individual who had spoken to him in the guise of an old man, and he did not doubt either that the woman was the witch, against whose pernicious projects the celestial child who had given him the ring had warned him. He was tempted, for a few moments, to go immediately to punish that perfidious woman and the other scoundrels that he believed to be in that place with her, but he did not remain long in that design, judging all those wretches unworthy of his vengeance. Then he thought of drawing away from their odious troop in order to find his companions or at least find the route by which he might return.

He had not been walking for long when he was abruptly attacked by three men who suddenly emerged from a clump of trees. The Prince defended himself with a heroic valor and intrepidity, and quickly reached a tree against which he could support himself in order only to be attacked from one side. There he fought with so much courage, skill and good fortune that, after having killed one of his enemies and knocked another to the ground, he saw the third take flight.

He did not bother to pursue him, and only thought of continuing his route, but he was very weary, and he had received a slight wound in the arm by which he had lost a good deal of blood, which weakened him extremely. Finally, after having covered a little more ground, he was fortunate enough to find a number of his companions, who were very surprised to find him so weak, tired and wounded.

When he had remounted his horse, in spite of the state he was in, he flew very rapidly to the palace, in which he found his mother in a terrible anxiety in his regard. The princess was alarmed to see him wounded, although the surgeons, who were summoned immediately, assured her that the injury was trivial. In spite of that assurance, Rosanie was sensibly afflicted by it.

No one, however, could divine the origin of that detestable assassination attempt against a prince who was equally gentle and obliging. He could not disentangle it himself, for, although he had seen clearly the sentiments that Bleakthought had for him, and had no doubt that she was discontented by the fact that he did not respond to them, he was far from thinking her capable of such a perfidious act.

While the Prince had been an anxious witness to the witches' Sabbat, however, and had been the target of the furies of a malevolent lover, his father the King had been passing much more agreeable moments. He had learned secrets and facts that had given him a sensible joy.

The same day that the Prince had been exposed to such deadly perils someone came to tell the King that a lady, whose beauty and charming manner made her extremely remarkable, was asking for an audience.

Having ordered that she be brought in, he was indeed very impressed by the attractions that shone in her person. She was accompanied by an old man of benevolent appearance, who appeared to be a man of condition, and another old man who, beneath his rustic appearance, presented the appearance of prudence and probity that immediately spoke in his favor.

"Sire," said the lady to the King, "You see before you a princess who has come to render you thinks for the obligations she owes to you and your wife the Queen."

"I do not believe, Madame," the King replied, "that the Queen or I have ever been fortunate enough to render you any service."

"It is true, Sire," the lady continued, "that I have not received personally the favors for which I have come to thank you, but they have been granted to someone who is dearer to me than myself, since it is Princess Rosanie, my daughter."

"What, Madame!" exclaimed the King. "The beautiful Rosanie is your daughter! That is very difficult to believe; although that charming person is still almost a child, you have too much beauty and youth for anyone to be persuaded that you are her mother."

"Sire," the lady replied, "I know what I ought to think about the obliging things that you are saying to me; they are the gallant and gracious lies that the agreeable habit of politeness always inspires in men of an elevated rank; but if you will deign to listen to me, Sire, I will inform you of serious verities, which will, I believe, surprise you very much."

The King having testified to the lady that her story would give him a sensible pleasure and that he was ready to hear it, she went on thus:

"You see in me, Sire, Queen Smilingimage, the widow of King Finedesign, whose sad destiny has caused so much talk. When the cruel Hollowdream defeated and killed my husband the King, took possession of his throne, and locked me in an obscure prison, he no longer thought of anything but consolidating his usurpation. As he knew that I was pregnant, he resolved to kill the child to which I gave birth if it were a son, but if but were a daughter he wanted to conserve her with great care in order to marry her one day to his son, who was then very young.

"I learned of the dire projects that the tyrant had formed regarding my childbirth, and shivered over either of the destinies that he was preparing for my child. I shed torrents of tears when I thought that if I brought a son into the world a barbarian would snatch away his life as soon as he was born, but I was scarcely less afflicted when I thought that if I gave birth

179

to a daughter, she would one day have the sad fate of being attached by odious bonds to the blood of a detestable tyrant. I therefore resolved that, whatever the sex was of the child that Heaven sent me, to try to remove the child from the power of the tyrant, even if it cost me my life, which, in the state I was in, was more burdensome than precious.

"The faithful knight that you see," the Queen continued, indicating the old man who appeared to be an aristocrat, "has always been attached to me with a zeal as active as enlightened; he has always had so much penetration in his intellect and so much prudence in his actions that my people had give him the nickname of Farsight, which has remained to him. That knight, therefore, who had avoided the cruelty of the tyrant by means of a disguise, bribed one of my guards and was able to come to talk to me in my prison.

"Delighted to see him, I made arrangements with him as quickly as possible in order put the child to which I was to give birth in his hands. The tyrant had ordered that I be treated with a great deal of respect because he wanted to protect me, in view of my pregnancy. Thus, the governor of the fortress where I was took care to ensure that I had all the comforts and facilities that could contribute to my health and my satisfaction.

"When I saw that I was very close to the time of giving birth I testified that I had an extreme desire to eat a wild boar pâté. Measures were immediately taken to satisfy me, and thanks to the cleverness of one of my maidservants, it was the faithful Farsight, disguised as a peasant, who was charged with making that pâté. Farsight gave it to my guards, who brought it to me.

"My chambermaid and I opened it without witnesses, and we found inside, as I had agreed with Farsight, a stillborn child that had just been brought into the world. The prescient knight had given me the means of preserving the body of the child exempt from corruption until I the moment came when I would have to show it.

"In the end, I gave birth successfully to a daughter, who had on her arm, above the elbow, a birthmark in the perfect design of a rose, which immediately caused me to give her the name of Rosanie. My chambermaid hid the child is a distant place, placed the dead child next to me, and then immediately began weeping and crying for help, saying that I had just given birth to a dead child.

"That news was taken to the tyrant, but he had no regret for it, for the stillborn child that had been brought to me was a boy, and as there was still a large party that hated Hollowdream and his tyranny, many people spread the rumor that I had given birth to a son, and that he had killed him. Meanwhile, the dead child was put into a coffin. My chambermaid, with admirable feats of trickery, removed him from it and put my living daughter into it instead of the little corpse, of which she disposed by throwing it into a secret place, without anyone having the slightest suspicion of it.

"Finally, the coffin was taken away, and although my daughter had been given a good deal of nourishment, I still trembled that her cries might betray our secret. By an extreme good fortune, however, she did not cry out, and Farsight, who, by means of his skill, had acquired the confidence of the governor, was charged by him with the care of the burial, which took place that evening without any ceremony.

"The fortunate and adroit Farsight took little Rosanie out of the coffin as soon as possible and, by virtue of the visible protection of Heaven, he found her in a very good condition. He gave the child all possible cares and did not rest until he had removed her from the country over which Hollowdream exercised his tyrannical domination—which this faithful subject did, Sire, in the manner that he will recount to you."

When the Queen concluded with those words, Farsight began to speak, continuing the story, still addressing King Prudent.

"I emerged successfully, Sire, from the realm of Fiction, taking the little princess with me and a nurse, whom I passed off as her mother. Although I had taken great care to acquire that woman, I hid from her the birth and fate of the child that she was nourishing. I arrived in your estates, Sire, and I traversed a part of them without finding anyone who appeared to me to be appropriate to conserve the precious deposit with which I was charged. However, I would have been delighted to be able to confide her to safe hands as soon as possible, for it was necessary, in the interests of the Queen and the Princess, for me to return to the kingdom of Fiction as soon as possible.

"Finally, one day, in order to allow the Princess and her nurse to rest, I had stopped under the trees bordering a highway, in the vicinity of two or three villages. While the nurse sat down, I was walking among the trees, and I had drawn some distance away from the woman when, finding myself behind two peasants, who were also walking, I heard one say to the other: 'Well, obstinate Taciturn, are you still in the humor that has earned you that nickname, and don't want to say anything about the cause of all this racket?'

"'What do you want me to say?' replied the other peasant. 'I'm content to feel sorry for my neighbor's misfortune without criticizing him or going out of my way to investigate its causes, so I know nothing at all of what you're asking me.'

"'Come on,' said the one who had spoken first, 'not everyone in our village is as close-mouthed as you are. I'll soon know what I want to know without you, but since you won't tell me anything, I'll hasten my steps and arrive in the village before you; that will give me time to chat, for it's necessary for me to go back promptly and I can see that, charged with your infant as you are, you won't be able to go so quickly.'

"After saying that, the peasant quit the other and started walking as rapidly as he could. As soon as the one carrying the little child was alone, I approached him and asked him a few questions I learned that the child was his daughter, to whom his wife had given birth no more than a month before; that the woman had had a malady in her breast that had obliged him to confide his child to a nurse in a village a few leagues distant from his own, but that, his wife's illness now being completely cured, he was coming back from fetching child in order to have her nourished by that wife, who was a perfectly good nurse.

"I listened to that entire speech with great attention. I examined the man's physiognomy; it pleased me, and I believe, Sire, you will find that I was right when you know that the good peasant in question was the same old man that you see behind my mistress the Queen. I also learned that he had been given the nickname Taciturn because of the penchant he had for silence and the restraint he had in talking. All that prejudiced me advantageously in his favor, and I resolved to engage him to be Princess Rosanie's guardian—without, however, confiding the entire secret of her birth to him. I therefore made him considerable promises, and put in his hands a good deal of gold and precious stones, including an infinitely precious bracelet that the Queen had given me in order to contribute one day to recognizing the Princess.

"After having won over Taciturn, therefore, and having assured him that the child for whom he was to care would one day be the cause of his fortune and that of his entire family, I asked him not to make anyone party to the adventure, not even his wife. He swore to me that he would only conduct himself in accordance with my orders; and that was the manner in which we disposed things, in order that our secret would remain between the two of us.

"Taciturn's daughter being exactly the same age as Rosanie, we decided that he would present the Princess to his wife as being their veritable child, which he had just brought back from the place where he had taken her to be breast-fed during her mother's illness; he and I had no doubt that the mother would be received since she had only seen her daughter at the moment of her birth. On the other hand, I would take Taciturn's daughter to Rosanie's nurse and take the little princess from that woman's arms in order to put her in those of the worthy peasant. Taciturn and I agreed that I would find the nurse a comfortable abode in a village that he named, some six

183

leagues way from where we were, and I assured him that his daughter would be cared for as well as if she were my own.

"On those assurances he put her in my hands and I took her to Rosanie's nurse, from whose arms I took the Princess, telling the good woman that I was changing her nurse. She was extremely surprised by that exchange. I told her that I had my reasons for making it, and after having taken Rosanie to Taciturn, I returned to find the nurse, whom I took to lodge in the nearest village. Then I went to the peasant's village, in order to inform myself fully as to his character. I learned that it was as good as I could have wished. After that I took the nurse and her nursling to the village Taciturn had named to me, and, having enabled the woman to live there comfortably, I returned to the realm of Fiction.

"I found that Queen Smilingimage was still in captivity there, and that the barbaric Hollowdream was exercising his usual tyranny. There was a party ready formed that hated Hollowdream mortally, but it was not sufficiently powerful to declare itself openly in opposition to the tyrant; it was necessary to think of fortifying it. Although a few of servants of the late King, including me, employed all our industry in that, we could not succeed, and many years went by before we were in a state to move.

"Tyrannical and eccentric as Hollowdream was, he had taken possession of many minds. In addition, as it was only known that the late King had distant heirs, that was discouraging; nevertheless, I dared not confide the secret of Rosanie's birth to anyone, in the fear that if it were betrayed, the tyrant might find a means of attempting the life of the Princess. Meanwhile, I had fairly frequent news of her, and made it known, in spite of the difficulties, to my mistress the Queen. That was the only consolation this princess had in her sad captivity.

"Some time after I had returned to the realm of Fiction, the nurse of Taciturn's daughter informed me that her nursling had died. The father of the child also wrote to me, and as I was preparing to bring the nurse back to her homeland, which was that of Fiction, the woman died in the village where I had left her. Thus, although she had never known Rosanie's birth, her death made the secret even more secure, as it remained buried in a profound silence.

"Finally, after a long passage of time, Hollowdream's family, which had multiplied and become very numerous, committed extravagances that revived the hatred that people had for the tyrant. The party that detested him had always subsisted and, having always remained united, although without ostentation, had grown and become stronger; finally, it saw itself in a state to carry forward its enterprise.

"We thought, therefore, of attacking Hollowdream's principal fortresses, and set forth on campaign under the leadership of General Greatideas, who had triumphed so many times during the reign of the late King. Initially, the general made considerable progress, and defeated Hollowdream's troops twice in pitched battles, but the tyrant of the realm of Fiction was not beaten; for, not only had he summoned to his aid various kingdoms of Europe, but had also brought auxiliary troops from the Arab lands, which signaled themselves by such exploits that, after having defeated and wounded General Greatideas, it was thought for some time that they might destroy the faithful subjects of King Finedesign and Queen Smilingimage to the last man. It is also true that they promised that if they were allowed to plunder the land of Fiction for a thousand and one nights, they would ensure Hollowdream an eternal triumph. But General Goodtaste having come to join Greatideas, with troops that he had brought from the land of Politeness, our party became the stronger again, and the auxiliary Arab troops, in spite of their numerous squadrons and their fantastic forms, were forced to yield before Greatideas and Goodtaste.

"When I saw that the party of the late King had the upper hand, I told the leaders that the King had left an heir, and told them the secret of Rosanie's birth. However, as we still suspected that there were traitors among our troops, we did not judge it appropriate to divulge that secret, for fear that the

185

Princess might be sacrificed to the tyrant. It was only resolved that someone would be sent in quest of Taciturn, in order to confirm the most considerable members of the party of the truth of what I had advanced, for with regard to the Queen, we could not yet have the joy of counting on a testimony as illustrious as hers. The governor and the guards of the fortress where she was imprisoned had been changed, and since that change it was no longer possible for me to have any communication with her in her prison.

"We therefore sent for Taciturn, but as soon as he arrived in the land of Fiction he was taken prisoner by soldiers of Hollowdream's party. We continued to make progress in the meantime, but in spite of the prudence and intrepidity of our leaders and the bravery of our soldiers, we found that the resistance lasted longer than we thought. In the end, it was not until ten days ago that the tyrant's party was conclusively defeated. Fortunately, we had recovered Taciturn, and subsequently, as we had taken the fortress where the Queen was a prisoner, we had the sensible joy of liberating the princess.

"She learned from Taciturn, with extreme joy, that Princes Rosanie similarly combines the beauty of the soul with that of the face. As the tyrant Hollowdream had fled the land of Fiction following his final defeat, we declared to the people of the realm that they were about to recover their true Queen in the person of a daughter that the late King had left. They learned that news with an infinite joy, for the memory of King Finedesign is extremely dear to the good citizens of the land of Fiction, and they have testified by a thousand splendid demonstrations that they will be delighted to live under the reign of a Princess emerged from his blood.

"Queen Smilingimage, who thought that she could not attain soon enough the moment when she would see her daughter, the Queen, wanted to leave with us in order to bring forward that joy by some time. We left the government of the realm of Fiction in the hands of Greatideas and Goodtaste, and the Queen Mother, with a small retinue and traveling for long days, arrived in your estates.

"Taciturn took us first to his village, where the Queen thought she would find Rosanie, and made it a pleasure to surprise the Princess; but we learned in the village, Sire, that your wife, the Queen, had taken her in, and that under the name of the Beautiful Spinner she has received a thousand marks of the generosity of that great Queen and yourself. My mistress the Queen, having learned at the same time that you were in this house of pleasure, directed her steps here urgently, in order to thank you as soon as possible for everything that Queen Rosanie owes to you."

"Yes, Sire," said Queen Smilingimage then, "I have come to this place with that design. I repeat once again that I cannot give you enough thanks; I thought that I would be able to give them at the same time to your wife, the Queen, but I believed that she was in this manor with you, and I also counted on finding my daughter, the Queen, with her."

"No, Madame," the King replied. "Queen Rosanie is not here, but it will not be long before you see that charming princess; she has remained with the Queen in my capital city, to which I shall accompany you tomorrow. "But Madame," he added, "I do not know how we can excuse ourselves to you and the Queen, your daughter, for all the faults that ignorance of the rank of that princess has caused us to commit toward her."

After this speech the King gave orders to have the carriages prepared, and the following day, after having regaled the Queen and her retinue magnificently, they all took the road to the capital city.

*

Rosanie was languishing there in a mortal anxiety. Although the Prince's wound afflicted her, because she was extremely sensible to everything regarding a lover so dear to her, that was nevertheless not the greatest subject of her affliction. She saw approaching from one minute to the next the redoubtable instant when the master of the wand would come to demand the return of the fatal piece of wood; and, having not been able to remember the name of the unknown individual, she saw that the inviolable engagement of her word and her oath would oblige her to follow him wherever he wished.

She shed torrents of tears when she thought that it would be necessary to quit forever the Queen who had heaped her with so much kindness and so many benefits, and for whom she felt such a sincere attachment. She would also greatly regret the presence of the amiable Siren, and she would be distressed to be removed from the care of Vigilentine; but the greatest dolor that tore her was in thinking that she would be eternally condemned to never seeing the Prince again and to live apart from him. Everything that she suffered as a result of that cruel idea was indescribable; she had not ceased weeping all night.

In the morning, while she was still preoccupied by those disastrous ideas, someone came to tell her that the Queen, who was in her son's apartment, had instructed that she be summoned.

As soon as the Queen saw her come in, she cried: "What strange news there is, my dear Rosanie! Alas, I had a monster among my maids of honor."

After those words, the Queen told her what we are about to repeat accurately. One of the Prince's would-be assassins, who had escaped, badly wounded, had dragged himself to the nearest village. There, the surgeons had declared to him that he would die of his wounds, and on that declaration, the wretch had started cursing Bleakthought, who had embarked him on an odious and criminal enterprise. He had reported the circumstances as we have already recounted them.

Afterwards, having seen the dead bodies of his two companions brought back from the forest, he had expired, detesting his culpable mistress. Someone, however, had promptly informed the unworthy young woman of her rascally lover's declaration; furious, she had left the palace immediately, and had flown to the home of her perfidious witch, had insulted her abundantly, and after having killed her, had killed herself.

Rosanie shivered a thousand times during that story. When it was over, the Queen, who wanted to go to the temple,

188

and also wanted to distract the Prince, in order that he should feel the pain of his wound less intensely, ordered Rosanie and Siren to remain with him, in order to amuse him, and invited Siren to sing.

The amiable young woman sung with all possible charm, but the Prince and Rosanie were hardly listening, being so preoccupied with other things that they were insensible for the moment to the soothing effect of the music. Siren, who perceived that they were very distracted, stopped singing, stood up and went to the window with another lady in order to gaze at the swans that were floating on the river and coming to eat from the hands of the palace servants.

As soon as the Prince thought that only Rosanie could hear him, he hastened to say to her: "Whence comes, beautiful Rosanie, the mortal sadness into which I see you plunged? Should not the urgent ardors of my heart, always so vivid and so tender, give you some joy, if you are not insensible to my amour?"

"Sire," said Rosanie, "can I see you in the state in which you are, and think about all the dangers you have run, without feeling an extreme chagrin?"

"Those dangers are past," relied the Prince, "And I have not even to fear any unfortunate consequences. But charming Rosanie," he added, "as I have nothing to hide from you, know how far my good fortune extends, in having avoided perils of so many kinds to which I have been exposed."

After saying that, he told her about his adventure in the enchanted palace in the forest, the traps that had been set for him by the pretended unfortunate princess, and the present of the ring of truth that the marvelous unknown child had given him. Then he told her the story of his other adventure, about the old ruined palace and all the diabolical speeches that he had heard there.

When he came to declaim the fine song, of which he had not forgotten a single word, he repeated the lines:

If a young and tender female
Only liking childish frolics,
Had kept it in her had,
That Ricdin-Ricdon is my name,
None would come into my lakes;
But the beauty will be mine
For such a name is unknown.

When he repeated those lines, Rosanie uttered a great cry, which was initially of alarm, and which made the two ladies watching the swans turn round. The Prince was reassured, however, seeing Rosanie cry out with a great surge of joy: "Heaven be praised for the infinite generosity it has for me!"

The Prince asked her for an explanation of those words, but he saw immediately that she did not want to give it in front of the two ladies, whom the exclamation had caused to approach her.

The ladies returned to the window, and then Rosanie recounted to the Prince, briefly, the adventure of the wand, and could not retain her alarm on learning that the man whom she had promised to follow was a demon, for she had never suspected it.

The Prince could not help criticizing her slightly for having made treaties so lightly with a man that she did not know at all, but as one is always ready to excuse someone that one loves, he attributed her imprudence entirely to her extreme youth and lack of experience. However, he was extremely delighted that, thanks to his fortunate memory, he had enabled her to avoid the greatest danger that she might run in her entire life. He immediately wrote the name of Ricdin-Ricdon on tablets that he gave to Rosanie. The beautiful young woman could not find enough expressions of gratitude with which to thank him.

"Alas, Sire," she said to him, "your generous valor has already extracted me once from the hands of a cruel abductor, but today your excellent memory has saved me from an enemy far more redoubtable."

When she had finished showing her gratitude to her illustrious lover, she went to join the ladies at the window and engaged them to return to the Prince. One of them did not remain there for long, but Siren stayed with Rosanie, and the three of them talked about agreeable things.

Toward midday, in the middle of their cheerful conversation, a venerable old man came into the room, dressed very properly, albeit simply.

As soon as Rosanie had looked at him, she ran into his open arms, saying to him: "Oh, my dear Father, what a joy it is to be able to embrace you after having thought that you were dead. Sire," she continued, addressing the Prince, "forgive the transports of a daughter who is seeing again the best father in the world and the most worthy of being cherished. In spite of the obscurity of his condition, I do not blush to have received birth from him; he is such an honest man, and full of a probity so noble, that the rectitude of soul and the elevation of sentiments nature has given him repair the baseness in which fortune has left him. You will also permit, Sire," she continued, "that I ask him for news of my mother, whom I cannot forget, harsh as she is."

"Madame," replied the old man, "you are not my daughter; you have qualities too great to have been born of a man like me. You are the daughter of a great King who is no longer in the world; but the Queen, your mother, who has just arrived in this palace and is with the Queen at present, will come here to embrace you and render you testimony of what I am saying to you."

Rosanie was so surprised by this speech that she could not speak at first, but finally, having collected herself somewhat, she cried: "How much I have to bemoan! What, Father, you want to belie the probity of which you have made such an exact profession all your life? You have come to impose before the Prince, to whom I have just been praising with so much pleasure the rectitude of your soul?"

"I am not imposing, Madame," replied the old man. "The Queen, your mother, whom I see coming in, will render you certain of it."

In fact, at that moment, Queen Smilingimage, King Prudent, the Queen, his wife and Lord Farsight came into the Prince's room, where those illustrious persons delivered themselves to transports of delight. Queen Smilingimage was enchanted to find Rosanie so beautiful, and without having the strength to say anything to her, clasped her tenderly in her arms.

The charming girl kissed her hands and moistened them with the tears that her joy caused to flow; for the King and Farsight told her about the splendor of her birth and informed her of her destiny. She was less impressed by the throne and the glory of reigning than by the generous pleasure of offering a scepter to a lover who had had the design of assuring her a crown even though she was a shepherdess.

As for the Prince, he felt such a great diversity of impulses full of tenderness and glory that he could scarcely suffer them. He applauded himself for having been able to divine the merit and charms of Rosanie through the thick veils with which her servile condition enveloped her; he was delighted to have made the beautiful young woman love him. Transported by having extended considerable services to her, and in the flattering hope of soon being united with her, he only envisaged the joy of being with the person he loved, without the splendor of the throne that fortune had just given his lover having any effect on him at all.

After Queen Smilingimage had given free rein to the expansions of her tenderness for some time, Farsight and Taciturn approached Rosanie and said to her: "Permit, Madame, that we allow the Queen your mother to see the mark that you have on your arm, and which gave you the name that you bear."

"Ah!" cried Smilingimage, "I have no need of any proof to recognize my blood here; even if I did not have the testimony of the honest men that you both are, Rosanie resembles so strongly the late King, my husband, that that resemblance alone suffices to convince me that she is my daughter."

However, in spite of what the Queen said, the chambermaid who had saved Rosanie's life when she was born approached the charming girl and, lifting the sleeve of her dress, she showed the company an arm whose whiteness effaced that of alabaster. Everyone stood up and surrounded the new Princess, and they saw on her arm, above the elbow, the figure of a little rose, perfectly depicted.

The two Queens resumed hugging one another; then Taciturn presented Queen Smilingimage with the diamond bracelet and the other gems that Farsight had put in his hands when he had confided Rosanie to him. The Queen Mother handed them to her daughter, who received them with a great deal of respect.

"See, Madame," said the worthy old man to the young Queen, laughing, "whether I did not have good reason when I incessantly refused for you all the good suitors of the village; I knew full well that whenever you were recognized, the least of the stones that I was keeping for you would make you richer than all their wealth combined."

Rosanie said a thousand obliging things to her good guardian, assuring him that she would give him abundant marks of her gratitude, and added that, his wife having been her nurse, she would also make her rich, as well as her son; nor did the young Princess forget to say many gracious things to Farsight and the faithful chambermaid. She gave a hundred caresses to Siren, who was regarded from that moment on as he favorite of the new Queen.

As soon as a little calm had been reestablished in that good company, King Prudent, without putting it off any longer, asked Rosanie's mother for her hand in marriage for his son, the Prince. The request was immediately granted, and the day of the marriage settled immediately, which gave an infinite satisfaction to the two lovers and the two mothers.

Afterwards, they dined with an extreme magnificence, and after the dinner, everyone retired to their apartments, in order to repose.

Rosanie had not been in hers for long when someone came to tell her than a man dressed in black with a very somber physiognomy was asking to speak to her. She ordered that he be shown in, and at the first glance she recognized him as the man of the wand.

Although she now knew his name, the sight of him caused her to shiver, recalling to mind what the dangerous donor of the wand was. Without saying a single word to him, she stood up, went to fetch the enchanted piece of wood and said to him, as she returned it: "Well, Ricdin-Ricdon, here is your wand."

The evil spirit, who had not expected that, disappeared, uttering terrible howls, and was thus taken for a dupe, which often happens, when those to whom he addresses himself, in order to make them fall into his traps, have not had any criminal intentions in allowing themselves to be caught therein, and have not recognized that it was him who wanted to acquire them.

Rosanie spent many years with the Prince, in perfect union and an extreme happiness. They made a marriage between Goodadvice and Siren, who always remained their favorites; they heaped benefits upon all those who had rendered them services, and Farsight, Taciturn, the Queen Mother's chambermaid and Vigilentine had reason to be content with the effects of their gratitude. The amiable royal couple were dearly loved by the largest and most noble fraction of their subjects, who were delighted to see the descendants of King Finedesign and Queen Smilingimage reigning over them.

However, as it is very difficult to please everyone and almost impossible to unite all kinds of suffrage, Hollowdream's party revived from time to time, and sometimes became powerful enough to contrive irruptions even in the capital city. It is even said that in spite of the gracious manners of the legitimate sovereigns of the realm and the cares of Generals Greatideas and Goodtaste, the Hollowdreams can never be entirely eradicated in the kingdom of Fiction; as long as that agreeable kingdom subsists, one can be sure that a party of them will be conserved there.

I, who am speaking, am perhaps one of the foremost in that party, amusing myself as I do in extracting from forgetfulness the ancient nonsense of King Richard, who, great conqueror, gallant and full of intelligence as he was, was also sometimes, like us, passably engaged among the Hollowdreams. But let us finish with those reflections in order to give a faithful account of what such an enlightened King said after finishing his story.

"My dear Blondel," that Prince said, after a few moments of silence, "that is one of the longest fables of those I have composed here. Such as it is, it was able to amuse me; works of that sort, frivolous as they appear to be, ordinarily divert those who produce them and those who listen to them; but to render them worthy of attracting the approval of connoisseurs of their genre, it seems to me that one ought always to think about mingling utility with the pleasures that they give to the mind. It is therefore necessary that one can extract from the adventures that contain them maxims that serve for the guidance of life.

"That is what I had in view in the tale of Ricdin-Ricdon. I have sought to make visible the dangers to which young person expose themselves who listen imprudently to all sorts of people and trust them with too much facility. However," Richard continued, "There is no need for me to explain such things to you. Full of penetration as you are, you have disentangled them easily. Furthermore, I have enclosed the moral that can be derived from that tale in the lines that I will declaim to you.

Then the King recited verses to Blondel with the following meaning:

> *Beauties, whom a sad blindness*
> *Of ambitious designs and the desire to please,*

Cause so lightly to make
A dangerous engagement,
And a temeritous step;
Oh, tremble for the outcome!
Often, beneath the seeming urgency
Of an officious and obliging soul,
Is the evil spirit, tempting you
To your eternal doom;
And if he tricks you deftly,
If some imprudent promise,
Leads you then to the cruel attempt
To which you fatal oath exposes you,
You will not find now,
To repair your errors,
Any young hero from realms above;
But you will only find
Certain fraudulent financiers
Seeking means to put you in their debt.
At that time, young and lovely things
Be more on your guard than ever.

When those verses were finished, Blondel, after having given his master's ingenious fictions the praise he believed to be their due, withdrew from the Prince's company and went once again to think about ways of saving him from his prison.

While awaiting the moment that he desired with so much ardor, he was would have liked to send news of the King to his mother, the Queen, and a few English lords who were his particular friends and who were full of fidelity and zeal for their sovereign, of whose fate they were unaware. However, Blondel dared not confide letters to England to just anyone, for fear of being betrayed. Even less did he dare confide them to ordinary ways, knowing that the Emperor's tyranny was such that he had all letters given to public couriers opened. Blondel was therefore in a cruel uncertainty, not wanting to commit to hazard a secret as important to his master's service as the place of his imprisonment. On the other hand, he would have been delighted to write to England in order to obtain advice and assistance.

Finally, seeing that he could not do it without an excessively apparent danger, he decided to keep silent, and forming ideas that were very flattering, in which he hoped at certain moments that perhaps he could succeed in removing the king from captivity solely by his own efforts; for he did not envisage with a mediocre pleasure removing from the Emperor's hands a prisoner that he had arrested with so much injustice and perfidy.

By dint of searching in his mind for means to execute that project, he believed he had finally found a reliable one. The keeper, who was convinced of his fidelity, often confided to him, with no scruple, not only the keys to King Richard's room, but also the keys to the galleries, and even the main door of the tower. Nevertheless, in spite of the confidence the man had in Blondel, he obliged him to return the bunch of keys to him every evening, and the keeper habitually put them under his bed-head. Blondel did not fail to profit from having the keys during the days, however; he made imprints in wax of all those that he thought necessary to his plan.

After that he found pretexts to obtain permission from the keeper for a short journey to Vienna, for he did not want to confide the making of the keys he needed to any of the locksmiths on Linz. The latter town was not large, and was so near to the tower that he saw too great a danger of being recognized there, and seeing his plan discovered. He did not hesitate, therefore, to take the resolution only to confide it to a workman in Vienna.

The keeper, who liked him, and who reposed various sorts of cares on him, saw him making preparations for the journey to the great city with regret, and begged him to make it short. Blondel promised him that, and announced his imminent departure and his projects to the King.

The Prince testified his gratitude to him by a thousand obliging caresses, and opened his heart once again to hope. The flattering ideas that it gave him put him in an agreeable

197

state of mind. Blondel, who was not leaving until late the following day, asked him to be kind enough to tell him another of the fables that he had composed in the tower. The King, who was grateful for all Blondel's procedures and only sought to please a man who was so devoted to him, yielded to his desire gladly, and related the tale that I am about to report.

If you would be kind enough to recall the warning that I gave before the tale of Ricdin-Ricdon, it would spare me the necessity of repeating that I am not conserving King Richard's terms in recounting the fables of his composition, but I shall declare here once and for all that in all the King's tales and stories that I am bringing to light, I am following the route that I followed in "Ricdin-Ricdon." If, like many other voyagers in the land of Fiction, my fate is to get lost in that land, which is more difficult to traverse than one might think, it is as well that I go astray in the route that I have chosen rather than another.

THE ROBE OF SINCERITY

A philosopher of the isle of Crete named Misandre, a naturally good man but eccentric in his manners and extraordinary in his sentiments, was nevertheless married to a wife who had beauty and virtue; but that wife had a character so savage and melancholy that, the foundation of ill humor combining with the misfortune she had in being united with a husband who had very little fortune and a great many caprices, she had become so exceedingly bitter and sad, and so bad-tempered that she had been nicknamed Chasseris,[43] and the name stuck.

Of the marriage of those two quarrelsome spouses nothing resulted but a unique daughter, and that was a great good fortune for them, for Misandre's indigence had increased incessantly with his years. He belonged to a noble family, but his father had scarcely left him enough to sustain him in his estate with same tranquility, and he had not wanted to take up a profession; he was scornful of almost everything that people in general esteemed the most.

The profession of arms seemed to him to be odious for a thousand churlish reasons that he alleged; the magistracy and the bar did not please him anymore, the one because it was not exercised in society in a manner in conformity with his ideas, and the other because eloquence appeared to him to be a despicable art. He treated as bagatelles, vain amusements and futilities what people called business, commerce and the fine arts, and he said that he only wanted to apply himself to seeking the truth; and what was strange about that was that he made the search for the pretended truth consist of a few

---

[43] The implication of his name is not immediately obvious, but might derives from one of the meanings of the verb *chasser*, which implies driving someone away.

wretched metaphysical arguments that nobody understood and which he did not understand himself.

However, believing that he possessed the most sublime enlightenment from the heights of his luminous mind, he gazed pityingly at the thick darkness of the rest of humankind. He deplored blindly those he saw applying themselves to becoming skillful in politics and history. He had no greater esteem for poetry than he had for eloquence, but, although he was very scornful of fine writing, he disparaged the other fine arts even more. He talked incessantly, in the most insulting fashion in the world, about painting and music, and, as if he wanted to avenge himself for the disorder that a spoiled imagination had created in his mind, he decried the imagination relentlessly.

Utterly bizarre as the visions of the philosopher were, however, he nevertheless did not fail to dazzle for some time a small number of individuals, who applauded as they listened to him pronounce grandiose words that they did not understand, wanting to receive lessons from him in order to try to comprehend them.

Misandre was, therefore, reputed to be a master of philosophy, and he obtained a utility from that which his family sensed. His pupils, however, who never understood anything of his fantastic reasoning, from which reason was always banished, soon lost their appetite for his tenebrous knowledge and did not take long to take their leave of such a master. Thus, Misandre fell more than ever into indigence, for his patrimony as diminishing every day. As he was far from having enough income to support his family, he often drew on his capital, and made so much use of that recourse that in the end, he found that he no longer had anything at all.

Meanwhile, his daughter entered into her nineteenth year. Herminie—that was her name—was beautiful, shapely, and had all the qualities that can render a young woman amiable. Nevertheless, no suitor had yet asked for her hand; the meager fortune and the bizarre humor of the philosopher had frightened away all those in whom the beautiful young woman's charms had given birth to an inclination to espouse her.

In spite of the poor state of her fate, Herminie did not feel any chagrin in finding herself without a lover; she had no ambition of coquetry and had been born with a certain firmness of soul that caused her to receive tranquilly all the disgraces that it pleased destiny to send her. She had not inherited anything of her father's mentality, nor did she have anything of her mother's bitter and surly humor; she only resembled her mother in virtue and beauty. She had large dark eyes so full of fire, tenderness and vivacity that by means of her brilliant and affectionate gaze it was easy to detect the intelligence and benevolence of the person that animated it. She had a perfectly formed nose, an admirable mouth, a complexion of dazzling whiteness and beautiful shiny and lustrous black hair. It was the agreeable mixture of black and white made by the extreme whiteness of her skin and the beautiful blackness of her hair that had caused her to be given the name Herminie.[44]

Although she had been raised in the bosom of a grim family, whose members very rarely went into society, the charms of which she partook had always caused her to be noticed advantageously, and by her beauty, her mildness and her engaging manners she had attracted universal benevolence since her childhood. She could not prevent herself from having an inclination for the majority of the things that her father hated the most; she cherished fine writing and music ardently, and had such a powerful passion for painting that from the age of seven she drew with pure genius—which had attracted terrible scolding from Misandre, who called the liking she had for the fine art a "pernicious penchant."

Chasseris, who was an exceedingly active mother, led harsh and laborious life, opposed to all pleasure, never taking any rest, and never let others take any; she intended that Herminie should be regulated by her model in all things, and wanted the beautiful girl only to learn to sew, to spin and to

---

[44] By analogy with "ermine."

keep a household in good order. On the other hand, Misandre wanted to fill her head with his hollow metaphysical reveries and the chimeras of his new system of the world; but the amiable Herminie did not feel any inclination to become the victim of philosophical visions, and was no more disposed to limit herself uniquely to the mind than to vulgar occupations.

She learned admirably well all the petty labors that were appropriate to her sex, and she worked therein with as much pleasure was skill, and was no less able in regulating the economy of a household, but she believed that after having fulfilled with exactitude the duties of her estate, it was then permissible for her to satisfy the innocent inclination that she had to equip her mind with knowledge as noble as it was diverting. She therefore read avidly in history, fables, poetry, orators and their writings, where she learned the morality that one ought to practice in order to live honorably and pleasantly in civil society.

Herminie obtained a marvelous fruit from all her reading, but it was necessary to hide it from Misandre and Chasseris with an extreme care. As she was as laborious as her mother and naturally very lively, she worked by day at a young woman's tasks, and read for a part of the night.

She had a neighbor named Philantrope, who had taken her in amity since childhood. That neighbor, who had a great deal of virtue and a very cultivated mind, had lent books secretly to Herminie as soon as she was able to read, and had always sought to give her pleasure in all sorts of occasions. Her obliging benevolence had given rise to the greatest happiness that Herminie had ever had, for not only did Philantrope have a knowledge of literature unusual in persons of her sex, but she also knew music perfectly and had very distinguished talents in painting. She knew how to pant in oils with a great deal of nobility, but above all, she painted miniatures in a manner so accurate and gracious that her paintings had the reputation among connoisseurs of being consummate works. She usually worked on portraits; she took much more pleasure in exercising her brush in that than on historical subjects, although she was also very skillful in painting history.

As obliging as she was enlightened, Philantrope had seconded as best she could the precocious penchant that Herminie had for painting, and had communicated to her with a great deal of care the knowledge and talent that she had in that charming art. In order to teach Herminie to draw well and paint graciously, however, it was necessary to take a great deal of trouble, for it was necessary to hide it completely from Misandre. As for Chasseris, she was not completely unaware that Philantrope was showing her daughter how to paint, but because the young woman and she had received a thousand favors from that obliging friend and she knew that she was a widow without children, rich and always disposed to give them new pleasures, she had not dared resist the pleas that Philantrope had always made to send Herminie to spend the day with her frequently.

The amiable pupil profited perfectly from the lessons of her mistress, but nevertheless, unlike that savant woman, she felt a particular penchant for treating historical subjects, so it charmed her more to represent Daphne changed into a laurel or Diana hunting in the forest with her nymphs than making a simple portrait, although she made elegance and nobility shine in all the genres in which she worked. Having already acquired great skill, therefore, at the tender age she had reached, and seeing the sorry state of her father's finances, she resolved to make use of her talents in painting to render a little aid against misfortune.

She made Philantrope party to her project, but that generous friend did not want her to carry it out. "I am very sorry," she said to her, while embracing her, "only to have such mediocre wealth, having the sentiments that I have for you, but such as that wealth is, I flatter myself that you would like to share it with me, and I hope that it will be sufficient for us to lead a comfortable life, with those who gave you birth. All three of you, then, come to my house, which I beg you to regard as yours."

Herminie testified to Philantrope the keen gratitude that such a generosity proposal merited, but, in spite of the situation in which she found herself, she could not bring herself to accept the kind offer, because of the capricious humors of Misandre and Chasseris, from which she feared that Philantrope might suffer too much, and would be discouraged by it after a few months of patience. However, she had wanted throughout her life to give the most ardent cares to her father and mother, who, in spite of their eccentricities, were very dear to her.

Philantrope begged her so tenderly and with such good grace to accept her offer that in the end she consented, but only after Philantrope had returned from a journey that her affairs rendered absolutely obligatory to a port distant from the capital of the island, and on the condition that she and her family would not be lodged in the house of her generous friend. Matters being settled thus, Philantrope left Herminie a sum of money that was more than sufficient to sustain the family in comfortable abundance until her return.

The two friends separated with the most ardent marks of tenderness, but as destiny seemed to be conspiring to persecute Herminie, scarcely had Philantrope arrived in the maritime town where her journey ended than, while walking along the sea shore, she was abducted by pirates.

Herminie, more out of amity for Philantrope than her own interests, thought that she would die of dolor when she heard that news. As for Philantrope's heirs, however, they were in haste to take possession of all her property as soon as possible, without giving any thought at all to making attempts to discover where the pirates had taken her. On the contrary, it seemed that they were apprehensive of being informed of it, for fear of being obliged to end her captivity by paying a ransom. Herminie, who had entirely opposite sentiments, had all the searches made that were in her power; in spite of all the actions and trouble she took, however, she was unable to learn anything about the fate of such a dear friend, and, in losing

204

any hope of ever seeing her again, she was overwhelmed by the weight of her chagrins.

Meanwhile, she sensed that she was about to fall back into the domestic anxieties from which Philantrope's generous cares had saved her for a time. Misandre had sold all of his remaining property and he had nothing left but a few items of furniture that were almost worthless.

While he took advantage of those woeful scraps for the subsistence of his family, with which he had retreated to the country, Herminie worked for several months on paintings, in which she treated gracious historical subjects, but although she succeeded with a great deal of taste and elegance, as she did not have a cabal to praise her, little account was made of the paintings, for which she was only given a price far below mediocre; for that century was already at the level that it followed for a long time thereafter, in which the rarest talents in the fine arts fell sadly into oblivion if they were not shored up by protections; already, false merit supported by a cabal oppressed true merit destitute of support.

Let us return to Herminie, however; her father, who had once revolted against her talents in painting, was offended to the utmost in seeing them so badly received, and, finally irritated to excess against his century, he resolved to avenge himself in the manner that we shall describe in due course, after we have talked at some length about the King of Crete, of whom our philosopher was a subject.

That King was a young prince named Clearque, born with some fine personal qualities. He had a pleasant face, valor and liberality, but, in addition, he was suspicious, mistrustful, stubborn in his prejudices and superstitious to such a degree that he gave himself blindly to all popular errors.

The prince had a sister named Elismene, who seemed to have received from Heaven all the gifts appropriate to charm. She had an admirable figure and a face in which all the features were symmetrical and agreeable. She had chestnut-brown hair, a complexion as pale as it was uniform, heightened by a hint of vermilion that rendered it dazzling, and one saw in her large blue eyes, softened by brown eyelids, as much fire as softness. The qualities of her soul were no less admirable than those of her person. She had a grandeur of courage above her sex, a heroic rectitude and generosity, and a gracious goodness that attracted all hearts to her.

That beautiful princess had often suffered from the caprices of her brother, the King, even though she was the gentlest and most complaisant person in the world. The prince changed his sentiments so often that it was not a mediocre affair to study them, but Clearque never abandoned his love of pleasures, particularly those of hunting and warrior games.

At the time when Misandre and his family were languishing in the country, one day when the King of Crete was giving his court a fête in which there were chariot races, combats with javelins, wrestling and other spectacles, a young stranger was seen to appear in all those various games, who distinguished himself as much by his skill as his good looks and his magnificence. He had all the honors of the day. He carried off the prizes with the applause of the court and the acclamations of the people, and manifested an unparalleled grace and generosity in all his actions and procedures.

In the evening there was a ball in the residence of the princess, and the young stranger shone no less there than he had in the other diversions. As it was from Elismene's hand that he had received the prizes, he had already had opportunities to talk to her, and he found another at the ball, and made as much intelligence and politeness visible in his speech as there was charm in his manners.

The King heaped him with honors and caresses, and expressed a strong desire to know who he was. He begged the prince for permission to remain in his court incognito for a few more days, and assured him that he would gladly satisfy his curiosity thereafter. Meanwhile, Clearque gave him an apartment in his palace and had him served there with great magnificence. The stranger's retinue was not numerous, but

all those composing it appeared, by their manners, to be people of great distinction.

The amiable unknown soon found an opportunity to tell
the princess that he adored her, and that he had only come to
the island of Crete to offer her a heart over which the charms
of her portrait had already triumphed in Thessaly. She could
not be offended by that declaration, for he told her at the same
time that he was Prince Telephonte, the son of the King of
Cyprus. He indicated to Elismene that he was sure of having,
for the knots that he desired, the agreement of the King to
whom he owed the light of day, who would not fail to send
ambassadors to ask for her. He added that he flattered himself
that King Clearque would not refuse his support in her regard,
but he protested that he did not want to owe the precious gift
of her hand either to the endeavors of the King of Cyprus or
the orders of the King of Crete.

"I only want, Madame," he said, "to obtain it from yourself; it is only by virtue of the respectful passion that I have for
you, and my tender services, that I dare to hope to acquire a
place in your heart. It is the dread that I have that an overly
scrupulous obedience might bear you to hinder your wishes
that made my hide my name and my birth from your brother
the King until I was instructed of your sentiments. If my glorious pretentions have the misfortune of displeasing you, that
prince will never know who I am; but if you deign not to dis-
approve of my designs I will make them known to the King of
Crete, and I hope that he will be favorable to them."

Elismene had listened with so much surprise and trouble
to the Prince of Cyprus' speech that it was some time before
she found the strength to respond. Finally, with a blush on her
face and confusion in her eyes, she told him in an embarrassed
fashion that she was absolutely submissive to the will of her
brother, the King, and that she would always glory in obeying
him.

Telephonte pressed her to declare naturally whether she
did not feel any aversion in his regard, swearing to her again
that if he were unfortunate enough to displease her, he would

refrain from asking her brother for her, not wishing to expose her to suffering that any violence should be done to her inclinations.

She assured Telephonte that she knew neither love nor hate, but only how to obey. Then, after reddening further, she added that in his regard, he was wrong to fear her aversion, since a prince such as him was more apt to give birth to esteem than hatred. After saying that, nonplussed, and trembling that she might have said too much, the Princess of Crete summoned her ladies-in-waiting—who, out of respect, had moved away—and for the rest of the day the conversation was general.

Meanwhile, the Prince of Cyprus, transported with amour for Elismene and delighted that the charming princess had not received the offering of his prayers in a disobliging fashion, told the King of Crete who he was. The King gave a thousand marks of joy at the news, and rendered with splendor to Telephonte's rank all the honors due to it.

Clearque was burning with desire to know the reason for which the Prince of Cyprus had come to his estates, but he dared not ask the Prince overtly. He contented himself with asking questions on that subject of a young knight in Telephonte's retinue who appeared to be one of this master's foremost favorites. That knight, whose name was Leandrin, did indeed have a large part in the confidence of Telephonte, but he did not think it appropriate to inform the King of Crete of the Price's secrets.

It was Telephonte himself who informed him. After a thousand petty things, which he remarked every day with an infinite joy, had persuaded him that the offer of his hand would not displease Elismene, he declared to the King of Crete the amour that he had for her, asked him for his protection with regard to the Princess, and added that if he deigned to approve of the designs he had for that charming sister, the King of Cyprus would send a solemn embassy to request her as soon as possible.

Clearque assured Telephonte, while embracing him, that nothing could be dearer to him than an alliance with a Prince as accomplished as him. He then took him to Elismene's apartment, and asked her to regard Telephonte as a Prince that he destined for her spouse, and who merited all her attachment by virtue of his fine qualities.

The Princess replied to the King, her brother, with a great deal of deference and modesty, but through her modesty and submissive manners it was evident that she had no distaste in obeying the order that had been given to her to have consideration for Telephonte.

The Prince said a thousand things to her that were as witty as they were gallant. Then he added: "In spite of the strength of the knots that attach me to you, Madame, I shall soon be obliged to quit you in order to obey the orders of the King, my father, who is recalling me urgently to Cyprus in order to witness the marriage ceremony of Princess Celenie, my sister, whom an ambassador for Lemnos is to marry in a short while, in the name of the King his master.

"But Madame," Telephonte continued, "rigorous as the difficulties that your absence will cost me are, I shall feel the rigor diminished by the glorious permission that your brother the King has given me. That great prince wishes that as soon as I arrive in Cyprus, my father will send an envoy to announce solemnly the honor and felicity to which I aspire."

After a few similar speeches, Clearque, who could not remain in the same place for long, went out and took Telephonte with him. As he went, the Prince made a sign to Leandrin to stay with Elismene, and the favorite, who was very intelligent, easily understood that his master wanted him to talk to the Princess about his love. He acquitted that task like the clever man he was, but, while depicting Telephonte's passionate sentiments with great skill, he did not forget to give a fine idea of the Prince's character. By recounting certain of his actions, he was able to insinuate subtly the rectitude and grandeur of his soul, the generosity and delicacy of his heart, the intrepidity of his courage and the valor of his arm.

It is true, however, that in spite of the extreme zeal that Leandrin had for Telephonte, the portrait that he made of him did not flatter him. The young prince had all the qualities of a hero, so he was tenderly cherished by his father the King, and adored by that monarch's subjects.

The Princess of Crete listened with a great deal of pleasure to all that she was told about the great prince, to whom she sensed strongly that her heart was taking a keen interest, and as Leandrin perceived that his conversation was not boring her, when he had finished the discourse just described he continued thus:

"The Prince my master, after having responded so nobly to the care that had been given to him for his education and given famous roofs of his courage, hardly emerged from childhood, in the last year of a war that the King of Cyrus terminated with a glorious peace, Prince Telephonte, who saw that the realm that he was destined to rule some day was about to enjoy a long calm, asked King Telanor's permission to travel in tome of the lands of Greece.

"The King loved the Prince so dearly that it was difficult for him to resolve to see him go away, but he finally consented to it, on the condition that his absence would not last long. The beautiful Princess Celenie, who has the most tender amity for the Prince, her brother, shed many tears on his departure, and the entire court, whose delight he was, was extremely regretful about it. As I had had the honor of being brought up with Prince Telephonte and he honored me with his good graces, I had never been separated from him, and I was destined to company him in his voyages.

"We traveled in various countries of Greece, in which my master displayed his intrepidity, the elevation of his soul and the solidity of his intelligence on many occasions. But as I have already recounted a part of his adventures, Madame, I shall pass on swiftly to another story, in which amour was doubtless the only guide of his conduct. Solicited by the King's desires, Telephonte was preparing to return to Cyprus when, passing incognito through Larissa, the capital of Thessaly, the young Prince, who likes painting very much, went to the home of the foremost painter in the city with the design of buying pictures there.

"He saw several worthy of his curiosity, but what struck him most vividly was the portrait of a ravishing brunette who had large blue eyes, whose brilliant charms and noble and spiritual tenderness one could not admire enough. In sum, Madame, you will understand why it would be impossible for me to describe all the graces of that painting when you know that it was the portrait of the illustrious Princess of Crete."

Elismene blushed at those words and interrupted Leandrin, forbidding herself with a great deal of modesty the praises that he gave to her beauty. He responded like a man who was not insipid in giving praise, and knew how to spread his incense with as much wit as politeness; then he resumed the thread of his discourse in these terms:

"Prince Telephonte having asked with an extreme urgency who the marvelous person was who was represented by the portrait, after he had received the reply that it was you, Madame, a woman holding a palette and brushes advanced and said to him: 'Sire, although the charms of the beautiful princess that you see represented here are without equal on earth, I can assure you that the beauties of her soul are far above those of her face. It seems that Heaven has wanted to unite in her person all the virtues and all the rare qualities that can render a princess accomplished.'

"The woman went on: 'I can speak of her knowledgeably, for, not only was I born a subject of her father, the King, but the late Queen, her mother, honored me with a great deal of benevolence; thus, I have seen at close range the admirable childhood of Princess Elismene and I have always seen her virtues increasing with her age. When my misfortune took me away from the island of Crete, they had reached such a high point of perfection that it seemed that they could not be augmented any further.'

"Telephonte listened with an extreme avidity to everything that the woman said to him and asked her a thousand

211

questions on the subject of the beautiful princess, for whom he already felt a boundless admiration. The stranger always replied in a manner that gave the Prince pleasure, and he was so obliged by all the agreeable things that she said that, becoming interested in her, he asked her by virtue of what unfortunate incident she had been taken away from her homeland.

"'Alas, Sire,' she replied, with a sigh, 'as I was walking on the shore of the sea on our island, barbaric pirates abducted me, and, in spite of my ardent pleas, never permitted me to send news to Crete in order to summon a ransom, doubtless fearing that if the King of Crete came to have particular knowledge of their rapines, he would think seriously about having them hunted throughout the surrounding seas. In sum, either by virtue of that consideration or others, the cruel men who had made me a slave never wanted to consent to my buying back my liberty, and they put me in the hands of a merchant, who, because of the talents I had in painting, sold me in this city to the famous painter whose pictures you see here.'"

"Ah!" Elismene interrupted, at that account of the painter's talents, "I believe I recognize the virtuous Philantrope, who was kidnapped on our coast by corsairs six or seven months ago."

"Yes, Madame," replied Leandrin, "that is the name of the sage Cretan woman who knows your rare qualities so well."

"And why is it," retorted the Princess, "that you have not informed us, as soon as you arrived in Crete, of the place of her captivity, in order that we could try immediately to put an end to it?"

"It is, Madame," said Leandrin, "because that is something that will not be possible for some time, as you will learn from the rest of my discourse." After saying that he resumed thus:

"Prince Telephonte immediately offered Philantrope to pay the painter whatever he demanded as the price of her liberty. 'Alas, Sire,' she replied to him, 'such is the misfortune that is pursuing me that I cannot take advantage of the effects of your generous kindness. That which ought to relieve the weight of my chains augments their weight; I made known to the painter to whom I belong all that I can do in painting, thinking to attract more consideration to myself. The man, as you see, is a grandmaster in oil painting, but he has no talent in miniatures and absolutely will not consent to render my liberty until I have rendered his daughter skillful in that genre. It is true that I found her vey inferior in it and that she is making great progress every day, but in spite of her assiduous application and the exactitude of my cares, a great deal of time will pass yet before she has the perfection that her father demands that I give her. Thus, I see with an extreme dolor that the moment of my liberty is still distant.

"'It is not,' Philantrope continued, 'that all the family do not treat me with the same consideration and the same regard as if I were a close relative, but, however mild slavery might be, it can never be pleasant, especially for a person like me, who was born with such a great love of liberty that, in spite of the veneration I have for the memory of the late Queen of Crete and the infinite zeal that I feel for the charming Princess Elismene, I thought of retiring from the court as soon as our great Queen was dead, hating even the image of captivity. I saw the King very infirm and foresaw above all that under the reign of the young Prince Clearque, the courtiers would have to endure many caprices.'

"Forgive me, Madame, for the sincerity of my story," Leandrin went on, "if I report to you even the scarcely respectful terms of which Philantrope made use in speaking of the King, your brother. After several other speeches that it would take too long to recount to you, she informed Telephonte that it was her who had bought your portrait to Thessaly. She told the Prince that when the corsairs had abducted her, she had the portrait with her in a rich box, which the barbarians had not failed to take with them, but that she had begged them so insistently to return the painting that the box contained to her that in the end they had been touched by her pleas and that,

213

having the portrait in her possession, she had made large-scale copies of it when she was in Larissa.

"'It is from those copies,' Philantrope continued, 'that the painter to whom I belong made the portrait that you see. So, Sire,' she added, 'you can easily judge that the Princes of Crete is even more beautiful than that portrait, for in making so many copies of the portrait of a beautiful person, some of the graces of the original always escape.'

"Telephonte, increasingly charmed by what he heard Philantrope say, summoned the painter and gave him whatever he wanted for the beautiful painting by which he was enchanted; he also bought several other pictures, and had Philantrope promise that she would make him as soon as possible a copy in miniature of the small portrait that she had in her possession. As for the original, even if she had been offered a kingdom, she would have refused absolutely to deprive herself of it.

"As I almost always accompanied Telephonte, I had been a witness to the conversation he had had with Philantrope. As soon as the Prince had returned to the house where he was lodging, he spoke to me with so much transport about the Princess of Crete that I knew full well that his heart was already captured. He said such astonishing things before the beautiful portrait, which he had placed in his cabinet, that I shall not repeat them to you, Madame, for fear of fatiguing the exceedingly scrupulous modesty that forbids us with so much severity to render your charms all the justice that is owed to them. I will only tell you that Telephonte no longer thought about anything but preparing to travel to Crete in order to come here to offer you the homage of his heart.

"Meanwhile, the Prince went incessantly to Philantrope's house in order to ask her questions about everything relating to you, and to implore her to finish your portrait in miniature promptly. As the woman has a great deal of intelligence, and is very attentive and extremely penetrative, by the air of grandeur that she saw spreading around my master's person and manner, and the magnificence of his procedures, she judged that he was of extremely high rank. She revealed her suspicions to him, and did so with such skill that he admitted his birth to her and the rapid penchant that drew him toward the Princess of Crete; nevertheless, as he did not want to be known in Thessaly, he asked her to keep the secret, and she did so very scrupulously.

"One day, when the Prince and I went to see Philantrope work on the little portrait that we wanted so ardently, we saw one on the woman's table that we mistook at first for the one in question. Telephonte picked it up urgently, but then, having looked at it attentively, he said: 'Charming as the person represented in this portrait is, she is still far from approaching the beauty of the Princess of Crete' As he said that, the Prince handed me the portrait, and it offered to me eyes the image of a brilliant brunette with dark eyes full of intelligence and fire, and infinitely touching.

"'The person represented in that portrait,' Philantrope told us, 'still contributes a great deal to my finding my captivity distressing; she is a friend that I cherish more than myself, and for whom my absence might have been fatal. To try to soothe slightly the pain that I felt in being deprived of the sight of her, I made her portrait here by the strength of my imagination alone. But alas,' she added, 'nothing can compensate for the loss of her conversation, always so full of intelligence, tenderness and politeness.'

"After saying that, she gave us in a few words a very fine idea of the character of her friend. Then she said to the Prince: 'Sire, if you go to Crete, I beg you to have the goodness to inform that amiable friend of my fate. Her name is Herminie, and I beg you to permit me to inform the obliging Leandrin of the measures he ought to take to find her father, who, by virtue of the poor state of his fortune, is languishing in obscurity in Crete. As for the charming Princess, the daughter and sister of my sovereigns, I hope that you will deign to inform her of the ardent zeal that I conserve for her in the midst of the chagrins of captivity.'

"A few days after that conversation, Madame," Leandrin continued, "as your portrait was finished, we set forth for Crete, where were arrived, fortunately at the time when everyone was preparing for the fête that your brother was giving. On the eve of that fête, Telephonte saw you in the temple, and found you so far above your portrait that he thought he might expire of delight and amour. The next day, he had the glory of attracting all gazes in that magnificent fête, and since that day, Madame, you know everything that has happened to the Prince, whose destiny you hold absolutely in your hands.

"In any case, Madame," Leandrin added, "deign to forgive me if I have mingled with my story something that does not concern you, having taken the liberty of speaking to you about Herminie. That is because I believed that, good and generous as you are, and also honoring Philantrope with your esteem, you will deign to pay some attention to the chagrin I have in having been unable to acquit the commission that the virtuous woman gave me. I have searched in vain on the island for Herminie and her father, with all possible care. In spite of the scrupulousness of my research, I have not been able to obtain any news of her."

Elismene assured Leandrin that she would give precise orders to seek information as to the fate of Herminie. After the beautiful Princess had said things to him that were equally obliging and modest, on the subject of his master and for his own benefit, he withdrew.

He found Telephonte in his apartment, who repeated a thousand times everything that he found charming and marvelous about Elismene, and made him repeat everything that the Princess had said in his favor. He saw her several times a day, throughout the time he remained in Crete, and received various innocent marks of consideration, and also received from the King a thousand testimonies of esteem and amity.

When they left, Clearque declared gallantly that whatever inclination he had to be his brother-in-law, he would only consent to marry his sister to him if he came to marry her in person. "And as you are very amorous," he added, "I hope that you will not refuse that mark of amity to the brother of your mistress."

Telephonte promised him positively that he would be close behind the ambassadors that his father the King would send; then the young Prince left, full of the tender hopes with which a lover can flatter himself.

As for Leandrin, he was not entirely content, although he had a great deal of joy at the fortunate success of his master's designs. By virtue of a feeling that he did not understand very well himself, he could not console himself for not having been able to learn any news of Herminie, even though the Princess had given the most attentive orders on that subject that her generosity had been able to inspire. Herminie was too well hidden for anyone to be able to discover what had become of her.

On the same day that Prince Telephonte left Crete, someone came to tell the King that a man whose appearance was somber and grim was asking to speak to him, in order, he said, to render him a service that he hoped would be agreeable to him. Clearque, who liked all novelties, ordered that he be sent in

"Sire," he said to the King, "knowing the praiseworthy penchant that you have for curiosity, I have come to offer you the means of satisfying it, on a subject that is ordinarily very interesting. I once loved philosophy, but having been convinced of the futility of its researches, I have attached myself to the art of enchantment, in which I have made admirable progress. I have been instructed by a grandmaster, who has taught me all sorts of secrets, except that of making gold. The fear that he had that I might quit him if I became rich—for my aid was of great utility to him in his work—caused him to keep that fine secret from me, but of the remainder, there is none that I do not know. I know how to divine the past and how to penetrate the future; I can foresee the accidents that might occur by virtue of the caprices of fortune, and how to provide remedies in order to avoid them. I have a reliable means of being informed as to the fidelity of women, and in giving that means I give at the same time the pleasure of seeing an ingenious and magnificent endeavor.

"As princes of your age," the philosopher continued, "must be more touched by those sorts of things than anyone else, it is the last of my talents, Sire, of which I have come to offer to make use in your service."

Clearque, transported with joy by the philosopher's proposition, asked him eagerly what means he could employ in order to execute his promise.

"Before explaining them to you, Sire," replied the man, "permit me to give you proof of the prodigies that I can accomplish."

"I consent to that with pleasure," said the King, "but I want someone I love to share that satisfaction with me."

After having said that, the prince gave the order to fetch one of his courtiers, named Dinocrite, who had not been his favorite for long. As soon as he appeared, Clearque told him about the marvels of the man that he saw, and Dinocrite recognized him as the philosopher Misandre, the famous eccentric so at odds with fortune.

"Sire," said the King's favorite, "it is necessary not to be astonished at the admirable knowledge of this savant man; he has always studied the secrets of nature with extraordinary care."

"I have studied the art of enchantment even more," said Misandre, "and I will give proofs of it now, if the King will do me the honor of granting me permission to do so."

Clearque having signified that he was ready to see and hear whatever he wished, Misandre performed before the prince and his favorite a thousand tricks with goblets, the most surprising in the world. As there had never been any fairground in Crete, or any place where anything similar had been seen, Clearque and Dinocrite could not get over their astonishment, and mistook all those feats of skill for the marvelous effects of the art of enchantment.

When Misandre had performed a great number of them, he said to the King: "Well, Sire, are you content?"

"I would be very wrong not to be," replied the King, "but I have a violent desire to know by what means one can clearly distinguish prudish women from coquettes."

"The method takes time, Sire," Misandre replied, "but it is infallible. It consists of making a robe that I, my wife and my daughter are equally able to do. The basis of that robe is merely a black fabric, which is clear and transparent, but all three of us are able to form thereon a light embroidery as brilliant as it is delicate, and which represents admirable things, of which I will give you a description when it pleases you.

"There is no miniature so fine that it is not outshone by that work, and, by the power of my art, such is the gift of that embroidery that of all married men, it is only those who have faithful wives who can see it; the others only perceive the transparent cloth, completely uniform. As for men who are not in the bonds of matrimony, if they have a sister of the humor of Helen, they do not see the embroidery in question. As for those who have neither a wife nor a sister, they are also deprived of the sight of the marvelous embroidery if their closest female relative is too favorable to her lovers. For husbands who have faithful wives, however, and brothers who have solidly virtuous sisters, even if all their aunts and female cousins are the most consummate coquettes, they will always see the ingenious embroidery of the robe in all its beauty; and as that robe reveals hidden verities to everyone, it has been given the name of the robe of sincerity, combining together the fabric and the embroidery."

"Oh, what a marvelous work!" cried the King. "I am in haste to see it, but how long will it take you to make it?"

"It will take my family and myself at least three months," replied Misandre, "to put all its perfection into it, but at the end of a month, Sire, you will already be able to judge it and be amused by it. In order to render you the finished work in the time I have specified, it is only necessary to lodge my wife, my daughter and myself in one of the most remote parts of your palace, order that we should not lack any of the necessities of life, and that we are furnished abundantly with gold and silk."

"I will give such good orders for your satisfaction," said Clearque, "that you will have reason to be glad. You have only to bring your wife and daughter to my palace today; all three of you will be comfortably lodged in a place that my officers will indicate to you."

Misandre withdrew, without making any further response to Clearque except a profound reverence, and left the young prince in an inconceivable joy at the beautiful acquisition he had made during the day.

For Dinocrite, it was not the same; he was a naturally suspicious and envious man; he was so jealous of his master's good graces that he incessantly spoke ill of everyone to his master, for fear that someone else might share his favor—or which he made very bad use, moreover. If he was jealous of his title of favorite, however, he was even more so of his wife. She was a very lively young woman of whose virtue he was more than half-suspicious; as he was eccentric, arrogant and incapable of any complaisance for her, he doubted that she loved him, and did not believe that she had a character sufficiently heroic to remain perfectly virtuous without any amity for her spouse. In spite of the scant esteem he had for her, he was very much in love with her, because she was beautiful, but that passion, which ordinarily renders those who possess it tender and polite, only seemed to render him more violent and intractable with regard to his wife.

One can, in consequence, imagine, given that he was amorous, eccentric and having scant esteem for his wife, how redoubtable the robe that the King had been promised seemed to him. He feared finding therein what he did not want to see—or, rather, he feared seeing nothing therein but transparent fabric.

Clearque, who did not judge Dinocrite's wife as poorly as he did, and who, on the contrary, believed her to be very sage, also believed that Dinocrite was sure of her virtue, and did not imagine that the robe in question could give him any anxiety. On the contrary, he thought that he shared with him the pleasure he obtained from the hope of seeing his curiosity satisfied, and, obtaining in advance a malign joy from seeing many husbands who would see nothing on the robe, he instructed him not to divulge the secret of the mysterious garment to anyone.

Meanwhile, Misandre, his wife and his daughter came to take possession of the apartment that had been given to them in the palace. The amiable Herminie only came with regret; her father, capricious as he was, loved her and held her in high esteem, and he had made her the confidence of the propositions he wanted to make to Clearque as soon as he had imagined them. She had made every effort to deter him from doing so, but she had been unable to succeed. He had always said that he would take extreme pleasure in tricking a prince full of errors, under whose reign virtue and merit had such scant consideration, and that furthermore, he would find even more satisfaction in ensuring their subsistence for three months, during which time she could work on miniature paintings and her mother on the works of embroidery that she did so well, which would put them in a position to obtain subsequently the utility of the work with which they occupied themselves. Misandre had even obliged his daughter to teach him scrupulously certain items of history and fable that he wanted to repeat to the King when the occasion arose.

Thus, having been unable to change her father's resolution, Herminie accompanied him sadly to the palace. The natural horror that she had for everything that had an appearance of deceit caused her to envisage with a great deal of dolor the role he was about to play there, but, although she had never felt a more troublesome chagrin in her life, she was no less beautiful for it, and her attractions were noticed by all the officers of the palace who saw her. The number of those who had that destiny was not large; Clearque had ordered that Misandre and his family be installed in the palace very quietly, and the Prince's orders had been followed scrupulously

While Clearque was looking forward to the pleasure that the enchanted robe would give him, however, Elismene was in a very different situation. Not only had Telephonte's merits made such a deep impression on her heart that his absence appeared to her to be hard to bear, but she also dreaded that if the Prince did not find in the King of Cyprus the dispositions for an alliance with Crete for which he hoped, the advice and authority of a respectable and crowned father might oblige Telephonte to renounce the amour that he had for her. The mere idea of a change of mind on the part of that Prince made her shiver. He had seemed so likeable and worthy of esteem that it seemed to her that he was the only man in the world who could render her happy.

She confided those anxieties to Anaxaride, the wife of Dinocrite, who had no less a share in the good graces of Elismene than Dinocrite in Clearque's. Although that agreeable woman was veritably attached to the Princess, however, the extreme buoyancy of her humor did not permit her to share her chagrins to any great extent. She contented herself with representing to Elismene that, beautiful and charming as she was, it was impossible that anyone could become infidel in loving her. Then she added that, even if that destiny arrived, the same attractions that had enabled her to acquire the heart of Telephonte would also enable her to make the conquest of a thousand other hearts, among which there would doubtless by some worthy of her choice.

Anaxaride's arguments were very little consolation for Elismene, who felt sure that she would never be able to love anyone other than the amiable Prince, who, alone among so many illustrious lovers who had offered her their prayers, had had the secret of softening her soul. However, she soon had reason to quit the anxieties she had in his regard; she received a letter from him, written as soon as he had seen his father the King; it informed her that the monarch in question, approving of the fires with which he was burning for her, would think about dispatching ambassadors to ask for her hand as soon as he had seen the departure of Princess Celenie, who was to set forth for Lemnos a few days after her marriage, which was to be celebrated the day after the one on which Telephonte was writing.

The Prince added to his news everything passionate that a gallant and tender lover can write to the object that charms him. The letter that he wrote to Clearque was also full of wit and amity, and as the ship that had bought those letters was a light vessel, which traveled at such speed that it seemed to be flying over the sea, and had had very favorable weather, they were pleasantly surprised by the diligence with which that news had arrived. Everyone praised the exactitude of Telephonte and his good fortune of his envoys.

As Elismene was adored by the entire court of Crete, and Telephonte had appeared infinitely likeable, everyone applauded the union of two such accomplished persons and testified their impatience in waiting for the moment to arrive.

Dinocrite was almost the only one who took no part in the general delight, but he was so occupied with his personal anxieties that he could not take his thoughts away from them; the memory of the robe of sincerity returned incessantly to his mind. Sometimes he burned with impatience for the embroidery to be finished; sometimes he trembled that it might be finished, so much did he fear being unable to see it.

In the end, overwhelmed by his anxieties, he could no longer sustain their weight alone; he told a friend in confidence that the King was having an enchanted robe made that would be the touchstone of the virtue of all women, and he explained to the friend the mystery of the robe. The friend, extremely impressed by that marvelous secret, confided it to a second friend, the second to a third, the third to a fourth, who told it to others, with the consequence that in very little time, not only all the men in the court, but many men from the city, were informed in detail of the gift that the robe on which Misandre was working would have.

What is unusual, however, is that all the men who had kept the secret of the robe so carelessly with regard to one another kept it admirably well from women; not a single per-

son of their sex was informed of the mystery of the embroidery that was being done in the palace.

Clearque had a furious desire to see it progress rapidly,
and went to see Misandre before the time when that philosopher had told him that one could begin to be diverted by it, but
Misandre, going to receive him at the entrance to his apartment, begged him urgently not to come in, assuring him that
not enough work had been done as yet to give him any pleasure, and testifying to him that he would be very grateful to him
if he refrained from looking at the work until it was in a state
to amuse him. Clearque, in accordance with what was asked of
him, did not go in, and went to seek his amusement elsewhere.

A few days later, the King made a journey to a delightful
palace that he had on the edge of the sea. His sister, the Princess, and the entire court went with him, and in that place he
indulged several times in the diversions of fishing, hunting
and solitary walks.

One evening, when the weather was as fine as it had
been frightful during the day, during which terrible winds had
raged, Clearque, while walking along the sea shore, only accompanied by Dinocrite, saw by virtue of the moonlight, three
or four fisherman gathered around a magnificently clad woman, who appeared to have fainted. Impelled by curiosity, the
King approached the fisherman, and saw that they were trying,
by their cares, to bring the woman round, who, unconscious as
she was, appeared to be a young woman of great beauty.

She immediately attracted the compassion of the young
King. He ordered Dinocrite to return to the palace promptly
and to fetch help more reliable and more active that the poor
fishermen could give her. He did not want, however, to interrupt the assistance that the good folk were giving the unconscious beauty, and he hastened to ask them by what adventure
she came to be in that place.

Two of the men replied to him that, the tempest that had
raged for the greater part of the day having prevented them
from going fishing, they had wanted to repair that omission

when they thought that the storm had passed, but when they had tried to put their boats to sea, still finding it too rough, they had remained on the beach to see whether it might calm down. Then they had seen the body of the young woman floating in the water, and pity had moved them to leap into their boat immediately, in order to see whether they could help her. In fact, they had grabbed hold of her clothes, and, having found that she was still breathing, had carried her to the shore, where she had opened her eyes after vomiting a great deal of water, but then had fallen once again into the unconsciousness in which he saw her.

Clearque, touched by the pitiful state that that the beautiful person was in, saw with displeasure that she was not coming round. As soon as several of his servants arrived, summoned by Dinocrite, and they had tried to revive by means of various essences, he had her put in a carriage in order to be carried to the manor, after which he recompensed the fishermen liberally for the care they had given her.

Clearque had the unconscious lady placed in the most magnificent apartment in the palace, and after withdrawing, sent Princess Elismene's ladies-in-waiting to her in order to undress her and put her to bed, where they continued to give her all the remedies necessary to her condition.

When the beautiful lady had recovered consciousness, she was very surprised to find herself in such a superb place, surrounded by people who were all unknown to her, but when she knew that she was in a house belonging to the King of Crete, where the Prince and his sister were staying, she asked for the favor of being able to speak to Elismene, and wanted to get up in order to be taken to her. The Princess, however, having been informed of her arrival and having enquired with a great deal of concern about her health, when informed of her design, forestalled it and went obligingly to her bedside.

As soon as the beautiful stranger saw her, she said: "I am no longer afflicted by my shipwreck, although it nearly cost me my life, since it has given me the fortunate opportunity to see an incomparable princess, about whom my brother, the

Prince, has spoken to me incessantly with so much admiration since his return to Cyprus, and for whom he has a keen and delicate passion, the force of which can only match the magnitude of the charms that have given birth to it."

"What, Madame!" exclaimed Elismene. "I see in you Princess Celenie! The manner in which the King, my brother, talked to me about you just now, and the touching beauty that I presently see in your face had already inspired a strong inclination in your favor, but Heaven, how I sense it increasing when I learn that you are the charming princess of whom renown speaks so advantageously, and the sister of a prince for whom I shall have such a perfect esteem so long as I live!"

"I cannot render enough thanks to my destiny," said Celenie, "for having brought me to you before delivering me to the King of Lemnos, with whom I must stay forever, since I am united with that prince by a sacred bond. But Madame," she added, "I seem to have understood by your discourse that I have been seen by the King, your brother. On what occasion, then, have I had that honor?"

"It is my brother the King who took you, unconscious, from the hands of fishermen who had saved you from the sea."

"I am very distressed," said Celenie, blushing, "that such a great prince has seen me in that condition."

As she was about to continue, Clearque approached her bed, in a very respectful manner, and as the blush that animated them gave a great splendor to all her attractions, the Prince, who had only seen her pale and disfigured, although she had seemed beautiful to him then, found her so far above her previous appearance that he was dazzled by her charms.

Elismene informed her brother, that, while thinking that he was only rendering aid to a likeable stranger, he had had the good fortune to be of service to the illustrious Princes Celenie, Queen of Lemnos. Clearque, by virtue of a sentiment as yet unknown to him, blushed at that news and was nonplussed. He pulled himself together, however, and said very politely to the Queen of Lemnos everything that the merit and the rank of that princess demanded, and after a brief conversation, having suggested to his sister that it was necessary to allow the Queen to rest, he and Elismene withdrew.

In the meantime, the news spread throughout the isle of Crete in very little time that the King had saved the Queen of Lemnos from a shipwreck, and many members of the princess's crew, who had also had the good fortune to be saved, by virtue of various adventures, assembled in the vicinity of their mistress. The ambassadors of Lemnos were among that number; when the Queen's ship had broken up they had sustained themselves on planks hand had drifted, fortunately, to neighboring beaches. Oddly enough, that the tempest that had broken the princess's ship had spared another member of her retinue, who, having not perished, had been able to reach a port near to the place where she had been wrecked.

In order to obtain their orders, all those people came to Manetusa, which was a superb city where Clearque ordinarily had his abode, not far from the manor where the Princess had initially welcomed her. The King of Crete and his sister had begged the Queen of Lemnos to come to that city, assuring her that the purity of the air that one respired here would contribute to a more prompt and entire recovery of her health.

As she was recovering by the day, her beauty and her delightful humor were also increasing, charming Clearque to such an extent that he could no longer dissimulate from himself that he was in love. The certainty that he had of that fact put him in despair, when he considered that the princess would shortly be removed from his gaze forever and put in the power of the fortunate rival to whom her oath had engaged her. He also made the reflection that perhaps Celenie had only engaged that oath with aversion, or at least with indifference, and that it might be the case that she would be unhappy all her life.

When he paused on that thought, he accused destiny a thousand times over of blindness, for it seemed to him that if he had had Celenie for a wife, the happiness of that princess could not have failed to be certain, by virtue of the tender and ardent attachment that he would always have had for her.

Then, he stimulated himself to search for means of preventing Celenie from belonging to the King of Lemnos, telling himself that there need be no scruple in removing that charming beauty from a prince who was doubtless not in love with her, in order to give her to a King who adored her.

He did not remain long in that design, however; sentiments of glory made him envisage that it was no longer permissible to take that princess from the King of Lemnos, who was her husband by the consent of the King, her father, and by her own, and he considered that he could not take the slightest measures to keep her on the island of Crete without his design being regarded throughout the world as a crime against the laws of honor and those of hospitality.

So many sentiments, so opposed to one another, gave him a dolor so great that he could not enclose it entirely within himself. He made Elismene party to it, exaggerating his amour considerably, and his despair in finding himself on the eve of losing forever the object that had given birth to it.

"If I were not the most unfortunate prince in the world," he added, "and destiny had, on the contrary, been favorable to me, some fortunate hazard would have enabled me to see Celenie a long time ago; I could have asked her father the King for her hand and would have obtained it. Judge, my sister, what perfect joy I would have had in seeing myself united by a double bond with Prince Telephonte, who is so full of merit, who has so much amour for you, and for whom you have so much amity."

Elismene replied to Clearque with extreme recognition, and sought to console him with a great deal of intelligence and tenderness, but he was not in a state to appreciate her consolations.

"No, no," he said, "it's in vain that you try to soothe my woes; I feel that I was born to be the most unfortunate prince in the world; until now I have loved nothing seriously; and the first time in my life that I am gripped by the most violent amour that could ever be, it is for a person from whom I must be separated eternally."

The dolor that that thought gave him did not, however, prevent him from thinking that it was time for the robe of sincerity to begin to give him pleasure. In order to provide a diversion for his chagrin, therefore, he went to see Misandre, who received him with a good deal of gravity, having made his daughter hide as soon as he had been informed of the King's arrival.

"Come in, Sire," he said, taking toward a work-table at which Chasseris was busy. "Come and see what there is of the marvelous work on which we have been laboring for your amusement."

At those words Clearque approached Chasseris' work very closely, and was seized by a terrible tremor when he could see nothing on that tale but a black cloth, perfectly uniform and transparent, very similar to what is nowadays called gauze. The prince, suddenly torn by devouring chagrins, did not doubt for moment that Elismene was not at all what she seemed, and, abruptly forming a thousand insulting suspicions regarding the glory of that innocent princess, he did not deign to make the slightest reflection that, by such a cruel injustice, he was outraging virtue itself. He only thought about hiding his disturbance and the pretended shame of his sister from the eyes of the philosopher enchanter; he limited himself entirely to that design and, in order to carry it out, after having pulled himself together somewhat, he said to Misandre: "My eyes are so dazzled by that beautiful work that I cannot discern clearly all its parts; that is why I beg you to make a detailed description of it as if the work were not present to my eyes."

Then Misandre, obedient to the King of Crete, spoke to him thus:

"As it is only those whose wives and sisters are veritably virtuous who have the pleasure of seeing the delicate embroidery of this robe, I thought, Sire, that in order to increase that pleasure, I ought to trace figures there that give an idea of the conduct of coquettes, the grimaces of false prudes and the unworthy tricks of hypocrites, those false worshipers at altars who flatter themselves foolishly that they are imposing on the gods by deceiving humans.

"To commence with the coquettes, therefore, I have represented, as you see, the flattering and adroit manner in which Helen hastened to give marks of tenderness to Menelaus in the days when she had already formed he design to abandon that unfortunate spouse and depart with Paris to go to Troy. You can also observe the seductive glances that she directed at that lover in order to draw him further into her nets. I believe that you are content with the attire of that princess, as well as the samples of architecture that the city of Sparta offers to your eyes and the spectacle of the agitated sea in which the distance is so well contrived.

"These other figures, which are not so well designed, represent the story of the Lydian Queen whose false prudery cost the life of her husband, the King. Her grimacing virtue claims to be so offended by the fact that her husband had enabled Gyges to see her in a state of indecency, whereas, in truth, she was so scarcely offended that she had no repose until Gyges had plunged his dagger into her husband's breast and had snatched the crown of Lydia from the house of the Heraclides to put it on his own head. Oh, a fine prudery that assassinates a husband in order to crown a lover! All these things, as you see, are well characterized here.

"As for these other figures," he went on, "which are only sketched as yet, it's the story of Pauline, the celebrated Roman hypocrite,[45] who spent her days in temples at the foot of altars, seemingly rejecting all her lovers in the most severe manner, but was nevertheless very tender with one, who took the name and face of a god, coming to tell him her reasons in the evening in a temple; that falsely pious woman was the dupe of the

---

[45] The story cited by Misandre here is contained in Antoine Du Verdier's *Les Divers leçons* [Various Lessons] (1604; reprinted 1662 as *Les Diverses leçons d'Antoine du Verdier, Seigneur de Vauprivaz*), where L'Héritier presumably found it, but seems to have been rarely reproduced since.

lover and the priest, because she wanted to be, only seeking to honor the image of virtue. She betrayed virtue itself without scruple.

"You will be able to decipher that subject much more clearly," Misandre added, "when it is finished; the appearance of the head and the attitudes of the figures will give you an entire understanding of it. But Sire," he went on, after falling silent for some time and seeing that Clearque was not speaking, "does the work, in which I have employed all the knowledge of my art, not have the good fortune of pleasing you? Do you find it too incorrect, or too ungracious?"

"I find it perfectly beautiful," Clearque replied, finally, "but I am presently occupied with a reverie, which prevents me from examining all its excellence. I will come back another time to consider the marvelous workmanship at leisure."

As he concluded that speech he withdrew, and left Misandre and his family to resume their ordinary occupations.

The King of Crete had scarcely returned to his apartment that someone came to tell him that the ambassadors from Cyprus, who had come to ask for Princess Elismene in marriage, had arrived. What the prince felt on hearing that news is indescribable. A host of dolorous sentiments agitated his mind; he could not consent to believe the anger he had against his sister sufficiently to sacrifice her to his indignation; nor could he resolve to give as a spouse to the Prince of Cyprus, who he held in such high esteem, a person so lacking in virtue and so unworthy of him.

The good fortune that the princess had had in being loved by such an accomplished prince rendered her even more culpable in his eyes; he could not forgive her for having betrayed a lover as likeable and tender as Telephonte was. At certain moments, he entered into fits of fury against her of which he was not the master. Everything seemed to contribute to irritate him against that innocent princess; for not only did he feel a mortal dolor at the supposed dishonor that covered her, but he had an extreme chagrin that it prevented him from seeing the marvelous embroidery of the robe of sincerity, which he would have been so delighted to contemplate without obstacle. In addition, the sentiments the Celenie inspired in him redoubled the bitterness that he had at the outrage that had been done to the brother of that princess.

On the other hand, the modest appearance and the virtuous manners of Elismene presented themselves to his imagination, and seemed to accuse him of injustice for the insulting suspicions that he was forming against his sister. As he did not doubt the gift that the robe of sincerity had, however, everything that spoke in Elismene's favor was only faintly heard.

Tormented by a thousand tumultuous impulses that agitated his soul, he was constrained to give an audience to the ambassadors from Cyprus before having been able to calm that disturbance. The only control that he had over himself was to be able to maintain an apparent tranquility. He received the ambassadors perfectly politely and granted them the request that they made for the princess, without having precisely determined in his heart whether he intended to keep his promise to them, or whether he would withdraw it someday, in order not to give Telephonte a wife unworthy of him.

Clearque was not the only one whose imagination was troubled by the robe of sincerity. Dinocrite, who, as the prince's favorite, had privileges above other courtiers, made use of the rights that they gave him to obtain chagrin much more promptly than the rest of the court. Like the King, he had been to see Misandre urgently, and had not seen in Chasseris' work anything but black cloth, transparent and uniform; and like the prince, in order not to inform Misandre of his supposed misfortune, he had testified that he saw on the fabric everything that the philosopher wanted him to see there; but he quit Misandre with a soul so full of rage against poor Anaxaride that he could not prevent himself from giving her evidence of it as soon as he returned home.

The young woman in question, in keeping with the character of her humor, was extremely cheerful that day, and said extremely pleasant things to him, appropriate to have given joy to anyone but a jealous spouse. Then Dinocrite, far from paying any attention to Anaxaride's joyful discourse, said a thousand harsh things to her, which she treated at first as jokes; but he added so many things to them frightfully insulting to her virtue that in the end, she was outraged by them, and ran to the palace in tears, to go to throw herself at Elismene's feet.

As she found the princess alone, she did indeed throw herself there, and begged her to obtain permission from the King for her to leave her husband, in order to retire to a solitude closed to the world, with women consecrated to the service of altars, adding that it was impossible for her to live any longer with a husband who was capable of suspecting her virtue in such a extravagant manner.

The princess, deeply touched by Anaxaride's story, sympathized with her misfortunes with a kindness full of affection; but after she had testified to her how sorry she felt for her chagrins, she told her that, rude as they were, it was necessary to resolve herself to support them rather than cause the scandal she projected.

"Consider," said Elismene, "how promptly a woman of your age and temperament would weary of leading a solitary life between four walls. However," she added, "when a person as young as you no longer wants to live with her husband, there is no other course of action for her to take than that of retiring from the world, if she is scrupulously attached to her glory; so, don't go in an unseemly fashion to engage in a divorce, of which the tedious life would soon draw you into another retreat of which you would soon repent. Continue to live in solid virtue and exact decorum, as you always have, and whatever just pride that the innocence of your mores might inspire in you, only oppose mildness and patience to Dinocrite's calumnies and rages. You will be praised and attract the sympathy of everyone; in addition, seek to dissipate the chagrins that your husband's strange humor will give you, by means of all the innocent pleasures that you can obtain with me and your friends.

"For as long as you are here, Madame," exclaimed Anaxaride, sadly, "I shall try to follow the orders that your prudence prescribes for me exactly, because your protection and your kindness will give me such pleasant consolations that they will give me the strength to support the barbaric treatment of my husband, but when you have departed for Cyprus, what will become of the unfortunate Anaxaride?"

Elismene represented to her that Dinocrite's eccentricities might pass. In the end, she gave her such favorable hopes, and said such obliging things to her that she almost restored calm to the soul of the chagrined wife, and the ambassadors from Cyprus, who arrived at that moment in order to pay court to their future princess, completed, by means of their conversation, dissipating any residue of disturbance that might have remained in Anaxaride's mind.

The first of those ambassadors, whose name was Cleophane, was full of distinguished merit. He entertained Elismene with a hundred amusing things, and as he mingled skillfully with his discourse various depictions of Telephonte's amour and great qualities, his conversation was doubly agreeable to the Princess.

From that day on, Elismene saw Anaxaride incessantly attached to her paces; she only found in the company of the Princess of Crete a refuge from the ill-treatment of her husband, who waited very impatiently for Elismene's departure in order to allow all his fury against Anaxaride to burst forth, not daring to outrage her as far as the ultimate violence under the eyes of the princess, by whom he knew that she was highly considered.

The sincere testimonies of tenderness that Elismene received from a prince who was very dear to her, and the presence of the beautiful Queen of Lemnos, gave her an extreme satisfaction, but that satisfaction was nevertheless considerably troubled by the anxious melancholy that she remarked in her brother's eyes, although she only took that disturbance for a effect of the love he felt for Celenie.

It was not, however, that passion which was now tyrannizing Clearque's soul most oppressively; the dolor that he felt at the injury he believed his sister to have inflicted on his honor filled his thoughts so forcefully that, seemingly entirely delivered at times to all that it inspired in him of the catastrophic, he imagined that he could no longer conserve sufficient sensibility for the flame that had burned within him.

He was mistaken; the amour had not quit him; it was only hidden in the depths of his heart. The violent fury that animated him against Elismene had suspended the tenderness that he felt for Celenie, but it had not lost any of its rights over him.

However, in order to satisfy the fury that was agitating him, he had all Elismene's words and actions observed with a rigorous exactitude. Nothing was reported to him that was not appropriate to convince him of the nobility of the sentiments and the delicate virtue of the Princess. Still prey to his eccentric caprices, however, he preferred to persuade himself that his sister no longer had the intrigues that he pretended to have discovered by means of the robe of sincerity than deign even to suspect that he might have been the dupe of a dangerous credulity.

While the King occupied himself with a thousand desolate thoughts, which gave him a somber and pensive air that worried the entire court, and while Celenie prepared with displeasure to set sail toward her husband, a light vessel arrived in Crete in which there were two aristocrats from the isle of Lemnos who came to inform the beautiful Queen and the ambassadors who were accompanying her that the King of Lemnos had died suddenly.

Celenie received that news with so much moderation and grandeur of soul that she attracted a general admiration. She appeared to be moderately afflicted; she spoke with much esteem and gratitude about the monarch who had given her the title of Queen, and responded to the envoys of the new King of Lemnos with so much dignity and mildness that everyone was unable to help admiring the noble firmness with which she lost a crown.

However, it was decided that the envoys from Lemnos would return Queen Celenie to the hands of her brother, Prince Telephonte, who was due to arrive in Crete the following day in order to marry the beautiful Elismene in person.

That princess was at the peak of her happiness; informed of the ardent amour that her brother had for Celenie, she believed that the death of the King of Lemnos had destroyed all the obstacles that might oppose the happiness of that prince. But she was very surprised when she saw that after receiving the news, Clearque still remained in the same somber and chagrined humor that had dominated him for some time, and her astonishment was increased by a conversation that she had with Celenie.

The two beautiful princesses had suddenly felt so much disposition to love one another that they had not taken any precautions in tightening the knots of their amity; sympathy had formed the bond in a manner so strong that each of them had a large enough opening in the heart for the other as there would have been if they had been friends for a long time. Elismene therefore announced to Celenie the tender sentiments for her of whose penetration Clearque had made the confidence to her, and exaggerated greatly the despair of that prince in the time when he had seen her destined to make the happiness of the King of Lemnos.

"I assure you, Madame," replied Celenie, smiling and blushing at the same time, "that your brother the King can only have told you these things to please you, knowing the amity with which you honor me, for I can answer to you for the fact that he has never said anything to me but things that a young prince as gallant as he is ordinarily says to all persons of my sex. I ought to inform you, in addition, that, since the death of the King of Lemnos, the King of Crete appears to only to want to find himself in my presence surrounded by a numerous court; he even seems to avoid my gaze, and when by chance, I encounter his, I see there a sadness mingled with fury rather than impressions of tenderness. However, Madame," Celenie added, still smiling, "you know that in the isle where I was born, people have the reputation of possessing the art of detecting the movements of the heart perfectly in the eyes."

"It is necessary, however, Madame," replied Elismene, jovially, "that your art has not served you well on this occasion, for in my turn, I can protest that, without being born on the isle of Cyprus, I have surely seen, in the eyes and in the speech of my brother the King, all the transports of a veritable amour."

"It is true," replied Celenie, "that those who only have the advantage of being born on the isle of Cyprus must cede their rights to a princess who ought one day to be its Queen, but Madame, if it is true that the route you are on to the throne of Cyprus has given you better than me the art of knowing that the King of Crete is in love, he must be a very discreet lover, for, except for a few sighs that he has occasionally uttered in my presence, which might as easily have been sighs of sadness as of amour, he has never allowed any mark of tenderness to escape him before me."

That speech of Celenie's threw Elismene into a strange astonishment; she did not know to what to attribute the extreme chagrin of her brother, and had an anxiety in consequence that troubled her repose.

The Queen of Lemnos had had good reason when she had assured the princess that Clearque had never given her any positive sign of amour. Although he was filled with it, deep down, the cruel ideas that the robe of sincerity had given him did not permit him to allow that sincerity to appear externally. It was, however, true that the death of the King of Lemnos had let him know more than ever how strong that ardor was.

Initially, with pleasure, he had felt love and hope reawakening in his soul, and in the first transports of his joy he emerged from his apartment in order to run to Celenie's, to offer her his heart and his faith and to ask her whether, by his services, he could obtain permission from her to send his am-

bassadors to request the consent of her father. While traversing the palace, however, as he was going to see the princess,
he chanced to encounter Misandre in his path.

The sight of the austere philosopher recalled so sharply
to Clearque's mind the redoubtable woes that the mysterious
robe of sincerity revealed, that, as suspicion and mistrust were
really the dominant aspect of the prince's character, he felt all
their power at that moment. For, without remembering in the
slightest all that renown published advantageously regarding
Celenie's scrupulous virtue, not paying any attention to the
noble modesty that was manifest in all the words and actions
of that princess, entirely delivered to his chimeras, he told
himself that it was quite enough to have a sister who diminished his honor without running the risk of giving himself a
wife who might cover him in shame.

With those fine reflections, on a slight pretext, he returned to his apartment, where he made a firm resolution not
to say a word about his tenderness to the Queen of Lemnos
until he had shown the robe of sincerity to Telephonte, without
telling him the mystery of it, in order to judge, by the proof
that it would make of that princess, whether the spouse of the
Queen of Lemnos would have been able to see the embroidery
of that terrible robe.

Clearque's foolish credulity and bizarre suspicion threw
great disorder into his court. He was in an agitation that was
remarked by everyone, but, in spite of the amity that Elismene
had for him, she feared him so much that she dared not ask
him the reason for it. What further augmented the timidity that
the Princess had always had in his regard was that she had
noticed that he often launched glances full of fury at her, and
that he spoke to her in an irritated tone, although he forced
himself not to say anything rude.

She did not understand how she could possibly have attracted his anger, but the chagrin she felt in consequence troubled all the pleasure that her prospects gave her. However, the
perfect esteem that she had for Telephonte enabled her to hope
that, by his prudence, he would return calm to the King's mind

once he was beside him. Thus, for all sorts of reasons, she awaited the arrival of the Prince of Cyprus with great impatience.

Celenie had scarcely less. Secretly irritated by the indifferent silence that Clearque maintained in her regard, after what Elismene had told her about the sentiments of that prince, and what she had believed that she detected herself when she first arrived in Crete, annoyed to have flattered herself in vain that her charms had conquered a king who seemed likeable, Clearque's presence embarrassed her and gave her a sort of chagrin, which made her wish ardently to return to the King of Cyprus as soon as possible.

Finally, it was learned via a courier that Prince Telephonte had arrived in the port of Crete. At that news, Elismene felt an infinite joy and Clearque a terrible emotion. Amour, amity, suspicions, indignation and anger divided his soul sadly, and if rays of hope were sometimes glimpsed there, dread soon caused them to disappear. However, the prince, who took no pride in the arrogant prerogatives of royal dignity, prepared to go and meet Telephonte very diligently.

As the time he had given Misandre to complete the robe of sincerity had just expired, he asked him whether the work was finished; the philosopher having responded that it would have reached its final perfection in a matter of hours, the King made him bring the fatal robe, at which he looked again, tremulously, in Misandre's presence. Perceiving, with a further dolor, that he could not see any embroidery there and that the garment offered nothing to his gaze but a uniform black gauze, without saying anything to the philosopher, he made him a sign to withdraw.

Immediately, he summoned several officers of his wardrobe. Without giving them the slightest explanation, he simply gave them the order to place the robe in one of the trunks that were being prepared for his journey.

Although Clearque said nothing about the robe in question to his officers, they all knew its mystery, by way of the channel that Dinocrite had opened, and they had learned how long the pretended enchanter had asked in order to finish it. They knew that the time had expired, and they had just seen Misandre going into the King's apartments carrying something and then come out again without it.

Informed of all those things, the officers did not doubt for a moment that the robe that they saw, and which the King had ordered them to pack for his journey, was the marvelous robe of which Dinocrite had spoken, and as none of them saw any embroidery on it, each of them, his soul seized by dolor, had no doubt that he was among the number of the unfortunates to whom the sight of the robe's rich ornaments was forbidden. However, all those men, knowing that the king was informed of the gift of the enchanted garment, thought of hiding their shame and misfortune, and they all proclaimed, as if in concert, the astonishing beauty of the robe. Then each of them applauded himself in secret for having had sufficient self-control to hide his disgrace from his sovereign and his comrades, whom they knew to be as well-informed as the King regarding the robe's effects.

The exclamations that the officers made regarding the pretended embroidery further augmented Clearque's despair and, a moment later, he believed himself to be almost alone in having women in his household whose conduct was errant, for he had his courtiers enter—who, being as well informed as the King's officers of the robe's properties, were no more clairvoyant than them in discerning the ornaments, and no less prompt than them to pretend that they saw marvelous things. Clearque felt an indescribable chagrin at seeing so many men free of a misfortune to which he thought himself subject. Dinocrite, who had been one of the last to arrive, felt transports a thousand times more violent, and immediately formed terrible projects against poor Anaxaride.

Finally, the King of Crete, beside himself to the point of fury at not even having the feeble consolation of finding companions in disgrace, without asking any questions about the embroideries that where being praised so highly, for fear of hearing the insupportable exclamations recommence, abruptly ordered that the robe be shut in the trunk, which was immediately done. Clearque went to bed early that evening, because he wanted to leave early in the morning.

Dinocrite returned to his dwelling, his soul more ulcerated than ever after seeing the fatal robe again, and the reflections he made on the happiness of those who contemplated the embroideries at their ease redoubled his rage. Thus, when he had gone into his room, which was only separated from his wife's by a light partition, without having the strength to do anything, he went to bed, although he sensed that he would not be able to sleep. He only occupied himself there with chagrined thoughts full of fury.

Toward midnight, he heard Anaxaride come in. She had just left the Princess, who, not having to make a journey the following day like her brother, had returned rather late. Anaxaride, who was fatigued by talking and drowsy, went to bed immediately, but after falling asleep she was awakened with a start by a dream, feeling a violent thirst. She got out of bed in order to look for a vase that was normally left in her cabinet full of water.

She searched for it for some time in vain, and was finally persuaded that her maidservants had forgotten to bring it after having filled it in the morning. As she could hear them still talking and laughing in their bedroom, which was above her own, she decided to go and ask them for the vase that she needed, because she did not want to pull the bell-cord that she usually used to summon them, for fear that the noise might wake her eccentric spouse.

She therefore went very quietly to the servants' room, who begged her pardon profusely for their negligence. Then one of them went ahead of her, carrying a candle in one hand and the vase in question in the other, which was filled to the brim with beautiful clear water, so fearful were they that the lady, who seemed very thirsty, might run out of it during the night.

As the slight noise that Anaxaride had made in opening her bedroom door had been heard by Dinocrite, however, and as the jealous husband's bedroom and his wife's had a common antechamber, he had got out of bed abruptly and had run furiously into Anaxaride's room. At first he had listened with extreme attention to see whether he could hear the voice of some man and that of his wife, but, unable to hear anything at all, he approached Anaxaride's bed, which he found to be empty. Then, transported by an excess of rage, he emerged from the bedroom and was traversing the antechamber as rapidly as was possible in the dark when he saw Anaxaride's chambermaid come in, who was lighting the way for her mistress.

As the maid was marching in the lead, and his imagination as seething, he mistook her for Anaxaride; he advanced toward her like a maniac and shouted at her in a menacing voice: "Ah, wretch, so this is how you betray me!"

The poor maid was so frightened by his voice and his action that she trembled and tottered, and, unable to be mindful of what she was doing, she bumped into a table, which knocked her over. As she collapsed, she dropped the candle and the vase that she was holding. As it fell the candle went out, while the vase, which was made of clay, shattered into a thousand pieces, with a terrible noise.

Dinocrite, who had seized the chambermaid's dress just as she had bumped into the table, had been dragged down by the young woman's fall, so that he fell too. The noise that the clay vase made in shattering alarmed him so much that he did not know what he was doing; he imagined that it was some lover of his wife, who had wounded him mortally, and, as the water spilled from the broken vase had drenched the visionary, he cried out, desperately: "Murder! Help! I'm drowning in my blood!"

At those cries, all the servants in the house came running. Several having brought light, it was not a spectacle devoid of humor to see Dinocrite lying on the floor, having sustained no harm except that of being inundated with water, and

242

surrounded by the debris of the broken vase. He was so preoccupied with his foolish imaginings that, in spite of everything
his servants could say to reassure him, he continued to shout
relentlessly for his wounds to be dressed and his murderer to
be arrested.

The chambermaid whose fall had caused his own had got
up as soon as other people arrived, so he did not know that she
had fallen there, and he called to her for help as well as the
other servants. As the young woman had a humor at least as
cheerful as her mistress, however, Dinocrite's chimerical terror and the involuntary bath of sorts, in which he believed
himself to be inundated with blood, caused her to burst out
laughing in spite of the attempts that were made to stop her.
That laughter caused Dinocrite pass from movements of fear
to those of anger, and her indiscreet hilarity would have exposed the maid to some unfortunate effects of his wrath if she
had not run away.

Finally, however, the jealous man, beginning to be persuaded that he was not wounded, no longer thought about anything but searching every corner of his dwelling to see whether there was some lover hidden there. In spite of the indignation that Anaxaride felt at the seeing the offensive suspicions
that her unjust husband had formed regarding her conduct, the
panic terrors of the eccentric and the humorous situation in
which she had seen him had caused her a desire to laugh
scarcely less violent than that of her chambermaid. The noble
education she had received, however, rendered her much more
self-controlled than persons of that sort, and she gave no external evidence of what she thought.

She maintained a profound silence, which she only broke
in order to say coldly to Dinocrite, whom she saw greatly agitated and searching everywhere: "Sire, it appears to me that
you would be much better off going to bed in peace than tormenting yourself as you are."

"Eh!" he replied, looking at her askance. "How can I be
in peace when you take so much care to take it away from
me?"

243

Without making any reply, Anaxaride went into her cabinet and sat down in an armchair, without deigning to go back to bed, so chagrined was she.

As for Dinocrite, after having searched the entire house in vain, he finally went back to bed. He was scarcely there that he abandoned himself to further anxieties. He had enough experience of society to imagine easily that among the large number of servants who had witnessed his suspicions and his fears, there were few who would keep the secret. He knew that he had many enemies, and did not doubt that before the King's departure, that prince would be informed of the scene that had just occurred in is home. Thus, he thought he could already see himself furnishing the gossip of the court and the city, and those ideas caused him transports of rage, which the memory of the chambermaid's laughter did not help to calm.

His fury increased further when he thought that people would dare to treat him as a visionary and a coward, and at certain moments he would have been ready to give everything he possessed to have the good fortune of surprising a favorite lover with his wife.

After spending an hour those cruel thoughts, as he was more deeply buried than ever in his hollow reveries, he heard a noise on the staircase. Full of the foolish ideas that he had in his mind, he exclaimed: "Ah, wretch, that's one of your seducers fleeing! He was so well hidden just now that he escaped my eyes and he's leaving now that he thinks everything is calm—but he won't escape me, and I'll be able to convince all those insolent laughers that I'm not a man to forge visions."

As he said that he got up again with an extreme precipitation, without making the reflection that he had no light, any more than the first time—for when he had gone back to bed, in spite of the fright he had had, his mind had still been so agitated that he had forgotten to order that candles be left for him. He therefore went to the door of the antechamber in darkness, and opened it.

As soon as he was on the staircase he heard someone walking, whom he followed, furiously. Thinking that he could feel someone's hair, he tried to seize it, but the person escaped him and he thought he heard them going down the stairs. He followed as quickly as possible, but scarcely had he gone down a few steps than he felt himself caught from behind and pushed so rudely that he fell down the stairs. He rolled down the steps and into a wall, against which his head collided so unfortunately that it made a terrible wound.

At the noise he made in falling and the cries he uttered after having fallen, and the barking of a large dog that had made itself heard very loudly at the moment of his fall, woke the entire household with start, and all the servants immediately came running—convinced, however, that it was some new chimera on the part of their master. They were very surprised, however, when they saw that his blood was, indeed, flowing and that he was dangerously wounded in the head.

Although Dinocrite was suffering a great deal from his injury, he was still more attentive to order that the assassin be arrested than to ask for help. It was rendered to him nevertheless with considerable urgency. No matter how carefully they searched for the supposed assassin, however, no trace of him could be found; they only found a large mastiff at the bottom of the stairs, from whose coat some hairs had been freshly torn out. As Dinocrite had asserted immediately that he had grabbed his assassin by the hair and it was perceived that a few hairs were still retained in his hand, and as it was also on the steps of the staircase that he had indicated that he had been pushed a moment after he had seized someone by the hair, on the basis of Dinocrite's story and some solid conjectures, no one had any doubt that the visionary had mistaken the mastiff for a man. He found himself so obliged to believe it, by virtue of a thousand circumstances that were recounted to him, that he thought he would expire from rage.

This is how it had happened. At the moment when the fall of the vase full of water had caused Dinocrite such great alarm that he had summoned the whole household to help him, his grooms had come running as well as the other servants. One of those grooms had a large mastiff that was very dear to him and which amused his comrades greatly. The dog usually slept in the stables beside him, but when Dinocrite's cries had caused the groom to run to his master, the dog had followed him. When everything seemed calm and the man had returned to the stables, the dog had gone to sleep on the staircase next to a chair that Dinocrite had had one of his valets bring. While searching the house, the jealous man had noticed that there was a kind of cupboard on the stairway that had once been destined to contain a clock; he had exclaimed that there might well be a man hiding in that redoubt, and had demanded that his valet stand on a chair in order to see whether he had guessed correctly.

When everyone had gone back to bed, they had forgotten to take the chair away. The dog, after taking a nap, had bumped into it when it woke up and had caused it to fall; that was what had made the noise that had caused Dinocrite to get up for a second time. Mentally preoccupied, having heard the mastiff moving, he had thought it was a man; he had seized it by the fur, which he had mistaken for hair; the animal had escaped and had then pushed Dinocrite from behind so rudely that he had fallen, as we have seen.

Meanwhile, Anaxaride, who could not sleep, because of the chagrin her husband's extravagances had caused her, had suddenly heard the second rumor that had gone up, but as she had no doubt that it was some new frenzy on the part of the visionary, she had resolved not to stir from her cabinet. Lending an ear nevertheless to what was happening, she heard two or three voices asserting quite seriously that Dinocrite was badly hurt. At that news, very alarmed, she ran to him precipitately, for, in spite of the eccentric's strange behavior, his wife's good nature was such that she still had benevolence for him.

She found him surrounded by all his servants, except for those who had gone in quest of physicians and surgeons. As what he was suffering greatly increased the bad mood that he was usually in, he received Anaxaride's cares very poorly. In spite of all the offensive things that he said, however, she did not want to leave him until she had taken all possible precautions for his relief and she had seen the first dressing applied to his wound, which the surgeons declared to be very dangerous.

Rumor of Dinocrite's adventure spread so rapidly that Clearque was informed of it as soon as he awoke. The prince, having planned to take the favorite with him on his journey, and who had amity for him, was very sorry for his misfortune, and went to visit him before departing. He gave him a thousand testimonies of good will, but when he asked him for details of his accident, Dinocrite replied in a manner so confused that Clearque imagined that he was still delirious, and quit him feeling very sorry for him.

The young king had a soul so agitated, and had such a great desire to be enlightened on the subject of Celenie, that, forcing his horses at the whim with his impatience, he soon joined Telephonte.

The latter prince was transported with joy at first but he was very surprised to see something somber and constrained in Clearque's expression and manner that he had not expected to find. Nevertheless, he hid his astonishment from the two courts and only confided his chagrin to Leandrin, for whom he had an entirely open heart.

"Oh, my dear Leandrin," he said to him, "what does the troubled reception that the King of Crete is giving me presage? Has the charming Elismene changed her attitude in my regard? What if that divine princess no longer wants to consent to render me the happiest and most glorious of all men?"

Leandrin sought in vain to reassure him; he remained so alarmed that he did not get a single moment of peaceful sleep all night.

The next morning, Clearque had the robe of sincerity brought to him precipitately. As soon as he had the garment he went into Telephonte's room. The latter prince, by means of countless obliging words and actions, sought to give him further evidence of a limitless amity full of deference, but Clearque received the gracious evidence of his urgency with so much trouble and distraction that it further augmented Telephonte's chagrin. However, he begged the Prince of Cyprus to rest for a day before taking the road to Manetusa again. The Prince, who did not want to contradict him in anything, agreed to his wish, and also consented to the proposition he made at the same time that they should take a pleasant stroll together.

The King of Crete took him to a solitary wood, and there they drew away gradually from their followers. When the King saw that they were sure of no longer being overheard by anyone, he said to the Prince of Cyprus with a forced smile: "How comes it, Sire, that in the nearly two hours that we have been together, you have not yet said anything to me about the magnificence of my attire?"

"I had so much application, Sire," Telephonte replied, "in searching your eyes for glorious marks of your amity toward me, and was so attentive to listening to your speech, that it is not astonishing that, occupied in the pleasure of gazing at an august visage in the joy of hearing a conversation full of wit, I have not paid any heed to your adornment. Nevertheless, if you imagine that there was indolence in that lack of attention, I will tell you, in order to justify myself, that even in the company of your sister, for whom I believe that I cannot be accused of having an indolent heart, I spent entire days without knowing what she was wearing; the attractions of her face and the luminosity of her mind occupied my entire soul so agreeably that, incessantly admiring the charms with which Heaven had adorned the divine Elismene, I no longer had the leisure to pay any heed to the advantages she might have received from her garments. If one relied on vulgar opinions, one could scarcely believe that a Prince of Cyprus born on the isle of Cyprus could be so insensitive to adornment, most of all that of beautiful women, but the vulgar do not have accurate opinions. On our island, as elsewhere, delicate amour is not influenced by borrowed splendor; it is only sensitive to the brilliance of the eyes and the intelligence of the beloved object.

"However, Sire," Telephonte continued, "after having sought to justify my scant attention to attire, since your speech engages me now to pay heed to yours and to tell you my sentiments in its regard, I confess that it appears to me that you are wearing a robe today that is very simple and rather lugubrious for a prince as young and as gallant as yourself."

Clearque had listened with an extreme impatience to all the gracious things that Telephonte had said. His discourse appeared to him to be frightfully long-winded, and he had been on the point of interrupting it twenty times over in order to be informed abruptly regarding his robe, but finally, after the Prince had declared to him naturally what he thought, it was as if he had been struck by a thunderbolt. Without having the strength to say anything, he went to sit down nonchalantly at the foot of a tree, where Telephonte followed him.

After having sat for some time without speaking, the Prince of Cyprus said to the King of Crete: "What is the matter, Sire? It seems to me that you are feeling ill."

"Oh, Sire!" exclaimed Clearque, "I have never suffered so much in my life, but it would be in vain if I tried to hide my dolor from you, since it is necessary, in spite of what I do, for you to share it with me."

"You will never have woes," Telephonte replied, "to which I shall not be sensible myself."

"Alas," said Clearque, sighing, "you will have to deplore yours as well as mine. Know, Sire, that the Elismene of whom you were speaking just now with so much amour, is a perfidious woman who, by the aberrations of her conduct, is unworthy of the tenderness that you have for her; and that the Queen of Lemnos, the sister for whom you testify so much amity and esteem, has betrayed her glory no less. I adored her, that culpable charmer, but I have just been convinced that she does not merit a pure incense, any more than my unworthy sister."

"Stop, Sire!" cried Telephonte, transported by dolor. "It is too much for me to learn at the same time of the cruel affliction that my honor has received and the loss of all my pleasures!" He went on, however: "But no, on the contrary, deign to inform me of all the circumstances of my double misfortune, in order that the deadly account will cause me expire in despair."

"It is necessary that I confess to you my confusion," said Clearque. "Without your disgrace, I would never have had the assurance to declare my own; but the conformity of our destinies gives me the strength to speak. Yes, the certainty that I have had today of the weakness of Celenie permits me to make you the confession of Elismene's bad conduct."

"Please, Sire," Telephonte interrupted, impatiently, "Do not keep my mind in suspense any longer. Deign to tell me in detail all that you have discovered about the odious aberrations of those two unworthy princesses."

After those words, the King of Crete gave the Prince of Cyprus a faithful account of the manner in which Misandre had come to offer him the robe of sincerity; he explained the mystery of the robe to him and announced to him that it was by virtue of the gift that it possessed that he had discovered the bad conduct of Elismene, and added that it was by the same means that he had just been convinced that Celenie was equally culpable.

Telephonte had a great deal of difficulty in controlling himself sufficiently to listen to the end to a story that seemed to him so extravagant and superstitious. However, he was transported by joy to see with what bizarre injustice the innocence of the two princesses had been suspected.

Finally, when Clearque had stopped speaking he said to him: "Is it possible, Sire, that a prince as intelligent as you can fall victim so cruelly to the black malice of a scoundrel? Oh, Sire, banish from your mind all the suspicions you have formed against the virtue of our sisters the princesses, since you have no other evidence against them that the chimeras that this fantastic philosopher has recounted to you."

"Do you believe, then, Sire, that I am blindly superstitious?" retorted Clearque, in an irritated tone. "Do you count for nothing the testimony of Dinocrite, my officers and a host of my courtiers, who have all seen admirable embroideries on this robe that neither you nor I have been able to see?"

"All those people, Sire," Telephonte replied, "are bold impostors. Do you believe that among all the men of your court and the officers of your household who have seen your robe that there is not one who has an infidel spouse or a coquettish sister? If it were true, therefore, that the robe has the gift that you attribute to it, and if it were true that those men were as sincere as they are false, there would have been a considerable number of them who would have confessed in good faith that they did not see any embroidery on the robe; but there was not one of them who did not tell you that he saw marvelous things there. That alone can easily make you doubt the fidelity of their reports."

"But why should the men of my court sought to impose on me with regard to the embroidery on the robe," said Clearque, "since they did not know that those who saw it uniform were declaring themselves the victims of the foolish conduct of women to whom they were linked by marriage or blood? They would have talked to me naturally, since they did not know the gift of the enchanted robe, the secret of which I confided to Dinocrite alone."

"It is enough for one man to have known your secret," Telephonte replied, "for it not to be surprising that it was able to spread throughout your court."

Finally, without reporting the conversation of the two princes entirely, it is sufficient to say that Telephonte, by virtue of his prudence and his mildness, was able to bring Clearque round to his own sentiments so effectively that the King was no longer in doubt that he had been tricked by the philosopher and deceived by the men of his court. Telephonte even made him sense, in a delicate manner, that it was the excessive attachment he had to his opinions and the vivacity with which he sustained them once he was prejudiced in their

251

favor that had caused those surrounding him to speak to him so insincerely, because they so often feared displeasing him by telling him the truth.

"For myself," Telephonte continued. "I have accustomed all those who approach me not to disguise anything from me, and have always testified such scant bitterness to those who have been able to tell me something annoying, that people have no hesitation in telling me the most disagreeable truths. That method has enabled me to avoid several accidents to which I might have fallen victim if people had not spoken to me freely.

"As I am in possession of that right, permit, Sire, that it might contribute to complete undeceiving you of your error. There is still a considerable number of people who have seen not you in the robe that you are wearing; I ask you for the favor of taking it off as soon as we have arrived at the manor from which we set off and to put it on myself when we are no more than a day away from Manetusa and are surrounded by your court and mine, the ambassadors of my father the King and those from Lemnos."

Clearque assured Telephonte that he would consent all that he desired; then he begged his pardon with a great deal of dolor for the reckless judgment that he had made of Celenie and Elismene, and begged him insistently to hide his weakness from the two princesses—especially the beautiful Queen off Lemnos, for whom he sensed fires whose ardor his cruel suspicions had not been able to extinguish, and which, at the moment, were making him feel transports more violent than ever.

After that discourse, the princes stood up in order to go and join their followers, but as they were walking in the wood, two peasants who were traversing it found themselves close by and stopped short to consider them.

One of them had seen the King of Crete the day before and had remembered he prince's face perfectly, so he recognized him at first glance, and said to his comrade, in a naïve and surprised fashion: "Oh! Look how our King, who was so richly dressed yesterday, is clad today! He almost resembles an old schoolmaster who has put on his festival costume in summer."

The peasant, who had all the indiscretion of the village, had spoken loudly enough for the King of Crete to overhear him. That prince was delighted, but was far from giving any evidence that he had heard anything. When he had taken a few more steps he turned round, summoned the peasant and asked him, in the presence of is comrade, a few questions about the hunting in the vicinity. Then he asked him whether he was married; the man, who seemed to be no more than nineteen or twenty years old, said that he was not. Clearque asked him if he had any sisters.

"Alas Sire," he said, in a sorrowful tone, "I have one who is a nursling. My mother, who had never had any child but me, took it into her head, after twenty years, to have a daughter six months ago, and that has caused many young women who made soft eyes at me not to look at me any longer, because I am no longer my parents' only child, as I was before."

The naivety of the peasant caused both the King of Crete and the Prince of Cyprus to smile. Then Clearque went on:

"Has your father so much wealth, then, that you regret deeply not being its sole heir?"

"Oh, yes, Sire," said the other peasant. "He's the richest laborer in the entire canton, so he's almost its king, as you are with all the fine society that goes everywhere with you."

Clearque and Telephonte smiled again at that fine speech, and after having given marks of their liberality to the two peasants, the princes rejoined their followers and returned with them to the manor. As soon as they arrived there, Clearque changed his clothes, as he had promised Telephonte, and immediately sent a courier to order the guards he had left with Elismene at Manetusa to arrest and imprison Misandre and his family.

However, the King, although he affected an exterior tranquility, was still in an extreme agitation. When he came to sound the depths of his heart, he sensed that he was not yet entirely cured of the suspicions that the robe of sincerity had given him. His soul was balanced between hope and dread. At certain moments he believed that Misandre was a rogue, at others he believed him to be a truthful man, very knowledgeable in the art of enchantment, and imagined that the Prince of Cyprus was the dupe of his incredulity. He could not cease to be astonished that the Prince had not conserved the lightest shadow of suspicion after the confession he had made him, and criticized him in his heart for the violent urgency he had to marry Elismene.

At least, he said to himself, *if that marriage renders Telephonte unhappy, he will only be able to blame it on himself, since, in spite of my sister's interest, I had the good faith to declare my suspicions to him. Oh, I ought to refrain from imitating him! In spite of Celenie's charms and the ardent amour I have for her, I cannot resolve to marry her until I am better enlightened regarding the robe of sincerity.*

However, he continued, *can I have clearer evidence of the knavery of Misandre than the testimony of that peasant, who is not married and only has a nursling sister? Let us investigate whether the man told me the truth on those two articles, and has not been bribed to tell me that he saw nothing on my robe. But if he was telling me the truth about his estate and has not been seduced to comment on my robe as he did, it is certain that the fatal robe, which has give me so much chagrin, is not enchanted, and it is only the production of Misandre's malice, who wanted to trick me.*

Oh, if that is the case, how happy I shall be! I shall be able to unite myself with a beautiful princess whom I love with so much passion! I shall be able to give all my esteem to my sister again, and in addition, I shall be able to avenge myself on the perfidious Misandre for the shame that my foolish credulity has attracted to me.

Clearque spent the entire night in that strange uncertainty, and the following morning, before leaving, he sent forth a man as adroit as he was faithful, by whose report he was convinced that the peasant had not been bribed to speak about the robe and had told the exact truth in all regards. The surety of that news gave the King of Crete the sweetest transports, and caused him to take the road to Manetusa with a joy that burst forth in his eyes, even though certain residues of suspicion returned to him several times, over which he had difficulty obtaining absolute mastery.

Telephonte was not the same; the chimera of the robe had not left the slightest scruple in his mind; the Prince was so far above such vulgar errors that he was incapable of believing in such a superstition. He was, in consequence, not occupied with anything but the pleasure of seeing Elismene again and the flattering hope of soon being united with that charming princess. It was not the bizarre credulity of Clearque that could give any diminution to his joy.

He had been annoyed that the King could have formed so lightly such offensive suspicions against the two princesses, whose virtue everyone had always admired, and at times he had found himself more inclined to quarrel with Clearque than to disabuse him. However, as the Prince of Cyprus had a great penchant for Clearque, and the King, except for the wrong routes he sometimes took, had many likeable qualities, as well as being Elismene's brother, amity had mastered indignation in Telephonte's heart, and the Prince, after having criticized the King of Crete's weakness, had felt compassion for his error and no longer thought of anything but freeing him from it completely. He had regarded the double alliance of Cyprus and Crete as the completion of his joy, and knew that his father the King would be pleased to see Celenie marry Clearque.

As soon as the Prince of Cyprus was within a day's journey of Manetusa he put on the robe of sincerity, but as he had an appearance considerably more aristocratic than Clearque that costume, simple as it was, did not hide anything of the noble and charming air that distinguished him so much from other men.

As had been anticipated, all the important people there were in Crete came to meet the two princes in a small town

255

not far from Manetusa. The ambassadors from Cyprus, whom their prince had ordered to stay with Elismene, only come to meet him there; they were accompanied by the ambassadors from Lemnos and several senior officers of Celenie and Elismene, who came to compliment Telephonte on behalf of the two princesses.

Although the fine deportment of the Prince of Cyprus shone so forcefully through his somber costume, they were nevertheless extremely surprised to see him dressed in that manner on such a ceremonial day. Leandrin had indicated his astonishment in the morning, but Telephonte had only responded with a smile; in spite of the confidence he had in his favorite, he had been able to resolve not to tell him anything about Clearque's bizarre foibles. However, as the Price of Cyprus had a certain gracious and easy-going manner, which, without him ever descending from his rank, rendered him familiar with everyone, there was no one who did not take the liberty of expressing surprise at the garment he was wearing.

The people of condition even criticized it quite seriously, especially Cleophane, the chief ambassador of Cyrus, who could not weary of telling him how poorly the costume suited him and how unsuitable it was on a day that was not very distant from that of the wedding. Cleophane was naturally so full of sincerity and rectitude that, even at the risk of displeasing his masters, he never hid truths from them that might have some utility to them.

Telephonte replied with the patience and mildness natural to him, however, to everyone who said anything disobliging or importunate on the subject of his attire. What was satisfying for the Prince was that Clearque heard all the arguments that were unanimously put forward by that host of individuals regarding the disagreeable simplicity of the robe, which completed convincing the King perfectly of the knavery of Misandre. That gave him such sharp resentments against the fantastic philosopher that he was terribly chagrined to learn from the people arriving from Manetusa that on the same day that he had left the capital in order to come and welcome

Telephonte, Misandre and his family had left the palace, without anyone having seen the slightest vestige of any of them since.

The King of Crete, who was violent, was transported by anger at that news, and gave severe orders to have the three fugitives arrested wherever in his estates they might be. Leandrin, who heard those orders given, was veritably afflicted, seeing that after having searched in vain for the amiable Herminie, about whom Philanthrope had spoken to him so advantageously, he only learned news of the beautiful young woman when the King of Crete was so irritated against her father that he appeared disposed to subject him to the harshest treatment. Leandrin did not know the reason for the King's anger, but it did not take him long to find out.

Clearque had been so agitated during his journey that he had not had the leisure to think about the woes of Dinocrite, and since he had been enlightened regarding the knavery of Misandre he had been very irritated against all those who had contributed to deceiving him by praising the embroideries of the pretended enchanted robe to him. He was, therefore animated by a good deal of chagrin against Dinocrite, but compassion dissipated a part of it, and caused him ask for news of his favorite; he was told that his wound was going very badly and that he was in great danger of losing his life. The king was sorry about that, and resolved to go to see him as soon as he arrived in Manetusa.

When he arrived there he was told that Misandre had just been arrested in a nearby village but that neither his wife nor his daughter had been found. Clearque, who only had an indirect anger against those two individuals, was not unduly troubled that they had not been caught, but he had a great deal of joy in having Misandre in his power.

Elismene and Celenie welcomed Telephonte with all possible pleasure. The Queen of Lemnos showed all the transports of her amity for such a cherished brother in with great enthusiasm. As for the Princess of Crete, she showed a modest joy, which, modest as it was, delighted the Prince of Cyprus no less.

Clearque was not received in the same way. Elismene testified a great deal of amity and respect to him, but something fearful and hesitant was visible in her manner, which took away a good deal from everything obliging that she said to her brother. As for Celenie, she received the prince in question with much civility and deference, but accompanied by a coldness so glacial that he thought it would drive him to despair.

All day long, Telephonte was unable to say a word in private to Elismene, but he explained himself so well by means of his eyes, and, by consulting with care those of the beautiful princess, he saw such favorable things in his regard therein, that he was able to console himself for not being able to enjoy the pleasure of her intimate conversation. As the Prince of Cyprus had donned a costume that day with all the magnificence and gallantry that the previous day's attire had lacked, his handsome face and adornment attracted all gazes to him.

When the time came to quit the ladies, however, Clearque went to see Dinocrite, and Telephonte retired to his apartment, accompanied by Leandrin and Cleophane.

"I sympathize with you greatly, Sire," said the ambassador, "for not having been able to say a single word about your secret sentiments to the princess, and not having been able to hear hers from her beautiful mouth. What I find even more astonishing is that you have not asked any of us who were with her how she spoke about you in your absence and how she spoke about her other lovers."

"Oh, Cleophane," replied Telephonte, "I have seen the divine Elismene; I have consulted her beautiful eyes, and I have no need of anyone to be informed of my fate. It is only lovers who are only half-submissive to amour who take the trouble to set spies around the beauties they love, because they want to be at least as much their tyrants as their slaves. But those who, like me, were born on the isle of Cythera and follow the laws of the god that reigns there exactly, have very different fashions."

As he concluded that speech, Telephonte leaned on a table and seemed so pensive that Cleophane and Leandrin, not wanting to interrupt him, kept silent. After a few moments of reverie, Telephonte resumed speaking, and told them, smiling; "Amour is animating my mind so forcefully that I have just put into verse the thought that I expressed to Clephane just now; it is necessary that Landrin, who makes such pretty tunes, makes one for these lines, in order to sing them tomorrow to the princess. Here they are:

> *When a lover has dully submitted is heart*
> *To the god who is worshiped on Cythera.*
> *To know his destiny, there is nothing dearer*
> *Than the eyes of his loved one can impart.*

"Oh, Sire!" exclaimed Cleophane, those are very gallant lines, which contain a very delicate sentiment; but from what I see, you will not be one of those husbands who want to learn their fate from the robe of sincerity."

"What, Cleophane," said Telephonte, "you also are informed about the chimera of that fantastic robe?"

"Yes, Sire, I am informed about it," Cleophane replied, "and I also know that it was the robe in question that, by virtue of a chain of events, has brought Dinocrite to the brink of the tomb."

"If he was able to enter into it entirely," said Leandrin, precipitately, "you will doubtless be very obliged to the robe, since it will have delivered the beautiful Anaxaride from her tyrant, and you from an odious rival, who, by his death, will put you in a position to become the husband of a charming and virtuous woman."

"For a man who arrived in this place today," said Telephonte, "Leandrin is strangely well informed of all sorts of news."

"I am so poorly informed," retorted Leandrin, "that I do not know what the robe of sincerity is, but if you refuse to enlighten me, I shall not make a tune for your lines, however beautiful they are. You know, Sire, that people who dabble in music are commonly accused of being capricious."

"Those who dabble in poetry," replied Telephonte, "are no less exposed to that accusation, but to mark that we do not merit it, we shall all act without caprices. I consent that Cleophane tells you all that he knows about the robe of sincerity; I propose that you tell us as much as you know about Dinocrite and Anaxaride; and I will make you party to my sentiments and reflections on all the things that you relate."

"I have almost nothing to add, Sire," said Leandrin, "to what I have already told you about Anaxaride. She is a beautiful and sage person, who has an eccentric and intemperate husband, for whom, so great is her virtue, she nevertheless had a great deal of consideration. That unfortunate beauty is loved by Cleophane, who has never dared to make the confession of it to her; but if he has amour for her, for her part, she has a great deal of esteem for him, and if she became a widow, I believe that she would not refuse to make the happiness of a man as gallant as him. As for Dinocrite, Sire, you know him; you know that he is no more a worthy favorite of his master than a worthy husband of his wife, and that, in consequence, it would be no great loss if he were to go to expiate in the other world the chagrins that he has caused so many honest people in this one."

"In good faith, Sire," said Cleophane, "if I had made Leandrin my confidant, he could not be better informed of my secrets, but I do not know whether I am as well informed about those of the King of Crete."

After that speech, Cleophane told Telephone what that prince knew as well as he did—which is to say, the news of Clearque's love for Celenie, and the disorder that Misandre had caused in the heart of the King with the pretended enchanted robe. What surprised Telephonte, however, was to learn that the princesses were informed of the King's weakness, and that both of them were very indignant at the insulting suspicions with which he had outraged their virtue.

"The quality of sister," Cleophane continued, "renders Princess Elismene more moderate, but for the Queen of Lemnos, she was so forcefully abandoned to anger that, without the prayers of the Princess, she would never suffer the presence of the King of Crete again. Queen Celenie is all the more irritated against that prince because Elismene had assured her that he adored her, and the Queen, having, seen a thousand tender marks in his gaze herself, had allowed him to glimpse that they did not displease her.

"I am telling you all these things with no disguise, Sire," Cleophane went on, "because I am not unaware that you are perfectly cognizant of the exact virtue of your sister the Queen and I am convinced that you would not have criticized the innocent penchant that she had felt for the King of Crete."

"Far from criticizing her," replied Telephonte, "I would have applauded her greatly. The King of Crete is a very powerful prince and, although he has a few faults, he is full of merit. That is why, just though my sister's anger is, it is necessary for her to forgive him. It will try to recommend that to her. Nevertheless, I am no longer astonished by the terrible coldness with which Celenie received him a little while ago. That prince was extremely mortified by it, but sincerely, he deserved it, and if he comes to me to complain of it, I know what reply I shall give him. However, if my sister will trust me, she will not make his punishment last too long, and I shall try to turn that quarrel promptly into gallantry."

After saying that, Telephonte became profoundly pensive again. Cleophane and Leandrin remained silent, as before, and when the Prince had maintained the silence for some time, he broke it by saying to them: "I am in such a humor to make verses today that I have just composed another on the subject of the Queen my sister and the King of Crete. I hope that Leandrin will make a tune for this one as well as the other."

Then he recited these lines:

When the young beauty who captivates a swain,
Deigns to admit that she is glad,
And, far from savoring a joy so plain,
The lover lets suspicion drive him mad,
That is an odious crime, which angry Amour
Always punishes severely.

Cleophane and Leandrin praised highly the fortunate facility for poetry possessed by a prince who was always far more occupied with the métier of arms than exercises of the cabinet. The Telephonte made the reflection that, as the greater part of the night had already passed, all three of them ought to be thinking about obtaining some repose.

Clearque was scarcely in a state to savor repose; he had been to see Dinocrite, whom he had found in such a poor condition that, far from conserving any bitterness against him, the favorite had strongly excited his compassion, especially when he had confessed to him that it was only to hide from him the shame with which he believed himself to be covered that he had pretended to see the marvelous embroideries of the robe.

Dinocrite could not help shedding tears in remembering that it was the fatal robe that had taken away all his peace of mind and was the cause of his death, and he uttered so many imprecations against Misandre that the king, thinking that it would give him some satisfaction, told him that he had been arrested. Then he begged the prince so insistently to bring him to his bedside that Clearque yielded to his prayers.

Misandre was, therefore, brought to Dinocrite, who made him a thousand reproaches for having snatched him from life and from a wife as sage as she was beautiful, whose virtue he recognized perfectly, after having suspected it so unjustly so many times.

Because of the state that Dinocrite was in, Misandre did not deign to respond to him with a single word, but when Clearque also wanted to make reproaches to him, the bitter philosopher said a hundred offensive verities to him, and made him a thousand arrogant remonstrations, which irritated the King, already mortally chagrined to the utmost degree by Celenie's anger, of which he knew that Misandre was the primary cause. He no longer conserved any compassion for the unfortunate old man, therefore, and told him that he wanted such a villain to be subjected, the next day, to capital punishment. Then he returned to the palace, where he did not sleep.

A short time after Clearque's departure, Dinocrite, whom the sight of the King and Misandre had caused great disturbances, expired in the arms of Anaxaride, who, in spite of the injustices of the way that he had treated her, had considerable pity for his fate.

As soon as it was daylight, Clearque ran to see Telephonte and told him that the coldness and indignation that he had detected within the external civility with which Celenie had treated him had given him the cruelest affliction

"I can see clearly, Sire," he added, "that by virtue of the misfortune that accompanies my fate, someone has informed the Queen of Lemnos about my insulting suspicions; but if your generous amity does not ensure that the beautiful queen forgives me, I shall die of despair. I have the most tender and most ardent love for her that anyone has ever had, and I feel such an acute and dolorous repentance for the outrage that my foolish credulity caused me to commit against her virtue that, offended as she is, she would take pity on the state that I am in if she only deigned to pay some attention to it."

Telephonte was assuring Clearque that he would make every effort to redeem him in Celenie's mind when Leandrin came into his master's room, holding in his hands the two tunes that he had made for the Prince's verses. Telephonte wanted him to sing them before Clearque, who, having praised the words and the tunes of the songs, added: "I can see, Sire, that you have put into exceedingly pretty lines very malicious maxims against me; but confess, however, that there is one of your songs that does not befit me entirely, which is the second one:

263

When the young beauty who captivates a swain,
    Deigns to admit that she is glad,
And, far from savoring a joy so plain,
The lover lets suspicion drive him mad,
That is an odious crime, which angry Amour
    Always punishes severely.

"That does not apply to me," Clearque added, "for the Queen your sister never made me such a tender and glorious confession."

"It is said, however," Telephonte replied, "that my sister the Queen had a great penchant for you, and that after the death of the King of Lemnos, she no longer imposed on herself the law of hiding all the marks of that penchant from you."

"It is true," said Clearque, "that sometimes I thought I saw in her beautiful eyes dispositions not to hate me, but how could I have been enlightened of my fate other than by a few favorable glances, since I, although burning with love for that princess, because of eccentric reasons that you will divine easily, had only ever declared by my gazes and sighs the ardent fires with which I was ablaze for her?"

"What, Sire!" cried Telephonte. "You have never told Celenie that you love her?"

"No, Sire," replied Clearque. "Nothing other than my eyes ever explained my sentiments; my mouth has always maintained a profound silence."

"I am delighted," said Telephonte, "to be informed of a silence observed with so much exactitude on either side. I will make that a subject of justification for you with my sister; it is necessary that I have a conversation with her before you see her again."

Telephonte quit Clearque and, accompanied by Leandrin, went to see the Queen of Lemnos, in whose company he found Princess Elismene. He said a thousand polite and gallant things to the Queen his sister and the Princess he adored, and whether he was acting as a brother or as a lover, he had manners so gracious and tender that he could not help pleasing them a great deal; so the princesses said a hundred obliging things to him. Then he had Leandrin sing them the songs that he had composed. The favorite sang them with a great deal of accuracy and charm, and as the maxims that they contained pleased the princesses, they liked the lines and the music even more and did not spare their praises.

Telephonte, who saw their minds in such a favorable disposition, chose that moment to complain graciously to Celenie about the coldness with which she had received the King of Crete. The princess had been waiting for that complaint with a great deal of impatience, for she was burning with the desire to speak against Clearque. So, as the presence of Princess Elismene and Leandrin did not embarrass her at all, she explained naturally to Telephonte the reason she had for being irritated against the King of Crete, and admitted to him that she had been informed of all his bizarre sentiments by one of Elismene's servants, who had overheard the entire conversation that he had had in the wood with the King of Crete on the subject of the robe of sincerity.

"That domestic," Celenie continued, "came with an extreme diligence to inform his mistress, word for word, of that fine conversation, and I was with the princess when he rendered an account of it. You can easily judge, Sire, the effect produced in my mind by the outrageous judgment that the King of Crete had made of the Princess his sister and of me."

"I have a great displeasure," said Elismene, "if that man's indiscretion in telling such a story before the Queen of Lemnos, for if I alone had known of the weakness of the King my brother, I would have hidden it forever from the charming Celenie."

"My amity," said the Queen of Lemnos, "would have reason to complain of that reserve."

"On the contrary, my sister," retorted Telephonte, "you would have been obliged to the Princess for hiding from you a slight weakness on the part of a King, otherwise full of merit, who adores you with the most violent passion."

265

After those words, Telephonte said a thousand things to Celenie in favor of Clearque; he exaggerated the charms of his person, the strength of his amour and he grandeur of his repentance, which merited that she show him mercy.

"But how is it, my brother," that princess responded, half-persuaded, "that you are now giving me advice that is opposed to the maxims that you put into your songs? For, after all, you say there:

> *When the young beauty who captivates a swain,*
> *Deigns to admit that she is glad,*
> *And, far from savoring a joy so plain,*
> *The lover lets suspicion drive him mad,*
> *That is an odious crime, which angry Amour*
> *Always punishes severely.*

"The advice I am giving you," said Telephonte, "is not contrary to the maxim that I advanced in that song, since it is true, my sister, that the King of Crete has not in his life been fortunate enough to hear you make the confession of any sentiments favorable to him. Be assured that if he had ever had the glory of hearing your mouth pronounce in favor of the amour that you know full well that he had for you, he would absolutely not have held to that oracle and would not have consulted the robe of sincerity; but, far from deigning to give him some mark of generosity by your words, you even pretended not to hear the sighs that he was able to address to you."

"If I did not understand those sighs well enough," said Celenie, "it was up to him to explain them more intelligibly; a heart solidly touched…."

"Oh, please, my sister," Telephonte interrupted, "don't examine with so much rigor the conduct of an admirable king who adores you, and who is the brother of an amiable princess for whom you have such a tender amity."

Elismene having joined her pleas to Telephonte's, Celenie finally consented to forgive Clearque, on condition that the King consented to banish Dinocrite from the court if he recovered from his wound.

"That unworthy favorite," she added, "is capable of giving his master pernicious advice of which I would be the victim."

"But you are not remembering," said Telephonte, "that Dinocrite is at the extremity, and that there is no appearance that he will come back from the state that he is in."

"It does not matter," said Celenie. "As his danger might not be as sure as people believe, I still want the King of Crete to make me that promise. And may it please Heaven, Sire, that that prince, so subject to prejudice, only admits to his presence men as well chosen as those you admit to yours. Then no one will inspire any more prejudices in him dangerous to his glory and fatal to the repose of his friends."

After having quit the princesses, Telephonte went to Clearque's apartment, but he learned that the King was not in the palace. While waiting for him to return, the Prince of Cyprus isolated himself, in order to write to the King his father, and Leandrin took the opportunity to go for a walk in the city.

Clearque, who had not thought that Telephonte would go to see Celenie so early, did not expect to see that princess until after dinner. Thus, having been informed of the death of Dinocrite, he felt obliged to render a visit to Anaxaride before going to a beautiful pleasure palace that he had not far from the gates of Manetusa. He wanted to go to that place himself to order the preparations that should be made for a fête that he intended to give for Elismene. As for Celenie, he flattered himself that, amid the joy that the games and diversions would inspire, he would be more easily able to enter into the good graces of that princess.

As he emerged from Anaxaride's lodgings he was struck by a spectacle that would have touched him deeply on another occasion.

As the King had ordered the previous day that Misandre should die, it happened that the unfortunate old man was being transferred at that moment from the prison to the tribunal where the death sentence was to be pronounced. He was being taken by a troop of armed men and a few subaltern judges, but the whole escort had been stopped by a confusion of horses and carriages, which obliged the king's carriage to stop too.

That gave the prince time to notice a young woman of extraordinary beauty speaking to the judges who had stopped, in a suppliant manner. As soon as she was informed of the proximity of the King she quit the officers of justice she was addressing and ran to throw herself to her knees in front of Clearque's carriage.

"Oh, Sire," she said to him, sobbing, "Open your heart today to clemency, and deign to pardon an unfortunate old man, who, in truth, played a criminal trick on you, but is more worthy of your pity than your anger. Nevertheless, if you wish absolutely that the crime be punished, here is the culpable before your eyes; it was me who conducted all the artifice of that deceit. Let your justice, Sire, deign to send my father away absolved, and that all the penalties that were destined for him fall on me."

Clearque could not help admiring that beautiful person, who spoke in such a generous and touching manner. Nevertheless, he was so irritated against Misandre that he did not yield to her prayers or her tears. On the contrary, he made an effort not to listen to the pity that spoke in favor of the afflicted beauty, and he replied, dryly:

"Misandre has deceived me too odiously to merit my clemency; as for you, I believe that you are less culpable than you are pretending to be, in order to save your father. However, I want to examine whether you are, indeed, one of his accomplices, and in order to clarify that you will be taken to prison, where you will not remain for long if you are innocent. All that I can do of the most equitable at present, for you and for Misandre, is to send an order to the judge to postpone the pronunciation of the sentence that has been rendered against him, in order that you can share his punishment, if it is true that you had a part in his crime."

Scarcely had Clearque finished speaking than the blockage that had stopped his carriage was cleared; the prince's horses resumed their movement and the desolate Herminie, surrounded by a crowd of armed men, was placed next to her father—who, not having heard anything that the King had said, believed that he would soon be put to death. In the midst of such a dire situation, he preserved a proud and grim constancy that was not without its grandeur. What gave him the most pain was to see that Herminie had come to save him, blind to all those perils.

The beautiful girl attracted the gazes of the entire crowd of people who were following Misandre, but among them there was no one else who experienced emotions similar to those that were agitating Leandrin. Hazard had caused him to find himself alongside Misandre and those who were escorting him at the moment when they were stopped, and scarcely had he cast his eyes on that troop than he had seen a young woman of admirable beauty, who begged those who were in authority there to permit her to company Misandre in order to justify him before the tribunal to which he was being taken, since she alone was guilty of the crime that was being imputed to him.

She accompanied those words with tears that she could not hold back, but those tears were so beautiful and so appropriate to soften hearts, her dolor had something so touching about it, that Leandrin was penetrated by it. He was naturally very sensitive, and even if he had not already been prejudiced in Herminie's favor, whom he suddenly recognized in the person of the unfortunate young woman, perhaps amour would not have neglected to submit his heart to a beauty that he had seen in that circumstance.

He felt himself suddenly inflamed by an ardor so fervent and so powerful that he would have given his life for the object that caused it, and when he saw Herminie run to Clearque's carriage he followed in her footsteps precipitately, and wished a great deal of harm upon that prince when he heard the rigorous response that he made to the charming and afflicted young woman. He dared not, however, risk addressing any plea in her favor to Clearque, even though the King had showed a good deal of consideration to him because of Telephonte. Leandrin thought it would be better to get his master and Princess Elismene to take action in the matter. He therefore contented himself with bowing deeply to the King of Crete, who thought he was only there out of simple curiosity.

When Clearque had taken the route to the house of pleasure for which he was bound, Leandrin mingled with the crowd that was following Misandre, and, keeping his gaze firmly fixed on Herminie, he abandoned his heart to the movements of amour and compassion that were tearing it in a strange fashion.

Meanwhile, following the King's orders, Misandre was taken back to prison instead of being led before the judges, and by the same orders, Herminie was also locked in that frightful abode. She had no sooner entered it, however, than, before she was separated from her father, Leandrin asked to speak to both of them. The rank that he held in association with the King of Cyprus commanded so much respect that no one dared refuse him what he asked, and he was taken to a place where he had the satisfaction of speaking to Misandre and his lovely daughter without witnesses.

They were both very surprised to see a handsome and magnificently dressed stranger approach them in a very respectful manner, but he did not give them time to make long reflections. He began speaking, addressing Misandre, and saying to him: "Savant man, I am extremely touched by the unfortunate situation that you are in, and I have come here to try to give you some consolation. I have the honor of being party to the good graces of the Prince of Cyprus, and I shall renounce forever an honor that is so dear and so glorious if, by means of the credit of my master the Prince, I cannot obtain from the King of Crete that he revoke the fatal orders that he has given against you and this charming person."

Turning to Herminie and looking at her kindly, he went on: "Madame, you see before you a friend of the dearest of your friends—by which I mean the virtuous Philantrope, who conserves for you in Larissa the tender amity that you have experienced in Crete."

"What, Sire!" cried Herminie. "The virtuous Philantrope is still alive! Oh, in the midst of the cruel misfortunes that overwhelm me today, I have a great consolation in learning that news! But Sire," she went on, "forgive the transports of an ardent amity, and the indiscreet exclamation I made, before giving my father time to render thanks for your generosity toward us."

When she had finished speaking, Misandre thanked Leandrin warmly for the interest that he was taking in his destiny, Herminie did not spare her thanks either. Leandrin told her how he had found Philantrope in Larissa and gave her a brief account of the situation she was in and the conversations he had had with her. Then he made Misandre and Herminie offers of services so obliging, and urged the beautiful young woman so insistently to charge him with her orders, that she eventually said to him:

"Sire, since the goodness of your soul engages you to assist unfortunates like us with so much ardor, I will take advantage of your generosity and inform you of all our designs, and I hope that you will be convinced that an unfortunate family, who were only thinking of exiling themselves from Crete without doing any harm to anyone, do not merit the treatment to which you see us exposed.

"When my father delivered that fatal robe to the King, the project of which had been inspired in him by the dangerous desire to avenge himself on his century, we had no doubt that during his journey the prince would be disabused of the belief that he had in regard to the robe. So, fearing the anger that knowledge of the error into which he had fallen would give him, we all slipped out of the palace, taking nothing with us except a few miniature paintings that I had done during our sojourn there, and a few works of embroidery that my mother had also made there.

"We returned to the home of a peasant not far from Manetusa and from there we sent the paintings and the needlework to be sold in the city, the price of which was intended to give us the means to go to Cyprus, where we wanted to spend the rest of our days. But the man we had charged with those things, instead of having sold them in Manetusa, brought them back to us, very frightened, telling us that that a public proclamation had been made in the city, by which all the King's subjects were expressly ordered to arrest us. He added that large rewards had been promised to anyone who denounced us and harsh punishments to anyone who hid us, and that he had refrained since that proclamation from showing the works that he had in his hands for fear that they would enable our discovery.

"The man, who was the one with whom we were lodging, gave us a thousand assurances of fidelity, and as, in fact, we knew that his probity was proven, we believed that there was no better decision for us to make than to remain hidden in his home until we had been forgotten. We flattered ourselves that no one would think of searching for us as close to Manetusa as the village where we were.

"However, we were greatly mistaken in our hopes. A short time afterwards, men came to seize my father in his retreat, but, the leader of those searching for us having initially come into our rustic house on his own and having seen my mother and me, he exclaimed that he did not want it to be said that he had caused harm to women like us, adding that no wife or daughter should ever have to suffer for the actions of the head of the family, since they were only obeying his will. He therefore invited us to hide, assuring us that he would tell his troop that he had only found Misandre.

"I wanted to go with my father, but my mother represented to me, in tears, that I would be much better able to help him by conserving my liberty than by going to prison with him. We both lay low, therefore, penetrated with dolor at seeing my father taken away. Nevertheless, we were far from thinking that his life was at risk, being unable to imagine that a fault of the nature of the one he had committed could carry the King to greater excesses of vengeance than keeping him in prison. However, as we sent incessantly to Manetusa to inform ourselves of everything regarding him, we learned this morning in our retreat of the barbaric order that the King had given against him yesterday. I flew to the city immediately, but only arrived here at the moment when my deplorable father was being taken before judges devoid of equity, who were to pronounce a cruel sentence.

"You know the rest, Sire," Herminie continued, "since you heard everything that I said to the King and the men conducting my father. But after having informed you of all our design, the favor that I now have to ask of you is that you deign to send someone reliable, as soon as possible, to inform my mother of the situation that my father and I are in. I left her this morning in an inexpressible dolor, and perhaps her despair in further augmented at present by the dire thought that she has of my father's death."

"Madame," said Leandrin, "permit me not to give to anyone but myself the care of going to console in her alarm a mother who is dear to you, but before taking the route to the place where you will inform me that she is, suffer that I go to request, for the learned Misandre and yourself, the protection of the Prince of Cyprus, the Queen of Lemnos and the Princess of Crete. I will only employ a short time in those steps, which I believe to be necessary for your security, and immediately thereafter I will mount a horse and render with extreme diligence to your virtuous mother."

Again, Misandre and Herminie testified a heartfelt gratitude to Leandrin; then, the beautiful young woman, having given him good information to enable him to find the place where Chasseris was easily, and having also give him the means to let her mother know that he had come on her behalf and that she could trust him, the new lover withdrew, but so transported by amour and so agitated by anxiety, that he had great difficulty enclosing all that he felt in his soul.

He obtained the protection of Prince Telephonte and the two princesses for Misandre. Although the robe of sincerity had caused a great deal of chagrin to the three illustrious individuals, they were generous enough not to want to conserve any resentment against the man who had thrown Clearque into a error that had cost them all repose.

After taking his leave of Telephonte, Leandrin departed, and arrived with extreme promptitude in the village where Chasseris was. That village was situated on a small hill that overlooked Manetusa, and from that elevated location the gaze could wander, without any obstacle, over a large expanse of open country, which was very beautiful.

The manor to which the King of Crete had gone was not far from the small hill, and before Leandrin had mounted his horse, Telephonte had learned that Clearque would be remaining in the manor for several hours longer than he had thought, because he had given his workers orders to build a machine, of which he thought it necessary that the commencement be carried out in his presence

Leandrin found Chasseris easily, but what surprised him agreeably was to find Philantrope with her. Chasseris was in mortal alarm for Misandre, and Philantrope was sharing it with a great deal of sensibility. In spite of her distress, however, she was delighted to see Leandrin. He explained immediately to Chasseris the subject of his mission, and gave her a brief summary of the situation in which Misandre and Herminie found themselves. He did not neglect to inform her of the kindness with which the Princess of Crete, the Queen of Lemnos and the Prince of Cyprus had engaged to protect them.

"It is to your generosity alone, Sire," she said to him, "that we owe the protection of all those great princes, and I am infinitely grateful for it, but alas, I tremble that, in spite of such powerful protection, the King, who is stubborn and violent, might sacrifice my unfortunate husband to his anger."

Leandrin reassured her as best he could; then he asked Philantrope by what adventure she had returned to Crete.

"It is," she replied, "by the misfortune of the young woman who was my pupil. She died, as she was about to arrive at a sufficient point of perfection in the art that I was teaching her, and the painter whose daughter she was, deeply touched by her death, attributed it to the wrath of Heaven, punishing him for having kept me in captivity for so long in spite of the offers of ransom that I had made him. He therefore rendered my liberty and, far from claiming that I ought to buy it back, he gave me what was necessary for my journey, and even made me a present of several rare and precious things.

"Among other curiosities, he gave me certain marvelous pieces of glass, shaped with so much art that, being cleverly encased in tubes, they bear the sight three of four leagues from the place where one is. He has also given me singular machines made of a sort of metal, which carry the voice over the same distance that the pieces of glass I mentioned carry sight. Those two machines, which are so useful for seeing and speaking at a distance, have been invented by a philosopher of Larissa, who has given a considerable quantity of them to the painter who made me a present of them. Vulgar people would doubtless mistake these admirable productions of science for the effects of magical art, of which Thessaly is accused of making great use.

"I had returned to Crete carrying these curiosities, therefore, and had taken the road to Manetusa joyfully, taking pleasure in the thought of surprising my friends there, when, passing the foot of this hill this morning, I encountered the peasant in whose house we are lodged. The man, who had been one of my laborers before my departure from Crete, recognized me immediately, and told me in secret that Chasseris was hiding in his house because of an unfortunate affair that exposed Misandre to the danger of a shameful death.

"I parted from the people who were accompanying me and came here to mingle my tears with those of my old friend and offer her my services. She cried out on seeing me that it was surely Heaven that had sent her to her aid in such a dolorous conjuncture. But alas, in spite of my good intentions, what can I do for her? I have no credit with the King, and do not even have the power, at present, of helping her with my wealth, for I have just learned from the master of this house that my avaricious heirs have avidly taken possession of it, with no certainty of my death. It is, therefore, on you alone, generous Leandrin, that we can found our hope."

Leandrin replied with a great deal of zeal and politeness to everything that Chasseris and Philantrope had told him, and spoke to the latter with so much ardor and expansion about Herminie's charms that she, having a great deal of penetration, had no doubt that he was in love. As she had the most tender amity for Herminie, the discovery she made of the amour that Leandrin had for the beautiful young woman redoubled the benevolence that she felt for him.

Meanwhile, in order to distract Chasseris for a few moments from the cruel thoughts that were tormenting her, she invited her and Leandrin to examine, by means of the marvelous glasses that she had brought, what was happening in the surrounding country.

Scarcely had Leandrin made the test of the gift that they had of bringing all objects closer than, turning those ingenious aids to vision in the direction of a plain, he said that they enabled him to see the King and his retinue, who were returning to the city. Chasseris, who was also looking through the admirable glasses, saw the same thing, and exclaimed: "Oh, unjust prince, perhaps on returning to Manetusa you will pronounce the cruel order that will take way the life of my deplorable husband!"

In fact, at that moment, Clearque, who had given all the orders that he thought necessary for the fête, was going back to the city diligently, and on the way, he was thinking bitterly about all the chagrins that the robe of sincerity had caused him. He trembled that he might not be able to recover Celenie's good graces, and that thought irritated him so strongly against Misandre that, in spite of the scant penchant for cruelty that he had by nature, and in spite of the compassion that Herminie had inspired in him, he was firmly resolved on the death of the old man. He told himself that he was obliged to set a rigorous example in order to teach his people that his confidence and credulity could not be abused with impunity.

As he was very occupied with these tumultuous thoughts, he distinctly heard a terrible voice, which cried to him: "King of Crete, refrain from giving death to the man to whom you will owe the glory and good fortune of your reign."

Clearque looked around in astonishment, and saw fearfully that there was no one there but his servants, who, like him, had all heard the sound of that strident voice. He had no doubt, therefore, that it was a voice from Heaven that was warning him to use clemency toward Misandre. It seemed to him that the celestial power was not just, to act so forcefully in the interest of a trickster, and he did not understand how he was going to owe the glory and good fortune of his reign to that bizarre philosopher.

Delivered to those somber reveries, he entered Manetusa with an expression so melancholy that everyone noticed it.

His chagrin was initially dissipated by Telephonte. That prince criticized him agreeably for the long time he had taken to return from his excursion, and said to him that, for a lover whose mistress was no longer irritated with him, he was scarcely in haste to savor the joy of reconciliation. Clearque, who had not anticipated that good news, was unimaginably delighted by it. He ran to throw himself at the feet of Celenie, who received him generously.

Elismene and Telephonte came to the Queen's apartment shortly thereafter, and were witnesses to the transports of amour and gratitude that the King of Crete expressed to her. They took advantage of the favorable moment to ask the King for mercy in regard to Misandre. He did not want to tell them at a voice from Heaven had already warned him to let him live; on the contrary, he told them that he was granting mercy because of their prayers.

"But I would like to know," he added, "what was meant by a person who, in asking for the life of that philosopher, talked about him as a man to whom I would owe the glory and good fortune of my reign."

"That person," said Telephonte, "told you the truth. Misandre, in throwing you into error on the subject of the pretended embroidery of the transparent robe, has saved you from a thousand other errors a hundred times more dangerous. That robe, such as it was, really has been the robe of sincerity for you; it has enabled you to distinguish the false flatterers of your court from those who are attached to the truth and who speak to their prince as men of honor. The aversion that you testify for the former and the esteem with which you mark the latter will accustom your subjects to speak to you sincerely, which is one of the most precious advantages that a king can have.

"Furthermore, in imposing his marvelous robe on you, Misandre has put you in a state to remember forever that it is necessary to mistrust the brilliant promises of those whose capability one has not put to the proof. Will not so many good effects, Sire, contribute to the glory and felicity of your reign?

"For myself," Telephonte continued, "I have an infinite obligation to the robe of sincerity, and never, Sire, have you given me greater pleasure than when you permitted me to put it on; such a garment permitted me to distinguish instantly my true friends from those who only seek to follow me in order to render me the victim of their dangerous flattery."

Clearque, finally persuaded that he would only obtain utility from Misandre's deceit, gave the order that he should be released from prison. Leandrin, who had just returned to Manetusa, was already in the presence of the King of Crete when he gave that order, and it was Herminie's lover, delighted to have such agreeable news to take to his mistress, who went ahead of anyone else who could announce it to her.

He also rendered an account to her and Misandre of his journey to see Chasseris and the return of Philantrope. Herminie, transported with joy by so many fortunate events, rendered a thousand thanks to Leandrin for all his generous cares, and told him that she owed he life and liberty of her father to him. She added that she could not thank him enough for having brought her joy to a peak by informing her of Philantrope's return.

"I assure you, Madame," he said to her, "that in spite of the zeal of my heart and the vivacity of my actions, it is not to me that you owe the liberty of such a cherished father; it is surely to the presence of mind and cleverness of the virtuous Philantrope that we owe his happy success."

After saying that, Leandrin gave Misandre and Herminie a brief account of the marvelous machines for sight and the voice that Philantrope had brought from Larissa. He told them how, by the aid of the first of those machines, Chasseris and he had seen Clearque returning to Manetusa, reported the dolorous exclamation that Chasseris had made, on the subject of her husband, at the sight of the King, and told them how that cry had caused Philantrope to make use of the machine that carried the voice so far to give Clearque a warning in Misandre's favor.

Leandrin added that while Philantrope was speaking into the machine in question, he had observed the King of Crete by means of the marvelous glasses, and that he believed that he had seen, by the prince's disturbance, that he took the voice he heard for a voice from Heaven. "And I am convinced," he went on, "that I was not mistaken in my belief, since, as soon as I arrived in Manetusa, I heard the King order that you were to be set free."

"By the story you have told me about those marvelous machines," said Misandre, "I am beginning to be persuaded that there are in philosophy more beautiful parts and more useful to cultivate, than those I have affected thus far. Instead of devoting myself uniquely to metaphysics and speculative physics, as I have always done, I also want to apply myself to optics and mechanics."

After Misandre had pronounced those great words, to which Leandrin did not pay much attention, the philosopher changed his discourse, and resumed thus: "Sire, I admire the justice that Heaven has had in delivering Herminie from the alarms she had on my subject, and that justice is all the greater because never has anyone merited less than my daughter the horrible affliction into which she has been plunged, since she did not contribute in any way to what attracted it to us. For the sake of fairness to her, I ought to inform you of what her modesty caused her to suppress in telling you the story of the sequence of our misfortunes.

"Know, then, that she always opposed with all her force the desire I had to toy with the King's credulity in order to avenge myself or the scant attention that the prince inn question has for the solid sciences. The character of a loyal subject, disinterest and good faith are so sovereign in Herminie that she had shed tears a thousand times at the petty trickery that the chagrin dominating me caused me to employ, and which she was unable to reveal it to those who had an interest in it. So, Sire, your generosity has made you act in favor of a person who is not unworthy of your good offices. Although she is my daughter, verity demands that I render you this testimony."

Leandrin had no need of anyone to show him Herminie's virtues in a new light; a thousand things that he had remarked had persuaded him so fully that they were perfect, that he had as much esteem as amour for the charming young woman.

Meanwhile, the people that the King of Crete had ordered to come and release Misandre arrived at his prison and restored him and his daughter to liberty. At the same time, Leandrin sent someone to take that good news diligently to Chasseris and Philantrope, and sent a carriage a short time afterwards to bring them to Manetusa.

As he conducted Misandre and Herminie to lodgings that he had arranged for them in the city, the lover, who had always constrained himself until then, could not prevent himself whispering to Herminie that in working to render her liberty to her, he had lost his own. Although that speech caused her to blush and embarrassed her, she took it for a simple gallantry and only responded to it in that tone.

The beautiful young woman had not been in her lodgings for long before she saw Chasseris and Philantrope arrive there. The latter could not cease embracing her and giving her caresses, but Chasseris, although she loved such an amiable daughter very much and was very glad to see her again, did not give her much evidence of it, for she was not naturally given to showing affection.

Philantrope, who was born to distinguish herself generously in amity and to do good in the world, was saying a great deal to Herminie about Leandrin when that knight came in, having come to tell the virtuous woman and the lovely young woman that the Queen of Lemnos and the Princess of Crete were asking to see them.

Misandre and Chasseris, whose character did not belie their names, were delighted to remain in their lodgings, and Philantrope, accompanied by Herminie, went to the palace, escorted by Leandrin. All three of them went to the apartment of the Princess of Crete, where the Queen of Lemnos was. At that moment, the only person with the two princesses was Anaxaride, whom Elismene had obliged to come and stay in the palace, but who did not want to show herself in the Princess's apartment when there were many people there, because of her recent widowhood. Celenie and Elismene received the two women that Leandrin had brought in an extremely obliging manner. They say a hundred advantageous things about everything they knew of the virtues and the enlightened intelligence of Philantrope, and gave a thousand praises to the beauty and good grace of Herminie.

Elismene, wanting to retain Philantrope for a while and give Celenie the pleasure of hearing her talk, said to her then: "Virtuous Philantrope, it is necessary, if you please, for you, who are so enlightened and have so much experience of the world, to decide between Anaxaride and myself which of us is right in a dispute that we have."

Philantrope having only responded to what Elismene said by a gesture of modesty and submission, the Princess went on: "Everyone is aware of the harshness with which Dinocrite treated Anaxaride while he was alive; and no less aware that, in spite of that husband's strange behavior, she has always had for him all the care and complaisance that the most exact vir-

281

tue could prescribe for her. Heaven has delivered her from that terrible husband, and after having fulfilled in his regard all that reason and decency demanded of her, one cannot believe that she has any reason for regret. Also, she has too much good faith to affect externally a dolor that she does not feel.

"The subject of our difference of opinion, however, is that Anaxaride does not wish to receive the prayers of Cleophane, solely because he is a foreigner. She says that she believes the tenderness that the expresses for her to be sincere, that she finds him worthy of esteem, and does indeed hold him in esteem, but that, even if she were offered a crown, she would not want to spend her life outside her native land."

"If Anaxaride does indeed find merit in Cleophane," said Philantrope, "it is quite astonishing that she refuses the offer of himself because of the difference in their homelands. When sacred bonds link one to a husband that one loves, one regards as a homeland all those in which one spends one's days with him."

"I am very sorry, sage Philantrope," said Anaxaride, "not to share the sentiment of the Princess and yourself, but whatever passion a lover might inspire I me, I assure out that it would never make me decide to quit the island of Crete for him."

"But do not the Queen of Lemnos and I," replied Elismene, "give you an example of quitting the homeland in order to accompany a husband?"

"Princesses as great as the two of you are, Madame," said Anaxaride, "have been accustomed to such ideas since their infancy, and as they are born to command, they are regarded everywhere with admiration and with pleasure, but for vulgar individuals like me, I know that one becomes a poor figure in a foreign land; they always appear extraordinary and ridiculous there."

"Even supposing that your anxiety were ever well founded," said Celenie, "do not call the isle of Cyprus a foreign land in your regard, since all the people of quality in Crete know the language that is spoken in Cyprus, and the manners are so much in conformity that…."

As the Queen of Lemnos pronounced those words, the King of Crete, the Prince of Cyprus and Cleophane came into Elismene's room.

"Madame," said Clearque to Celenie, "as I know that you honor Cleophane with a particular esteem, I hasten to tell you that the Prince your brother has just assured me that he will obtain the consent of the King your father for me to give a present to the generous Cleophane. When that minister has, with my ambassadors, accompanied the Princess my sister to Cyprus, he has consented to return to spend his life in Crete. He will hold with regard to me the same position that Dinocrite had, which he will doubtless fulfill much better. I sense so keenly today the harm that lies and flattery have done me on a thousand occasions that I want to attach to me forever a man whose sincerity and rectitude I know so well, and I cannot render enough thanks to Prince Telephonte enough, to whom I shall owe the hand of the most beautiful princess in the world and the services of a minister who is as skillful as he is full of probity."

"Sire," replied Telephonte, smiling, "I assure you that it is not to me that you owe the decision that Cleophane has made to devote his days to your service. In spite of the zeal and respect that he has for you, I do not believe that he would have quit the court of the King my father for yours, if he had not been convinced that, for whatever reason, Anaxaride will never quit the isle of Crete, and will only consent to render him happy when she sees him established on this island."

"In truth, Sire," said Anaxaride to Telephonte, "there is a good deal of mischief in the interpretation you are offering of the urgency that Cleophas has to render his services to the King."

"Since the wishes of the Prince, my brother," said Celenie, "and apparently the orders of the King, my father, will engage me to spend my days in Crete, I am delighted that

Anaxaride and Cleophane are remaining here, for I hold them both in infinite esteem."

"I can assure you, Madame," said Elismene, "that whatever affection I have for Anaxaride, I will see her remain in Crete joyfully, since her presence here will give you pleasure."

"My sister," said Clearque to Elismene, "if you are losing Anaxaride in order to leave her to us, I count on you taking with you to Cyprus another beautiful Cretan, who will compensate you for the loss. Prince Telephonte has just told me that Leandrin is passionately in love with this beautiful young woman." He indicated Herminie with his hand.

"Yes," said the Prince of Cyprus, "Leandrin loves her as much as she merits being loved, and I have taken responsibility for rendering him happy. I do not believe," he added, "that Philantrope or Herminie's parents will refuse to consent to such a well-matched marriage."

"Sire," said Philantrope, "by the right that amity gives me with regard to Herminie, I can answer on this occasion for the consent of her parents and her obedience; they will all be very honored by alliance with a knight of Leandrin's condition, as accomplished as he is."

Leandrin, transported by joy at that response, rendered as many thanks to Philantrope as the place where they were permitted.

Afterwards, Philantrope and Herminie wanted to withdraw, but Elismene ordered them to remain, as she had already done once, and the Princess ordered Leandrin in a low voice to go immediately to make sure of the consent of Misandre and Chasseris to his marriage, and to return in order to report what they had to say on the subject.

Meanwhile, Cleophane marked with a great deal of respect his gratitude to the King of Crete and the Prince of Cyprus, and did not neglect to let Anaxaride see in his eyes the sentiments that he had for her.

Clearque and Telephonte left in order to give a few orders; Cleophane went with them, and when there was no longer anyone there but the Queen of Lemnos and Anaxaride, the

Princess asked Herminie, kindly, whether the choice of Leandrin for her husband was not contrary to her inclinations. Herminie only replied to the Princess with a profound modesty, but Philantrope assured her that she knew her sentiments well enough to be certain that she had an infinite esteem for Leandrin. Then Elismene invited Philantrope to come with Herminie to settle in Cyprus.

"That is my design, Madame," Philantrope replied. "The ardent zeal that I have for you and the tender amity that I have for Herminie would not permit me to make any other decision, and I dare to add that the generosity with which Prince Telephonte deigned to honor me during his sojourn in Larissa further increases the desire I have to execute that design. I do not share the sentiment of the beautiful Anaxaride; I always regard my fatherland as the place where the people most dear to me are, and it is all the more permissible for me to be indifferent regarding my residence because I only have distant relatives in Crete, who have rendered themselves unworthy of my affection by the harsh and avaricious measures that have taken against me. Herminie's father and mother will also go with you, Madame, without even having foreseen such a fortunate opportunity; they had already made plans to go and live in Cyprus."

"I can assure you," said Celenie, "that you will all find the isle of Cyprus a charming abode."

As she said that, Leandrin returned to inform Elismene of the joy with which Misandre and Chasseris had consented to his alliance.

Shortly thereafter, Clearque and Telephonte returned to the Princess's apartment and the King of Crete, seeing Herminie there, said: "Beautiful Herminie, as with all the errors into which the robe of sincerity has thrown us, there remains to us as much chagrin as displeasure in not having seen the beautiful embroideries that your father promised that we would see; it is necessary that you repair that omission. I have just learned that during your sojourn in the palace you and your mother made admirable works in embroidery and miniature. It is necessary, if you please, that you allow the Queen and the Princess to see them."

Immediately, Herminie sent a messenger to her lodgings for the requested works, and as soon as they were seen, they attracted everyone's admiration. As Misandre, in making Clearque a description of the supposed embroidery of the robe of sincerity, had affected to remind him of the actions of several women who, by their character, brought shame upon their sex, it seemed, on the contrary, that Herminie had sought to revive in her works the deeds of heroines who, by their virtue and the grandeur of their courage, had done honor to it. It was that beautiful girl who had designed the figures from the embroidery of the three robes on which her mother had labored with so much skill and art that the figures seemed animated.

On one of those robes one saw the virtuous Alcestis giving her life to the Fates in order to save her husband from the tomb. Another offered to the eyes the ingenious skill with which the chaste Penelope was able to deceive the foolish hopes of her audacious suitors. The third robe, finally, represented the story of the tender Alcyone, who delivered herself to a terrible death in order not to survive a husband whom she had loved dearly.

The King and the Princess of Crete, the Queen of Lemnos and the Prince of Cyprus could not stop praising those admirable embroideries, but they had reason to exclaim again when they considered Herminie's paintings. The first represented Artemisia, so famous for the superb tomb that she had built for her husband King Mausolus; the second was a portrait of the generous and tender Hypsicratea, the wife of the great Mithridates; and the third was the faithful history of the illustrious Queen Zenobia, as celebrated for her courageous valor as for her rare knowledge.

All the pictures were painted with so much artistry, nobility and intelligence, and were so correct and so gracious, that they enchanted the gaze of all those who saw them. After the two princesses and the two princes had given them a thousand praises, Telephonte said, gallantly: "Misandre was not risking anything when he said that we would see enchanted works; he had only to show us those of his daughter to convince us that he was right."

"And moreover," added Clearque, "he had only to make us see these same works to convince us that all the centuries have produced infinitely virtuous women."

Herminie begged the Queen of Lemnos and the Princess of Crete to permit her to offer them the robes and the paintings that had the good fortune to please them. The princesses did her the honor of accepting those fine presents with a very good grace, which they divided between them

A few days later, Telephonte married Princess Elismene with an infinite joy, and as soon as they had the consent of the King of Cyprus, the marriage was celebrated of Clearque with the Queen of Lemnos, who was delighted to see with the King of Crete a favorite as wise as Cleophane. Herminie married Leandrin, whom she loved as much by inclination as by gratitude, and as soon as Anaxaride had given her mourning the time that decorum demanded, she married Cleophane, with whom she lived very happily. Philantrope, Misandre and Chasseris went with Herminie to Cyprus; Philantrope enjoyed all the charms of society there, but Misandre and Chasseris in spite of their good fortune, did not change their character.

All of them, however, remembered forever the robe of sincerity, which had caused such changes in the mind of the King of Crete.

"That, my dear Blondel," continued King Richard, "is the entire tale of the robe of sincerity, and this is the moral of the tale, contained in the lines that I shall recite to you.

When once one is spoiled
By prejudice and by vanity,
One is untrue and often bizarre.
  Frankness and equality
Are gifts of Heaven whose usage is rare;
They alone, however, make out happiness.

> *Whoever wants always to be flattered,*
> *Will go astray in strange routes.*
> *A prince is ill-served if he is not told*
> *The truth exactly.*
> *But among courtiers, rarely is prepared*
> *The robe of sincerity.*
> *If it comes from the mean capricious hand*
> *Of an eccentric pedant, a stubborn philosopher,*
> *Fortunate is the hero full of firmness,*
> *Who has such an ornament to put on!*

"It is necessary to admit, Sire," said Blondel, "that you are admirable in everything; I believe that there is only you, among the heroes of the world, who is so well able to take cities and win battles, and can compose such agreeable fables and pretty verses when you take it into your head to dabble in that. In truth, you ought not to carry off so much glory all at once, and content yourself with that of a great conqueror without taking more from us...."

Blondel was unable to continue his speech; he suddenly heard a terrible noise, and, emerging abruptly from the King's room he saw that two prisoners were being brought into the tower, whose handsome faces and noble air were easy to observe, even in the dim light that illuminated that that dark place.

The End of *The Dark Tower*

APPENDIX: LETTER TO MADAME DE G***

I know, Madame, that the large number of your pious occupations does not prevent you from sometimes amusing yourself by reading the works of the mind, and that you would like to be informed of the character of the novelties that it produces. The churlish humor that appears in certain persons that are called pious, which renders them grim, is not found in you, although you fulfill your duties with a profound and solid piety. Thus, I take pleasure in announcing to you today that people began some time ago to develop the same tastes as yourself.

One sees little *histoires*[46] spreading through society whose design is to prove agreeably the solidity of proverbs. Our ancestors, who were ingenious in their simplicity, perceiving that the wisest maxims are poorly imprinted on the mind if they are presented nakedly, dressed them, so to speak, and caused them to appear under ornaments. They exposed them in little *histoires* that they invented, or in the recitation of a few events that they embellished. And as these stories only had for their goal the instruction of young people, and it is only the marvelous that strikes the imagination very well, they were not miserly with it; prodigies are frequent in their fables. However, their design appears to me to be well conceived and rather fortunately executed for the time, for there is nothing more capable of rendering the mind just and enlightened than to fill it with sage maxims, and nothing is more capable of

---

[46] I have left several French terms used for works of fiction untranslated in this appendix, as the letter illustrates the changes in meaning to which such words were being subjected in salon parlance, creating a confusion that still exists today and makes translation into the equally-confused set of English terms awkward.

instructing young people than to teach them the good fortune or ill fortune of people who have followed or neglected those rules of life.

Events for the most part bizarre; proverbs purified of traits of common sense: there are ample subjects for reflection and moralizing for you! I have been charmed that fashion is entering so well into your taste, for I have not forgotten the conversation we had in S.C.'s house concerning proverbs, of which you know a large number of pretty ones in various languages. I remember perfectly how astonished you were that people are not making *nouvelles* or *contes* based in those antique maxims. People are finally getting round to it, and I have hazarded to place myself in their ranks, in order to mark my attachment to charming ladies of whose good qualities you are aware. Persons of their merit and character seem to bring us back to the times of the fays, when one saw so many perfect people. Today, great merit is very rare, and I believe that before it becomes more common it will be necessary to see again the fortunate times in which troubadours recounted so many marvels to us.

But I am talking to you about troubadours as if I were sure that you are acquainted those gentlemen. In spite of the great enlightenment you have in antiquities, however, it might be that they are unknown to you. At any rate, I will tell you something about them; you need not read it if you judge that it has nothing new for you.

The name is Provençal and it signifies *trouveurs*, or inventors. Without making citations that would not be to your taste or mine, only suffer that I sent you what one of the most illustrious scholars has said on their subject in the beautiful dissertation that he had made on the origin of *romans*.[47] For

---

[47] At this point, the essay's use of the word *roman* seems to refer to what are now known as Medieval prose romances, although it subsequently undergoes the shift that allowed it to become the modern word for "novels," while the essayist also

myself, what I propose to tell you is that the troubadours were the authors of the little *histoires* that I have mentioned. They were intelligent men; in those days Provence had more of them than the rest of France, and still has a great many. They filled their stories with astonishing prodigies of fays and enchanters; and as, in those days, fine minds were highly cherished, troubadours were welcomed everywhere; they went through the region reciting their tales in the homes of people of quality, and they charmed all those who listened to them. In a short time their reputation became so great that when there were entertainments in the courts of sovereigns, they were not thought to be complete if people had not heard some of those marvelous tales.

Those gallant troubadours, however, saw much overbidding in their projects. Before them, no one had heard mention of *romans*; they were made. From century to century those sorts of productions were embellished and they finally reached the peak of perfection to which the illustrious Mademoiselle de Scudéry has brought them, with so much splendor that posterity will agree with us that the admirable *romans* of that savant woman are veritable poems in prose, but a prose as eloquent as it is polite.

In spite of the progress of *romans*, tradition has conserved the *contes* of the troubadours for us, and as they are ordinarily full of surprising events, and they contain a good morality, grandmothers and governesses have always recounted them to children to put into their minds a hatred of vice and a love of virtue. They no longer serve any other function.

But as, by an almost inevitable destiny, works that are taken to their perfection infallibly degenerate, *romans* have lost many of their beauties. They have been reduced in scale, and in that state there are few of them that conserve the graces of style and the attractions of invention. Against a *Princesse*

---

introduces the term *romance*, which, in French, usually refers to a kind of song that is known in English as a "ballad."

de Cleves[48] and two or three others that have charmed by the grandeur of their sentiments and the accuracy of their expressions, an infinite number of *romans* has been seen to appear devoid of taste, regulation and politeness.

That decadence of *romans* having caused a disgust for them, it has been thought advisable to return to their source and bring back into vogue *contes* in the style of the troubadours. An illustrious Academician,[49] by a quantity of fine works the admirable enlightenment that he has in the fine arts, has put *contes* of that character into verse, which meet with universal approval. Afterwards they were made in prose, and that mode has finally become general.

That of *romances* has followed. As that word is perhaps less familiar to you than that of troubadour, I will also say something about it.

The Spaniards call *romances* certain tender, gallant and even satirical songs, in which there are several sets of words for the same tune. A similar name is given here to pastoral songs, in which a certain naïve and rustic tenderness is dominant. It is also given to songs that are not pastoral, in which only a gallant and naïve playfulness is dominant. Various words are also set to the same tune, and a tune is always chosen that is celebrated for its antiquity and the great simplicity of the words it had before, which were apparently made in the era of the troubadours or very nearly.

Modern *romances* try to imitate the simplicity of antique *romances*; with delicacy, in truth, but at least attempts are

---

[48] *La Princesse de Clèves*, published anonymously in 1678, was one of the key works involved in the evolution of the *roman* as popularized by Scudéry toward the modern novel, in terms of its length and the structure of its narrative. It is set in a much more recent period of history than Scudéry's novels and does not seem to be a *roman à clef*. It is generally attributed to Marie-Madeleine Pioche de La Vergne, Comtesse de La Fayette (1634-1693).

[49] The reference is to Perrault.

made to conserve the natural and naïve tenderness that pleased Molière and of which you can get an idea in a song that he put in the mouth of the Misanthrope:

If the King had given me
His great city of Paris
And had wanted me to quit
The amour of my darling,
I would say to King Henri,
Take back your Paris
I'd rather have my darling, yes,
I'd rather have my darling.

It seems that these old words were very much to his taste:

I esteem that more than the florid pomp
Of all the false gems that everyone proclaims.

In fact, so many songs tasteless in their tenderness have been seen that it seems to me that it would be better to return to the style of the troubadours than to cling to such insipidity. What is desirable is that, in bringing us back to the taste of Gaulish antiquity, we would also be brought back to that fine simplicity of mores that is said to have been common in those happy times.

The narratives that have been made always tell us that vice is eventually punished, and virtue triumphant. You will see examples of that in the four *nouvelles* that I am sending you. There is nothing marvelous in the enchantments of Marmoisan or Artaut;[50] everything there happens in the natural

---

[50] In *Oeuvres meslées* the story of "Marmoisan" is followed by a verse narrative entitled "Vice puny" [Vice punished], featuring a character named Artaut, which I have not included in the present collection

order, but in the two others the fays play their part, and in addition, those two *historiettes* revolve around proverbs.

Do not be surprised if I have set Finette in a time as scantly remote as that of the crusades. You can imagine that I am not unaware that they only commenced at the end of the eleventh century; but, apart from the fact that I have tradition for me, which puts the story of Finette in the time of the crusades, I have the famous example of Tasso, which introduced enchanters into his *Jerusalem Delivered*,[51] whose setting is the same era, and that of Pierre Le Moyne, who also admits enchantments in his poem of Saint Louis,[52] although that great king lived more than a century after Godefroy de Bouillon. In any case, it is not astonishing to hear talk of fays in the eleventh century, since there are still people today sufficiently lacking in common sense to believe in those sorts of visions.

But what appears to me to be more capable of astonishing is to see that these Gothic fables, which have only been made to bear good morals, are nevertheless often filled with scandalous adventures. For example, you know full well that in the foundations of the fable of Finette, her two sisters are far from being as virtuous as I make them. There is no mention of marriage; they are two unworthy individuals whose odious weakness is recounted with shocking circumstances.

I believe, to tell you more about what I think on that score, that those tales have been filled with impurities in passing into the mouths of the little people, in the same way that

---

[51] *Gerusalemme liberata* (1581) by Torquato Tasso is an epic imitative of Virgil set during the first crusade with insertions inspired by Ludovico Ariosto's flamboyant adaption of the substance of French Medieval Romances, *Orlando Furioso* (1516). The mixture was very popular, particularly in French translation, where it eventually became a standard object of study in schools.

[52] The baroque epic *Saint Louis, ou La Sainte couronne reconquise sur les infidèles* (1653), by the Jesuit Pierre La Moyne, was a significant precursor of Tasso's work.

pure water is always charged with ordure in passing through a dirty channel. If the common people are simple, they are also vulgar; they do not know what decorum is. Pass lightly over a licentious action full of scandal, and the story they tell subsequently will be full of all its circumstances. Criminal actions were recounted for a good end, which was to show that they are always punished; but the people, from whom we get them, report them without any veil and even link them so firmly with the subject thus unveiled that it does not cost much now to recount the same adventures while enveloping them. They are well invented and do not strike us any less covered than uncovered; the decorum of the words does not take anything away from the singularity of things; and if the people, or the troubadours, had expressed themselves like us, their *contes* would only have more value.

It must nevertheless be admitted that if those eras did not have as much delicacy as ours with regard to expressions, they had a more general one for actions, since they were eras of good faith and generosity;[53] one only thought of inspiring virtue without affectation, and no one was wounded by the terms and manner in which it was exposed. Nowadays it is not the same, when one talks about morality, the manner in which one does it hardly ever escapes being criticized severely.

But all those who produce something, whether in public or in private, ought to expect that destiny, and they ought not to worry about it. One writes in order to instruct oneself and to

---

[53] L'Héritier is by no means the only belated reader of Medieval prose romances to have made the mistake of thinking that the mythology of pious chivalry that they promoted must have had some reflection in actual behavior. Obviously, the troubadours knew perfectly well that it was an ironically fantastic negative image, and that the actual barons and knights who constituted their audience, far from being chivalrous, were vicious thugs for whom pillage, rape and murder were a way of life, bloodily pursued in crusades for which piety was merely a thin disguise.

amuse oneself; one also writers to instruct and amuse one's friends. That is ordinarily the objective one proposes to oneself; when one has arrived at it, one ought not to be embarrassed. What does it matter if people with no taste are discontented with works that were not made for them? They do not have the talent to profit from them, even less that to produce something similar; it is therefore necessary not to deny them the pleasure of criticizing, well or badly, it is the only way in which they can hope to make themselves distinguished.

If I wanted to take the liberty of naming names, I could give you a long list of those critics, and enable you see at the same time that all their finesse consists of examining a work on the principles of schoolboys and on the ideas they think they have obtained from Horace or Juvenal. One hears them saying in a grave tone "Don't you see that that isn't the nominative? What construction! That is obscure; Horace would not have talked like that!" Those who want to cover hen in incense say: "Monsieur *** does not compose; he is not a poet, but he is a connoisseur, he is such a judicious critic!" Consult them, however, and they fatigue you with wretched remarks, and the majority cannot even speak French.

With those sentiments, you can imagine that I am not very alarmed by the censures that might be made of my works; to those into whose hands they fall, whether they be savant or ignorant, people of intelligence or devoid of common sense, I give full liberty.

However, if there are not minds equally polished and delicate in your province, I beg you to refrain from letting them see any of these *nouvelles*. There is no mention therein of Phoebus, and vulgar provincials only like works filled with pompous gibberish that they do not understand. It requires great enlightenment to know the differences between styles and the usage one ought to make of them. Well-extended naivety is not familiar to everyone. I do not believe that *nouvelles* from the source of the troubadours, or *romances,* ever find their account among those who are unable to emerge from the ordinary character that certain provinces produce.

Sciences embellished by politeness have excepted the one where you are from those faults; people there could well accommodate them to the fashion dominant at present. But warn your friends that they ought not to judge that fashion solely by the works that it has enabled me to produce; they would be wrong; they will see another delicacy therein. I am only putting others on the trail; is it not better to be the first to walk new paths? You will at least take account of my having been so quick to enter the lists in order to make *historiettes* on the subject of proverbs, since that vivacity enables you to see how much I love you, and how much I am,

Yours, etc.

SF & FANTASY

Adolphe Alhaiza. *Cybele*

Alphonse Allais. *The Adventures of Captain Cap*

Henri Allorge. *The Great Cataclysm*

Guy d'Armen. *Doc Ardan: The City of Gold and Lepers; The Troglodytes of Mount Everest/The Giants of Black Lake; The Abominable Snowman*

G.-J. Arnaud. *The Ice Company*

André Arnyvelde. *The Ark; The Mutilated Bacchus*

Charles Asselineau. *The Double Life*

Henri Austruy. *The Eupantophone; The Olotelepan; The Petitpaon Era*

Barillet-Lagargousse. *The Final War*

Barbot de Villeneuve.*The Naiads/Beauty & The Beast*

Cyprien Bérard. *The Vampire Lord Ruthwen*

S. Henry Berthoud. *Martyrs of Science; The Angel Asrael*

Aloysius Bertrand. *Gaspard de la Nuit*

Richard Bessière. *The Gardens of the Apocalypse; The Masters of Silence*

Chevalier de Béthune. *The World of Mercury*

Albert Bleunard. *Ever Smaller*

Félix Bodin. *The Novel of the Future*

Pierre Boitard. *Journey to the Sun*

Louis Boussenard. *Monsieur Synthesis*

Alphonse Brown. *City of Glass; The Conquest of the Air*

Émile Calvet. *In a Thousand Years*

André Caroff. *The Terror of Madame Atomos; Miss Atomos; The Return of Madame Atomos; The Mistake of Madame Atomos; The Monsters of Madame Atomos; The Revenge of Madame Atomos; The Resurrection of Madame Atomos; The Mark of Madame Atomos; The Spheres of Madame Atomos; The Wrath of Madame Atomos* (w/M. & Sylvie Stéphan); *The Sins of Madame Atomos* (w/M. & Sylvie Stéphan)

Jean Carrère. *The End of Atlantis*

Félicien Champsaur. *Homo-Deus; The Human Arrow; Nora, The Ape-Woman; Ouha, King of the Apes; Pharaoh's Wife*

Didier de Chousy. *Ignis*

Jules Clarétie. *Obsession*

Jacques Collin de Plancy. *Voyage to the Center of the Earth*

Michel Corday. *The Eternal Flame; The Lynx* (w/André Couvreur)

André Couvreur. *Caresco, Superman; The Exploits of Professor Tornada* (3 vols.); *The Necessary Evil*
Gaston Danville. *The Perfume of Lust*
Camille Debans. *The Misfortunes of John Bull*
Captain Danrit. *Undersea Odyssey*
C. I. Defontenay. *Star (Psi Cassiopeia)*
Charles Derennes. *The People of the Pole*
Georges Dodds (anthologist). *The Missing Link*
Charles Dodeman. *The Silent Bomb*
Harry Dickson. *The Heir of Dracula; Harry Dickson vs. The Spider*
Jules Dornay. *Lord Ruthven Begins*
Alfred Driou. *The Adventures of a Parisian Aeronaut*
Odette Dulac. *The War of the Sexes*
Alexandre Dumas. *The Return of Lord Ruthven; The Man who Married a Mermaid* (w/P. Lacroix)
Renée Dunan. *Baal; The Ultimate Pleasure*
J.-C. Dunyach. *The Night Orchid; The Thieves of Silence*
Henri Duvernois. *The Man Who Found Himself*
Achille Eyraud. *Voyage to Venus*
Henri Falk. *The Age of Lead*
Paul Féval. *Anne of the Isles; Knightshade; Revenants; Vampire City; The Vampire Countess; The Wandering Jew's Daughter*
Paul Féval, *fils. Felifax, the Tiger-Man*
Charles de Fieux. *Lamékis*
Fernand Fleuret. *Jim Click*
Charles-Marie Flor O'Squarr. *Phantoms*
Louis Forest. *Someone is Stealing Children in Paris*
Arnould Galopin. *Doctor Omega; Doctor Omega and the Shadowmen* (anthology)
Judith Gautier. *Isoline and the Serpent-Flower*
H. Gayar. *The Marvelous Adventures of Serge Myrandhal on Mars*
Louis Geoffroy. *The Apocryphal Napoleon*
G.L. Gick. *Harry Dickson and the Werewolf of Rutherford Grange*
Raoul Gineste. *The Second Life of Doctor Albin*
Delphine de Girardin. *Balzac's Cane*
Emmanuel Gorlier. *The Nyctalope and the Tower of Babel*
Léon Gozlan. *The Vampire of the Val-de-Grâce*
Jules Gros. *The Fossil Man*
Jimmy Guieu. *The Polarian-Denebian War* (2 vols.)
Edmond Haraucourt. *Daah, the First Human; Illusions of Immortality*
Nathalie Henneberg. *The Green Gods*

Eugène Hennebert. *The Enchanted City*

Jules Hoche. *The Maker of Men and His Formula*

V. Hugo, P. Foucher & P. Meurice. *The Hunchback of Notre-Dame*

Romain d'Huissier. *Hexagon: Dark Matter*

Jules Janin. *The Magnetized Corpse*

Gustave Kahn. *The Tale of Gold and Silence*

Gérard Klein. *The Mote in Time's Eye; Starmasters*

Fernand Kolney. *Love in 5000 Years*

Paul Lacroix. *Danse Macabre; The Man who Married a Mermaid* (w/Alexandre Dumas)

Louis-Guillaume de La Follie. *The Unpretentious Philosopher*

Jean de La Hire. *The Fiery Wheel; Enter the Nyctalope; The Nyctalope on Mars; The Nyctalope vs. Lucifer; The Nyctalope Steps In; Night of the Nyctalope; Return of the Nyctalope; The Nyctalope and the Tower of Babel*

Etienne-Léon de Lamothe-Langon. *The Virgin Vampire*

André Laurie. *Spiridon*

Gabriel de Lautrec. *The Vengeance of the Oval Portrait*

Alain le Drimeur. *The Future City*

Georges Le Faure & Henri de Graffigny. *The Extraordinary Adventures of a Russian Scientist Across the Solar System* (2 vols.)

Gustave Le Rouge. *The Dominion of the World* (w/G. Guitton) (4 vols.); *The Mysterious Doctor Cornelius* (3 vols.); *The Vampires of Mars*

Jules Lermina. *The Battle of Strasbourg; Mysteryville; Panic in Paris; The Secret of Zippelius; To-Ho and the Gold Destroyers*

Maurice Level. *The Gates of Hell*

André Lichtenberger. *The Centaurs; The Children of the Crab*

Maurice Limat. *Mephista*

Listonai. *The Philosophical Voyager*

Jean-Marc & Randy Lofficier. *Edgar Allan Poe on Mars; The Katrina Protocol; Pacifica 1, 2; Robonocchio; Return of the Nyctalope;* (anthologists) *Tales of the Shadowmen 1-14; The Vampire Almanac* (2 vols.)

Ch. Lomon & P.-B. Gheuzi. *The Last Days of Atlantis*

Charles Malato. *Lost!*

Maurice Magre. *The Marvelous Story of Claire d'Amour; The Call of the Beast; Priscilla of Alexandria; The Angel of Lust; The Mystery of the Tiger; The Poison of Goa; Lucifer; The Blood of Toulouse; The Albigensian Treasure; Jean de Fodoas; Melusine; The Brothers of the Virgin Gold*

Victor Margueritte. *The Bacheloress; The Companion; The Couple*
Camille Mauclair. *The Virgin Orient*
Xavier Mauméjean. *The League of Heroes*
Joseph Méry. *The Tower of Destiny*
Hippolyte Mettais. *Paris Before the Deluge; The Year 5865*
Louise Michel. *The Human Microbes; The New World*
Tony Moilin. *Paris in the Year 2000*
Michael Moorcock's *Legends of the Multiverse*
José Moselli. *Illa's End*
John-Antoine Nau. *Enemy Force*
Marie Nizet. *Captain Vampire*
Charles Nodier. *Trilby and The Crumb Fairy*
C. Nodier, A. Beraud & Toussaint-Merle. *Frankenstein*
Henri de Parville. *An Inhabitant of the Planet Mars*
Gaston de Pawlowski. *Journey to the Land of the 4th Dimension*
Georges Pellerin. *The World in 2000 Years*
Ernest Pérochon. *The Frenetic People*
Pierre Pelot. *The Child Who Walked on the Sky*
Jean Petithuguenin. *An International Mission to the Moon*
J. Polidori, C. Nodier, E. Scribe. *Lord Ruthven the Vampire*
P.-A. Ponson du Terrail. *The Immortal Woman; The Vampire and the Devil's Son; The Police Agent*
Georges Price. *The Missing Men of the* Sirius
René Pujol. *The Chimerical Quest*
Edgar Quinet. *Ahasuerus; The Enchanter Merlin*
Jean Rameau. *Arrival; in the Stars*
Henri de Régnier. *A Surfeit of Mirrors*
Maurice Renard. *The Blue Peril; Doctor Lerne; The Doctored Man; A Man Among the Microbes; The Master of Light*
Restif de la Bretonne. *The Discovery of the Austral Continent by a Flying Man; Posthumous Correspondence* (3 vols.); *The Fay Ouroucoucou* (2 vols.)
Jean Richepin. *The Crazy Corner; The Wing*
Albert Robida. *The Adventures of Saturnin Farandoul; Chalet in the Sky; The Clock of the Centuries; The Electric Life; The Engineer Von Satanas; In 1965*
J.-H. Rosny Aîné. *Helgvor of the Blue River; The Givreuse Enigma; The Mysterious Force; The Navigators of Space; Vamireh; The World of the Variants; The Young Vampire*
Marcel Rouff. *Journey to the Inverted World*

Marie-Anne de Roumier-Robert. *The Voyage of Lord Seaton to the Seven Planets*

Léonie Rouzade. *The World Turned Upside Down*

Han Ryner. *The Human Ant; The Superhumans*

Henri de Saint-Georges. *The Green Eyes*

Louis-Claude de Saint-Martin. *The Crocodile*

Frank Schildiner. *The Quest of Frankenstein; The Triumph of Frankenstein; Napoleon's Vampire Hunters*

Nicolas Ségur. *The Human Paradise*

Pierre de Selenes: *An Unknown World*

Norbert Sevestre. *Sâr Dubnotal: Vs. Jack the Ripper; The Astral Trail*

Angelo de Sorr. *The Vampires of London*

Brian Stableford. *The Empire of the Necromancers (1. The Shadow of Frankenstein; 2. Frankenstein and the Vampire Countess; 3. Frankenstein in London); The Wayward Muse; Eurydice's Lament; The Mirror of Dionysius; The New Faust at the Tragicomique; Sherlock Holmes and The Vampires of Eternity; The Stones of Camelot* (anthologist) *News from the Moon; The Germans on Venus; The Supreme Progress; The World Above the World; Nemoville; Investigations of the Future; The Conqueror of Death; The Revolt of the Machines; The Man With the Blue Face; The Aerial Valley; The New Moon; The Nickel Man; On the Brink of the World's End; The Mirror of Present Events; The Humanisphere*

Jacques Spitz. *The Eye of Purgatory*

Kurt Steiner. *Ortog*

Eugène Thébault. *Radio-Terror*

Edmond Thiaudière. *Singular amours*

C.-F. Tiphaigne de La Roche. *Amilec*

Simon Tyssot de Patot. *The Strange Voyages of Jacques Massé and Pierre de Mésange*

Louis Ulbach. *Prince Bonifacio*

Théo Varlet. *The Castaways of Eros; The Golden Rock.; The Martian Epic* (w/Octave Joncquel); *Timeslip Troopers* (w/André Blandin); *The Xenobiotic Invasion*

Pierre Véron. *The Merchants of Health*

Paul Vibert. *The Mysterious Fluid*

Villiers de l'Isle-Adam. *The Scaffold; The Vampire Soul*

Gaston de Wailly. *The Murderer of the World*

Philippe Ward. *Artahe; Manhattan Ghost* (w/Mickael Laguerre); *The Song of Montségur* (w/Sylvie Miller)